WHAT
SHE
GAVE
AWAY

WHAT SHE GAVE AWAY

A THRILLER

CATHARINE RIGGS

THOMAS & MERCER

Text copyright © 2018 by Catharine Elizabeth Manset Morreale
All rights reserved.

Published by Thomas & Mercer, Seattle

www.apub.com

Amazon, the Amazon logo, and Thomas & Mercer are trademarks of Amazon.com, Inc., or its affiliates.

ISBN-13: 9781503901896
ISBN-10: 1503901890

Cover design by Shasti O'Leary Soudant

Printed in the United States of America

To Phil, Jessica, and Ali:
my lifelong partners in crime

PART ONE

PART ONE

Crystal

I've targeted the sperm donor. I blame him for the fat. Not the six-hundred-pound kind that shows up on TV. Or the curvy kind that's trending in magazines. I'm talking about the basic kind that makes me invisible. Just fat enough that girls don't hang with me and boys won't take a second look. Just fat enough to get the glare when I climb onto an airplane or a crowded bus.

I try to avoid mirrors, but they've seated me in an office with a mirror directly behind the desk. It has a weird curve to it, warped on the sides and in the middle. It makes me look fatter than I am. I mean, why is the office designed this way? Do they want their clients to feel insecure? Will it make them deposit more money? Help them to choose a bigger loan? I paste on a smile. That usually lifts my fat pads so my cheekbones show through. But smiling in this mirror only makes me look crazy. The door squeals open, and I stand.

"Ms. Love?"

"Yes?"

"I'm George Taylor. The bank's chief lending officer."

I hold out my hand to an aging hipster dressed in a tight black suit and pink satin tie. Dirty-blond hair, nicely textured. Blow-dryer and curling iron at work. That and a little gel. Stinky gel, the kind that wrinkles my nose. Should I tell him about the bit of salad stuck between his teeth?

"Please take a seat." He picks up my résumé and gets right to business. "You've had five years' experience as a loan analyst?"

"Six if you count a year of training." He's disappointed, I know. I have the qualifications but not the look.

"Why move to Santa Barbara?"

"I'm tired of the Bakersfield heat."

"You have family here?"

"A few friends."

He glances at my belly with a question in his eyes. I know what he's thinking. I carry a lot of weight in my gut. But he's taken his HR classes. He knows the rules. That's a lawsuit waiting to happen. I do my best to sound earnest.

"I'm one of those rare people who grew up wanting to be a banker. I love working with numbers. They mean everything to me."

"So you've taken accounting?"

"I was an accounting major at Bakersfield College. Got my AA degree six years ago and went right to work at the local bank. I've never looked back."

He nods, staring hard at my résumé. Time to nudge him in the right direction.

"I'm not looking for a job. I'm looking for a career. I'm a hard worker. I'm focused. I'm single. No children. I'm the most efficient person I know. I believe Pacific Ocean Bank is the right fit for me. Only five branches and ten years in business, but you're the top-performing bank in the region. Impressive."

He forces a smile. "Our president's an industrious man."

"So I've heard."

George taps his pencil on the table. "We prefer four-year degrees."

"My accounting major and years of experience should more than make up for that."

"And we have a strict dress code . . ."

"Which I will follow."

"No casual Fridays."

"I've never been a fan."

"The other analysts are men. Any problem with that?"

"None at all." Fish on the hook. Now reel him in slow.

"Do you work well in high-pressure situations?"

"I prefer them."

"Weekends?"

"No problem."

"Team player?"

"Absolutely."

"What about references?" He points to my résumé. "May we contact your most recent supervisor?"

"I wish." I make a sad face. "My ex-boss passed away a few months ago from a horrific accident. A terrible situation. He was a mentor to me. The head of Human Resources said to call her with any questions. She understands my need to move on."

He scribbles something before looking up. "When can you start?"

"Next week." There's something wrong with his left eye. I'm guessing it's made of glass. I bet it's a flaw that bugs him. I file away the thought.

I'm flipping through a file, trying to tune out the banter between the boys. I call them boys even though the obnoxious two are older than me. Eric and Tyler. Frick and Frack. Aryan twins. They seemed surprised when George introduced me this morning, and I caught some eye rolling and a laugh behind my back. The third analyst is small and quiet. He's from India or someplace like that. I don't recall his name.

The loan analysts' office is tucked away in the belly of the bank, a basement without windows or doors. No cubicles separate our desks;

there's no privacy at all. Stark walls, clutter-free desks, no personal photos, screen savers locked on the bank's logo. Even the coffee cups match—all white, no inscriptions. Not a Starbucks disposable in sight. The boys call our office "the Stable." I'm not sure where that name came from.

George has given me a pile of loan files to review. It's no secret the last analyst was a slob. I would have fired him too. I work through papers stacked every which way to bring order to the files. Financial statements belong on the left. Tax returns on the right. Credit reports get filed in the back, smoothed with the press of my hand. I imagine sex to be like this, satisfying and complete.

"How about Katie?" Tyler asks his buddy. Their desks sit back-to-back. He's the blonder of the two boys. Ruddy skin, thinning hair, and a little puffy at the edges.

"She's a prude. Don't waste your time." Eric rubs the bristles shadowing his chin. He's either a lazy grub or a fan of the morning-after look.

"Then who should I take?"

"Try Lolo. She always puts out."

"Bingo." The boys share a gulping laugh.

They spend the rest of the morning planning their trip to Vegas, texting friends, and booking hotels. When they finally leave for lunch, the quiet analyst turns to me. I've studied the bank website by now. Dipak Patel, junior analyst. UCLA graduate, class of 2014. Eric and Tyler are UCSB frat boys turned senior analysts in less than five years. And then there's me. A reject with a community college degree. The pecking order is clear.

"How's it going?" Dipak asks.

"Fine," I reply, snapping shut a file. "Thank you for asking."

"Don't mind those guys. They're rude to everyone."

"I don't mind them." But I do.

"Let me know if you have any questions. Always happy to help."

By the end of the week, Dipak and I have bonded over our love for numbers and loathing for the boys. We look peculiar together. I'm as big as a truck, and he could pass for Santa's elf. And his social cues are off. He dresses sloppy, he cracks his knuckles, and he eats stinky food at his desk. But that mile-wide chip on his shoulder? I can make use of that.

I take a chance and invite him to Ted's for a drink, and his smile nearly splits his face. The first beer gets him talking about family, the second about the social scene. By the third he's moved on to bank management. I try to stall him there.

"Is the bank president a genius like they say?" I ask, nursing my beer. Ted's is exploding with the Friday-night crowd. I have to lean close to hear his answer.

"All bullshit," Dipak replies with a slur to his words. We're seated at a corner booth that faces the bar. His chin barely tops the table.

"But to found a bank? That takes some kind of brains."

He makes a face. "He looks nice in a suit—that's all. And he's willing to do whatever they want. He's nothing but a puppet."

"Who are 'they'?"

"The developers who control the bank's board. You'll get to know them soon enough. Part of our high-value clientele."

I want to ask him more, but we catch sight of Eric and Tyler surrounded by a gaggle of girls.

"They're idiots," Dipak says, envy steeling his eyes.

"How do they keep their jobs?"

"They're part of the Great White Hopes."

"The what?"

"The white guys they groom for senior management. Half-baked skills at twice the pay. It's sickening. It pisses me off."

"So why'd they hire you?"

He takes a slug of beer. "I'm the bank's nod to diversity."

"And me?"

He raises an eyebrow. "Well, they hire women every now and then. But usually they're hot, no offense."

"None taken." His insult settles in with the rest.

"I mean, George hires outside the box on occasion. He'll pick smart people even if they don't fit the mold. He'll get fired for that one day."

"So you like him?"

"Yeah. I like him. He's a good guy. One of the very few."

"What's the story on his eye?"

Dipak sets down his mug and wipes his mouth with his sleeve. "I heard he got beat up in college. A fight outside a gay bar or something like that." He slides off the bench. "Those beers are running right through me. I'll be back in a sec." He stumbles off, and I lean back and take in the scene. A girl dances past me in a tiny black dress that barely covers her crotch. She bumps against Tyler and laughs. Then she bumps against him again. She's pretty but slutty in a way I don't like. I pick up my beer and finish it off and begin a round of my favorite game. What's the worst thing that could happen to that girl? What would destroy her life?

Kathi

May 2, 2016

I'm waiting on the back terrace for the gardeners to arrive. They've gotten sloppy these past few weeks. Weeds grow between the bricks. Leaves float in the pond. The fire pit overflows with ashes. And now they're late. It's all too much.

I wander to the far side of the lawn to take in the morning view. A silvery sheen hangs over the tree-studded estates of Montecito. The ocean sparkles blue; the islands stand clear—just a hint of fog to blur the air. I try to ignore the eight o'clock train paralleling the coast. Its ghostly horn always grated on Rich's nerves, but I used to like the sound. Made me dream of traveling to distant lands. Paris. London. Rome. Rich had promised we'd visit those places one day. Now we never will.

I sip from my mug of freshly brewed coffee. It tastes like nothing, of course. My therapist says there's an upside to every misfortune. You just have to look. So the upside to losing my sense of smell to last year's virus? I've lost my taste buds too. Food tastes like sawdust and drinks like something worse. If only I'd come across that secret before. All those years spent counting calories. Popping pills. Measuring steps. Now I've lost twenty pounds, and I'm on the road to lose ten more.

I love the way my clothes drape across my skin. No pinching. No squeezing. I feel lighter than air. Rich would be proud. He never liked the extra weight, always poking at my stomach or giving me his death stare whenever I ordered pasta or dessert.

The upside to living alone? That one's harder to nail down. I can have two glasses of wine now. Sometimes even three. And I don't have to wait until six o'clock. Of course, wine tastes like tap water, but I've learned I'm not in it for the taste. All those years traipsing through Napa, attending tastings in Santa Ynez. Arguing over Pinots. Snubbing the white zins. And the money we spent stocking our wine cellar? I buy boxed wine these days. Not in Montecito, of course. I would die if my friends ever caught me. I drive to the far side of Santa Barbara and buy gallon-sized boxes of chardonnay—usually three or four at a time.

I plan to head to my wine store later today after my appointment at the bank. I'm not in the mood to speak with George, but there's some problem with our accounts. As if I would have any answers. Rich and I had one of those old-fashioned marriages you don't hear about anymore. He was the one who brought home the bacon, and I took care of our house. So why question me about our finances? I can't pull answers out of a hat. It's all too much. I feel like crawling back to bed. Instead I use a trick my therapist taught me and give my wrist a little pinch. I'm thin, damn it. Model thin. And what could be better than that?

It was a dark and stormy night. The night was dark and stormy. It was night, and it was stormy. It was a stormy, dark night. The storm moved in at dark. Stormy, it was dark. It was stormy, and then it grew dark. Before it was dark, it was stormy. Stormy. Dark.

My hand cramps, so I set down my pen. I've been waiting at the bank for a good half hour. Seen a dozen customers come and go. This never would've happened under Rich's watch. He was meticulous in his attention to detail. Never a second late. Less than two months gone, and the bank is imploding. I'll bet Rich is turning in his grave.

I pinch my wrist.

Another upside to living alone? I finally have time to write. I bought a pretty leather notebook that I store inside my purse. I used to love to read and write. Kept journals recording my every thought. It drove Rich a little crazy. He was so passionate back then. Wanted to know everything I was thinking and didn't want to share me with a book. I kept journaling for a while after we married. And then one day I stopped.

I no longer want to write the great American novel. I'm much too old for that. I'd settle for a sweet romance series, something bound in pinks and greens. The hero would be dark and handsome, his lover small and perky. No real sex, just lots of passionate kisses. And no tongue. I'm not a fan of that. The novel would end with the hero carrying his bride into the bedroom. Just the thought makes me shiver. I bet there's a market for that. Not everyone wants graphic sex. But first I have to come up with the perfect pen name.

Skylar Savage. Sunny Skies. Bunny White.

"Mrs. Wright?"

I snap shut my notebook, my cheeks growing warm. A hefty young woman stands over me with her hand outstretched. She has pretty blue eyes but an unfortunate figure—an apple shape, just like Rich's sister. I haven't heard from Ann since the funeral, but she and Rich were never close. He liked to tease her about her weight, and she wasn't fond of that. I wonder if she'd mind if I shared my secret for success.

"I'm Crystal," the woman says. "Crystal Love. We've met before."

"We have?" *Crystal Love.* I picture her name atop my pink-and-green novels. It's perfect. Just perfect. Now if I can only nail the first line.

"At the Dignatarios party at the zoo last summer? I was one of the bank volunteers?"

I shake my head. "I'm sorry . . ." I don't remember the woman, which is strange. She's so very big; you'd think I would.

"That's okay. I attended the funeral, but it was crowded, so I didn't get a chance to offer my condolences. I want you to know I admired your husband."

"Thank you. That's sweet. What do you do here at the bank?"

"I'm a loan analyst."

"Loan analyst? Really? I thought all of the analysts were men."

A smile tweaks her face. She has nice white teeth. "A few of us girls do understand numbers."

"Of course. I didn't mean . . . I'm sorry. That was stupid."

"No worries." Crystal takes the seat beside me. "I don't want to be presumptuous, but if I can be of help, please call." She hands me her business card. "Your husband was a great man. A mentor to me. I'd do anything to return the favor."

"Thank you." My eyes grow misty from her kindness. "I appreciate your offer, but I think I'm doing fine."

Crystal pats my knee and stands. "Good to hear. But the offer's on the table if you need it. Now, who are you meeting with?"

"George Taylor. He's late."

"I'll go get him. He's usually right on time."

She disappears, and I whip out my notebook and practice my new pen name.

Crystal Love Crystal Love Crystal Love.

Behind George stands an unfamiliar man with a stern face. He's in his midforties and wears the standard bank uniform: white shirt, blue tie, and a gray suit. His head is shaved and his body chiseled. Tan skin but not a wrinkle in sight. Must have Italian blood. He's handsome in that stern professor kind of way, which would make him a good character for my novel. Not the lover, of course. My lover is much younger. But someone serious. Maybe the father? Or an uncle? Or the bad guy? Are there bad guys in a romance novel? I'll have to check on that. I glance at my watch. It's after four. I hope this doesn't take too long.

"Thank you for coming," George says.

George has always been gracious. I never liked it when Rich made fun of his eye. "It's good to see you again, George."

"I'm sorry we made you wait. Please take a seat."

I perch myself on the edge of the chair with my purse upright in my lap. I want them to think I'm in a hurry and have somewhere important to go. George takes a seat at his desk, but the stern man remains standing, peering at himself in that awful mirror hanging right behind George's head.

"That was a wonderful memorial service," George says.

"Thank you." It really was.

"Would you like some coffee or water?"

"I don't think so. Will this take long?"

"I'm not sure. Typically the head of compliance handles these types of interviews, but she's out on a leave of absence."

Interview? He makes this sound so formal. I catch the stern man peering at me in the mirror. I begin to fidget with my purse.

George works his manicured hands together. "I'd like to introduce you to Special Agent Aaron Sykes. He's with FinCen, the FBI's Financial Crimes Enforcement Network."

FBI? My heart skips a beat.

Sykes turns to face me but doesn't offer his hand. "Please be patient. I have a lot to go over."

"You do?"

"Just stay calm, Kathi," George says. "We need to ask you a few questions to get an understanding of the situation."

"Situation?"

Sykes jumps in. "I'll take over from here."

"Be my guest." A bead of sweat slips from George's forehead and slides the length of his face.

"What do you know about your husband's work at the bank?"

"Not much," I say in a tiny voice.

Sykes glares at me like I'm a criminal. "You were married to him for close to thirty years. You must know something."

I try to compose my thoughts. "I know very little except that he was the president. And a founder. He rarely talked about what he did day to day."

"What about during this past year? Any talk about special loans?"

"No . . ."

"Problems at work?"

"Problems?"

"Did he mention that he was under investigation?"

"Why, no." The blood rushes to my head. "Whatever for?"

"How about the two-million-dollar home equity loan? Any idea where those loan funds went?"

I shake my head. "I barely remember signing the documents."

"One million of that was a refi," George says.

"Let Mrs. Wright answer the questions," Sykes snaps.

George's lips grow thin. "Of course."

I look from George to Sykes. I don't like the tension in the room. "Rich was always having me sign things," I say. "I never read them. I just did what he asked."

"Really?" Sykes says. "So I suppose you don't remember signing a falsified loan application."

"Falsified?" I struggle to my feet. "I think I should go."

"I have a few more questions."

I glance at George, and he nods. I sink back down in my chair.

"Now then." Sykes peers at the notes in his hand. "Can you explain the contents of your safe deposit box?"

"My what?"

"Your box? Your safe deposit box? Number 101? The one you have here at the bank?"

"I don't know anything about a box."

Sykes gives George a quick tap on the shoulder. George shoots the man an irritated look before turning to me. "I know you've been going through a rough time, Kathi. And sometimes things can slip your mind. But you and Rich have had a box here since the bank opened its doors."

"Yes, well . . . maybe." I try to rack my brain, but my thoughts have grown fuzzy. "Maybe we do. I really don't remember. But if you say so, it must be true."

Sykes folds his arms. "So you never used the box?"

"Not that I recall."

"Never visited it during the past year?"

"No."

He pulls a sheet of paper from his briefcase and hands it to George. George unfolds it and pushes it toward me.

"Is that your signature?" Sykes asks.

I nod.

"Do you see the date?"

"Yes, but . . ."

Sykes leans over George and digs his eyes into mine. "According to the records, you accessed the box at nine a.m. on March 14, 2016. Does that date mean anything to you?"

"Of course." I swipe at the tears blurring my eyes.

"So you acknowledge you accessed your box the morning of your husband's death."

"No, I didn't. I swear I didn't."

"Are you aware it's against the law to keep money in your box?"

"There was money?"

"Two hundred thousand, to be exact."

"But that's crazy. It's so much. How did it get there?"

"Why don't *you* explain that to *me*?"

"But how can I? I don't know anything." My heart races, and I can't catch my breath. "I'm not feeling well. Can I leave?"

Sykes shrugs. "I suppose that's enough for now." He slides his business card my way. "If anything comes to you, please give me a call."

I stare at the card and then look at George. "Do I need a lawyer?"

He sighs, his glass eye twitching. "Yes, I think that would be for the best."

When I return home from the bank, I try calling Rich's lawyer. But of course, it's after five, and lazy Leo is gone. I don't mean that. It's the wine talking. Leo's not lazy. He swims at the club after work. I know that because Rich spent many evenings there, too, working on his perfect body each and every day. Running in the morning. Swimming at night. Biking on Saturday and Sunday. God forbid he miss a single workout and spend a few hours with his family. Oh, Rich. Dear Rich. What in god's name have you done?

I head for the kitchen and trip on a stray shoe. My wine sprays across the white couch. Rich always warned me there'd come a day when one glass wouldn't be enough, that I'd move on to two or even three. Well, I've fooled him this time. It's not three glasses. It's four.

I slosh around the house, knocking into furniture and walls. Where to go? What to do? Call Jane? Call Laurie? I can't. I just can't. I don't want anyone to know. I bumble up the steps and mill around upstairs until I find myself in Jack's room and fall across the bed. His room hasn't changed since he left for college, except for the red-and-gold USC banner hanging on the wall. University of Spoiled Children. That's what we called it when I was in college a hundred years ago. And that's what Jack's become. A horribly spoiled child who won't speak to his mom.

I was a good mom. Possibly a great mom. I'm sure of that, I think. I feel dizzy. I feel sick. I try to focus on Jack's swimming trophies grouped by year on his bookshelves. The housekeepers polish them each and every week until they gleam. All those years I spent shuttling Jack to swim meets. Bakersfield, Fresno, San Diego. And then when he got better, Arizona, Florida, New York. I was the proud mom. I couldn't help but gloat. And then whoosh. A scholarship to college. A failed attempt at the Olympic Trials. He got out of the pool that day and never stepped back in. He wiped his hands of his sport just like he's wiping his hands of his mom. Now that he has the bittiest part in the bittiest TV series, he thinks he can toss me away. His father would be so disappointed. Tears slip down my cheeks, and I wipe them away.

I picture Jack as a baby, all wet and happy in my arms. He used to love his bath, used to giggle and laugh until tears streamed from his sparkling blue eyes. *Oh, why can't babies stay babies? Why didn't I have a few more?* I swipe at the tears again. *Don't think about that. Just call him. Yes, call him. He can't mean what he said. He wasn't thinking clearly.* I fumble my cell from my pocket and scroll through his text messages and stop on three words.

HOW COULD YOU?

How could I? Why don't you ask your father? He was the boss of me, then and now. The blood pumps loud in my ears, and I begin to sweat. What did that cardiologist say at the Go Red luncheon? More women die from heart attacks than cancer. Maybe that's what's happening to me. Maybe I'm having a heart attack. Maybe I'll die. That would show Jack. That would make him feel bad.

I'll text him. Yes, a text is better. My heart begins to calm down.
PLEASE CALL ME, I type. IT'S AN ENERGY.
I hit send and then stare at the words.
EMERGENCY, I retype.
He hates all caps, but I'm only mimicking his bad behavior. I wait on his bed for the call, the phone resting against my chest, the light

draining from the room. I should eat dinner, but I'm too tired to get up. How do I know if my text has been blocked? He swore he'd do that. Did he follow through? Would my message come back? Would my phone let me know? *Call me. Jack. Call me. Call me. Call me, please.* I'll have to find out about blocking. I'll google it tomorrow.

It's dark now. I close my eyes, and the buzzing simmers down. I rub my hands across my hip bones and smile. The upside is that I'm thin and getting thinner. What could be better than that?

December 1, 1979

Mom died a year ago now. Dad died that night too. I've read things get better with time, but I'm nearly always sad. Aunt Genny thinks it might help if I write my feelings in a journal. I'm not sure writing will make any difference, but I promised I would give it a try.

The sheriff said it was the black ice that killed them. That the wheels were old and worn. I'm guessing he was right because Mom and Dad always argued over that ugly old van. Mom said we needed something safer, but Dad said VWs were the best. At the funeral I heard Aunt Genny call Dad a penny-pincher. I've never heard her say a bad word since.

The psychologist says what happened wasn't my fault, but deep down I know it was. A few days before the accident I got into my biggest fight ever with Mom. I mean, thirteen and they still treated me like a baby? Wouldn't let me go to sleepovers. Couldn't get my ears pierced. And the sitters were the worst. Mom and Dad never let me stay home alone. Mom said it was because I was their one and only. I said I didn't care. I yelled some horrible things that night, so Dad sent me to my room. A few days later they surprised me and left me on my own.

I was reading Gone with the Wind when the sheriff showed up. It was the third time I'd read it that year. I used to love most everything about that novel. I'd climb inside the words and let them sweep me into another world. Loved everything except for the so-so-sad ending. That's why I read it over and over. I kept wishing the ending would change. That Rhett would stay with Scarlett. That Bonnie wouldn't fall off her pony. That they would love each other and have lots of babies and live happily ever after. Of course now I know I can wish all I want, but endings never change.

Crystal

I've rented a small studio near downtown Santa Barbara. *Studio* makes it sound too nice. It's actually a converted garage with old appliances and a sloped floor. All that luxury for $2,000 a month plus utilities. It's crazy money—almost half of my take-home pay—but this town is crazy. For the same amount of money, I could rent a three-bedroom house in Bakersfield. With a pool. But I shouldn't complain. With a vacancy rate under 1 percent, I was lucky to nab the place.

My landlord lives next door in a rustic Craftsman with crumbling steps and a rotting porch. The drought-stricken lawn is scorched to amber; a sagging picket fence borders the yard. The only touch of color is a red bougainvillea that consumes one side of the house. A family of rats lives in the middle of all those thorny spines. Big ugly ones with long yellow teeth. I've seen them lurking in the early morning when I leave my studio for work.

Just for fun, I looked up the house price on Zillow. A whopping $900,000. Are they crazy? Close to a million for this dump? How any normal person can live in Santa Barbara I just don't understand.

My landlord, Martha, is older than my faux granny by a decade, but her brain's still intact. No family, as far as I can tell. The house overflows with old textbooks, magazines, and newspapers, and the air's thick and musty with mold. Martha says she taught high school history for decades until the school district forced her to retire. She's lonely, I can tell, but I'm not looking for a friend. I don't ask her any questions and keep my answers short.

"I'll have you fill out an application," she said on the day I toured the room. "But I have some tough questions for you first. I don't use a management group, so I can't run credit checks. You'll just have to promise to tell me the truth."

"Of course."

"If you lie to me, I'll see it on your face. After teaching fifty years, I've honed my sixth sense."

I nodded and pasted on a smile.

"Married?"

"No."

"Children?"

"No."

"Dating?"

"No."

She stepped closer, and I flinched at her old-lady stink. "I don't want men around here," she said. "Understand me? I'm very old-fashioned that way."

I stepped back. "You won't have to worry about me."

"Credit clean?"

"Close to eight hundred."

"Ever arrested?"

"No."

"Committed a felony?"

"No."

"Spent time in jail?"

"No." At least not as an adult.

"Hmmm. What else."

I didn't like being grilled one damn bit. Reminded me of the inquisition that had sent me to juvie. I wanted to tell Martha where she could go, but I needed the place, so I kept my mouth shut and played a round of my favorite game. Stroke? Broken hip? Dementia? Or did eviction top the list?

As soon as I moved in, I scrubbed the place and painted it white. Then I unpacked my three trim boxes and arranged my sixteen true crime novels by the color of their spines. White sheets. Porcelain dishes. New silverware. One pot and one pan. Nothing on the walls. No TV. No computer. Clean and stark and perfect. So much better than my faux parents' disaster of a home.

Actually, *home* isn't the right word. They had a disaster of a *house*. Not that they were poor—at least not in the beginning. But they hated their jobs and their marriage even more. The central battle of their private war became who should do the housework. Anna spent her free time shopping. Alan spent his sifting through porn. That left their one and only adoptee to clean the place as best as a little kid could.

I tried. I really did. I picked up after the slobs morning, noon, and night. Still, the plates piled up and the garbage spilled over, and one day I finally gave up. I spent much of my ninth year huddled in a corner of the living room plucking strands of hair from my head.

No knight in shining armor came for me like you see in the movies. No kind neighbor. No policeman. No teacher. No friend. And after the divorce? Anna didn't want me, and neither did Alan. So Granny took me in and tried to make things right.

At Granny's, I grew mean and ugly and twisted, like a worm. My hunger grew boundless; junk food became my only friend. That was when the mind games started. At first I focused on the Disney girls who danced across the screen, hating their perfect faces, flawless bodies, and storybook families. One girl in particular drew the most loathing from me, a perky blonde with a winning smile and an endless supply of friends. How would she feel if someone slashed her face? Or stole her voice? Or hurt her parents? What was the worst? The very worst thing that could happen to ruin that girl's life? Death seemed too easy. At least the quick deaths I saw on TV.

After a while I got tired of pretending and started playing the game with Granny. Hid her favorite clothes—that made her confused. Tossed her wedding ring—that made her cry. And the fire? I hadn't meant to hurt her, but of course that was what I did.

I've finished with the decorating, and now I'm ready to begin. After I plow through a box of glazed donuts, I head to the library five blocks away from my studio. I may be big and heavy, but I don't mind walking. Counting steps clears my head.

The library is the perfect place to begin my research. Big and grand and impeccably organized, it gives me a sense of peace. I use my fake ID to get a library card and then vie for computer time with a batch of the town's homeless.

A girl taps my shoulder. "Are you new here?" she asks. She wears a frayed cap pulled tight over her head, and bits of blonde hair poke through the seams. She's so tiny I think she's a child until I spot the wrinkles around her eyes.

"Nope."

"My name's Mimi. What's yours?"

She smells like a bag of week-old trash. I wish her far away.

"This is the nicest library, don't you think? It's my favorite place in the world." Mimi claps her hands together and gets shushed by the security guard. "They don't like us," she says, dropping her voice. "But they can't stop us from coming. We have rights too."

I grab my cell and peer close like something important has happened. "I'm busy," I say, turning my back.

"Oh. Sorry." Mimi slinks off to the bathroom. Minutes later she's jabbering with some homeless friend.

When it's finally my turn for a computer, I hunker down and get to work.

Kathi

I'm seated in Leo's office wishing myself someplace else. His words drone on like the buzzing of a bee. *Embezzlement. Fraud. Complicity. Theft.* God knows I could use a goblet of wine, but it's only two in the afternoon.

"What do you mean I'm under investigation?" I ask him.

"Let's see . . ." Leo slips on a pair of gold-rimmed glasses and rifles through the papers in my file. He's sixty going on eighty, a divorcé living alone. He has jowls and thinning hair and walks with an awkward limp—not the type of person who typically made it onto my husband's advisor team. Rich liked to be surrounded by good-looking people. But Leo has a pedigree that can't be denied. Harvard undergrad. Stanford law. Chicago MBA. In this town, he's the best you can get.

He sighs and sets down his pen and places his fingertips together in a thoughtful way. He has small hands—perfectly smooth and white. They look odd next to his gnomelike face. "We'll get down to business in a moment, Kathi, but first I'd like to hear how you're doing. How are you handling life?"

"I'm fine. Just fine."

"Really?" He searches my face with his hangdog eyes. "Because you're looking a little frail."

"I . . . I think I'm doing okay . . ." I choke on my lie and dab at my eyes. Then the truth tumbles out of my mouth. "It just seems like everything's falling apart. My debit card wouldn't work yesterday, and a bill collector's been calling day and night. And then my housekeepers asked for a raise, and the gardeners didn't show this week. And then there's the broken air conditioner. I begged Rich to replace it last summer, but he insisted it would last another year."

"Can't Jack help out?"

I swallow and straighten my shoulders. "He would, but he's so very busy. He has a major part in a successful TV series, you know."

"Impressive." Leo jots something down. "How about relatives? Anyone live nearby?"

"I don't have anyone," I say, wiping my nose. "My parents died when I was young, and the aunt that brought me up passed away in 2010."

"I'm sorry to hear that. But surely you must have an abundance of friends willing to offer support."

I nod fast and hard. "Of course I do. I'm just saying after all of these years, it's terribly hard to live on my own."

"It *is* hard." For a moment I think he might share a personal story, but he retreats into his businesslike self. "I suppose we should return to the subject at hand. I spoke with George Taylor at length yesterday. He was quite helpful. A pleasant man, I must say."

"And?"

"Well . . . apparently the FBI believes you may have colluded with Rich."

"Colluded? Me?"

"Not that they've proven anything . . ."

My thoughts spin round and round like the wheels of a runaway bus. "But Rich never talked to me about his work. I know nothing. I really don't."

"Do you recall signing a loan application that contained erroneous information?"

My voice grows shaky. "Yes, I do. I mean, I didn't know the information was wrong. As I told that Agent Sykes, Rich was always having me sign documents. It's not like I read them. I just did what I was told."

Leo blinks several times. "I believe you, Kathi. I really do. I know how wealthy men behave in this town. But these days it's unlikely a judge or a jury would let you off with that excuse. Any prosecutor would argue that you're a college-educated woman living in the twenty-first century."

"I know, but . . ." I pinch my wrist. But what?

Leo pages through my file and pauses. "Oh, yes. George says they've located video footage of you accessing the safe deposit box."

"That's impossible. It's just not true."

"It was recorded at nine fifteen on the morning of Rich's death."

"But I wasn't there."

"Where were you?"

"At home, of course. I rarely get out of the house before ten."

"Is there anyone who could testify as to your whereabouts?"

"Maybe the gardeners."

"You spoke with them?"

"I don't recall."

"But they were there?"

"I'm not sure."

"Now, Kathi—"

"It wasn't me. *I swear!*" I begin to sob. I can't stop myself.

Leo takes a deep breath. "I'm sorry. I don't mean to upset you."

"Well, you *are* upsetting me," I say, snuffling. "I would think you of all people would believe me."

"I do believe you, Kathi. But I must ask you these difficult questions. It's my job." Leo takes a box of tissues from his top drawer and slides it across his desk. "I'm not saying you did anything wrong. I'm just trying to get a full understanding of the situation." He searches my face, trying to read my mind. I drop my gaze and fidget with the hem of my shirtdress. It's a little too short and snug.

Leo's cell phone throbs. "Excuse me a moment," he says. "I have to take this."

He steps out of the office, and I focus on the floor-to-ceiling bookcases lining the windowless wall. They're filled with an assortment of leather-bound books, some of them old and frayed. On the top shelf sits an ugly gold clock, naked cherubs surrounding its base. Its ticking reminds me of the annual cricket invasion at Aunt Genny's Iowa farm. Tick. Tick. Tick. The thing grinds on my nerves.

"What kind of clock is that?" I ask Leo upon his return.

He takes his seat. "It's a French ormolu clock from the 1850s. My wife bought it for me the summer we lived in Paris."

My smile freezes, and my face grows warm. He must know that *I know* there's no wife. She left him for a younger woman a few years ago. Older wife snags babe in the woods, as my friend Jane likes to say. Their breakup was all the talk of the town. And such an ugly divorce. His wife got the house and the kids. I'm surprised he didn't move away.

Leo clears his throat with a froglike croak. "Have you ever heard your husband mention something called a SAR?"

"SAR? Never. What's that?"

"It's an acronym for *suspicious activity report*—something a bank files with the federal government when they get wind of questionable activity. It's typically used to target terrorists and money launderers. Part of the Bank Secrecy Act."

My brain has that fuzzy feeling again. "They think Rich was a terrorist?"

"No. But banks are required to file a SAR when they suspect insider abuse."

"Insider abuse? That's impossible. My husband was a good and decent man. Who would accuse him of such a thing?"

"My understanding is that the ball got rolling through some anonymous tips to the feds. The feds then contacted the bank's compliance department, which had no choice but to investigate. Apparently the compliance officers found enough evidence to file a SAR."

"Did Rich know about this?"

"Not at first. Investigations are strictly confidential."

"So when did he find out?"

"About four months ago."

I mull this over. "Two whole months before he died?"

"Yes. He never mentioned anything to you?"

"No."

"Did you notice any change in his behavior? Had he been acting a little strange?"

Strange? I slowly shake my head. Had he? Maybe. Maybe not. He'd been spending less and less time at home, but that had been going on for years. "There must be some kind of mix-up," I say. "Rich maintained the highest of ethical standards. He would never do anything wrong."

"And the money in your safe deposit box?"

"I told you I don't know anything about that."

Leo searches my face. "But Rich did."

"I don't know. Maybe he didn't."

"Then how would you explain its presence?"

"*I don't know.*"

Leo's eyes narrow. "Please don't raise your voice."

"I'm sorry."

He shuts my file with a snap. "The thing is, Kathi, I'm a business attorney. I handle leases and contracts and that sort of thing, so this issue is outside of my purview. Even so, Rich and I were friends for many years, so I'm willing to try to help. But only if you're honest with me."

"I swear I'm telling the truth." Tick. Tick. Tick. I wish that clock would explode.

Leo gnaws his lower lip. "All right, then. Let's move on to another difficult subject. As of today, the FBI has frozen your assets."

"What assets?"

"Bank and investment accounts."

"You mean I don't have any money?" My heart flutters. I think I might just faint.

"Unfortunately, no. They're also placing liens on your home and your vacation cabin."

"They can't do that, can they?"

"They can and they will."

"But how? Why?"

"Among other things, they believe you knowingly signed a fraudulent loan application."

"But I didn't."

"Unfortunately, they think you did."

I can barely catch my breath. "So I have no money? Nothing?"

"Not until the investigation is complete."

"But how can I possibly live?" I feel like I'm in a dream. A nightmare without an end. I pinch my wrist, harder this time, but I don't wake up.

"The FBI has agreed to release twenty thousand dollars to cover your personal expenses."

"That's not much, is it?"

"Not with your current lifestyle."

I rack my brain. "What about Rich's life insurance? Shouldn't I be getting that soon?"

Leo shakes his head. "There'll be no distribution until a determination is made about the cause of Rich's death."

"I'm not following you."

"They need to rule out suicide."

"*Suicide?*" My eyes grow blurry. "But it was an accident. He would *never* kill himself."

"He was under a lot of pressure."

"It doesn't matter. He didn't do it. I'm one hundred percent positive of that."

Leo nods. "I'm sure you're right. But the train's video footage tells a complicated story. Why was he on the tracks at that time of night? And why wouldn't he stand up?"

"I don't know. Maybe he tripped. They haven't found those homeless women?"

"No. Neither of them have turned up. So for now, we'll need to be patient. In the meantime, I'll keep checking in with the insurance company. Hopefully they'll know something soon." Leo glances at his watch. "I'm sorry to have to cut our meeting short, but I have back-to-back appointments this afternoon, and I'm running a little late."

"I understand. Thank you for seeing me on such short notice." I dab at my eyes and stand, feeling a little wobbly at the knees.

Leo comes around his desk and takes me by the arm. "You'll get through this, Kathi. It's hard, but I promise you will."

"I hope so."

He walks me to the door and opens it wide. "One thing. Don't discuss the investigation with anyone. Not even with your closest friends."

"What about Jack?"

"Well, yes. I suppose he'll need to know. But no one else. Promise me?"

"I promise."

"Good. And one last piece of advice. Consider letting the gardeners go. And your housekeepers too. You'll need to eliminate all extraneous expenses. Understand? That includes no shopping except for the basics."

I try to work my mind around a life with no money. If there's an upside, I don't see it. I have a sudden, terrible thought. "But won't my friends and neighbors know I have a problem?"

His sad eyes get sadder. "I'm guessing they already do."

May 15, 1980

Aunt Genny tries. She really does. But it's lonely out on the farm. She's always telling me to invite my girlfriends over. Have an old-time slumber party with popcorn and ghost stories. I tell her people don't like to drive the distance—she lives over twenty miles from Des Moines. But the truth is I haven't made any friends. It's hard enough to start over in a new school, but when kids learn about my parents, they think I'm some kind of freak. I mean, they're nice enough to my face, but I always know when they've found out. They get this scaredy-cat look in their eyes. Like what happened to me just might rub off. Like losing a family is some kind of disease.

Crystal

May 19, 2015

Dipak is the closest thing I've ever had to a friend. We're tied together at the hip. I don't play the mind game with him anymore, and I don't wish him hell on earth.

He's had a hard life. Not as hard as mine, but still. Parents that emigrated from India to live the American dream. Just enough money to make the down payment on a one-star motel in the desert. A childhood spent cleaning toilets, changing sheets, and tossing condoms. Targeted by high school bullies for his brains, ethnicity, and size. We have a lot in common, except his parents love him more than life itself. They pepper him with texts and phone calls all throughout the week. Can you translate this? Can you explain that? He says he hates the badgering, but I know that isn't true. His voice goes soft when he speaks to his mother. Oozes respect when his father takes the phone.

"Can you believe it?" he asks me one day over lunch. "My parents think they're role models of immigrant success." He laughs. "Who are they kidding? A run-down motel in the Mojave? A son that slaves away in a second-rate bank? Meanwhile they spend their days scraping shit off floors while thanking the Hindu gods for their blessings."

"Maybe what they left behind was worse."

"Maybe."

We're alone in the office this week. The boys are in San Francisco for advanced analyst training. Dipak almost quit when he got passed over. George had to talk him down.

"Check this out." Dipak sets one of Tyler's loan files in front of me. It's nowhere as neat as my own. I want to organize and smooth the papers, but I know better than that.

"What am I looking for?"

"Start with the credit report."

I page through it and see a mess. The guy's got $50,000 in credit card debt, five charge-offs, a foreclosure, and collection accounts. "A loser. So what?"

"Now look at Tyler's analysis."

I flip through the twenty-page loan report. There's a short explanation blaming the bad credit on the recession and predatory banks.

"That's bullshit," I say.

"What about the tax returns?"

I compare the tax returns to the income analysis, then the financial statement to the balance sheet. I find a few key mistakes. Or deliberate adjustments. I do a quick scan of the spreadsheets. The mistakes on the page interrupt the beauty of the numbers. That makes me fume. "Is Tyler stupid or a liar?"

"Both."

"Why do this?"

"I'm guessing he wants George's job."

"So we're making the loan?"

"It got approved at the board meeting last week. Seven million for spec construction."

"But that's impossible. The guy clearly doesn't qualify."

"It's not impossible. It happened."

"But George didn't sign it." As the chief lending officer, George was supposed to stamp his recommendation on any loan that made it to the board.

"He refused to. But look who did."

I spot the president's signature scrawled across the recommendation box. "Something's not right," I say, my cheeks burning with excitement.

"Exactly. Something's not right."

"What's not right?"

We both look up in a panic. Dipak recovers first.

"Why, hello, Mr. Wright." His voice is shaking. "Can we help you with something?"

I've never been this close to the president before. He rarely makes small talk with the staff.

"I'm looking for Tyler," he says, his blue eyes sparking with annoyance. He's dressed in a dark suit with a white shirt and red silk tie. His peppered hair is neatly combed.

"He's away at training."

"Oh, yes." His lips twitch, and he holds out his hand. "You must be Dipak. I've heard good things about you."

Dipak beams like he's been blessed by the pope.

Rich releases his hand and turns to me. "And you are?"

I take hold of his hand. It feels moist and limp. "Crystal Love."

"I heard we hired a female analyst. Welcome aboard. How do you like it here?"

"It's a wonderful place to work." I want to point out I've been here for two months, but I'm sure he'd think that rude.

"Good to hear." He tries to extract his hand, but I fold my other hand over his.

"I'm so happy to finally meet you, Mr. Wright."

He looks confused and tugs his hand away. "Call me Rich," he says. "We aren't so formal here." Pulling a handkerchief from his pocket, he wipes his hand while he scans the room. His gaze settles on the open loan file.

"You working on this credit?"

"No," Dipak stutters, shutting the file. "We were just putting it away."

"Well, that's what I'm here for. The board has a few more questions. May I borrow it?"

"Of course." Dipak hands him the file.

"Thank you. And keep up the good work."

Dipak waits until Rich leaves before dancing a jig. "Can you believe it? He's 'heard good things.' How cool is that?"

"I thought you didn't like him."

"I don't, but . . ."

I turn my back on Dipak. "Credit files aren't allowed out of our office."

"But he's the president."

"And who are you? The next Tyler?"

We skip the beer after work.

Kathi

May 8, 2016

Dear Harlequin Editor,

I've just reviewed your website, and I am excited to learn that you are actively seeking new novelists. I don't have an agent, but after reviewing your categories, I believe my novel, Honest Love, will fit perfectly into the Heartwarming series. Honest Love is a wholesome and heartfelt romance featuring Emma and Robert—think Scarlett and Rhett. In summary, a handsome young bank manager falls in love with a beautiful teller, but they must hide their love from the evil bank president, who forbids all interoffice dating. Through both passion and perseverance, they defy the rules and emerge with bonds that cannot be broken. The young couple doesn't believe in sex before marriage, so the grand finale comes right after their private beach wedding when Robert lifts Emma into his muscular arms and carries her into the bedroom of their recently renovated Victorian cottage. The final scene is of Robert shutting the door with his foot.

I don't yet have the manuscript written, but if you are as excited as I am about my project, I'm sure I can complete the novel in eight to ten weeks. Your website mentions it takes up to twelve weeks to respond to an inquiry, but I would greatly appreciate a response within a week to ten days. Please note that I am willing to accept an advance in the $10,000 range as long as I receive it in a timely manner. I look forward to hearing from you soon.

Yours kindly,
Kathi Wright, a.k.a. Crystal Love

I sit back and review my note written on expensive linen stationary. Mailing a nicely written letter rather than sending an email will make all the difference in the world. They'll know I'm serious about the business of writing and not just some blogger looking for a quick buck.

I address the envelope and place it next to the stack of unopened bills. Then I pour myself a goblet of wine and relax in front of the widescreen TV. *Housewives* or news? *Housewives.* I'd rather not hear what's going on in the world. I watch for a while, and then my cell phone chirps, and I just about fall off the couch.

"Jack?"

"Mom?"

I'm so happy I repeat his name with a giggle. "Jack. I knew you would call."

"What the hell's going on?"

"Jack, I—"

"First off, you need to stop calling and texting me day and night."

"I thought my calls were blocked."

"I don't want you calling me. And no more texts."

"All right . . . it's so good to hear from you."

"I don't have much time. Just explain what's going on with my account."

"Your account?"

"The one at Dad's bank."

"Oh, that."

"Yes, that."

"Was Dad giving you money, sweetie?" As if I didn't know.

"Don't call me sweetie. And you know that he was."

"You never opened your own account?"

"That *was* my account."

"Yours and your dad's, right? Your dad was on it too?"

"What if he was?"

"Well, I'm afraid all your father's accounts have been frozen."

"But it's *my* account."

"And your dad's. They must have frozen that one too."

There's a hissing on the phone, like steam coming from a kettle. "Frozen?"

"Yes." I start to cry. "That's why I've been calling you, Jack. They're saying some terrible things about your father."

"Who is?"

"The bank and the FBI."

"What the hell?"

"Don't swear, Jack."

"I'll fucking swear if I want to."

"Now, Jack—"

"What the hell were you guys up to?"

"It wasn't me. It was your father."

"Bullshit. You're as much of a liar as he was."

"That's not true . . ."

He's silent a moment. "So there's no money?"

"Not right now."

"You're broke too?"

"They let me keep a little, not much."

"This is great. Just great."

"I could sell something if you need cash right away."

"I'm going now, Mom."

"I could sell some jewelry."

"Don't do that."

"I'll split the advance on my book."

"Your book?"

"Yes, I'm writing a romance novel—"

"Stop!"

"What?"

"I don't want to hear about your bullshit dreams anymore."

I take a gulp of wine and nearly choke.

"Mom?"

"Please, Jack. I need you. It's terrible here. It seems your dad's been keeping secrets."

"You both were keeping secrets."

"That's not true."

The phone goes dead after that.

I cry for a while until my tears run dry. Then I wipe my eyes and get up and check the time. It's nearly eight. I'm feeling dizzy from another day of little food, so I pop a frozen dinner into the microwave and pour another goblet of wine. I throw open the glass pocket doors that front the living room and kitchen and wander out onto the terrace. No sign of the gardeners again today. The cactus garden is disintegrating before my very eyes—is it from too much water or too little? I make a half-hearted attempt to pick up a few stray leaves before I sink into my favorite lounge chair. The cushions haven't been turned in over a month, and they feel rough and sticky with dust. I finish off my wine and watch as the clouds spread their golden glow across the ocean while the mountains take on their evening shade of pink. It's warm out, and the strains of a string quartet waft through the air. Somebody's having a party. No invitation for me.

The microwave dings, but I only sink deeper in my chair. Maybe I'll do some shopping this week, just enough to cheer me up. One new outfit won't bust my budget. Then again, maybe it will. I should probably pay a bill or two, but which ones? There's my therapist, of course. She keeps sending nagging texts. I thought we were friends but apparently not. I set down my glass, close my eyes, and force myself to think. But aside from saving a few pennies, there's no upside to losing Jack.

October 13, 1981

It doesn't matter that Alberto and I don't speak the same language. He gets me. I can see it in his beautiful eyes, brown and round and dreamy with really long black eyelashes. You'd think he wears mascara, but of course he would never do something like that. I can't stop dreaming of his kisses. His lips are as soft as silk. I hope he can meet me on the porch again tonight. It's only been a week since he told me he LOVED me and I told him I LOVED him too.

Aunt Genny doesn't know about Alberto, but I'm sure she wouldn't mind. She worries that I haven't made any close friends. That I've never been out on a date. Never been to a single school dance. I want to tell her about Alberto, but he says we must keep our love a secret. His mom and dad would kill him if they ever found out because they don't want him dating white girls. They want him to work hard and stay with his own. We're just like Romeo and Juliet, except we're going to have a happy ending. I know that 100 percent!

I borrowed an English-Spanish dictionary from the library so we can practice lots of different words. Alberto doesn't read very well, but it's ABSOLUTELY not his fault. His family follows the harvests, so he has never spent much time in school. I don't think that's fair, so I'm going to ask Aunt Genny to let the Garcias live with us year-round in the apartment above the barn. She's always saying she could use some extra help. Then Alberto could go to my high school and learn to love books as much as I do. We could go to all of the dances together. Maybe we'll even get married one day!!!!!

Crystal

As I drive by the house for the third time this month, I try to put two and two together, but I don't get four. Math is my safety blanket. It calms me. Makes sense of the chaos. It tells me what's ahead and archives what's behind. So when the numbers don't add up, it more than tilts my world.

The flat and gray house, built in a drab modern style, doesn't fit with the charm of its Moorish neighbors. The lawn's been replaced by the peach-colored gravel that's shown up all over town. Cacti and succulents line the driveway, all measured and exact, their perfect symmetry giving them the appearance of plastic. I crunched a couple with my foot one moonless night, and sure enough, they were real. I bet the gardeners dig up the outliers and toss them in the trash. Not that I think it's wrong. I understand the need for proportion. That's the part of this I get.

The piece of the puzzle that doesn't fit sits squarely with the wife. Not that I pictured arm candy in a marriage of thirty years. But I expected her to mimic him—tall and lean, hard and cold. Instead, she's soft and frumpy and cowers like a puppy that's been broken by its master. It's clear she tries—designer clothes, expensive makeup, the auburn hair streaked with gold. I'm guessing her face has been "done" at least once, if not twice. She's still pretty but fading fast in a land that worships youth.

She isn't the woman I imagined. What has he done to her? Or what has she done to herself? Does she carry the secret for both of them? Is it eating her up inside? I want to take her by the shoulders and shake her hard. I start to play a round of my favorite game. What is the very worst thing that could happen? With the husband, it's easy. With the wife, I draw a blank.

A car drives up. I recognize the emblem emblazoned on its side as belonging to one of the private security services the local 1 percenters use. A man in a uniform steps out.

"Can I help you, ma'am?"

The security guard is tall and broad with the beginnings of a drinker's belly. A thirtysomething piece of work with a man bun to announce he's cool and arm tattoos to say he's tough. A gun? No. They don't carry. Nice cheekbones, though.

I pick up the book I keep handy for such encounters: *The Grand Architecture of Santa Barbara*. "I'm a student of architecture," I say. "This neighborhood is mentioned on page sixty-six. What a view, don't you think?"

Not a trace of a smile, just a lift of an eyebrow. "A neighbor called in. Said they've seen your car parked here before."

"Impossible. It's my first visit."

"They have footage."

I want to knock myself on the side of the head. Security cameras. Of course.

"Can I see your college ID?"

Is he dumb as a doorknob or slick as a snake? "I'm not in school. I'm just an amateur. I study beautiful buildings."

"Well, you can't do that here."

"Why not?"

"It's private."

"This is a public street."

"Want me to call you in?"

"I'm leaving."

"No. Stay where you are. I'll call you in."

Stupid girl. I turn the key and zoom off. He hops in his car and tails me to the Lower Village. I'm nervous. Sweating. *Stupid. Stupid. Stupid.* I pull onto the freeway, heart pounding. He doesn't follow me, thank god. I take a few deep breaths and wipe my forehead. It worries me when I make a mistake. There's no room to be wrong.

Kathi

I've met Jane for brunch at the Fairmont, and I'm feeling tipsy from my first glass of champagne.

"Oh my god," Jane says, "how thin you are. You look stunning. I'll trade my Jimmy Choos for your secret."

It's so nice to hear Jane say those words. She has a Parisian look about her—always chic and thin. She's never said a word about my weight, but I've glimpsed some smugness in her eyes.

We are seated in the Fairmont's partially enclosed terrace with the ocean a stone's throw away. Around us sit the best of Montecito, the women primped and beautiful, the men tan and distinguished. The buffet spreads out against one wall, colorful and lavish and full of lobster, quiche, and crab. I probably can't afford it. But Jane's a busy woman and Sunday brunch her only opening for weeks.

It's a warm day, and she wears a white linen frock and red sling backs that go well with her tan. The dark hair framing her ageless face is pulled back in a ballet bun. In my new Versace pantsuit, for once I feel close to her equal.

Jane dabs her napkin against her plumped-up lips. "I know you've been going through a horrible time. I just can't believe what happened to Rich. I'm so sorry we didn't make it to the funeral. With Franklin's plane on the fritz, it's such a hassle to get back to the States from Cabo. I hate flying public these days, don't you?"

We both know it's not that the plane is in the shop. It's Franklin. He's nearing ninety, and a quick-moving dementia has set in. Jane's only fifty. She's wife number three and younger than the youngest of his four children.

"So tell me," she says, taking hold of my hand. "Tell me how you are doing. I really want to know."

"I'm . . ." I must choose my words carefully. We've been friends for years, but anything juicy will spread around town like wildfire. "I'm doing fine, considering."

Jane glances at my plate, piled high with delicious food. "What's your secret?" she whispers. "A new pill? A shot? Whatever it is, I want it."

I tell her my secret, and she seems disappointed. She may inject herself with fillers, but she draws the line at snipping taste buds.

"I maintain my weight the old-fashioned way," she says, giggling and slipping the tip of a finger into her mouth. "You get the taste but not the calories."

I love Jane. She's funny and has always been kind to me, unlike some of the other women in town. She's had an unusual life. "Poor little rich girl," she calls herself. When she turned sixteen, her father joined a commune, and her mother kicked her out of their Montecito mansion. Next thing Jane knew, her high school boyfriend had moved into her old bedroom. Her mother's affair with the underage boy had lasted for many years. Nowadays, the mom would've been arrested, but those were different times. When Jane told me that story, I'd been shocked. She just shrugged and said, "Welcome to Montecito. Turn over any rock, and you'll find something worse."

By my second glass of champagne, I'm ready to spill the beans. I lean across the table, secrets slithering off my tongue. But then Jane's best friend, Eileen, steps through the doors with her handsome husband, Arthur. Dressed in a stunning black frock, Eileen whips her blonde hair this way and that, scanning the tables to see who is worthy of her notice. Her gaze settles on Jane, and she offers up a fake smile and a beauty pageant wave. Then she whispers in her husband's ear, and they head for the opposite side of the room.

"Bitch," Jane mutters.

"Did something happen between you two?"

Jane picks up her cell and flips through a thousand pictures until she settles on the one she wants.

"See this?" She points to a lavender tablecloth and matching napkins. "I'm so furious I can't see straight."

"You don't like the color?"

"Color? Are you kidding me? It's so much more than that. You know Eileen is this year's chair of the Diamond Ball. Well, it's gone straight to her head. I'm in charge of the decorating committee, and last week, after months of consideration, we chose the color of our linens. Then Eileen stepped in and overruled us. Said our color choice was too dull. Can you believe that? It's outrageous. It's never happened in the history of the ball. Let me show you her dreadful choice."

Jane flicks through a few more photos and flashes another lavender setting. I honestly can't tell the difference between the two, but I nod anyway.

"That's awful," I say.

"Revolting."

"Will she change her mind?"

"It doesn't matter because I've quit the committee. I refuse to be treated with such disrespect." She drops her voice to a whisper. "And you know what? I've heard rumors that the Van Meters are in financial trouble. Arthur's latest spec project has bombed. Eileen must be throwing a fit. I'll bet their marriage is on the rocks. How sad is that?"

"That *is* sad."

"I suppose so. But I'm sick of her superior attitude." Jane thrusts her cell into her purse. "But enough of that. I'm not going to let that woman ruin our brunch. So tell me. How is poor Jack? He must be devastated by the loss of his father."

I nod and take a bite of the lobster. It tastes like a bland bit of rubber. My hands start to shake, so I set down my fork. "He's taking it hard, but he'll recover."

"It must be a blessing to have him by your side."

"It is." I gulp down my champagne.

"I probably missed out by not having children. I mean, what's going to happen to me after poor Franklin passes away? I'll be all alone in that big, rambling house. And if I get sick? Who's going to take care of me?"

"You have the stepchildren."

"They've never liked me. And to be perfectly honest, I've never liked them. Right now, they're circling like vultures. Won't they be surprised when they see the will?" She finishes off her champagne and signals to the waiter to refill our glasses. "Did you ever wish you had more?"

"More champagne?"

"More children."

"I guess I always wanted a big family. I was an only child myself. And Jack begged us for a brother or sister. He was a little lonely growing up."

"So why didn't you have another little one?"

I hesitate before diving in. "There were complications when Jack was born. And then Rich came across some studies that said single children have higher IQs. And of course, there's the money issue. It costs a lot to raise a child."

Jane taps her nails against her champagne glass. "I don't mean to speak ill of the dead, but Rich was rather controlling . . ."

There's no way I'm going there, friend or not. "Truth is I couldn't," I say firmly. "I came down with an infection a few weeks after Jack's delivery. I couldn't have any more after that."

"Oh, Kathi. I'm so sorry. That was horribly inconsiderate of me."

"No. Please don't worry. It's all right." She waits for me to say more, but I nibble on a slice of rye toast instead.

"Anyway," she continues, perking up. "You should consider yourself lucky. You have a handsome, successful son. A Hollywood insider. I'd give anything to have a child like that. What if he gets nominated for an Emmy? Just think of it. What would you wear? Gucci? Saint Laurent?"

"I haven't thought about it . . ."

"Well, I would. Oh, to have a boy like Jack to support me in my darkest days. I don't have anyone. No one at all." Jane's eyes glisten for a moment, and then she returns to the subject of the ball. I pretend to be interested, but my thoughts slosh around like water in a tub.

It's nearing noon when Jane asks the waiter to split the bill. He returns with my credit card and a frown on his face.

"My mistake," I say. "Try this one."

He returns with that one too. A flush of shame creeps up my neck and spreads across my cheeks. I think back on the weekend's shopping spree. Leo will be disappointed, but what else could I do? I had to buy new clothes to fit my smaller figure.

"Oh, Kathi." Jane reaches out and pats my hand. "I'm sure it's just some complication with the estate."

"Yes. A complication."

"Who's your lawyer?"

"Leo Silverstein."

"Frumpy Leo? He's very good. Did you hear his ex-wife is getting a divorce? Apparently her trophy gal was a cheat." Jane turns to the waiter and instructs him to put the entire bill on her card.

"I'll get it next time," I say, pinching my wrist.

"Of course you will."

I want to die right then and there. Melt into the floor. I rack my brain but find no upside to being broke. No conceivable upside at all.

April 21, 1982

It's just so hard to decide. I only know I want to go to a faraway place where no one knows a single thing about my family and where I don't get that pitying look. I'm sick of lonely Kathi. I want to be someone else.

Since my dream is to become a writer, Aunt Genny thinks I should go to NYU. She lived in New York for a year after college before returning to run the family farm. I think she regrets giving up big-city life, but it's really not for me. I'd rather live in a beautiful place like California. Swim in the big, wide ocean. Maybe even learn how to surf. And UCSB is right on the beach. RIGHT on it! The pictures in the brochure are SO beautiful. I think it's the perfect place for me.

Crystal

When I arrive at work a few minutes late, Dipak looks up and whispers, "Surprise audit."

He stands at the entrance to our office dressed in his shabbiest suit and scruffiest shoes, eyes wide and lips drawn tight, cracking his knuckles nonstop.

Four members of the compliance department rummage through our desks. They're all middle-aged and dowdy, dressed in shades of black and brown. They scurry about like ants in search of sugar, looking for morsels of mistakes. If they find one, it'll be a feeding frenzy—they'll all pile on top.

This is our second audit, so I already know the routine. First they'll check the basics: files locked in cabinets, desks cleared of clutter, no confidential papers sitting loose in the drawers. After that they'll move on to loan files. They'll hand us lists of ten customers each—no substitutions allowed. Then they'll whisk the chosen files to the bowels of compliance, where our work will be chewed and digested. A small mistake might earn a slap on the wrist. A big one will result in the loss of a job. That's what happened to my predecessor. It will never happen to me.

Sue is the oldest and crankiest of the bunch, a devil of a woman with spotting scopes for eyes. She digs through my drawers and pauses at my hidden stash of candy. As she holds up a king-size chocolate bar, her lips twitch into a grin. "Breakfast?" she asks.

Dipak snickers, and I almost kick him. "No," I say, pretending to play along. "I'm saving that for lunch."

She drops the bar in the drawer and gets back to work. "Where are Tyler and Eric?" she asks, pouncing on Dipak's desk.

Dipak glances at me and shrugs. "They're usually in by nine," he says. "Ten at the very latest."

"Are you serious?" Sue straightens up, hands on hips. "You millennials drive me crazy."

There's a sudden commotion, and the head of compliance totters in on her trademark four-inch heels. Vanessa Sophia Allen has a smile that's whiter than white, hair that's blonder than blonde. A body that's thin as a rail except for the fake boobs that explode from her blouse. The two boys trail behind her like dogs hot on a scent.

You're a professional, I want to tell her. You're old. At least forty. You should be mashing those boys into paste, not playing into their hands.

"Thank you for the coffee," Vanessa says, flashing Tyler a starstruck smile. She wouldn't be smiling if she knew the boys had christened her Shipwreck Barbie for her listing walk and pointy breasts.

Vanessa turns to Sue. "How's everything going?"

"Fine. We've finished with the desks. We're collecting the files."

"Good to hear. This needs to go fast." She taps her foot a few times and then turns to me. "How are you enjoying your new job, Crystal?" Her eyes are a strange shade of green this morning. She must be wearing contacts.

"It's not so new anymore. But everything's just fine."

"You don't mind being the only girl in the Stable?"

"I don't mind at all."

"That's because we think of her as one of the boys," Tyler says.

"Not hard to do," Eric adds.

Vanessa laughs, and my mind slips into game mode. Maybe I'll send her an anonymous note and let her in on her Stable nickname. Might not destroy her life, but it sure would ruin her day.

The audit drags on through the morning, and I'm bored beyond belief. I'm about to excuse myself when Sue holds up her list. "There's a problem here," she says. "I'm missing two files. Jared Franks and Arthur Van Meter."

"Those are my clients," Tyler offers.

"So where are the files?" Sue asks.

"Rich's secretary took them."

"You let her?"

"Of course."

Sue's eyes narrow to slits. "Per bank policy, all original files must remain in this office."

Tyler folds his arms and offers her a sly grin. "So why don't you tell that to the president yourself."

"That's your job."

"You think?"

"I don't like your attitude."

"And I don't like yours."

Vanessa jumps in. "Let's all try to stay calm."

Sue's face has turned the color of an Early Girl tomato. "But bank policy says that—"

"I know what bank policy says," Vanessa snaps. "You might recall I wrote it."

"Well, of course, but—"

"Just take the boxes and go."

Sue straightens her back, picks up a box with a grunt, and hurries out the doorway, almost knocking George to the ground.

"Everything all right?" he asks as he steps in.

"Good morning, George," Vanessa says stiffly.

"Good morning, Vanessa," he replies. "Are you about done?"

"Yes, we are."

"Everything in order?"

"It better be. Regulators arrive next week."

"I'm aware of that." His glass eye twitches.

The compliance team gathers up the remaining boxes and carries them out of the office. Not a mention of the missing files to George. I squirrel that away in my head.

Kathi

I've subscribed to a writing magazine that has some wonderful articles on how to write your first novel. One of my favorites suggests background sketches on all the key characters. Know their history, their wants, their desires. It gives a list of twenty-five questions to ask. Where were they born? Family intact or divorced? Good student or bad? Cat or dog? Straight or gay? Children? And then there's "innermost desire." You need to know your characters' dreams—what they really want in life. By the time I fill out the questionnaires, *Honest Love* should be a snap to write.

The article suggests you try it on yourself first, but you have to be brutally honest. Easy enough. I'm sure I can do that. I pour a goblet of wine and head for the terrace. It's a warm afternoon but not too hot. Just perfect in the shade. I settle on a bench beneath our ancient oak and get to work on my questionnaire.

Name: Katherine (Kathi) Smith (Wright)
Birthplace: Ames, Iowa
Childhood angst: Parents died in a car crash
Family status: Married. Husband recently deceased.
Good student or bad: Good

Cat or dog?: Neither (Rich didn't like pets)
Straight or gay: Very straight
Children?: Yes
Names and ages: Jack, 29
Best friends: Jane & Laurie
Dream job: Novelist
Innermost desire:

I pause on that last one. What do I want? What do I really want? I suppose what I want is to have my family back. But that's never going to happen. Not with Rich gone.

The doorbell rings, and I startle, dropping my pen. It rolls beneath the bench, and I get on my knees to retrieve it. The doorbell rings again. And again.

Oh, go away, I think. I don't want to answer the door. I've been doing that lately. Pretending I'm not at home. Whoever it is, they're insistent. I hide my wine at the foot of the bench and head back into the house.

When I open the door, Mabel McCarthy is on the other side, our elderly neighbor from three houses down the block. I'm not in the mood for a neighborly chat, but there's no escaping her now.

"Mabel, so nice to see you again."

She holds a homemade pineapple upside-down cake in her tiny, clawlike hands. She was born in Montecito and has lived in the same house for fifty-some years. At one time her family owned most of the surrounding property, but they sold it off in bits and pieces to fund their lifestyle over the years.

Dressed in a bright-orange muumuu and dirty slippers, Mabel doesn't seem to notice three scruffy cats that weave through her legs. She claims to own five cats—the legal limit—but Rich insisted she owns more than ten. They wander through the neighborhood leaving mounds of poop wherever they go. Rich used to sprinkle hot pepper flakes around our garden to keep her felines at bay. I thought that cruel, so when he'd leave for work, I'd take the hose and wash away the flakes.

"I hope you like cake," she says with a near-toothless smile. The cake is sunken on one side and just a little too brown. "I made it myself. Would you mind if I come in?"

"Please do. Can I get you some coffee or tea?"

"Tea would be nice."

I try to shut the door on the cats, but all three scamper in. I start to say something, and then I don't. What does it matter anymore?

"You have such a beautiful home," Mabel says. "Everything white. Such a bold choice."

"Thank you." The house is a mess, but she doesn't seem to notice. I try to picture the room through her eyes. Rich insisted on our spare, modern style with floor-to-ceiling glass pocket doors. They're a horror to keep clean, but on a nice day you can open the doors wide so that the living room and terrace become one. I prefer a comfy cottage look, but Rich insisted a bank president's residence must set a certain tone.

Mabel plops onto our living room couch, and I take the cake to the kitchen. By the time I return with mint tea and slices of cake, the cats have settled into a ball on her lap. The cutest one, black and white with orange spots on his back, shoots his head up and yawns at me before resettling with a purr.

It doesn't take long for Mabel to begin reminiscing on her favorite subject of old Montecito, when artists and hippies ruled the land. In the 1950s, her father—a mediocre landscape painter at best—was smart enough to save his pennies and buy up acres of cheap land on Mountain Drive. When times changed, he went from starving artist to local real estate baron. Mabel was one of his four children. Her siblings have all since passed away.

She's in the midst of retelling a story about the trouble she got into jumping from the end of the old Coral Casino pier when she abruptly switches direction.

"I'm so sorry about Rich," she says, reaching across the glass coffee table to take my hand. Hers is a little moist, and I can't help but wonder when she last bathed. "Was the funeral nice?"

"It was." I gently pull my hand away and wipe it with a napkin. "So many people in the community came to pay their respects."

"I'm so sorry I couldn't be there."

"Well, I appreciate your thoughtful card. I'll get around to writing a thank-you note one day soon."

Mabel waves her hand like she's swatting a fly. "Don't bother yourself. That's a silly old tradition. Now, tell me, where is Rich buried?"

"Santa Barbara Cemetery."

"Oh, I love it there, don't you? I have my plot picked out right next to my dear Edgar. We'll have an ocean view together for eternity."

"That's sweet." How stupid of me. I'd been so devastated by Rich's death I didn't give a thought to location. I chose a grave site that backs up to the street. Rich would've preferred an ocean view.

"Anyway," Mabel continues. "I would've attended the service, but I can't drive anymore. After my last little mishap in the Upper Village, they've taken my privileges away."

I heard from a neighbor that her last little mishap involved hitting a fire hydrant and flooding the nearby streets.

"No worries," I say. "I know your thoughts were with us."

"Of course. I always liked Rich. He was a big help with my money."

"You were a client of the bank?"

She shakes her head. "Goodness no. I've had my accounts at Wells Fargo since I was a girl. Rich gave me investment advice—that's all." She finishes her cake and eyes mine like she wants to eat that too.

"You mean he helped you find rates on CDs?"

"Heavens no. CDs pay next to nothing these days. Most of my money was invested in a thirty-year treasury bond paying close to eight percent. When it matured last year, I didn't know what to do with the proceeds. Interest rates had fallen through the floor. Then Rich told me about a special investment where I could make ten percent or more."

"My Rich?"

"Yes. I was so very thankful." She drops her voice to a whisper. "It's not pin money, you understand. I gave him a million dollars. It's nearly the last of my inheritance."

I set down my fork. "You gave a million dollars to Rich?"

"I did." She tilts forward, and the cats scatter every which way. "The thing is, I was receiving regular interest payments until four months ago. I tried calling the bank, but Rich was always on the phone or busy and never returned my calls. And then, well, and then he was suddenly gone. I didn't think it proper to bother you with questions while you were in a state of mourning. But enough is enough. It's all the money I have in the world, and I have a stack of bills to pay." She sits up straight. "So I'd like my money back as soon as possible. I'm sure you can understand."

"Of course." The woman must be crazy or suffering from dementia. Nothing she says makes sense.

"Can you get it for me? My money?"

"I don't know . . ."

She folds her hands together. "My daughter says what's happened to me is called elder abuse. If I don't get my money back soon, she intends to call the police."

"Police? No. Please don't do that. There must be a misunderstanding. I'll look into it for you."

She smiles sweetly. "I knew you would. It's not like Rich was a thief. Are you going to finish your cake?"

"It's all yours." I hand her the cake, and she gobbles it down while I worry and wring my hands. "Do you happen to know the name of the investment?" I ask when she finishes up.

She swipes the back of her hand across her lips, leaving a swatch of red lipstick behind. "I know it's some kind of real estate investment. Bella Verde or Casa Grande. Something like that."

"Do you have any documents I can look at?"

"No, I don't. I'm a born scatterbrain, so Rich agreed to hold on to them for me." She stands, wobbling a little. "Now if you'll be so kind to help me round up my cats. They're so very mischievous. They'll be the death of me one day."

As soon as Mabel and her cats are out the door, I hurry up the stairs to Rich's office. He called it his "man cave." No women allowed. So when I open the door and flick on the lights, I feel a rush of guilt.

The office is so very Rich. White walls, sleek furniture, aluminum file cabinets, and an oversized window with an expansive view of the coast. But the mess—Rich would have hated it. The night he died, the police insisted on going through his things, so drawers yawn open and file cabinets sit ajar. Papers litter the surface of his desk. They asked to take his computer and have yet to return it. I make a mental note to call them tomorrow.

I think back on that night. "Where were you at nine?" they asked, as if I had something to do with his death. "Was your husband depressed? Were there money problems? Was he having an affair? Were you?"

"No, no, no, and no," I answered between racking sobs.

I rustle through the papers on Rich's desk and slide open the top drawer. Pencils, pens, paper clips, and rubber bands lie in precise rows. I move on to the file cabinets, opening and shutting the drawers. There are masses of papers going back decades, all perfectly sorted and labeled. When I open the last cabinet, I come across a thick file labeled CASA BELLA.

I pull the file out and scatter the pages across the white wool rug. Loan documents, I think, with $100,000 typed across the top of one, $200,000 on another. I see names I recognize: Peter Sterling. Jennifer Ross. Susan Evers. And then I spy Mabel's name next to a handwritten number: $500,000. Didn't she say a million? I'm sure she did. What could this possibly mean? Does it have something to do with the bank?

My face floods with heat. My heart thrums in my chest. I start breathing fast and hard. I try pinching my wrist, but the pain doesn't stop the bad thoughts from piling up. I return the papers to the file and shove it into the cabinet. Then I rush out of the office and down the stairs and throw open the refrigerator door. Grabbing an open box of wine, I pour one goblet and then another until Mabel's words fade away.

December 10, 1983

It's only been three months since I met Rich, but I feel like I've known him forever. He's SO sweet and SO good-looking, and I'm SO lucky to be dating such an incredible guy. We met on the very first day of classes. I was lost, and he helped me find my way. That's the kind of person he is. Thoughtful, kind, and caring. Never thinking of himself.

We're a lot alike in so many ways. I mean, he doesn't love books like I do. He's an econ major and plans to go into business and make a lot of money one day. But we're both serious about our studies, and we hardly ever party. And he doesn't have much family, just a younger sister and a mom he rarely sees. He's coming home with me for Christmas. I hope he likes Aunt Genny. I'm sure she'll like him. He's such an incredible guy!

Crystal

I got frustrated. The going was too slow. I wasn't able to break through the bank's information wall. So I decided to shake up the players. Give myself a promotion. Play a round of my favorite game.

The day of the revelation, I arrive at work early so I can sit back and watch events unfold. I'm excited to look through my emails, but I don't allow myself the pleasure. I'd rather savor the moment when it arrives.

To kill time, I open a box of celebratory treats from Jorgensen's Danish Bakery. Their flaky pastry crusts literally melt in your mouth— just enough sugar to counter the salt. A slice of heaven on earth. I chose an assortment of danishes: raspberry, rhubarb, apricot, and cherry. I said they were for a staff meeting, but the cashier gave me a knowing look.

"My favorite is the cream cheese," she whispered.

I've gained weight since my arrival in Santa Barbara. The hordes of thin people make me nervous. I slump over my desk to chow down on the cherry pastry and then hide the rest in my drawer. I don't want Dipak to see me eating. He thinks there's beauty hiding under my fat. Sometimes I glance in the mirror in just the right way and think there's a chance he might be right.

I lick my fingers and then open a loan file to keep my excitement contained. At work I play a modified version of my game. A home for

Jack but not for Jill. A car for Peter but not for Paul. Not that I lie or fudge numbers—I'm in no way like the boys. But if I think a client should win the game, I can nudge a decision to the finish line. Just a few telling words, a missing set of scores, a focus on the highs rather than the lows. It's not a science like some people think. It's a form of art.

My hands embrace the application. My eyes caress the numbers. A plumber wants a building, a place to store his goods. I haven't met the man, but his life seems neat and clean. A sprinkling of credit. Schedule Cs that show profit. Taxes paid on time. A wife who teaches nursery school. Two children in public school. They own a modest home with a reasonable mortgage and don't own a lot of frivolous toys. No sign of student loans to eat away their futures. I'm about to bless the file when Dipak slogs in.

"Morning," he says with a sullen look.

"Morning," I reply.

He sinks into his chair with a sigh.

"Something wrong?" I ask.

"Something not?" He takes a bite from a bagel and downs it with a slug of coffee. "I just don't want to be here," he says, crumbs spraying from his lips. "I'm bored and sick of work."

Happiness wells inside me. "You never know, Dipak. Life can change in the blink of an eye."

He pauses and looks at me. "What do you mean by that?"

"Nothing." I bury my head in my file. Today should cheer him up.

He turns to his computer, wiggles his mouse, and seconds later breathes deep. *"Holy shit!"*

"What?" My pulse speeds up.

His voice drops to a whisper. "Have you seen this?"

"Seen what?"

"Come here."

I haul myself out of my chair and stand behind him.

"Wait," he says. "Maybe you shouldn't . . ."

But it's too late. I see what's on his screen. It's the bank's newest loan assistant, a fiery redhead just out of college. She's spread full-frontal naked across a pile of white sheets. Glossy lips wide open, one hand caressing a smooth white breast, the other on her upper thigh. She looks like someone you'd see on a porn site. But it's not porn. It's just little Amanda from the corner office spread across Dipak's computer screen.

"Where'd you get that?" I ask.

"In my email. I bet you have it too."

"It's gross." So very gross. Not the worst photo I found on Tyler's phone but definitely the most incriminating.

"Damn it," Dipak says, his hands shaking. He nervously clicks until the image disappears from his screen. "It came in an email from Tyler, from his private Gmail account." He glances at me over his shoulder. "Holy double shit. He blasted it to everyone in the bank."

I try to sound innocent. "Why would he do that?"

Dipak points excitedly at his screen. "He sent it at midnight. Maybe a drunk dial. Who the hell knows? But he's in a shitload of trouble—that's for sure."

Breaking into Tyler's phone had been easy. So was sending the photo to my private account and wiping away the evidence. He has a habit of leaving his cell on his desk, and his password is in his drawer. I had a harder time figuring out how to spew the email from his personal account at midnight when the library closes at eight.

There's a scream far down the hallway and then the sound of hurried footsteps. I'm guessing it's Amanda. I feel sorry for her. I really do. She doesn't deserve this. She's collateral damage. A pawn in my game of life.

George's head pops through the doorway, his face pinched and grim. "Where's Tyler?"

"Monday and Wednesday he works out at CrossFit," I reply. "He doesn't get in until ten."

"Ten?" George's forehead wrinkles. He looks like he's aged a decade in a day. "Tell him to come to my office as soon as he shows up."

"Of course."

I log in to my computer and scan my emails. The IT department didn't waste a second. Tyler's indiscretion has been swept away.

Kathi

June 15, 2016

I wake to a pair of dreamy brown eyes, the kind of eyes I fell for before I met Rich. The eyes of a boy I crushed on in high school. Alberto. Alberto Garcia. I was sixteen when he arrived with his family to work the autumn harvest, and it was love at first sight. I thought we'd be together for eternity, but then his father caught us kissing on the front porch. His family disappeared that very same night. I never heard from Alberto again. His leaving shattered my heart.

I picture Alberto brushing my lips, kissing my nipples, caressing my thighs. Then the dream slips away, and I'm staring into the gardeners' worried faces. They hover above me, waving shears and rakes, the morning fog swirling around them like smoke.

"Nine-one-one?" the shorter one asks, holding up his phone. I can never remember his name. Is it Jose? Jorge? Jesus? Do the same ones come every time?

"No," I say, my hands fluttering like hummingbirds. "I'm fine. I was just resting."

I sit up, and my goblet falls from my chest and shatters on a flagstone. The two men glance at each other knowingly. One of them even smirks.

"No mas," I say in terrible Spanish. I wave my hands in the air. "No trabajas aqui today hoy."

They nod and back away like I'm some crazy woman. Well, I'm not. Or maybe I am. I wait until the side gate clicks shut and then collapse back onto the lounge chair.

I must have fallen back to sleep, because this time I wake to the burning sun, my mouth parched and dry. I push myself up and head to the kitchen, where I startle one of Mabel's wandering cats. It's the calico one. He's curled up against the unopened bills on the kitchen table and stretches when I get close.

"Shoo," I say, flicking my hands at the thing, but the cat just purrs. I grab the broom and raise it as he stares at me with his lemony-green eyes. Then he jumps from the table, winds around my legs, and meows. I set down the broom and crouch on the floor and run my fingers through his silky fur. He arches under my hand, begging for more.

"You're so handsome," I whisper. "Are you hungry?"

I search through the cupboards and the refrigerator, but I haven't been shopping in over a week. All I have are a few frozen dinners and a half dozen boxes of wine. I'm even out of coffee. I'll have to go out in the world.

After promising Mr. Calico I'll head to the store and pick up some food, I swallow two aspirin and climb the stairs to the bathroom, where I shower and dab on some light makeup. Then I pull on a pair of capris and my favorite Lululemon top and head to the Upper Village for a quick shop.

The Upper Village lies a mile from my house, a quaint minitown filled with expensive dress shops, trendy restaurants, and a high-end organic market. I rarely shop there due to the limited selection, but I'm in a hurry, and the next-closest market is another two miles away.

I pick up a dozen items, including a few cans of cat food, and wait in a rather long line. The checker looks trendy and cool, her black-and-purple hair shaved to stubble on one side. I smile and swipe my debit card, and the checker rolls her heavy-lidded eyes.

"Declined," she says in a dull voice. "Try again."

"But I just got a new one."

"Did you call it in?"

"Yes, but . . ." I don't need to run my card a second time to know what has happened. How could I have drained my account so quickly? I could swear I didn't spend more than $5,000 on my recent visit to Saks.

"Do you have another card?"

I rifle through my wallet, but all I find are frozen credit cards and a five-dollar bill.

"I'm sorry," I say, humiliated, as the line behind me grows. "I'll put the groceries away and come back later."

"Right," the girl mutters under her breath.

"No need for that," a man's voice booms from behind. "I'll take care of this." I look up to find Eileen's handsome husband standing beside me waving his card. He swipes before I can blink.

"Why, thank you," I stammer. "But there's no need . . ."

He taps in his PIN and then turns to me with a grin. "Now let me help you with your bags." His eyes are the color of a wind-whipped sea, his hair a shade of wet sand. I can't help but be mesmerized by his boyish grin.

"I can handle them," I say, my cheeks growing warmer. "I only have two bags."

"Of course you can. But let me help you anyway." He picks up my grocery bags and walks me to my car. If only I had washed the Volvo. It's so dusty it almost looks gray.

Fumbling with my keys, I drop them and giggle. I grab them and open the back hatch and at once wish that I hadn't. It's piled high with the stray clothes and trash I've accumulated since Rich passed away. My savior doesn't say a word as he sets the bags inside.

"Thank you," I say, shutting the hatch with a snap.

"No problem." He takes my hand in his. "I've seen you with Rich, but I don't believe we've ever been formally introduced. I'm Arthur Van Meter."

"I know who you are." I gawk like some awestruck schoolgirl. "I mean, I know you through Eileen."

"Of course you do. You've served on several of her committees."

"Yes, I have." I'm surprised he remembers me in any way.

He leans close. "I must tell you I found Rich's funeral quite moving. It was heartwarming to see so many in our community come out to pay their respects."

"I appreciate that."

"I'm sure I don't have to tell you he was a great man. He did so much for this community. I'll bet he never turned a nonprofit away."

"He was very generous," I say, feeling proud.

"Let me buy you a cup of coffee. I'd love to share some of my stories about Rich."

I think about the milk in my bag and the kitty waiting at home. A half-hour delay shouldn't be a problem. "I'd like that."

How could I not accept?

We stroll over to Le Petit Bayou and are seated at a bistro table draped in red-and-white checkered linen. The tables ring an eighteenth-century limestone fountain that the owners purchased in Provence. The outside temperature is approaching ninety, but a vine-covered arbor keeps the courtyard shaded and cool. Arthur orders iced coffees and a platter of fresh tropical fruit from a young waiter in a black pantsuit.

"So how are you doing?" he asks when our coffees arrive. He's dressed in a red Lacoste polo shirt and perfectly pressed tan slacks. His sandy hair is laced with gold, his teeth straight and white.

"I'm coping," I say, trying to calm my nerves.

He reaches out and pats my hand. "Good for you. This must be a terribly difficult time."

A yoga class lets out from the gym next door, and a clutch of young women lines up for coffee and tea. They're all dressed alike in their tight black leggings and fluorescent crop tops. Several glance our way, and for the briefest of moments, I feel smug. Yes, Arthur Van Meter is sitting with me, not you. Yes, I'm at least twice your age. I tilt my chin to keep my jawline tight. "It's just such a change," I say. "One moment Rich was here, and the next he was gone."

"I can't imagine how hard that must be." His eyes are so caring that I open my mouth and begin to spew.

"To be honest, I never thought I could feel this lonely. It's not like Rich was home much. He was a very busy man. But sometimes I reach out in the middle of the night, and it shocks me to find he's gone."

"Oh . . ." Arthur's gaze has drifted to a leggy coed cuddling her friend's silky black terrier.

"*Sooooo cute!*" the woman cries.

I think his interest has strayed until he says his next words. "Animals don't belong in food establishments. Don't you agree?"

"I do," I say breathlessly. "But I'd never say it out loud. Dogs are like children around here. I keep my thoughts to myself."

Arthur's eyes spark gold. "You're a bit of a rebel, aren't you?"

"I am?"

"I like women that don't fit the mold."

"You do?"

"Yes." A smile lights up his face. "Anyway. You were saying something about being lonely in bed?"

My face flushes red. "Not just in bed." I don't want to give him the wrong impression. "But everywhere. All the time. Rich took care of all the little things. Gas in the car. Instructing the gardeners. Replacing lights. Paying the bills. The bills are the worst. They just pile up and up. I don't even know where to start."

He nods, his chiseled face growing serious. "You have to be careful. I've read that con men will send fake bills at times like these, hoping someone is confused enough to pay."

"Exactly," I say, wringing my hands. "I'm just not sure what I'm looking at—or looking for."

Arthur leans back and studies me. "I've been in the real estate business for most of my life. I've even done a little work with Rich and the bank. How about I come over and help you sort through your bills?"

"Are you serious?"

"I am."

"You mean now?"

"Why not?" He pulls a twenty from his wallet and sets it on the table. "My golf game got canceled, and I have a few hours to spare."

"You're so kind. Are you sure Eileen won't mind?"

"Absolutely. She's too caught up in the details of her latest gala." He shakes his head with a grin. "Apparently there's been talk of mutiny. She's working hard to get the troops back in line."

"Well, all right." I get to my feet. "But I have to warn you my house is a mess."

"I won't judge. If anyone deserves to have a messy house, it's got to be you."

Arthur and I sit cross-legged on the floor of Rich's office. He's sorting through bills, tearing up junk mail, and making a pile of urgent past dues. He presses me about the mortgage.

"Your first and second mortgages are ninety days past due. If you don't pay these bills soon, you could lose your home."

I take a deep breath. "Rich's bank wouldn't foreclose on me, would they?"

"If the first deed holder files for foreclosure, they'll have to do the same to protect their position. It's not worth taking a chance. You need to pay these right away."

I pick up one of the bills and stare at it. The numbers seem so large. "How much money are we talking about?"

"I'd say forty-five thousand, give or take."

My jaw drops. "Forty-five thousand? That's crazy. Where will I get that kind of money?"

"It's not that much. You must have savings."

"Yes, of course." I bite my lip. "But it's all tied up in the estate." I want to share the issue of the frozen assets, but Leo's warning runs through my head.

"Don't you have a living trust?" Arthur asks.

"A what?"

"A living trust."

I shrug. "I guess so. We have a will. Is that the same thing?"

Arthur laughs. "I forgot you Montecito gals don't worry about such things. But I'm positive Rich would've set one up. He was a banker, for god's sake. But possibly he had some other means for holding assets. Is there a chance he squirreled away cash outside of his bank?"

"You mean like under the bed?"

"That's cute, but no. I'm thinking he could've opened an account somewhere under a separate legal name."

"Maybe . . ."

"Or hidden money in your home safe?"

"The safe only holds our jewelry."

"How about an offshore account? He ever mention that?"

"A what?"

"A bank account held in another country?"

"I don't think so. I would've remembered that."

"Okay, then. Let's get back to the safe. Houses like yours often have more than one. Helps to fool the more dim-witted burglars."

"We've lived here a long time. You'd think I'd know."

"Unless Rich thought it safer to keep you in the dark. If you'd like, I could help you look around."

God, no. I picture the messiness of the rooms. "That's okay," I say. "I'll poke around a little later."

He smiles. "All right. But I suggest you speak with your attorney. Rich was a wealthy man. Money should be the least of your problems. Worst case you could borrow against the estate."

"I'll talk to him about that."

"Is there anything else I can help you with?" he asks, his voice so kind it almost brings me to tears.

"You've done so much already," I say, picking up a handful of bills.

"All I've done is give you a little of my time. Now, tell me. What else do you need?"

I hesitate. "There is one thing. Maybe you can explain these papers to me." I get up and retrieve the Casa Bella file from the cabinet and hand it to Arthur. He quickly flips through the contents. "Seems to be some kind of real estate investment."

"Could some of our money be tied up in that?"

"It's hard to tell . . ."

"Is it possible Rich owes someone something? I mean, is it possible I owe money to anyone?"

He reads for a while, shuffles through the papers, and reads them a little more. "I'll tell you what," he says. "It'll take me time to go through this file, and our son's soccer game begins at three. What if I take it home with me and review? I'll call you if I find something important."

"Are you sure it's not too much trouble?" A weight lifts off my shoulders.

"Not too much trouble at all." Arthur holds out his hand and helps me up. "One thing," he says. "I suggest you don't mention I've been here. You know how this town works. All gossip, rumor, and innuendo, especially if it gets around that I was alone with a beautiful woman."

"Of course." Beautiful?

"So we'll keep this our little secret."

"Yes."

"Good. Rich helped our community in so many ways. It's an honor for me to have a chance to give back."

My eyes mist over. "Thank you." I follow him to the front door. "I can't tell you how much your kindness means to me."

He sets his hand on my shoulder and gives it the lightest of rubs. "Anything you need," he says. "I mean that. Please don't hesitate to call."

I shut the door, and my mind turns to my novel. I picture my hero's lips pressing against the lips of my heroine. He runs his hand along her inner thigh. I shiver. They will have a love that lasts forever. That's one thing I know for sure.

March 26, 1984

I thought it would be easier to make friends at UCSB. It was at first. But then my roommate started sneaking her boyfriend into our dorm room late at night. Like I couldn't hear them doing it under the covers. UGH! So gross. But now Carol refuses to speak to me, and half the dorm has taken her side. It's not fair!!

I know Rich feels bad about how it's all turned out. I had asked for a transfer to a new room, but he insisted I turn Carol in.

Said no one should have to put up with such filth, and she should be the one to move, not me. Or course he was right, but it doesn't matter. Somehow I've become the bad guy. I've even received threatening notes.

Rich says I shouldn't worry and that I don't need anyone but him. He's right, of course, but I still feel awful. I had hoped by my sophomore year in college, I would be part of a big group of friends.

Crystal

July 6, 2015

It's been five days since Tyler's indiscretion. He never made it back to the Stable. HR intervened along the way. I couldn't stand not knowing what was going on, so the morning of the incident, I offered to walk a set of loan documents to the executive offices and conveniently dropped the papers outside of George's closed door. I crouched to pick them up and smiled when I heard a man choking on tears. Tyler was begging. Really begging. My mouth watered like I was getting ready to lick icing off a cake.

An hour later I received a text from one of the many bank snoops. Tyler was slinking out the back door. I ran—well, I lumbered—upstairs so I could peer out the window and watch the holiday parade. Poor Tyler staggered with shoulders slumped, gripping his storage box of shame. He looked broken, shattered, defeated. His new aura was a pleasant reminder of my ex-Bakersfield boss.

Days later I heard Tyler had packed up his things and moved back to Kansas. Amanda gave her notice by the end of the week. Rumor is she received a six-figure settlement. It all worked out in the end.

On the following Monday, we're hard at work when George orders the loan support staff to appear at a mandatory meeting. Including the loan assistants and mortgage servicers, there are twelve of us in all, down two in just one week. Shortly before ten, I follow Dipak and Eric upstairs to the small conference room that doubles as an overflow storage space for old file boxes. When our contingent arrives, George is pacing the room.

"Take a seat," he orders without looking up. His green tie is askew, his hair slightly ruffled, and one of his shoes is untied. According to the company gossips, management blames him for Tyler's dabble in porn. I honestly feel bad about that.

"It's taken me nearly a week to pull my thoughts together," George says once we've gotten settled. "I apologize for that. But to be perfectly honest, Tyler's actions were so ignorant and repugnant I had to do some hard thinking on the matter." He looks up, his glass eye rimmed in red. "I've decided I've given this department too much slack. It's over now. Do you understand?"

I nod with the others, but I'm thinking Dipak and I shouldn't be here. We've done nothing wrong. Well, of course *I've* done something wrong, but *they* don't know that. And little Dipak is squeaky clean. His life's an open book, and he never strays far from the rules.

George stops pacing and, with hands on hips, eyes us with disdain. "My understanding is that the analysts' office has been nicknamed 'the Stable.' That Tyler's behavior didn't come as a surprise. Does anyone here want to counter that claim?" He waits a few beats before continuing. "I want you to know that the IT department has gone through your computers. They've read through your emails and viewed your downloads. You'd think this was a college dorm, not a conservative workplace."

Eric's face has gone pale, and he lowers his head to the table. He must've really screwed up.

"If it weren't so difficult to find adequate employees, there would be more firings happening today. But you're lucky. We're not going to let you go. At least not for now. Instead, what I expect is that beginning today, all twelve of you will behave like professionals. Understand?"

There's a murmuring of agreement but no eye contact. No one wants to be singled out.

"You will arrive at work by eight," he continues. "Your lunch break won't exceed an hour. Your workday will not end before five. And your computer will be used for work purposes only. Have I made myself clear?"

I nod, feeling queasy. This morning's chorizo-and-egg burrito sends a warning signal from my gut.

"Good." George shakes his head and begins pacing again. "It's going to take me weeks to hire a new analyst. In the meantime we need to divvy up the files. Who has room in their portfolio for a few of Tyler's credits?"

My hand shoots up. "I do."

George looks at me, and his expression softens. "Tyler managed some fairly complicated loans. You comfortable taking those on?"

"I am."

"All right, then. Come with me."

"Right now?"

"Right now. There's a meeting in the executive conference room, and I need an analyst to sit in."

I follow George out the door. We're halfway down the hall when he pauses and turns to me. "Before we join the meeting, I'd like to speak with you for a moment." He steps into his office and signals that I should follow. "Please take a seat," he says, settling into his chair. A bead of sweat trickles down my back. He couldn't have found out, could he? Have my plans been blown to bits? I hold my breath until he speaks.

"I wanted to check in with you," he says. "You're the lone woman in that office. And after the stunt Tyler pulled, I can't help but wonder what else he's been up to."

I shake my head, relieved. "Nothing terrible. I mean, he was rude and unfriendly, and sometimes he told questionable jokes."

"Sexist?"

"And racist."

"Why didn't you report him?"

"I needed my job."

"There wouldn't have been any retaliation."

I just stare at him. We both know that's not true.

He hesitates before continuing. "So tell me. Was Eric involved?"

Eric? Now that's an interesting question. Maybe I can unload him too. But I'll have to think on that angle a little more before I make such a bold move. "Eric was like Dipak and me," I say. "He just played along."

George nods, looking relieved. "In the future I hope you'll confide in me if another uncomfortable situation occurs."

"I will." I get to my feet, stomach grumbling.

"Wait a moment," he says. "There's one more thing." He opens his desk drawer. "I don't want you to be offended. I'm only doing this to help your career. You're smart and good at your job. I think you know that."

I nod because I do.

He slides a business card across the table. "If you're going to work on Tyler's credits, I need you to dress the part."

I gaze at the business card in confusion. A Nordstrom private shopper?

"We all know that it's expensive to live in Santa Barbara, and salaries are primarily spent on rent and food. So the bank has agreed to offer a five-thousand-dollar clothing allowance for its up-and-coming officers. But you have to work with this personal shopper. She'll help you choose the right look. And we're only talking about work clothes. How you dress on your own time is up to you."

"What about Dipak?" I ask, feeling defensive. "Will he be getting a clothing allowance too?"

"He will."

There's a sudden crack in my wall of anger, which I quickly work to mend. I consider telling George that he of all people should know that nice guys finish last. That even with his perfect hair, groomed nails, tailored suits, and good intentions, some staff members call him Cyclops and laugh behind his back. But in the end, I only say thank you.

"You're welcome." He glances at his watch. "Let's get going. The meeting is about to begin. Kevin is the loan officer on the credit. You know him, right?"

"Yeah, I know him." Kevin is Dipak's original model for the Great White Hopes, a balding man in his early forties with sloped shoulders and a pasty complexion. Part kiss ass, part fool.

"He'll take the lead along with Rich," Arthur continues. "Your role is as an observer. Sit away from the table, and don't speak or make a face. Take notes. If you have questions for the borrower, Kevin will field them later on."

We step into the executive conference room adjacent to Rich's office. With its walnut paneling, heavy curtains, and western landscape paintings, it oozes snooty money. Rich and Kevin are already seated with their client. Getting to their feet, they do a quick round of introductions. When I take a seat in one of the metal overflow chairs that line the wall, it squeals and pinches my thighs. I lick my lips, tasting spicy chorizo, and curse the storm brewing in my bowels.

"So good to have you here, Arthur," Rich says, his eyes caressing the man. Arthur Van Meter must be everything every man has ever wanted to be. Determined eyes sparkle above razor-sharp cheekbones; his cleft chin juts like a rock. He's wearing old jeans and a faded polo shirt yet looks more elegant than the men in suits. He carries his looks in a casual way, as if they mean less than nothing to him. I shouldn't like him, but his neatness draws me in. Not a stitch out of place, not a pound too much. Let's see what he has to say.

Kevin fidgets with his files while Rich and Van Meter engage in a smattering of small talk that drags on for what seems like hours. I try to concentrate on their words, but it's made difficult by the gurgling in my gut. They chat about upcoming vacations, their latest cars, and the last time they played golf. They touch on their respective families and make plans to meet for lunch. The only comment of interest is Rich's boast about his son's promotion from C-list actor to series coproducer. I don't believe him. I've been lurking on his wife's Facebook page, and she hasn't mentioned a thing. It's an easy lie to fact-check. He's either a poser or a fool. When the chatter finally dies down, Kevin jumps up and asks to see the plans.

Van Meter rolls them out on the table, settles back in his chair, and folds his hands together, his wedding ring flashing gold. It's the thick signet kind that royalty used to seal letters a few centuries ago. "I'm not one to pat myself on the back," he says, "but I think I've done an amazing job. This is by far my best work." His face has morphed from handsome to gloating. It's not an attractive look.

"Four stories and twenty-one units?" Kevin says, his hands caressing the plans. "That's huge for downtown. You can get that approved?"

"We already have," Van Meter says with a smile. "I've been working with a few local developers to set the stage for these types of infill projects. The city has a housing crisis, and we're offering a solution. We call it 'affordability by design.'"

"Affordability by design." Rich sucks on the term like it's a piece of candy. "I love that phrase. It has a nice ring."

"Doesn't it? We borrowed the idea from some shrewd San Francisco developers. It's been a win-win all around. The city gets kudos for increasing the housing stock, while the developers get to circumvent the permitting process and build denser developments on smaller lots. We've even made headway in preliminary discussions to raise height restrictions to five stories. Can you believe that? Just a year ago, suggesting four stories was like breaking one of the Ten Commandments. Co-opting the affordability language has been a godsend for a long list of stalled projects. I wish we had thought of it before."

"I was at that city council meeting and heard your presentation," Kevin says, patches of pink lighting his pale cheeks. "It was brilliant. Simply brilliant."

"Why, thank you." Van Meter takes on a modest look. "But I was just a member of an incredibly talented team. Enviro-Friendly Planning was our biggest resource. They did all the legwork while taking cover under the workforce-housing facade."

"But you were the visionary," Kevin interjects with a look verging on love. "It must've taken a lot of work to get those council members to follow your lead."

Van Meter chuckles. "I'm sure you're aware that they're not the sharpest knives in the drawer. They're easily swayed by a few nice meals and well-placed charitable donations. Add to that the repurposing of our mayor's socialist language, and we've been able to turn public opinion our way."

"Impressive," Rich says.

Should I ask them to get a room? I consider blurting out those career-ending words when my stomach begins to growl. Low at first, but then it grows loud enough that there's no way the men can't hear. I shift uneasily in my seat and check the clock. Can't we move this along?

"How affordable is affordable?" George asks in an overly loud voice. I'm guessing he's trying to provide cover for my gastric problem.

Van Meter laughs. "Depends on how much money you have."

George's glass eye twitches. "Let me ask my question another way. Does the term *affordability* come with any restrictions on sales price or income level?"

"Of course not. That's the beauty of the concept."

"Beauty?"

"Yes, beauty. We've set the presale price for the smallest units at a million dollars. The larger units will go for well over that."

"But only the wealthiest one percent can afford those prices."

Van Meter cocks his head. "True. But I can promise you we'll have *no* problem selling out."

"I understand that. I just want to clarify that there's no real intent to help solve the workforce-housing issue."

"Sure there is. Our intent is to solve the problem for the working rich."

George's face remains frozen while Rich chuckles and Kevin doubles over with laughter. Van Meter turns to Rich with a sigh.

"George doesn't have much of a sense of humor, does he?"

"He's had a tough week."

"That's too bad." Van Meter begins to speak in slow, mincing words. "Well, just so you understand, *George*, we're doing nothing illegal. We've never called this program *affordable* housing. It's affordable *housing by design*. In other words, the units are smaller and less expensive to construct, so they *could* be sold in the affordable range. But we live in a capitalist country. The condos will sell at a price the market dictates. And the fact that the design will allow our buyers to readily blow through walls . . . well, let's just say in the end the prices for the smallest units could easily top two million."

George frowns. "Blow through walls?"

Van Meter nods. "Our design allows a buyer to snap up two or more units and combine them into a wonderful living space. Combine all four top-floor units, and the penthouse would be outrageous."

"Doesn't that defeat the purpose of designing smaller units?"

"In what way?"

"You're supposed to be providing housing for more people, not fewer."

"It's not our fault if someone wants to purchase four units and combine them into one. We'll be adhering to the program's strict building codes. What more would you ask us to do?"

"Building codes *you* helped to develop."

"Is there a problem with that?"

George looks like he might like to strangle someone. I don't blame him. I wouldn't mind strangling someone myself. My stomach burbles. Kevin eyes me. Dear god, get me out of this room.

"What about the old adobe on the property?" George asks, his bad eye locked in a continuous twitch.

"What about it?"

"I believe it's a historical landmark."

Van Meter offers a thin-lipped smile. "Not anymore. We hired a consultant to confirm that the original structure has been modified so many times it no longer holds any historical value. The Board of Architectural Review agreed with our recommendation." He snaps his fingers. "Problem solved."

George's eyes narrow. "My mother was on the committee that worked to get that designation a half century ago."

"Luckily your mother is not a member of the board. Even luckier is that our architect is the board's chair."

"But that's a clear conflict of interest."

"He recused himself at the time of the vote."

Rich has been quietly eyeing his fingernails like he wants to gnaw them off. Now he straightens his shoulders and tosses George a more-than-irritated look. "I have a meeting with the regulators," he says. "We need to wrap things up. Arthur, could you fill us in on the financing structure?"

Van Meter nods. "There's your construction loan, of course. I'm hoping you get that approved sooner than later. As for the equity, I've formed a new syndication: Casa Bella Ltd. I already have a lineup of investors who want in on the project. It'll be quickly oversold. We're promising them a ten percent return, but it could go much higher than that."

"Interesting." Rich gets to his feet and extends his hand. "Thank you for coming, Arthur. This has been very helpful. I'm looking forward to our lunch next week."

"So am I."

I can't wait anymore. I heave my way out of my chair, my stomach rumbling like a truck. I push past Rich, nearly knocking him down. I should be brutally embarrassed, but for whatever reason, I'm not.

Kathi

June 21, 2016

It's a beautiful summer morning in the Montecito foothills. Eagles swoop. Squirrels chatter. A leaf blower rumbles from the estate next door. It's half past eleven, yet I'm sipping on only my first cup of coffee of the day. No reason to jump out of bed when the hours stretch before me like a desert road.

I head out onto the terrace and try to take pleasure in the sun sparking diamonds across the azure sea. But a sense of doom swirls around me like the haunting of a ghost. It slows my walk, rounds my shoulders, and colors my soul in shades of gray.

I pinch my wrist hard. *Snap out of it! Perk up! Think of all that you've had and still have!* I must shower. Clean up. Trade in my old sweats for new. Or better yet, slip on a cute top and a new pair of linen slacks.

Then a train rumbles down the coast, blasting its mournful horn. My spirits droop. Why bother? There's nothing to do. No one to see. No place to go. I pinch my wrist again. *Do something! Anything! Get to work on your novel.* Yes, that's it. I'll write a chapter or two, and by then it will be time for an early drink. I head back inside and grab my computer and plant myself on the couch. Lifting my fingers, I begin to type.

When Robert left his office for lunch, his gaze fell across the teller line and paused at the sight of the new girl. His heart quickened when she introduced herself as Emma. "Emma," he repeated. "What a beautiful name." She smiled, and he almost melted at her innocent beauty. *I'm going to marry you one day*, he thought.

I'm deep into my writing when I'm startled by a knock on the door. And then another. And then the sound of pounding echoes through the house. "*Police*," a man yells. "*We have a warrant. Open up!*"

I slide off the couch and sink onto the floor. Grasping my cell, I dial 911. "Help me," I whisper. "Someone's trying to break in. They say they're the police."

"Stay calm, ma'am," a woman replies in an even tone. "Tell me your address."

The line goes silent for so long I'm sure I'm going to faint. My face is mushed into the carpet. I spy dust bunnies under the couch. Cereal crumbs. Drops of dried coffee. Sprays of white wine gone yellow with age. How long has it been since I let the housekeepers go? Five weeks? Six?

The woman's voice returns. "It's legit," she says. "It *is* the police. They have a warrant. Go ahead and open your door."

"A what?"

"They have a warrant. Hello? Ma'am, are you listening to me?"

"Yes. Please help me. I'm scared."

"Just do what they say, and you won't get hurt. Start with opening your front door."

"But why are they here? What do they want?"

"All I can tell you is to open your door. I'm on the phone with them right now. Follow their instructions, and you'll be fine."

I push myself up and stagger to the door, my cell trembling in my hand. I want Rich. I want Jack. I want Leo. I want someone, anyone, to save me.

I pocket the cell and ease open the door to a dozen officers dressed in black tactical vests and baseball caps with the word POLICE emblazoned across their chests. A woman hands me a paper and mumbles something about a warrant. Before I can ask a question, someone shoves a video camera in my face.

"Please don't," I say, covering my cheeks with my hands. "I'm not even dressed."

"Sorry, ma'am. It's all part of the process." The police push by me, and I pinch my wrist until it hurts. Across the street my neighbors film the embarrassing scene from behind an unmarked police car. I slam the door shut and slump against the wall. Think. Think!

The policewoman looks at me without blinking. "I'm Detective Rubio," she says, pointing at the badge on her chest. "I'm the lead investigator on this case. Your name is?"

"Kathi," I reply in a small voice. "Kathi Wright."

"Katherine Wright?"

"Yes."

The detective—she must be younger than Jack—holds out her hand. "Let's go into the kitchen. It's a better place to wait."

She leads me to the kitchen. The drawers and cupboards have been thrown open, their contents strewn across the gray marble counters. Six boxes of wine stare at me like an accusation. I want to tell the detective that I save the wine for visitors.

"Is there someone I can call?" she asks, kindly. "A neighbor or a friend?" She has a pretty face with a smattering of freckles and eyes the color of my favorite amber ring. What is she doing here? Why isn't she a teacher or a nurse? Why not do something nice with her life? Why would she dress in men's clothes and spend her days searching through private homes?

"There's no one," I say. My throat tightens, and I begin to cry.

"I'm sorry," she says. "I know this is difficult. We'll be in and out of here as quick as we can."

"But why are you here? What have I done?"

"You've been named on the warrant."

"But I have nothing to do with the SAR thing. I don't know what Rich did at the bank."

"I don't know about the issues at the bank. We're here to investigate an accusation of financial elder abuse."

"But I'm just a wife," I sob. "I know nothing. Nothing at all."

Detective Rubio seems to believe me, because her voice goes soft. "If you've done nothing wrong, then you have nothing to worry about." The video camera returns and looms above her shoulder. I turn my head away.

"Do you have to film me?" I ask.

"It's in your best interest and ours. Now, if you could just answer a few questions . . ."

I nod and stare at my cold cup of coffee. Would it be strange if I asked for a few minutes to shower and apply my makeup?

Detective Rubio pulls out a small pad of paper. "Do you know anything about your husband's former real estate investments?"

I shake my head.

"Please answer yes or no."

"No. Should I call my lawyer?"

"You're welcome to do so. But right now we're only trying to piece together the information. Your cooperation could help confirm your innocence and allow us to quickly move on."

I picture my snooping neighbors. I have to get this over with as fast as I can. "All right," I say. "Go ahead. I'll answer your questions. I have nothing to hide."

"Okay. Let's start over. Were you aware that your husband was funneling private money to local real estate investments?"

"No."

"That he was investing in projects owned by his friends?"

"No."

"Finding investors to fund the projects?"

"No."

"That he skimmed some of this money and used it to fund your lifestyle?"

I shake my head hard. "That's impossible. He was the president of a bank. He made more than enough money to support us."

Detective Rubio's features grow stern. "Actually, our initial analysis indicates his salary was not nearly enough to cover your living expenses."

"That can't be true," I say, thinking she's not so pretty. "We had plenty of money. More than we ever needed."

Two policemen stagger into the kitchen with boxes piled high with papers. They hand the detective a list, which she quickly scans. "Is that everything?" she asks.

"Yes," they answer in unison.

She hands me the paper. "Please review this itemization and sign the receipt."

I scan the list. "You can't take my computer."

"We'll return it soon. I promise."

"You don't understand. I'm writing a novel. I haven't saved it anywhere else."

"I'm sorry about that. Now, let's finish up. I have only a few more questions, and then we'll be on our way."

"All right," I say. She'd better hurry. I'm about to get sick.

"Have you destroyed any of your husband's papers?"

"No."

"Removed anything from his office?"

"No . . ." I think of Arthur and pinch my wrist.

"You're sure?"

"I'm sure."

"Do you know Mabel McCarthy?"

"Of course. She's my neighbor."

"Did she tell you she invested a million dollars with your husband?"

"Yes, but . . ." My voice has grown shrill.

"But what?"

"She's old, and I didn't believe her."

Detective Rubio folds her arms and looks at me in a disbelieving way. "And she spoke with you about this last week?"

"It might've been two weeks ago . . ."

"Did she ask you to look for the investment documents?"

"Why yes, but—"

"Did you find them?"

"I . . . I never looked."

Detective Rubio stares at me until my cheeks grow warm. "All right, then," she says. "We'll be in touch." She turns to leave and then pauses at the door. "By the way, do you know Arthur Van Meter?"

My pulse races. "Eileen Van Meter's husband? I know *of* him. Why do you ask?"

She stares at me hard for several moments before stepping outside. Once she's gone, I slam the door shut on my neighbors' prying eyes and gossiping mouths. Then my knees buckle, and I collapse in a heap on the floor.

March 3, 1987

With graduation looming, I have a HUGE decision to make. Every day I wake up more stressed and confused. That's not weird, is it? I mean, Rich is so lucky. He took the banking job in Reno without blinking twice. I love that about him. He's so self-assured and always knows exactly what he wants. But it's different for me. If I take the job at Random House, Rich says he won't wait. He doesn't believe in long-distance relationships. I can understand, I guess. But if I follow him to Reno, I pass on the career of my dreams.

Oh, what to do? What to choose? Aunt Genny is rooting for New York. She says men will come and go, but the editorial position is a once-in-a-lifetime opportunity. But she's old. She doesn't understand. And she's a little hard on Rich. It's ABSOLUTELY not true that he's controlling. He just loves me so much he wants me to be near him when he embarks on his new career. I doubt I'll ever find a man who loves me like he does. No wonder I'm stressed out. How can I make such a choice?

Crystal

I feel overdressed in the black knit suit my private shopper picked out for work. Pearl necklace and earrings. Hair clipped back. Makeup discreet and fresh. Someone might think me pretty if it wasn't for the sweat pooling under my armpits.

"It's so nice to finally meet you," Dipak's mother says with a shy smile. "Our son speaks so very highly of you."

Dipak has dragged me to a family dinner at his favorite restaurant, Playa Verde. I tried to avoid the occasion, but he begged me to come along.

"They don't think we're dating, do they?" I asked him earlier in the week.

"Of course not. They just want to meet one of my Santa Barbara friends."

"And I'm it?"

"Kind of . . ."

The restaurant may be casual, but the dinner feels very formal. Dipak introduced his parents as Mr. and Mrs. Patel, and there were handshakes all the way around.

"Tell us about your family," his mother says. "Do your parents live nearby?"

"No, they don't." I could use a beer, but Dipak warned me his parents frown on alcohol, so I'm sipping an ice tea instead.

"Where do they live?" Dipak's mom is way tinier than he is. I doubt she's even five feet tall. She sits perfectly straight, shoulders back, chin up, dark hair piled atop her head. She's dressed in a red-and-gold sari that makes her look like an exotic queen.

"In Bakersfield," I reply, hoping that ends the subject.

"We know Bakersfield very well," Mrs. Patel says cheerily. "It's not so far from us. Is that where your family comes from?"

"They did."

"But they don't live there now?"

I shift uncomfortably in my seat. "I don't think so. Not anymore."

"You don't know?" Mr. Patel's dark eyes search mine, his face molded in concern.

"Dad . . . ," Dipak says.

"Let the girl tell her story."

"I was adopted," I say. "And it didn't work out." I bite into a tortilla chip and yearn for a dozen more.

"Adopted?" Mrs. Patel looks confused. "So your birth parents have passed?"

Dipak squirms in his seat. "Jesus, Mom, that's enough."

"Don't swear at your mother," Mr. Patel snaps. He turns his attention to me. "So why weren't you wanted? By your birth parents, I mean."

"Dad!" Dipak covers his face with his hands. "You can't ask those kinds of questions in America."

"It's okay," I say, although it's not. "I wish I knew the answer to that question, but I don't."

"So no family?"

"No family."

The Patels glance at each other. I've just failed test number one. Number two if you count my size.

"Sorry, Crystal," Dipak whispers in my ear.

"It's okay."

The waitress arrives with our food. Enchiladas for the Patels, a mixed-green salad for me. I'm not sure why I ordered the diet platter. These people aren't that dumb.

"What about college?" Mrs. Patel tries. "Did you attend UCLA with Dipak?"

More torture. "I went to Bakersfield College."

"A community college?"

"Be nice, Dad," Dipak tries. "You never even went to college. And besides, Crystal's way smarter than me."

Mr. Patel sets down his fork. "If I had grown up in this great country and had all of your advantages, I would have worked very hard and attended Stanford, Harvard, or MIT."

Dipak leans close. "My dad thinks UCLA is a second-rate school."

"It *is* a public institution," Mr. Patel says, "is it not?"

"Come on, Dad. It's one of the best."

"So you say."

Dipak shakes his head.

I take a huge bite of salad and feel a sudden sense of doom.

"Crystal?"

I haven't heard that voice in years, yet I recognize it right away. Marco.

I consider spitting my food into my napkin, but I choke it down and follow up with gulps of ice tea that dribble down my chin onto my neck.

"Heimlich?" Marco jokes.

I look up into Marco's doe-like eyes, and my past rears dark and ugly. His arms are as muscular as ever, his waist still flat as a wall. I'm shocked to see he's dressed in Santa Barbara police officer blues. "Hello," I reply in a surly tone. *Now please just go away.*

"I've been wondering what you were up to. Mind if I join you for a moment?" He doesn't wait for an answer and pulls up a chair.

The booth suddenly feels small—like I've gained twenty pounds while I sat. Dipak and his parents haven't moved or said a word.

"Pardon me for interrupting," Marco says. "I'm Officer Marco Castagnola. Crystal and I go way back." His smile is big and wide, a slash of white in his darkly handsome face. I try dabbing at my mouth with my napkin and hope that lettuce doesn't hang from my teeth.

Mrs. Patel recovers first. "Very nice to meet you. This is my husband, Mr. Patel. And our son, Dipak. He went to UCLA and is now a bank executive."

Dipak shifts uncomfortably. "I'm not an executive, Mom. I'm only a—"

"Shush," Mr. Patel says with a wave of his hand. "Never correct your mother in front of a stranger."

"Are you from around here?" Marco asks.

"We live in Mojave," Mr. Patel replies, sounding cautious. "We've come to Santa Barbara to visit our son. We're here to see the Fiesta parade."

"Well, if you like plodding horses and drunken caballeros, you're in for a major treat." Marco turns his attention to me. "It's been a long time, Crystal."

"It has."

"You're looking good."

Liar. I crank a smile.

"So what are you doing here?"

"Eating."

He throws back his head and laughs. "Nice to see that you've kept your sense of humor." His tone grows more serious. "Are you visiting?"

"I work here."

"Nice change of scenery."

"It is."

"So you moved here?"

"Yes."

"Recently?"

"In March." I'm so uncomfortable I could puke.

Marco nods. "Good choice. I moved here a couple of years ago now. It's a beautiful town, don't you think?"

"What kind of policeman are you?" Mrs. Patel asks politely.

Marco breaks eye contact with me and turns to her. "I'm a restorative police officer."

"Restorative?"

"I work with the chronically homeless, typically the ones suffering from mental illness or drug dependency."

"That sounds like an interesting job."

"I started my career as a juvenile probation officer. This has been a nice change of pace."

I can feel Dipak shifting next to me. He must be wondering what the connection is. I'll have to think of something good.

Marco stands and takes a card from his wallet. "I'll let you get on with your dinner." He sets the card in front of me. "Give me a call, Crystal. I'd like to catch up. How many years has it been? Four? Five?"

"Seven."

"Seven? Wow. How time flies. Well, you look great. I always knew you'd do well in life. I look forward to our chat." He steps away and almost makes it to the exit before pausing and looking back. "By the way," he calls, "in case you lose my card, where exactly do you work?"

I begin to cough, so Dipak answers for me. "Pacific Ocean Bank."

Marco nods and steps into the night.

Kathi

I arrive unannounced at Leo's office with a headache. His receptionist seems surprised he agreed to see me on such short notice. She has me take a seat across from a stern-looking executive dressed in a dark-blue suit. The man refuses to acknowledge me and won't even respond to my brief hello. His head is stuck behind the pages of a *Wall Street Journal,* which he rattles every few minutes.

The rattling reminds me of my dearly departed Rich. On his grouchier mornings, my not-so-sweet husband would do the very same thing: hide behind his paper and demand I stop my "relentless" chatter. He actually did that on his very last day on earth. In fact he was even meaner that morning, telling me in no uncertain terms I was to "shut my babbling mouth." That alone tells me his death was no suicide. If he had planned to step in front of a train, wouldn't he have said a few kind words? Left a loving note? Made a call to his only child? At the very least, he would have taken a moment to kiss me goodbye.

Leo's office door finally opens, and he steps out, his face a mask of concern. "Sorry for the wait, Kathi. Coffee, tea, or water?"

"Nothing, thank you."

I clatter behind him in a pair of too-tall heels, drop into a chair, and wait. Leo glances up at his ugly clock before settling in his chair and regarding me with a forced smile. "So how are you this morning?"

"Terrible." Tick. Tick. Tick.

"I can't say I blame you."

Words tumble from my mouth. "Did you know the police would raid my home?"

"I had my suspicions."

"Why didn't you warn me?"

"And have you worry about every knock?"

"But this is different. It wasn't the FBI."

Leo opens my file and retrieves a piece of paper. "The warrant came from the district attorney. That *was* a surprise to me."

"So what does it mean?"

"It means that there's more than one investigation going on. Accusations seem to be coming in from all sides."

"But this is unbelievable. It's totally unfair."

He pushes his glasses up on his nose and leans forward. "Is it?"

I lean back. "What do you mean?"

"You know that old adage—where there's smoke, there's fire. There's sure a lot of smoke in the air."

"I thought you were on my side."

"I am. But I'm growing increasingly concerned by some of Rich's past actions and how they may have an impact on you."

"So you believe he did something wrong?"

"Do you?"

"I . . . I don't know."

Leo sighs and flips through my file. "I spoke with a friend at the DA's office. There are allegations of elder abuse."

"I know." I pinch my wrist. "That's what the police told me when they raided my home."

"The accusations were made by an elderly neighbor of yours. Mabel McCarthy. She says she gave Rich a million dollars to invest. The money seems to have disappeared."

I make a face. "That woman's not right in the head."

Leo pulls off his glasses and sets them on his desk. "Did you know about her accusations prior to the raid?"

I feel like a schoolgirl caught cheating on a test. "Yes . . ."

"When did you find out?"

"Well . . . Mabel stopped by my house a couple of weeks ago and mentioned she had invested some money with Rich, and it seemed to have disappeared. Of course I didn't believe her. I think she's crazy."

"Damn it, Kathi." Leo rubs his eyes. "Why didn't you tell me?"

"I didn't think it was important. The woman has dementia. She's lives in la-la land."

He shakes his head. "The police don't think so."

"The police have it wrong."

"You're sure of that?"

"Yes."

"So Rich never spoke to you about Mrs. McCarthy's investment?"

"No. I'd remember that." It's on the tip of my tongue to tell him about the file I gave to Arthur, but then he'd know I lied to the police.

"All right," Leo says with a shake of his head. "I'll look into this further. But first I need your promise that you'll inform me of any future allegations or items of interest."

"I promise." A river of guilt flushes my insides.

"On another subject"—Leo closes my file with a snap—"Jack called me yesterday."

I straighten my shoulders and swallow. "You know Jack?"

"Rich introduced us several years ago. We've chatted a few times."

"I didn't know that. What did he want?" Tick. Tick. Tick. I just might knock that clock off the shelf.

"He's trying to understand the money situation."

"You told him there isn't any?"

"I did." Leo clears his throat. "He mentioned that the two of you aren't speaking."

"That's not exactly true."

"No?"

"*Jack's* not speaking to *me*."

"Thank you for the clarification." Leo's eyes search mine. "He suggested I ask you about the family secret."

I try to keep my face straight. "Family secret?"

"He said it could have an impact on the estate."

"I don't know what he's talking about."

"If there's something I should know, now's the time to tell me. I think I've made it clear I don't like surprises."

"There's nothing."

"I can't help you if I don't have the full picture."

"Well . . ." I slump in my seat. "If you must know, there *is* a family secret, something that happened long ago. But it has nothing to do with the bank and nothing to do with an investment. It's something very personal between Rich and me."

"And Jack knows?"

"He found out the day of the funeral. He's angry right now, but he'll get over it. He has to understand there was no other choice."

"And you're sure there's no need for me to know the substance of this secret?"

"Yes."

"Positive?"

"Absolutely." Tick. Tick. Tick.

When I arrive home, I shoot right for the refrigerator and treat myself to a goblet of wine. It's too early, of course. But what does it matter? No one cares what I do. I wander out to the terrace and settle on the bench shaded by the old oak tree. There's a yellowish sheen coating the ocean today that looks like a vast stretch of oil. There must be a wildfire somewhere. They seem to burn more often than not.

I wait until I'm sufficiently numb before I review the events of the day. Should I have revealed our secret to Leo? Should I have mentioned the real estate file? Leo is on my side, isn't he? But why didn't he mention before that he knew Jack? My thoughts swish round and round until they're muddier than our filthy pond. I drain my goblet and wobble to my feet. The only thing clear at the moment is the need to refill my glass.

May 30, 1987

Rich swears he would've asked me to marry him even if I hadn't gotten pregnant. And he didn't cheat on me—I don't care what Monica says. I believe him with all my heart. We're going to get married at the courthouse, and then we're packing our things and moving to Reno. I'm a little sad no one is coming to the wedding, not even Aunt Genny. Rich says it's better that way. That we love each other so much we don't need anyone else. He's right, of course, but still...

I wish I could get him to like Aunt Genny, but he thinks she's really weird. I mean, it's true she never got married and runs the farm on her own and dresses like a man. But she's always been good to me, and I know it will hurt her feelings when she finds out we've eloped.

I feel bad about passing on the Random House job, but I'm sure to find something just as good. And if not, then I'll get started on my novel. Think of all the hours I'll be able to write with a sleeping baby by my side!!!

Crystal

It's the hottest day of the year. There's a wildfire raging up the coast. White fire clouds boil above the mountains, and gray ash sifts through the smoky air. And yet where do I find myself standing on this blazing afternoon? At the entrance of the Santa Barbara Zoo selling drink tickets and stamping hands.

"Why am I here?" I ask.

"You're giving back to the community," Dipak says.

"What has the community done for me?"

"Jesus, Crystal. Don't get started with your negative stuff. Can't you just enjoy?"

"I hate being forced to volunteer."

"You're not being forced."

"Really?"

It's a well-known fact among the bank employees that Santa Barbara's weeklong attempt to celebrate the town's Spanish heritage is the president's favorite time of the year. The days are packed with parades and *mercados*, the nights with booze and dance. Rumors say the boss is angling to be next year's king of the Fiesta parade. That means the bank needs to dump money into sponsorships and the employees must volunteer. To not do so is to have the wrong boxes checked in your HR file. Team player? *No.* Future leader? *No.* Decent raise? *Absolutely not.*

Dipak shakes his head. "Come on, Crystal. This is a fun night. We get to party once we're done with our shift. Do me a favor and try."

"What's fun about it?"

"If you don't shut up, I'm walking away."

"Sorry. I guess I'm hot and cranky."

"You should've changed like I did. You're supposed to dress in theme."

I eye him up and down. Dipak is dressed in slim-fit jeans, cowboy boots, and an orange fringed shirt that's the color and texture of a carrot.

"In what way does your outfit suggest Old Spanish Days?"

"In what way does yours?"

"I didn't try."

"Well, I did."

I'm wearing a white shift that would've been cool enough if I hadn't paired it with a dark blazer. I don't care what my personal shopper says. I don't like the look of my arms.

We fall silent for a while. "Aren't the costumes great?" Dipak finally says.

"You think?" Sure, the colors are bright, and lots of skin shows through, but what I can't get past is the absurdity of watching white people playing at ethnic—sexy getups from Mexico and Spain with a few raunchy pirates thrown in.

"Everyone looks wonderful," says our starstruck coworker Shelby.

The recent college grad with the mooning eyes and perfect skin works part-time in the bank's marketing department. She's friendly to everyone, including me. Shorter than Dipak, with an even tinier build, she's small enough I could squish her like a gnat. Or take her in my hands and smoosh her. Dipak's been flirting with her all afternoon. I just might punch him in the nose. It's not like I see him as boyfriend material, but his crush still pisses me off.

A voice booms from behind. "It's so great to see our wonderful staff volunteering at this incredible event."

I turn to find Rich with his hand outstretched, waiting to be stamped. His words may sound nice, but his face looks stern, his eyes unhappy. He's dressed in a black matador suit trimmed in thick braids of gold, a red cape flung across his back. A Mickey Mouse cap tops his head. Does he know he looks like a doofus? Is that why he's making the sour face?

He drops his voice to a whisper, his lips thin and tight. "Get this line moving," he says. "We don't have all day."

The stamp slips from my hand. I bend down to retrieve it.

"Hurry up," he hisses.

His wife steps out from behind him, and my stamp almost slips again. "Don't worry, Rich," she says in a singsong voice. "We have plenty of time. It's not yet six."

"It's ten after." Rich shoves his wrist at me, and I stamp it without taking my gaze off the wife. "I'll meet you up there," he calls, quickly disappearing into the crowd.

The wife takes a tissue from her purse and dabs the moisture from her eyes. "It's my fault he's late," she says with a painful smile. "I couldn't decide which outfit to wear." She's poured herself into a pink satin dress, her arms bound by tiered, ruffled sleeves. Silver eyeshadow coats her eyelids, and streaks of rouge brighten her cheeks.

"My name's Kathi," she says, holding out her hand. "And yours?" Sadness reeks from the woman like sweat, but I don't feel a twinge of pity.

"I'm Crystal." I grip her soft, white hand with its three-carat diamond and jam the stamp hard on her wrist.

"Ow," she puffs, like a child who's been stung.

"Sorry," I say, hoping for a bruise. "My stamp's almost out of ink."

"That's okay." She rubs her wrist. "I'm fine. Just fine. And thank you for volunteering. It's such a wonderful event, don't you think?" She flashes the kindest of smiles. I want to slap it off her face.

It's after eight by the time the lines disappear and we break down the volunteer tent. By then my feet are swollen and my hands aching from the endless hours of stamping. The weather has shifted—a chill grips the air, and a smoke-laced fog has moved in. I want to go home, but I'm on cleanup duty, so there's no choice but to stick around.

I trail behind Dipak and Shelby, breathing hard from the uphill walk. They snuggle close and giggle like schoolkids, making me feel a little sick. Somehow I've become the third wheel in this party. I wish myself home and in my bed, a bag of tortilla chips in my hand.

When we finally reach the fiesta, I ditch my mooning coworkers and head to the bar for a double margarita. The drinks have been flowing for several hours, and more than a few people are stumbling drunk. I snoop around outside the VIP tent, but there's no sign of Rich and his wife. So I wander across the lawn to take in the action on the makeshift dance floor.

An aging rock band plays eighties covers, and dancers dart in and out of the twinkling lights. Dipak and Shelby spin by me, laughing, and the ache in my belly grows. I head off in search of another drink, trudging past clutches of chattering couples. After snagging a fresh margarita and a sugar-dipped churro, I veer down a darkened pathway. I stroll past the monkey cage and the lion exhibit and pause at the meerkat enclosure. A few of the furry animals stand sentry outside their burrow. They're tiny and look like a cross between a rat and a ringtail monkey. One picks nits off the back of his friend. Another cuddles her baby cub. I take a seat on a nearby bench to watch them, sipping my drink and stuffing my face.

The alcohol begins to work its magic, so I settle back and relax. The moon slips in and out of the fog; the music swirls from above. I close my eyes and begin to fade.

The sound of urgent voices snaps me awake. A pool of shifting moonlight silhouettes a couple standing beneath a cluster of ancient palm trees. Tall and thin, they whisper something and fall into a lusty embrace. I want to leave them to their lovemaking, but there's no discreet way to escape. I hoist myself up and step deep into the shadows that ring the backside of the bench.

"I'm tired of waiting," the woman says, pulling away from her partner. "I'm sick of it. Really sick." Her voice reminds me of someone I know. I can't pinpoint it right away.

"I'm only thinking about us," the man responds, his voice quieter than hers. "She'll get half of my assets in the divorce."

"That's so unfair," the woman says. "It's not like she's worked a day in her life, and for god's sake, she's nothing special. I mean, I can't believe what she wore tonight. She looks like an overweight marshmallow. She doesn't deserve a single cent."

"Which is why I need more time to strip my assets."

"So you're moving ahead with the second mortgage?"

"A soon as I possibly can."

"But when's that?" The woman's voice has turned whiny.

"I'm working through the logistics now."

"Can't you hurry?"

"I *am* hurrying."

"Don't snap at me."

"Then stop nagging me."

There's a pause, and when the woman speaks again, it's in a much sweeter tone. "I'm sorry, honey. I don't mean to pester you. I just love you so much that I can't stand for us to be apart."

"I feel the same way, Vanessa."

Vanessa? Are you kidding me? Shipwreck Barbie is bonking a married man?

The couple begins a round of sloppy kisses. Ugh. When they pull apart, the moon lights up the man's face. I take a deep breath, nearly collapsing. *Really, Rich? You're screwing Barbie? You're more of a scumbag than I thought.*

PART TWO

Crystal

I've hit the home run. I'm on the final stretch. I can see the finish line from here. Funny I'm thinking of sports metaphors when I've never played a sport in my life. Rich has applied for a home equity loan. But not just any loan. A $2 million beast. What's the money for, Rich? A renovation? A new car? Funding a new life with your mistress?

Of course, the bank didn't assign the loan to me. The senior analyst gets the first crack. But keeping Eric instead of sending him packing with Tyler has been one of the smartest things I've ever done. Eric has lost all of his cockiness. Without his sidekick, he's bitter and needy. Says hello when he arrives at the office. Good night when he leaves for the day. Asks us about our weekends, tells us about his family, and shares stories when the day gets slow. And tonight is a first—we're out on the town sharing drinks. For some unknown reason, he invited Kevin, the king of the Great White Hopes. Maybe he's angling for some insider tips.

Ted's is quiet for a Friday night. Classes haven't started at UCSB, and the tourist season is winding down. Eric and I sit on one side of the table, Dipak and Shelby on the other. Kevin is too bulky to fit in next to us, so he pulls up a chair. The lovebirds whisper back and forth, sneaking kisses when they think we're not looking. I honestly don't care that our friendship's been diluted. I just wish they'd cut the PDA.

"Can you believe the prez?" Eric slurs. He has that red-faced look that pale guys get when drinking rules their lives. "Makes four hundred thousand a year plus bonuses, and he's up to his eyeballs in debt."

"I've been to his house," Kevin says, setting his tumbler of wine on the checkered tablecloth. "Had to bring some loan documents there once. Beautiful home with an incredible ocean view. I'd give anything to live in a place like that."

"Must've cost him his shirt," I say, trying to push the conversation along.

Eric nods. "I'm guessing he needs to make up for his undersized dick."

Kevin turns red and nearly chokes; Dipak spits his beer across the table. Shelby's wide eyes grow even wider. I just sit back and enjoy.

"What?" Eric asks, swaying back and forth, his hands pressed flat on the table. "I say something funny? Don't tell me you guys didn't know."

Kevin frowns. "You shouldn't say things like that. Someone might hear you."

"Like who? Shipwreck Barbie?" Eric laughs. "I promise she wouldn't be caught dead in here."

"Shipwreck Barbie?" Shelby looks confused. "Who's that?"

"I'll tell you later." Dipak looks worried. He recently received a promotion and raise and doesn't need anyone screwing it up.

"Anyway," Eric says, finishing off his beer, "you ever notice Rich's small hands and feet? How he never uses the men's bathroom when anyone's there?"

"He has an executive bathroom," Kevin says primly, shredding a paper napkin to bits.

"Exactly. Nobody can get a visual of his minuscule dick."

Kevin's mouth drops open. "That's disgusting."

"Why?"

"Have some respect."

"For a loser of a man?"

"That's a terrible thing to say."

"Is it?"

"So why even work at Pacific Ocean Bank?"

Eric shrugs. "Personally, I'm in it for the money. That's it. I'll bet it's the same for everyone at this table. We're not craftsmen. We're not writers. We're not celebrity chefs. We're not creating a single morsel of beauty in the world. We're not doing good for anyone but ourselves. The truth is we're bloodsucking ticks. We're here for a paycheck and nothing more."

Kevin tosses his bits of ripped napkin to one side, and they flutter like angels to the floor. "Well, I don't agree with you. I happen to love my job."

"Really? Something wrong in your head?"

Dipak reaches across the table and taps Eric's hand. "You should stop now," he says. "You're getting mean."

"You think?"

Kevin fumbles for his next words. "You . . . you won't be working at the bank much longer if you continue to talk like this."

"I'll find another job doing the very same thing."

"Not at a premier bank like ours."

Eric snorts. "Premier bank? Are you kidding me? We're not even close. We're a third-tier bank led by a fourth-tier man. How can you look up to a leader who's mortgaged to the hilt *and* a total letch? You've seen how he eyes the girl tellers. It's way beyond gross."

Kevin bristles. "Rich is a man beyond reproach. He and his wife have been together for decades. And I'll have you know that his executive bathroom is nothing more than a well-deserved perk. If he's not at work, he's giving back to our community. He's a man of compassion. He's a man I admire."

"Giving back?" Eric scoffs. "What a load of crap. He's doesn't give a damn about the teenage addicts, unwed moms, and endless supply of homeless. If it weren't for the feds shoving the Community Reinvestment Act down his throat, Rich wouldn't dole out a nickel in this town. And don't get me started on the fawning and the recognition. It makes the prez feel good to get those humanitarian awards."

"What's your point?" Kevin asks in a low voice. He looks about as uncomfortable as anyone could get.

"My point? Well, my point is . . ." Eric's voice drifts off, and so does his gaze. "He's just a Montecito wannabe. A poser through and through. I'm sick of working for guys like him, self-important jerks with their heads stuck up their asses. Trophy wives. Trophy cars. Trophy homes. Truth of the matter is it's all about the size of their dicks. I guess that's my point."

"Then why do you stay in town?" Kevin asks. "Why don't you move somewhere else?"

"And do what? I'm bogged down with so much student debt I can barely breathe. Where else am I going to be paid a hundred thousand a year plus bonuses for doing as little as I do here?"

"I have to go," Kevin says, getting to his feet.

"You have a curfew?" Eric asks.

"No." Kevin pulls a five from his wallet and drops it on the table. "The baby was up all night, and my wife is exhausted. And I always read to my son before bedtime."

"Read him a book for me," Eric says. "Something about how you can grow up to be anything you want in life. My mom used to read me that book. What a fucking crock of shit."

"Maybe we should go too," Shelby says, not waiting for Dipak to reply. She gives him a shove, and he slides out of the booth.

"Want to walk home with us?" Dipak asks me.

"I think I'll stay."

"You sure?"

"I'm sure."

"Bunch of losers," Eric mutters as our coworkers walk away. He looks at me bleary-eyed. "Sorry. I didn't mean that. I know Dipak's your friend."

"That's okay." I buy another round of drinks. "You know what you were saying about Rich? About the debt?"

"What about it?" Eric's eyes fix on a drunken blonde stumbling across the far side of the room.

"Is it really that bad?"

"Sure is. He's got a million-dollar first and a matching home equity loan he's looking to double in size. And then there's the vacation home in Aspen and his Stingray and the sailboat he keeps in a slip at the harbor. Everything's loaded with debt."

"He makes that kind of money?"

"That's the problem. He doesn't."

"So his wife has a trust fund?"

"No such luck."

"Then how can . . ."

"I don't know. I just write the crap analysis, and the board approves it."

"So you . . . ?"

"Play with the numbers when I need to? Sure. Why not? I like my bonus."

"What about Reg O?"

He focuses his bleary eyes on me. "You work for FinCen now?"

"I just thought we couldn't give insiders more favorable terms and conditions than we give to the average joe."

"You're a walking training course, aren't you? Why don't you move over to compliance?"

"But I'm right, aren't I? If the bank makes a loan that Rich doesn't qualify for, then they're breaking the law."

A suspicious look creeps across Eric's swollen face. "Maybe the bank's doing something wrong, but I'm not. I'm just a cog in a machine. I'm following orders."

"Whose orders?"

"Rich's, of course. Who else?"

"So you won't turn the loan down?"

"Hell no. And neither will the board." His blond head bobs like a balloon.

"But what about George?"

"They have ways of keeping Cyclops out of the mix." He finishes off his beer.

"But George is your boss."

"In name only."

"And compliance doesn't intervene?"

"Rich has that department wrapped around his little finger."

"Meaning?"

"Meaning I gotta take a piss." Eric lurches from his chair and makes a beeline to the bathroom. Halfway there, he gets waylaid by a bunch of guy friends and parks at their table. They pour him a drink from a pitcher of beer. He glances my way once—they all do—and then there's laughter and a few unintelligible words. I don't have to hear them to know what they're saying. I've heard all of the fat jokes before.

A group of girls swarms my table. Fresh-faced, long-haired, pitch-perfect makeup. They're all dressed in sparkly shirts, tight pants, and knee-high boots—a gaggle of geese primped and preened for a Friday night on the town. One of them wears a silver cowboy hat with the words BIRTHDAY GIRL scrawled across the front. "You leaving?" she asks me nicely enough. I nod, and she claps her hands.

"See," she shouts, twirling in a circle. "It's like magic turning twenty-one."

I struggle to slide out of the booth. I've had way too much to drink. The bench screeches and squeals, fighting me for every inch. When it finally releases me, my face is steaming. I take a step and pitch forward and hit the tile floor, a beer mug shattering in my hand.

There's a pause in sound, a definitive break, as if the world skipped a beat. The birthday girl drops to her knees and presses her hand against my back.

"I'm so sorry," she says, her happy voice gone. "I didn't mean to trip you. Are you all right? Should we call for help?" Her cell phone slides from her lap and clatters by my side.

A shard of glass has sliced deep into my hand; blood spreads across the floor. "I'll get a towel," the girl says. She rushes off, and I close my bloodied fist around her cell. Seconds later a man reaches down and tries to help. "We've called an ambulance," he says in a worried voice.

"I'm fine."

"Let me help you up."

"No!" I get up and shake him off, pushing through the crowd until I'm through the doors and out on the sidewalk.

I hurry up State Street, blood dripping from my hand. An early fog has moved in, and the mist swirls around streetlamps that shimmer like ghosts. A group of teenage homeless call out in sad voices, begging me for a handful of change. They may look innocent and poor, but the young ones can be vicious. Good. Let's hope they are.

"Take this." I toss the stolen cell phone their way.

"Thanks, lady," one of them calls as I rumble on like a tank. "Hey, wait a minute," he yells a second later. "There's blood on this thing. What the fuck's going on?"

I don't answer the creep. Instead, I let my anger sizzle low in my belly like a fiery hunk of coal. What is the worst? The very worst? And then I'll move on to the wife.

Kathi

I'm desperate for a mani-pedi, but there's no money left in my account. No room on any credit card. No unworn outfit to return. I wander through my mess of a house trying to force myself to think. Should I call Leo? Rich's sister? Try reaching out to Jack? Tell a fib to Jane or Laurie? A whopper to a long-lost friend?

God, no! What's wrong with me? I'm losing my mind. No need to do something so drastic for a visit to the salon. The loneliness must be driving me crazy. It's time I pour myself a drink.

I take in the golden sunset with Mr. Calico nudging my feet. My foster kitty is so delightful. Not a bit of judging going on. I ruffle my fingers through his silky hair and give him an extra can of food before I pour myself another goblet of wine and settle into my evening fog. Then a simple idea creeps into my head.

I get up, stumble through the house, and drag an oversized box off of a storage room shelf. Inside is an assortment of castaway purses, and within minutes I come across three one-dollar bills along with a crinkly ten. But it's the handful of coins that turns the lightbulb on. *Of course!* Rich's coin jar. It's been waiting for me all along.

Rich had a thing about coins. The way they jingled reminded him of Christmas, his least favorite time of the year. Each night he'd empty the change from his pockets into a gallon-sized jug stored in his office closet. Years ago, when Jack went above and beyond, Rich would reward him with a bag of coins he could exchange at the grocery store. Sweet little Jack thought it magic how his coins would clatter through the machine and emerge as dollars at the other end.

Of course it might get the gossips going if anyone saw me feeding a coin machine, so I dump the contents of the jug into a tote and drive to a discount grocery store in a Latino neighborhood on the Lower Eastside. Next thing I know, I'm standing in a wobbly line with a dozen of the city's poor and needy. I slowly edge forward, staring at the ground shamefaced. I reassure myself that it's no different from the times I exchanged coins with Jack. But, of course, it is.

When it's finally my turn to work the big green box, I stare at the instructions, confused. They're different than the ones I remember. The machine is computerized now.

"Are you stupid or what?" a man calls from behind. "Get moving."

I scour the instructions a second time but can't make sense of the words. A tiny girl with bushy blonde hair steps up. "Push this button," she says kindly. She's obviously homeless, dressed in rags, but she has a sweet smile and a pixieish face. "Now dump your coins in here." She signals where they should go. The poor thing is missing a finger. I can't imagine what led to that.

"Hurry up," the man barks. "I got kids to feed."

I pour in the coins, and the machine gets going much slower than I would like. Tinkle, tinkle, tinkle. The coins swirl round and round until they disappear into a grate. When the tinkling stops, I expect to see dollars, but instead a slip of paper slides out. I stare at it, confused. "Over there," the girl says with her innocent smile, pointing at a cashier. "You can either buy groceries, or they'll give you cash."

"Why, thank you," I say.

"I better go," she whispers when a security guard appears. She scurries out the automatic doors.

"But you're next," I call out.

"No, she's not," the guard says, making an ugly face. "She's just harassing the patrons. She does it all the time."

"My turn, lady," the mean man says, pushing me aside.

"Excuse me?" How horribly rude.

I get into the express lane, the receipt clutched tight in my hand. Someone taps me hard on the back.

"This ain't the refund line, lady," a man says. He's fat and nasty looking with tattoos encircling his thick white neck.

"What?"

"You can't get a refund here. Take your voucher over there." He points at an information booth, where there's another line ten deep.

"It's not a refund," I respond, my face steaming hot.

"Looks like a refund to me."

"Well, it's really none of your business." I hand the cashier my ticket, and he counts out seventy-five dollars and twenty-six cents. "No groceries?" he asks with a quizzical look.

"Not right now."

I hurry out of the store to find my homeless friend lurking right outside the doors.

"What's your name?" I ask.

"Mimi."

"Well, thank you, Mimi." I hand her a ten-dollar bill. "I appreciate your help."

She jumps up and claps her hands like a little girl. "Thank *you!*" she screeches. "Now I can eat." Grabbing her oversized duffel bag, she hurries back into the store.

I stand there for a moment, smiling to myself. See? I just proved a point. No matter what anyone says, Rich and I were good people. We always gave a hand to those in need.

I step through the frosted glass doors of Tammy's Nails to find the place already humming. *Oh my god!* It's Friday. How could I have forgotten? For years, Tammy's was my first of many stops to get ready for the weekend parties. Hair, facials, Botox, and eyebrows would fill up the rest of my day. But now there are no parties in my foreseeable future. No dinners out. No invites to lunch. Not even a committee to serve on. I thought people liked me for *me*, but now I wonder. It's as if I've stepped back through the decades and returned to my lonely teenage self.

When the doors shut behind me, a dozen sets of eyes turn my way, and the chatter slows to a crawl. I force a smile, wondering if I was spotted at the coin machine and the gossip has spread around.

There's a ten-minute wait, so I head to the back of the salon to pick out a nail color. I take my time and finally settle on Wicked Red. I'm returning to my seat when I look right into the eyes of my good friend Laurie Lux. Laurie's married to one of Santa Barbara's leading plastic surgeons. She's tiny and cute, with a flip of brown hair and twinkling gray eyes.

"Hi, Laurie." I'm surprised to find her here. I thought she must be traveling. She hasn't returned my calls for weeks.

"Hello." She holds a newspaper in her hands, which she quickly folds and sets on her lap. "Good to see you."

"You too."

There's not a speck of friendliness in her tone. I want to ask her what's wrong, but something tells me to keep moving.

"Lunch soon?" I ask.

"Sure." She closes her eyes and taps the chair's massage button. Her body begins to vibrate. I nod and wave my fingers as if she isn't acting strange and head straight to the magazine rack in search of the latest *People.*

I scan the rack, and my breathing slows at the headline on the front page of the *Santa Barbara Times*: DECEASED BANK PRESIDENT AND WIFE

UNDER INVESTIGATION FOR ELDER ABUSE AND FRAUD. Beneath that is an unflattering photo of Rich and me taken at some long-ago benefit gala.

I watch the nail polish slip through my fingers as if it's happening to someone else. It hits the floor and shatters, and the red polish explodes across the room. No one says a word. Everyone stares. Then a worker runs over, drops to the ground, and runs a rag around my feet.

"*You pay,*" she hisses.

Fumbling for my wallet, I drop my sixty-five dollars on the counter and hurry out the front door. It hasn't even shut behind me before the chattering starts up.

Oh my god, oh my god, oh my god. Where to go. What to do. I spin around and run smack into a muscle-bound chest. Arthur Van Meter takes hold of my arms.

"Kathi?" he says. "Are you all right?"

"I don't . . . I don't know." I burst into tears.

"You poor thing. How can I help you?"

"No one can help me," I sob.

"I saw the paper this morning," he says. "Is it true the police raided your home?"

I nod in shame.

"My god. You weren't arrested?"

"No."

"Interrogated?"

"Just a few questions."

"Then the police were just on a scavenger hunt. They don't know anything for sure. The *Times* should be ashamed to publish such trash. I'm going to call the publisher this afternoon and give him a piece of my mind."

"You'd do that for me?" I ask, snuffling.

"Of course. I know the owner. I have a little pull."

"Thank you." I grab a tissue from my purse and wipe my nose, taking comfort in the warmth in Arthur's eyes.

"A thank-you isn't necessary. I will always stand up for a friend in need." The door to the salon swings open, and Laurie steps out. She begins to turn away but pauses when she spies Arthur.

"Why, Arthur Van Meter," she says in her sweetest voice, her eyes fixed on his. "It's been way too long. It's *so* nice to see you. And I'm *so* very glad you and Eileen will be attending the Summit House benefit." She smiles brightly. "Hope you plan to spend big."

Arthur turns to me. "Kathi, you've met Laurie before, haven't you?"

I drop my gaze. "Of course. We're old friends."

"So you must be attending the benefit."

"Ummm. No." My cheeks grow warm. "I don't believe I received an invite."

"Of course you did," Laurie says in a syrupy voice. "Unless it got lost in the mail."

Arthur looks from Laurie to me and back again. "Remind me," he says. "When is the big event?"

"Next Saturday," she replies, beaming. "I'm the chair, and I promise it'll be the most exciting fund-raiser of the year." She lowers her voice and winks. "We have a few special surprises planned."

"Saturday?" Arthur seems to consider. "Well, that's too bad. Eileen and I will be traveling that day."

Laurie's hand grasps her neck. "But you sent your RSVP."

"Maybe next year." Arthur turns to me. "You ready?" Taking me by the arm, he leads me away.

I glance back at Laurie. She looks like she's been slapped. "I can't believe you just did that," I say, swallowing a giggle.

"She got what she deserved. Now, let me give you a ride home."

"That's so very sweet, but I'm sure you're busy."

"Not so busy I can't help a friend."

"But my car . . ."

"We'll take your car. I'll Uber back."

Arthur puts his arm around me and guides me to my car. It feels so good to be treated with kindness. I really can't thank him enough.

October 16, 1987

Pregnancy is so much harder than I thought it would be. I've gotten slow and sluggish and as big as a house. And I'm horribly bored. I know the rent's cheaper, but I wish we hadn't moved to the outskirts of Reno where everyone and their mother is older than time. We can't afford a second car, so I'm stuck here alone for hours on end. I hate this ugly tract home with its yellow walls and orange carpet. And there's only so many soap operas a girl can watch. I could start my novel. I really should. I pinky promise I'll start it tomorrow. Maybe a good idea will pop into my head overnight. How did Tolstoy get his ideas? Or Dickens or Flaubert? I bet things will change once the baby is born. They have to. I love Rich to death, but I need something more.

Crystal

"Morning," Dipak says cheerfully. He's seated at his desk, surrounded by towering piles of loan files.

"Morning."

"Want to take a coffee run?"

"No."

"What's wrong with you?"

"Nothing."

"I mean, what happened to your hand?" He's staring at the bandages.

"Nothing." My fall at Ted's landed me in urgent care, but I'm not in the mood to share. Eric glances my way and opens his mouth and then closes it just as quickly. *Don't you dare*, I think. *Don't you goddamn dare, or you'll be playing a round of my favorite game.* I gather up a stack of files. "I'll be back in a while. I have a meeting."

"With George?"

I walk out the door without answering. Not that I should be mad at Dipak, but I am. I didn't hear from him once over the weekend. Not even a measly little text. And I'm tired. After hours of waiting in an overcrowded urgent care to have my hand stitched up, I spent the rest of the weekend at the library reading up on Arthur Van Meter. The guy has a long history in Santa Barbara—some of it good, much of it bad. Hit the home run on several development projects and rode a few others into the ground. There are multiple accusations of fraud but no indication he's ever been convicted. So what's the connection between him and Rich? I'm betting it's more than golf and lunch. Stepping into George's office, I avoid looking into his warped mirror.

"Ready for the meeting?" George asks, not getting up.

I nod. "Aren't you coming?"

"I've been told to stay away."

"Can I ask why?"

"Apparently I upset Arthur at our last get-together."

"But you were only asking for details on the project. What's so wrong with that?"

"Let's just say Arthur and I have a history. The bank has worked with him a few times before."

"And it didn't go well?"

He taps his pencil against his desk. "No. It didn't go well."

"So why would we extend him another loan?"

"Banks have short memories when there's money to be made."

"But there *will* be another recession one day."

"Of course. But I've been told I'm old and out of touch and way too cynical. Apparently, times have changed. The economy is booming, and Arthur has become a new man."

"Do you believe that?"

His bad eye twitches. "Just be careful."

"Of . . . ?"

"Of yourself. The only thing you own in this business is your integrity. Don't let anyone talk you into giving it away. Once you cross the proverbial line in the sand, it's all downhill from there. People will have certain expectations of you. And to be honest, that type of employee may have a job during the boom years, but they're the first to lose it in a bust. Then the hunt is on for ethical analysts and loan officers to staff the ranks. So don't do anything you don't believe in. Don't let anyone sway your analysis."

I think about Eric and how he rubber-stamps bad loans. And then I think about who I really am. For a moment I feel ashamed. "Kevin's the loan officer on the Van Meter credit. Aren't I supposed to just do what I'm told?"

"You don't work for Kevin. You work for me. You work for the board. You work for the shareholder."

"And I work for Rich?"

George makes a face. "That goes without saying. Just remember: your job is to be honest and ethical. Let the rest take care of itself."

"I appreciate the advice. Thank you."

"No need for thanks. You're good at this. You've got the analysis skills and cynicism to separate the good loans from the bad. One of the best analysts I've seen in my career."

A flicker of warmth begins to melt my heart, and I try to slap it down. I don't want to owe anything to anyone. I turn and head to the door. My hand is resting on the doorknob when George says one last thing.

"By the way, that Eileen Fisher ensemble looks nice on you. Very professional. Good choice."

"Eileen Fisher? Is that what I'm wearing?"

"Yes."

I straighten my shoulders and try to say thank you, but my throat has grown too tight. I hurry out the door, confused. George is a manipulator, I tell myself. He doesn't give a damn about me. And as for that boring ethics speech? If he is so very high and mighty, why hasn't he turned this place in? I mean, let's be honest here. George has sold his soul.

I'm the first to arrive at the executive conference room, so I take a seat and wait. And I wait. And I wait. What the hell? I can hear raised voices in a nearby office. What? A family fight? A door slams, and Kevin hurries in, his ear stuck tight to his phone.

"Yes, sir. Of course. I understand. It's just that . . . no. You're right. We'll have the documents ready later today. Yes. I know. Of course. I apologize for that, but it wasn't my fault. You see, my assistant forgot to . . ." He stops talking and stares at his phone, his face swollen and red. Plopping into a chair, he shakes his head and mutters swear words under his breath. He's dressed in a bulky gray suit and wrinkled blue tie and stinks like he's bathed in cheap cologne. There's some kind of bird poop or baby barf on his shoulder. I should mention the muck, but why help out a guy who blames his assistant for his own mistakes?

Kevin opens a file and then frowns at me and signals I should move close. I heave myself up and take the chair next to his, trying not to breathe.

"Did I get the time wrong?" I ask. There's a photo on his phone of two pasty-white children scowling at the camera.

"No, you didn't," he says, flipping through the file. "Arthur is running late."

"Thanks for letting me know."

He glares at me with a question in his eyes. Was I daring to rebuke him? Of course not. I make with my most innocent eyes to tell him I know my place. Kevin's quiet for a while, and then he seems to buy it.

"About Friday night," he says.

I slide my bandaged hand behind my back. "What about it?" Maybe he heard about my crash and burn. Maybe he thinks it's a joke.

"You're good at your job, so . . ."

"So?"

"I'll be blunt. You shouldn't hang out with Eric. Dipak shouldn't either. He'll only hurt your careers."

"He was drunk."

"That's no excuse. He said some things that could get him fired. I'd be careful if I were you."

His warning seems almost sincere. Maybe he's getting tired of his whipping boy role. Wouldn't hurt to have him on my side.

"I appreciate the advice," I say, batting my baby-blue eyes.

"You're welcome. Now, let's get down to business." He opens the file and flips through a few pages.

"So what's this meeting about?" I ask.

Kevin screws up his face. "Well, it was *supposed* to be about the financing structure. But now I'm told we'll be discussing the appraisal."

"There a problem?"

He shrugs. "It came in a little low. I brought a few copies so we can discuss."

I'm about to ask another question when Van Meter hurries in. "Good morning," he says with a smile. His gaze slides from Kevin to me. "Sorry I'm late. I was one of the featured speakers at the Women's Economic Ventures' fund-raiser, and the event ran longer than I expected."

We get to our feet, and Kevin extends his hand. "No problem."

Van Meter shakes Kevin's hand and then takes hold of mine. "We've met before," he says with a smile. "Your name's Crystal, right?"

"Crystal Love." It's hard to not be taken in by his haunting good looks. Until I remind myself I'm being played.

"That's a fantastic name. It belongs in a movie or in a play. Anywhere but in a bank." We all laugh at his little joke. "Anyway," he continues, "I'm guessing you're the brains of the operation."

"You're guessing right."

He chuckles a little more. "I like a woman with spunk." He turns his attention to Kevin. "I hate to embarrass you, but there's something on your shoulder."

Kevin glances down and begins to flail his hands. "I'll be right back," he says. He dashes from the room, leaving his minty stench behind.

Van Meter studies me. "You didn't notice his little problem?"

"Actually, I did."

"But you didn't care to intervene?"

"He has a baby at home," I reply, as if that excuses my inaction.

"Ah, yes. New parenthood. Not the easiest time of life." Van Meter retrieves some papers from his leather satchel and lays them on the table in two even piles. The second one is slightly misaligned, and my hands itch to set it right.

"Shall we get started?" he asks, settling back.

"It might be better if we wait for Kevin."

"I'm afraid I have back-to-back appointments this morning."

"I'm sure he won't be long."

"I'm running out of time."

I glance at the door. Where the hell is he? "All right," I say after a moment. "Go ahead."

"Do you have the appraisal with you?"

"I do." I take one of the bound appraisals from the file and slide it his way. Van Meter flips through the hundred-page booklet, pausing somewhere near the end.

"I don't get this," he says. "The comps are way off." He looks at me expectantly, as if I could change the outcome. "Have you reviewed it?"

"I have."

"Then maybe you can explain why they used comps from Goleta and Carpinteria." His nice-guy demeanor has disappeared, and his friendly eyes have turned cold.

"Maybe they were the only ones available."

"That's impossible." He shuts the appraisal and studies me again. Despite myself, I grow uneasy. "There are three similar projects within a one-mile radius," he says. "Why didn't they use any of those?"

"I'm not sure."

He tilts his head and his eyes narrow. "Are you new at this?"

"No."

"Even a novice analyst would question these comps."

Now my eyes narrow. "I suggest you discuss this matter with Kevin."

"I would, but he's not here, is he? But you are welcome to pass along the following message. I spent ten thousand dollars on these worthless pages, and I have no plans to spend ten thousand more. I'd like to appeal the outcome."

"I don't think you can do that."

"Of course he can." Rich steps through the doorway with an annoyed look. He glances from Van Meter to me and back again. "Where's Kevin?"

"Who knows," Van Meter replies.

"In the bathroom," I add.

Rich shakes his head. "You are not in a position to argue with a customer."

"I wasn't arguing."

He waves his hand dismissively. "I'll take this up later with George. And yes, Arthur, you are correct. It *is* possible to contest the outcome of an appraisal if the basis of the analysis is flawed. I read the appraisal over the weekend, and I believe you have a very good case."

"I knew you would see things my way. Flexibility is why I bank here."

"Flexibility is my middle name. Now, gather your papers, and let's finish this discussion in my office." Rich turns to me. "Tell Kevin to meet us there."

I pick up the file and begin to follow.

"Not you," Rich says over his shoulder. "Just Kevin. He can fill you in later." Rich puts his arm around Van Meter's shoulder and leads him through the door. "That was a great speech you gave this morning. I was impressed."

"And I was impressed by the size of your donation."

I stand still for a few moments, seething. Then I take the file, step into the hallway, and lurk outside Rich's door. I overhear the two men laughing. "If your analyst has got to be dumb, why can't she be good-looking?"

"I've warned George about hiring the fat ones, but of course his attention is on the boys." More laughter.

I'm about to kick open the door and get myself fired when Kevin taps me on the back. "I'm sorry," he babbles, his face beet red. "My wife called, and the baby's sick again."

I don't say a word. Just shove the file into his gut and jam my way back to my office. Dipak glances up when I storm through the door.

"What's wrong with you?" he asks.

"Where's the SARs manual?"

"The what?"

"The manual dealing with suspicious activity reports?"

"What do you want with that?"

"Just tell me."

"It's on the back shelf."

I grab the binder and throw it open on my desk.

"You know something about a surprise test?" Eric asks.

I give Eric my death stare. "Maybe I just feel the need to understand the regulations. Aren't we paid to do that?"

"You don't have to bite my head off."

"And you don't have to tell me what to do."

"Bitch," he mutters.

"Jerk," I mutter back.

Dipak sighs and buries his head deep in a file.

Kathi

It's late. Long past midnight. The fog has swallowed the moon. I'm standing on the railroad tracks holding a baby in my arms. A strobe light pulses, and a train whistle blows. The shrieks grow louder and louder. An axe cleaves my head. Move! *Move! MOVE!* But something feels terribly wrong. My feet are glued to the tracks.

"*Help me!*" I scream.

"Over here!" Rich yells from the shadows.

"*Save me, Rich. I'm stuck. Save the baby!*"

"The baby's too heavy," he calls. "Get rid of it, *now!*"

"*Help me, please!*"

"Toss it or you'll die."

"*No!*" My knees hit the tracks, and I startle awake. My heart's pounding. I'm sweating. My breathing comes fast.

I try to talk myself down. *Your feet aren't glued to the railroad tracks. You're sleeping on the living room couch. It was only a dream. A nightmare. Nothing more. Nothing less.* But I still feel the weight of that baby and hear the shrieking of the train. Only the shriek's not coming from a train whistle but from a smoke alarm inside my house.

Beep. Beep. Beep.

I get up and stagger onto the terrace. No wildfire is bearing down. Then I try stuffing my head under a couch pillow, but the shrieking refuses to stop. Something's wrong. This isn't normal. The alarm system has gone wacko. We had a malfunction a few years ago, but I have no idea how it got fixed. I get up again and stumble through the rooms until I pinpoint the throbbing source. The blaring alarm clings to the ceiling above the kitchen sink. *Sweet Jesus.* What am I supposed to do? I try flicking light switches on and off. Nothing. Why, Rich? Why'd you leave me? It's hell living on my own.

I climb onto a chair and fiddle with the thing but can't pull off the plastic cover. Beep. Beep. Beep. It's a nail piercing my brain. Think. *Think!* And then it comes to me. *Batteries.* That's it. That's what I need. Do I have any? I don't know.

I get down and rummage through the drawers like a junkie looking for drugs. Beep. Beep. Beep. Soon enough, I give up on the batteries and search through Rich's toolbox. Grabbing a hammer, I step up on the chair and almost tumble off. I right myself and swing the hammer at the loathsome plastic disk. It barely cracks. I swing again, harder this time. It cracks a little more. The third time I wallop the alarm, the disk flies onto the floor. It skids across the ground and hits a wall. The wailing continues.

Stepping off the chair, I lose my balance and topple onto the kitchen floor. A sharp pain shoots through my elbow, but I don't give a damn.

Beep. Beep. Beep.

"Shut up! Shut up! Shut up!"

I make a run for the linen closet and grab a blanket and wrap it around the wailing beast. Then I carry the alarm into the garage and stuff it deep in the trunk of my car.

Back on the couch, I can still hear the faint pulse of a wail. I need to sleep, but the nightmare continues. I can't tuck the visual away, so I head back to the kitchen and grab an open wine box. Then I settle on the couch and fill my goblet to the brim. Drink one down and pour another. I don't recall much after that.

"Mom. Mother?"

"Stop it," I groan. "It's too early to get up. Go downstairs and watch cartoons."

"Mother?"

I force my eyes open, a headache wedged between my ears. A blurry face swims above me.

"Jack?"

"Are you all right?"

"*Jack!*" I push myself up, my hands grappling with the couch. "You're home. I knew you would come back to me." I wrap my arms around him, but his body stiffens, and he pushes me away.

"What the hell is this?" he asks, his blue eyes flashing. "What's happened to the house? What's happened to you? Why are you sleeping on the ground?"

"I was just resting for a moment." I use my foot to push the wine box behind the couch. It knocks the goblet over, and wine sloshes across the rug.

"It's ten in the morning. Are you drunk?"

There's no denying he's an actor, with his expressive face and so over-the-top-dramatic personality. He's been that way since he was a child. Rich used to call him a drama queen, which was mean but not entirely wrong.

"I'm not drunk," I say. "I had a glass of wine last night and forgot to clean up."

"You mean a mug."

"Well, yes. A mug."

"Out of a box?"

137

"I have to watch my pennies." I don't like his man bun. It makes him look like a girl.

He places his hands on his thin hips and swivels like a top. "This place is a dump. Where are the maids?"

"The housekeepers? They've been gone for weeks." I try to keep my voice cheerful. I don't want to scare him away. "Same with the gardeners. We can't afford them. We can't afford anything. We're penniless, Jack. Penniless." I like the way the word *penniless* rolls off my tongue. It sounds like it comes from a Dickens novel. I should use it in my book.

"Well, it stinks like garbage in here."

"Does it?" I sniff, but of course, nothing.

"Hell yes. Is that dried blood on your arm?"

I pull down my sleeve. "It's nothing. I'm fine. Let me make you some coffee. Or breakfast. Yes, let me make you breakfast. I have a few eggs left. You're not eating enough. You're way too thin."

"I'm a vegan, Mom. Remember? And I don't drink coffee."

"How about tea?"

"No, thanks."

Jack's face is crunched into an unbecoming scowl. I hope he doesn't do that too often, or it'll ruin his movie star looks. He was such a moody boy. Quite needy. When he was little, he'd cling to my legs when I took him to the beach or the zoo. Cried nonstop the first couple of months of kindergarten. Would get his feelings hurt right and left. So when he finally found swimming, I thought he had found himself. It changed him from a shy boy into one brimming with confidence. But he never shared much of what was inside his head, and truth is I never wanted to know. That's the kind of family we were. We each had our secrets, and we kept them to ourselves.

He eyes me like I'm crazy. "Have you had some sort of psychotic break?"

"Of course not." I scan the room and see what he's seeing. Piles of empty wine boxes teeter next to the trash. Dishes overflow in the sink.

Stains cover the rug. Clothes lie strewn here and there. The pocket doors are so dirty I can barely see out. And layers of unopened mail cover the kitchen table.

Jack picks up a bill from the towering pile.

"Have you been keeping up with these?"

"When I can."

He makes a noise and grabs the wine box and shakes it at me. "I can't believe you're drinking this crap. What's wrong with you?"

His words remind me of Rich's belittling tone, and anger stirs inside. "Ever since your father's accident, I've been having a terrible time. And you haven't lifted a finger to help me. If you'd only call me now and then . . ."

Jack stomps his foot like a little boy. "Can we have some honesty here? Huh, Mom? Can we do that for once in our lives?"

"I don't know what you mean." I straighten my shirt.

"Dad killed himself, Mom."

My insides wilt. "You don't know that."

"Dad killed himself. He stepped in front of a train."

"There's no proof of that."

"He stepped in front of a train because of the crap he pulled at the bank."

"His death is under investigation. There are witnesses, you know."

"Witnesses. Ha. Some homeless drunks."

"You don't know that either."

"For once in your life, face reality. Think about it. Why else would Dad have been in that sleazy place at that time of night?"

"I don't know."

"I suppose the other option is he was meeting some woman—"

"Jack!" I turn away. "I've had enough of this. Did you come home just to hurt me? If so, I don't need it. I promise I've been hurt more than enough."

Jack grabs my arm and spins me around. "I came home because I need to know the truth."

I jerk my arm away. "What truth?"

"Stop it, Mom."

"I don't know what you're talking about."

"The fuck you don't. I want to know about my sister."

I take a deep breath. "There is no sister."

"A half sister *is* a sister."

"Who said you had one, Jack?"

"It doesn't matter who told me, does it? The fact is you can't deny she exists."

"She doesn't exist to me."

"What does that mean?"

"It means what I said."

"I have every right to know my sister."

"It's not what you think. Don't go there, Jack. I'm begging you. Please."

"What the fuck are you talking about?"

"Stop using that word."

"I'll stop when you give me what I want."

"Oh, Jack." I sink onto the couch. "Your father and I doted on you. You had the best of everything growing up. Private schools, vacations, clothes, cars. What more could you possibly want?"

"How about a dose of honesty. And a name. Or an address. Some sort of contact information. I'll take it from there."

I drop my head in my hands. "I think you'd better go."

Jack slams his fist against the wall. *"Look at me, damn it."* His face has gotten all twisted and red. "I can totally understand why you don't give a damn about my sister. But she's important to me." He shoves his finger at his chest. "To me, Mom. Can you understand that? She's important to me. I want my family."

"You have your family."

"No, I don't."

"You have me."

"You're not enough!"

"Please lower your voice. The neighbors will hear you."

"I don't give a damn if they do."

"Think of our reputation."

Jack throws his head back and laughs like a crazy man. "Reputation? Are you kidding me? When will you stop pretending we live in Beaver Cleaver land? I didn't have a happy childhood. Our family was a mess. Dad was a bully. A control freak. He was a narcissistic prick. He treated me like shit and treated you even worse. And then I find out he couldn't keep his dick in his pants."

"None of what you're saying is true. Your father was *not* an adulterer."

"Oh, come on, Mom. He cheated on you. He fucked some woman and got her pregnant. What do you call that?"

My cheeks grow warm with shame. Can I let Jack leave here thinking such awful things about his father? I don't know. I'm totally confused. "He didn't cheat on me," I try. "He loved me. There are things about the situation you just don't understand."

"Bullshit."

I get to my feet and point at the door. "I think you should leave. We can talk later, once you calm down."

"I don't want to talk later." Jack's knees seem to buckle. He looks like he's going to cry. "You're acting like a battered woman, Mom. You're taking on the blame when it's all Dad's fault."

"I am *not* a battered woman. Your father never laid a hand on me."

"You don't have to be beaten to be battered." He wipes his eyes and drops his voice. "I shouldn't have yelled at you. I'm sorry. You're as much a victim as I am. Maybe you thought you were protecting me by holding back on the truth. But Dad's gone now, and I want—*I need*—to meet my sister."

I turn to the mirror and shudder at the sight of the disheveled woman staring back. "You're wrong about your father," I say, not looking at Jack. "He was a wonderful man. The ideal husband. He was one hundred percent true to me."

"Then how do you explain his love child?"

It's on the tip of my tongue to tell him. But then I don't. "You see, after you were born, I went through a depression. Something very dark. I got an infection and couldn't have any more babies. I was incredibly sad." I sigh deeply and spread my arms wide. "It was me, Jack. I pushed your father into the arms of another woman. But he never loved her. He loved me. He loved us."

"You 'pushed' him?" Jack says slowly.

"Yes."

"You understand that's bullshit, right? A man can't be 'pushed.'"

I straighten my shoulders, taking strength in my lie. "Well, it's the truth. He got another woman pregnant, but he didn't love her, and we never heard from her again."

"So you just walked away from my sister?"

"She's not your sister, Jack."

"Then what is she?"

I shrug. "All I know is she's not your sister. She's something . . . something else."

Jack stands quiet for a moment, his face drained of color. "I'm done," he says in a quiet voice.

"What does that mean?"

"You figure it out." Without another word he spins on his heel and storms out the front door. I wait until his car drives off. Then I sprint for the bathroom and vomit until there's nothing left of me.

February 7, 1988

It's so hard to believe baby Jack is already one week old. He's so delicate. So beautiful. So perfect in every way. I can't stop staring at his exquisite face, his perfect hands, and his tiny feet. I love him so much it hurts. And the best part is that Rich has returned to his former sweet self. All the coldness has disappeared. Aunt Genny said he cried the night Jack was born. I don't think I've ever seen him cry before. I'm just so happy I came to Reno. So happy I finally have my very own family. That I have Rich and Jack in my life.

Crystal

And so it begins . . .

"We have to file anonymous complaints on Rich," I say.

"What do you mean 'we'?"

Dipak and I sit on a bench at Alice Keck Park munching on chopped Italian salads and sipping mango ice teas. I suggested it this morning as a nice place to spend our lunch, and he looked at me like I was crazy. We aren't the healthy picnicking types. But the day was nice, and I was pushy, so I finally got him to agree. We ordered lunch from our favorite deli and sat in a shady spot overlooking the pond.

The park's pretty and not too crowded. It's a square block of specimen trees and plants bounding a koi-stocked pond. I like to spend time here on the weekends, wandering around or reading in the shade. But today we are here because I need the privacy. Only Dipak can hear what I've got to say.

I take a few bites of my salad, savoring the balsamic-infused mix. Then I set down my fork and begin. "There's fraud at the bank."

"That's a little strong, don't you think?"

"No, I don't. It's all around us. Eric has admitted to fudging numbers. I've seen Kevin do the same. And Rich's loan should never have been approved."

"Eric's an idiot," Dipak says, chewing away, "but it's no business of ours."

"He may be an idiot, but that doesn't mean we can look the other way."

"Sure we can. People do it all the time."

"Have you heard of guilt by association?"

"I'm not associating with anything bad."

"It's not just Rich's loan. You've seen some of the other files. Tyler was a flat-out liar."

"And Tyler's gone." Salad bits spray from Dipak's mouth. The clothing allowance may have improved his appearance, but his manners remain stuck in the gutter. I signal he should dust off his shirt.

"Tyler didn't work in a vacuum," I continue. "Someone was telling him to bend the rules."

"Do you know that for sure?"

"I do. Rich has been pushing to get loans approved for his friends. He needs money to fund his expensive life. He may be taking bribes."

"You don't know that."

"It's an educated guess."

"You should write thrillers. You're making stuff up in your head."

"Am I? You should see the Arthur Van Meter loan. It's a disaster, but it got approved."

"So take it up with George." Dipak scrapes the last remnants of the salad from the plastic container and sets it aside. "Can you pass the potato chips?"

I open the chips, take a few, and hand the bag over. "George may be in on this too."

"Impossible," Dipak says. "He's an honest guy. He just can't afford to lose his job."

"You know something I don't?"

"I know something I shouldn't tell."

"We're friends. Remember?"

Dipak clears his throat. "I underwrote a home equity loan for him last year."

"Don't tell me he didn't qualify."

"He qualified."

"So? That shouldn't keep him from leaving or outing his boss. He must've made a lot of money over the years. I would think he could retire tomorrow."

Dipak shakes his head. "You're wrong about that."

"Then what? He a gambler? A drug addict?"

"See what I mean? Your brain is wacko."

"Then tell me what's really up."

"It's no cloak-and-dagger story. He takes care of his mom. That's all."

"And that's expensive?"

"She has Alzheimer's."

"So?"

"Do you know anything about anything?"

"Guess not."

"Well, it's a crazy-expensive disease. George took his mom into his home years ago, but that stopped working when she needed twenty-four-seven care. Last year he applied for a loan to get her into an upscale dementia facility. It cost him a hundred thousand dollars to get her in the door, and he pays at least that much annually to keep her there. It's crazy money. Poor guy."

"Won't the government pay for that kind of thing?"

"Not much. Without George, she'd probably be out on the street or in some dump. He'd never allow that to happen."

"So he can't jeopardize his job by exposing the truth."

"Exactly."

"Then Rich has him right where he wants him."

"He has him by the balls."

"And Rich knows that?"

"He's not stupid."

"No wonder George hasn't turned Rich in." I lean back on the bench, considering. A squirrel skitters up to our feet and steals a fallen chip. "So that leaves the two of us to do the right thing."

"It may leave *you* to do the right thing. I don't plan to get involved."

"Come on, Dipak. You're better than that. You can't just sit back and pretend you don't see the scams going down."

"Why do *I* have to be a hero?"

"Why not? You're young. Don't you want to make a difference?"

"Isn't that a job for compliance? Why don't you tell Vanessa?"

"Because she's in on it."

"I don't believe you."

"It's true."

"You're sure?"

"Absolutely." I tell Dipak about the affair.

"Holy shit. You sure about this?"

"Saw it with my own eyes."

"That's disgusting."

"So you'll help me?"

"No way. The fact that Vanessa knows about this makes it even worse. I've got a good job, and I like living in this town. I don't want to screw things up."

I can't let Dipak off the hook. A single complaint will get filed in some government drawer. Two complaints and they'll perk up their ears.

"But you *are* involved," I say. "You've heard the rumors. You've seen the files. You know as much as I do, maybe more. Rich didn't qualify for his home equity loan, not by a long shot. Then there's the long list of insiders who have gotten loans when in truth they didn't qualify either. And now that Casa Bella project's getting shoved down the bank's throat when the numbers don't add up. We know too much, you and me. We can't pretend we don't."

Dipak gets up, tosses his salad box into a nearby trash can, and returns with a worried look. "I'm telling you it's none of my business. I can't afford to throw away my career. I'll be blacklisted if anyone finds out."

"No one will find out. And if they do, they can't touch us. We're protected under the safe harbor laws."

"You believe that?" Dipak asks, eyeing me closely.

"I do."

"Well, I don't."

"And you call me a cynic?"

He balls up his hands, his voice rising. *"I said I don't want to get involved!"*

I lean back. "Sorry to upset you."

"It's not like I've done anything wrong," he says, pacing. "I haven't lied in an analysis. Faked any numbers. But if I file a complaint and the shit hits the fan, I could get myself fired."

"Believe me: you won't. They wouldn't dare."

"So what if we out them, and the bank implodes? I'll lose my job anyway."

I didn't think I'd need to push him this hard. No matter. I press on. "Look. I'm going to do this whether you help me or not."

"Then do it."

"You've had your SARs training. You know that if you see something wrong, you could be charged if you don't report it."

Dipak stops pacing and works his hands together. "Look, I can't afford any trouble. I need this job. I'm thinking . . . well, I'm thinking of getting married."

"Married?" That rattles me. "Are you kidding?"

"I'm not."

"To Shelby?"

"Who else?"

"But you've only been dating a couple of months."

"Long enough to know she's the one."

His announcement hits me like a blow to the chest. It's only a matter of time before I lose what's left of our friendship. The thought scorches my heart. But I can only shrug and file away the hurt. This is not the time to get distracted.

"I'm sorry, Dipak," I say. "I really am. But you need to face reality. I'm going to file a complaint. And if I have to, I'll file a second one under a made-up name. And a third and a fourth. Whatever it takes. I promise you it won't be long before the bank is crawling with feds. They'll go through every single file with a fine-tooth comb. If they figure out you knew something and you didn't report it, life as you know it will be over. You'll be facing fines and jail time. That's just the way it is."

Dipak sinks onto the bench and drops his head in his hands. "Ah, shit. Don't do this to me."

"I'm not doing anything except helping you to see the truth. For all we know, we're already under investigation. If we don't speak up, they'll assume we're complicit in a cover-up."

"Then maybe I'll just leave," he says in a muffled voice. "I'll quit and move home and stay out of the whole damn mess."

"And do what? Scrub toilets in Mojave?"

"I'll find another job. Maybe somewhere in LA."

I press on. "It may still come back to haunt you. Just because you walked away from your job doesn't mean you won't be prosecuted." I'm really stretching here.

Dipak's head drops lower. "Shit," he says. "I'm screwed. Totally, royally screwed."

"Not if we handle this right."

He eyes me sideways. "And you know how to do that?"

"I think I do."

"You think?"

"I know I do."

He's quiet for so long I'm not sure which way this will go. When he finally speaks up, his voice sounds so defeated that guilt surges through my gut. "All right," he says. "I'll do it. You write the thing, and I'll sign it."

"Great," I say, faking enthusiasm. "You're making the right decision."

"Am I?"

"You are. We'll file the complaints, and I promise you the two of us will come out on top."

Which is a lie, of course. I have no idea what will happen.

Kathi

July 4, 2016

I'm standing on the edge of our terrace, taking in the view of the promised land. It's the Fourth of July, and it's so hot I can barely breathe. Parties dot the wooded landscape. Music here. Sparklers there. Flames peek from barbeque grills. It's hard to imagine not a single invite—we received a dozen last year. I'm a nothing. A nobody. A speck of dirt on the earth. Rich is lucky he never lived to see the new world. It would've sent him to his grave.

It's after nine, and the fireworks are just getting started. The first ones flash red, white, and blue, lighting up the length of the breakwater, casting colored shadows on the harbor below. I picture families standing arm in arm, oohing at the glorious sight. But the gnats are out in full force tonight, so I soon retreat inside. I shut the pocket doors to keep out the bugs and head upstairs to cool off in a cold shower. Then I dress in shorts and a T-shirt and make a beeline for the wine. All week I've worked to prove my son wrong and limit myself to a single drink. I'm not a drunk. I like to drink. There's a difference. I've found it easier if I start drinking later, when there's less time to kill before heading to bed. So I dither around as long as I can before taking my very first sip.

Earlier this evening I put the box in the freezer, and what comes out now is slushy snow. *One glass. One glass. One glass.* I repeat that mantra in my head. I fill up my goblet to the tippity top and try not to lose a single drop. It cools me as I wander through the simmering heat of the house. If only I could get the damn air conditioner to work. I wonder how much that would cost. More than the remaining pennies in Rich's coin jar—that's for sure.

To distract myself from drinking too fast, I fold some laundry, sweep the floor, and toss junk mail in the trash. Then I decide to return order to the bookshelf, still a mess from the awful police raid.

Most of the books belong to Rich—boring self-help tomes that teach businessmen how to invest in stocks and real estate or turn employees into gold. I make a note to donate them to the local thrift shop. Give the bookshelves room to breathe.

I'm finishing up with the straightening when my hands come across a hidden stash. Years ago I'd concealed seven journals behind my collection of art books to keep Rich from throwing them out. Aunt Genny gave me my first journal on my fourteenth birthday. She thought that writing might help to ease the pain of my parents' deaths.

I take the journals upstairs and set them in order on the nightstand. It's been a quarter century since I cracked their spines. Climbing into bed, I open the first journal and find a faded Polaroid tucked between the front cover and the end sheet. It's a photo of Aunt Genny hugging me at the entrance to her farm. Lights twinkle above us. There's snow on the ground. I bet she was trying to cheer me up, but I look so very sad.

I never saw Aunt Genny after her cancer diagnosis and spoke to her only once or twice that entire year. Never got a chance to say goodbye. Of course, I couldn't help it. I was busy with multiple fund-raisers, and Jack was still swimming back then. Plus Rich never grew to like Aunt Genny. He claimed she eyed him with contempt. Eventually, he persuaded me to stop seeing her. I regret that decision now. A wave of guilt rises before me. I gulp my wine and swim away.

I slip the photo between the pages and begin to sample snippets of passages. After working my way through the first six journals, I stare with unease at the seventh. No need to read that one. Just more depressing entries that exaggerate the sad parts of my life. Sure, times were a little rough after Jack was born, but for the most part Rich and I were happy. Deliriously, ecstatically happy. I'm absolutely certain of that.

I'm not sure why I saved the journals. I should have gotten rid of them years ago. When I get a chance, I'll toss them in the trash. Or better yet, I'll burn them. I don't want Jack to get his hands on this nonsense. He'll think I never loved his father. He'll think I never loved him.

It's time I focus on the upside again. Yes, that's what I must do. Like tonight, for instance. The upside of not going to a Fourth of July party? I'll feel much better in the morning. I'll wake up early and write. The police still have my computer, so I've handwritten the second chapter of my novel. Tomorrow I'll get started on the third.

I stumble downstairs, refill my goblet, and take my place on the couch. Two drinks doesn't make me a drunk, no matter what my son has to say.

May 20, 1988

Last night Rich put his fist through the wall. That's the second time since Jack was born. He says it's my fault because I push his buttons. That I need professional help. He thinks Jack cries all the time because I'm a bad mother. I really don't think that's true. It's just that I'm so sad. So lonely. Some days I can barely drag myself out of bed. If only Rich would spend more time at home and help me out every now and then. But he says I signed on to the homemaker "job," and on the weekends he deserves a rest. He's taken up golf and tennis. He has new friends I've never met.

I don't know who I am anymore. I don't know who he is. I love Jack with all my heart, but I'd give anything to start over. I wish I had taken that job in New York. I wish I hadn't married so young. I wish I had a friend to talk to. I wish I hadn't gained so much weight.

Crystal

December 7, 2015

Pushing Dipak put the final nail in the coffin of our friendship; he mostly stays clear of me now. There's no chatter in our office. No lunches. No beers. He spends his free time with little Shelby, leaving me out in the bitter cold. I miss the times we spent together, and it hurts more than I care to admit. You'd think I'd lost a lover, not some workplace friend. I've tried directing my anger at Dipak. Pictured Shelby squashed in my hands. But I know I have no right to lash out, no authority to seek revenge. I willingly traded our friendship for a base hit in my payback game.

I mailed off our complaints two months ago now, and nothing has come of them yet. If the feds were poking around the bank, I would've gotten wind of it by now. At night my worries scuttle around my head like mice searching for morsels of grain. *What if the feds never follow up on our leads? What if they absolve Rich of his sins? And what about the innocent bystanders? Could George get dragged through the mud? Could Dipak lose his job?* It surprises me to have such thoughts. I mean, when did I start caring about others? I don't like this side of me. Feelings like these can only mess with my plans.

Yesterday I spent hours in the library researching my latest hunch. There's an unknown LLC involved in Van Meter's syndication, and its name delivered a clue.

VSA LLC.

VSA? Those are Vanessa's initials. Coincidence? I thought not. I scoured the state website for information—well hidden, that's for sure. Eventually I learned that VSA was owned by a second LLC. And that second LLC by a third. After hours of relentless searching, I found my pot of gold: the managing member of the original entity was none other than Richard P. Wright. My, my, Mr. President. How low can you get? And all that to trade in a wife.

Now on a sunny morning in December, my depression has drifted away. I've been digging through the Casa Bella file to confirm what I found. VSA LLC owns a one-third interest in Van Meter's $3 million syndication. I'm guessing Rich invested the proceeds from his home equity loan into the first LLC. He then funneled the funds through the sham corporations until it made its way to Casa Bella. Smart move if you need a way to shelter money from a potentially greedy wife. Thank you, Rich, for giving me a second avenue to wreak havoc on your life.

"Busy, Crystal?" Kevin stands at the office doorway, his presence a downer to my day. I snap shut my file.

"Apparently not."

"Want to check out the Casa Bella project?"

I perk up. "Sure. When?"

"Right now."

"Let's go." I pick up my purse.

"Should we drive?"

"It's only five blocks. Let's walk."

"That's not too far for you?"

I stare at him until his cheeks grow red, and then I turn and walk out the door.

Once outside, I hurry along at a breakneck speed just to prove an important point. I've been eating better lately and walking a couple of miles a day. Add to that the drought in Friday-night drinking, and my clothes have begun to feel loose. I don't remember having that sensation before. It's actually kind of nice. Even nicer is the sound of Kevin huffing and puffing by my side.

"It's not a race," he grumbles.

"Everything's a race," I reply.

When we arrive at the construction site, I'm surprised to see the old adobe has been demolished and replaced by an open pit. Two tractors work deep in the chasm, pushing dirt from side to side. A pile of boulders at least ten feet high rests on the east side of the project.

Kevin climbs up a few rickety steps and knocks on the door of a raised metal shed. Van Meter appears, dressed in canvas pants and a flannel shirt, a safety helmet perched on his head.

"Isn't this exciting?" he asks with a sparkling smile. "Demolition means there's no going back." He skips down the stairs and stands beside Kevin with folded arms. "It's my favorite part of a project." He turns and eyes me coolly. "I haven't seen much of you, Crystal. I thought you might have been reassigned."

I haven't laid eyes on Van Meter since that day I got dissed. I fight an urge to knee him in the balls. "No such luck," I reply in my most sarcastic voice. And fuck you, asshole. You're now a target in my sights.

"This is awesome," Kevin says, wonder in his eyes. "Those tractors are huge. I mean, they're the biggest I've ever seen."

Van Meter turns to him. "You like tractors?"

"Doesn't everyone?"

"I suppose. We're digging a subterranean parking lot on a tight schedule, so we lined up the biggest ones in town."

"Must cost you a mint."

"They do."

"Well, I'm impressed you've gotten this far without drawing on your construction loan."

"I've wrangled good terms from our subcontractors. Plus I'm using my investor funds first."

"Smart move."

Van Meter chuckles. "Don't worry. I've run through most of our funds. I'll be needing that construction loan soon."

Van Meter and Kevin keep talking through the dust and the noise, but my mind has wandered away. Investor money almost used up and no building yet in place. If there was ever a time to throw a wrench in the works, that time would be now. But how?

"What about security?" Kevin asks. "Shouldn't there be a fence?"

"Of course," Van Meter replies. "As soon as the digging is finished, we'll install a chain-link fence, along with a full-time security guard. If nothing else, we need to keep an eye on our problem neighbor. He lives right over there." He points at a tiny Victorian cottage nearly hidden behind the looming rock pile. "The old man's crazy. Wouldn't sell his house even though we offered him double what the dump is worth. I bet he'd dynamite our project if he could get away with it."

The old man's house is in way worse shape than the one I call home. Its roof slants over a porch that has buckled with age and weather. When they finish building the four-story structure, his place will be forever darkened by its shadow. If the man were smart, he would've sold out. But maybe he couldn't imagine starting a new life.

"So when do you expect security to be in place?" I ask, pretending to take notes.

Van Meter shrugs. "Two weeks, maybe three."

I nod, considering. There's not much time to come up with an idea that will blow this project apart. Not much time at all.

Kathi

July 7, 2016

Dear Harlequin Editor,

It's been weeks since I first contacted you about my proposed novel Honest Love, and I am deeply disappointed that I have yet to receive a response. I realize your staff must lead very busy lives, but I am also busy, and I would like to know as soon as possible about your interest in my novel.

I sit back and wipe the sweat from my eyes. By noon it's supposed to be well over one hundred, so I'm enjoying the garden while I can. Not that my house won't be as hot as a furnace, but it'll be even worse out here on the terrace. The sun has fried the life from our garden. The cacti curl at the edges, turning brown from the inside out. The succulents have morphed into a crispy shade of tan. The oak tree looks sad and ragged. Dead weeds poke from between the bricks. An ugly scum covers a pond even the birds don't dare to drink from. Such a horribly hot summer. The heat seems to get worse every year.

If I don't hear from you soon, I'm afraid I will have to go to a rival publishing house. Or I might choose to self-publish. Either way, I would hate for you to lose out on what I believe will be a bestselling novel. My terms are negotiable, and I am now willing to accept an advance in the $5,000 range. This offer is only available if you respond within the next two weeks. Please let me know as soon as possible if my offer will work for you.

Yours kindly,
Kathi Wright, a.k.a. Crystal Love

I set down my pen and nod off on the garden bench only to be slapped awake by the rumble of a train winding its way up the coast. I don't feel right. My mouth is dry, and I'm dripping with sweat. A dip in a pool or a stroll through the cool ocean surf sounds heavenly. If only I lived close enough to walk to the beach, instead of having to get in my car and use up my final gallons of gas to make the three-mile trip.

I never wanted to live so far up the Montecito hillsides, but Rich insisted on the 93108 zip code and an imposing ocean view. Early on, he decided Mountain Drive was where the right kind of people lived. That was important to Rich. He thought it would boost his career. And there is no way on earth I can argue he was anything but right. He became one of the youngest presidents ever to lead a California bank. But did his success make us any happier? I don't know the answer to that.

Gnats buzz in my ears, and I swat them away. Mr. Calico, who's been curled at my feet all morning, looks up and yawns. We're growing to be the best of friends. In fact, he may be the only friend I have. I know Jane's been out of the country for weeks, but couldn't she respond to an email now and then? And Laurie? After the fiasco at Tammy's, I doubt I'll ever speak to her again.

The phone rings. And rings. And rings. Someone leaves a message. A bill collector, I bet. Nowadays they call nonstop. I have to face the fact that I can't stay here. I've got to sell the house sooner than later. There's no way I can come up with the $45,000 to keep the banks at bay. George has left messages I haven't returned and sent letters I haven't opened. He sounds nice enough, but his last message said something about his hands being tied. It's not like I blame him for the mess I'm in. If there's anyone to blame, it's Rich. The truth is we could never afford this home. Why had he thought we could?

The heat is unrelenting, so I get up and wander inside. I sink onto the living room couch and flip through TV channels looking for something to cheer me up. Click. Click. Click. I pause at *Pawnshop Party* and picture Rich laughing by my side. He used to love that show. Liked to make fun of the wretched people who had to sell their family heirlooms for cash. Would slowly sip his Pinot and comment on their accents and their clothes.

It seems strange he could be so judgmental when his own mother had cleaned homes for a living. I'll bet after his dad abandoned the family, his mom sold a thing or two. I'm wondering if that's where Rich's harshness came from.

A commercial pops on for the local pawnshop. An idea blooms in my head.

I hurry upstairs and rummage through the safe until I locate his treasured box. It holds his eighteen-karat Rolex Yacht-Master—the pride of his working life. He bought it with his very first bonus and only wore it to the most exclusive events.

"Where did you find such a wonderful watch?" people would ask.

"It's a gift from my grandfather," he'd reply.

As if his long-dead grandfather—a humble almond farmer—had had the money for such an extravagant gift. I stare at his watch, wondering. Would Rich mind if I sold his precious possession? I don't think so. Not with the mess I'm in.

I can't go downtown without pulling myself together—what if I come across someone I know? So I shower and blow-dry my hair in such a way that my gray roots don't show. Then I file my nails, apply my makeup, and slip on my Versace pantsuit. Stepping into a pair of Michael Kors, I do a quick twirl in front of the full-length mirror. Being thin certainly helps.

I take the back roads that lead to Santa Barbara and park my Volvo in an obscure downtown lot. Once out of the car and clattering my way to the pawnshop, I'm melting inside my clothes. The air is still and hot, and the sweat pools under my arms and runs down the length of my back. It was stupid to wear the Versace. Everyone I pass is dressed in shorts.

Still, as I'm tottering along in my too-tall heels, I can't help but get excited. I picture my hair nicely cut and colored. A full mani-pedi—not at Tammy's, of course. Add to that a stocked refrigerator, a full tank of gas, and a clean house. The garden weeded. The windows washed. Maybe a bit of Botox to clear the frown lines from my face. My dreams propel me forward until I reach the shop.

The arched window is stuffed full of musical instruments, fur coats, and jewelry, the word LOAN splashed across its face in big red letters. Loan? I don't want a loan. I just want cash. I continue past the shop, feigning a lack of interest. Reaching the end of the block, I turn and totter back, passing the doors a second time. And then a third. And a fourth. On my fifth pass a man steps out with an e-cigarette dangling from his lips.

"Quieres algo?" he asks.

His shaved head accentuates his sloped forehead, and sleeves of tattoos conceal his arms. He's tight and wiry like a bantam rooster. He breathes out a massive cloud of smoke, and I wave at the smog in the air.

"Can I help you?" he tries again, this time in accented English. He pulls off his sunglasses and smiles. He doesn't look mean, just interested.

"Why, no. I'm just . . ."

"Puedes entrar." He holds the door open, and a bell tinkles from above. He signals that I should follow. I hesitate but shuffle forward, panic flaring in my head.

The store is built long and narrow. Jewelry lines the glass cases to my left. Electronics fill the shelves to my right. Guitars hang neatly on the wall, while bikes and surfboards dangle overhead. The glass shelving that covers the back wall contains piles of handguns, rifles, and knives.

"Abuelita," he calls to a tiny, silver-haired woman hidden behind an antique cash register. "Puede ayudar?"

Her hair is pulled tight in a bun. A green-and-yellow parrot perches on her shoulder and nips at a shiny gold earring that sags from her ear. "Sí. Sí." The woman offers me a sweet smile and holds out a surprisingly youthful hand. Heavy rings weigh down each finger. Her wrists are layered in gold.

"Quiere sell?"

I nod. The parrot stares at me with its beady black eyes. It opens and shuts its beak.

"Quiero ver," she insists.

I tug the Rolex from my purse and set it on the counter. She takes it from the box and looks at me in surprise. "Que hermoso." She closes her eyes and gently rubs the gold band between her fingers. "Bueno," she says. Opening her eyes, she becomes quite businesslike. "Yours?" she asks.

"No . . ."

Her eyes narrow.

"I mean, yes." My face grows warm. I never asked Leo if "frozen assets" also meant "frozen possessions." Could I be breaking the law?

"No es tuyo?" She points at me so I get what she's saying.

"It belonged to my husband. He loved it very much. But he's gone now." I look at her to see if she understands. "He's gone," I repeat.

"Gone," she says slowly. She sets down the watch and pushes it my way. "Divorcio?"

"No. No divorce. My husband passed away not very long ago."

She folds her arms, and I sense my jackpot slipping away.

"*He's dead!*" I blurt out with the power of a bullhorn. The parrot flutters into the air. "My husband died."

"Oh, muerto," she says, the smile returning to her face. She grabs hold of her parrot.

"Yes. Muerto."

She gives her bird a kiss and settles it back on her shoulder.

"Es bueno." She reaches for the watch and slides off her stool. "Esperate. Wait."

Weaving her way through a maze of boxes, she slips through a near-hidden back door. She argues with someone in Spanish and after a few long minutes returns to her stool and makes an offer.

"Tres mil. No mas."

"What?"

"Three thousand. No more."

Three thousand? I almost faint.

Thirty minutes later I step outside with a stack of one-hundred-dollar bills tucked in my purse, my smile so wide it could split my face. I'm floating on air. The upside to selling Rich's Rolex is money. And what's the harm in that?

"Kathi?"

I spin around, and the smile gets sucked from my face.

July 29, 1988

To top it off, the doctor said it wasn't unusual for a six-month-old to have colic. Really? I don't believe him. Every book I've read says the crying should've stopped by now. There's something wrong with Jack. I'm sure of it. Of course Rich doesn't agree, but he's hardly ever home, so how would he know? I'm so exhausted I can barely think. My head feels like it's spinning. There he goes again! Nooooooooo! Stop it! Please! I just put you down. Why can't you sleep for hours like other babies? If only Rich would let me take the happy pills. I know I shouldn't need a crutch to pull myself together, but would it hurt for just a month or two?

Crystal

December 12, 2015

I return to the library to research ideas for blowing up Van Meter's project. Saturday is the library's busiest computer day. Even though I get there an hour before opening, a crowd has already formed outside the doors—mostly homeless, with a few van dwellers, college students, and backpackers thrown in. I line up next to the homeless girl who's pestered me before. She's skinny, mouse faced, and weirdly missing one pinky. She drags a filthy green duffel bag behind her like Linus drags his blanket.

"Remember me?" she asks in her squeaky voice. "I'm Mimi." Her eyes are the palest blue; her hair billows out like a dandelion gone to seed. Her stink is part urine, part sweat. A sparkly pink top hangs from her scrawny frame, and a rope cinches her baggy blue jeans to her waist. I'm guessing she's been homeless for years.

"I've seen you here a lot," she says. "And you always stay a long time. Don't you have a computer at home?"

I don't need attention. I don't need a new friend. I want to swat her away like some bothersome fly. I focus on my bloodred copy of *Helter Skelter* and pretend I'm immersed in the pages.

"Is that a good book?" she asks.

"Yes."

"What's it about?"

"Nothing."

"Nothing?"

"Nothing."

"No, really. What's it about?"

I stare at her long and hard. "It's about a crazy man and his wacked-out girlfriends who kill a bunch of people and chop them up and make them into human soup." That last part's a lie, but I'm hoping to scare the girl away.

"Sounds interesting. Maybe I'll read it. What's your name?"

That's enough. I dig through my purse and pull out a five and hand it to the girl. She'll think I'm a sucker, but at least it'll get rid of her for now.

"Thank you," she says, dancing away. "I'm going to buy two sausage biscuits and a coffee. Want anything?"

"Nope." I return to my book.

The library doors open, and we all file in. Some of the craftier patrons have already reserved their times. The rest of us line up and input our information one by one. The earliest I can reserve a spot is eleven o'clock, and I can't schedule my second hour until I'm done with my first.

When I finally get my hands on a computer, I rush to begin my search. I try various words and phrases. *Construction stalled. Project halted. California condo building stopped.* All sorts of stories pop up, from the silly to the murderous, yet nothing I can use. And then? I hit pay dirt.

It's an old article from the *Los Angeles Times* about a project that imploded in the nearby town of Ojai. A worker there came across a stash of Chumash bones that shut the project down.

I do some further sleuthing. Turns out it's not so unusual to dig up a load of Indian bones. The Chumash hung around this part of California for many thousands of years. In fact, it's so common to

166

dig up a burial site that the state has developed rules for construction-site finds. First and foremost? Construction must stop. Then building officials get notified and the coroner shows up, followed by an archeologist and the head honcho from some Indian commission. That guy has the power to stall out the project for months or even years.

What a find. The perfect fit. I return to the original article. Back in the nineties, an Ojai grading contractor dug up a pile of tools, bowls, and bone fragments from what turned out to be a Chumash burial site. The developer knew the find would screw his project, so he bribed the worker to keep his mouth shut. Unfortunately, a disgruntled employee outed his scheme. The grading contractor turned state's evidence and received six months' probation in exchange for his testimony. The developer ended up with a dead project, a million-dollar fine, and six months in jail.

In addition to the developer's losses, his investors lost millions. The community bank that extended the construction loan almost had to close its doors. To top it off, there were enough lawsuits to paper Ojai's narrow streets. *Perfect*, I think. So very perfect. Almost better than the SAR because of the domino effect.

Rich will lose his job, then his mistress, then his home. In the midst of that, I'll send a note to his son that should prompt an interesting chat. In the end, all he'll have left is his simpering wife. I picture them playing house in a Fresno trailer park, where summer temperatures top triple digits and the nearest body of water is the public pool. To be poor, without a job, and living with his wife? That's got to be Rich's highway to hell. I shiver with excitement just thinking about his fate.

Looking up, I catch sight of Mimi. She blows me a kiss, followed by a wave. I drop my gaze to the computer screen and get back to work.

So how will I pull this off? How will I nail the critical details without giving myself away? I start to rub my hands together, but then a voice chirps from behind.

"Time's up. My turn."

Mimi again. I get up and reserve my next spot at the computer, which is just after two o'clock. Then I head outside to an empty bench to relax and eat my lunch. I'm gnawing on a peanut-butter-and-jelly sandwich when I jump at a screechy voice.

"Hi there," Mimi says, creeping up from behind.

Damn it.

"Mind if I join you?"

"I thought you were using the computer."

"I got bored." She skulks past me like a stinky skunk and sidles onto the far side of the bench. "I wanted to thank you for the five dollars," she says. "Usually library people aren't so nice."

Mimi's eyes are rimmed in red, her fingernails lined with dirt. She eyes my sandwich with interest. Why can't she leave me alone? She sighs and leans back on the bench, swinging her feet like a little girl. "Isn't the sun nice today?"

I flash my book. "I'm trying to read."

"Go ahead," she says. "I understand. I should get back to the computer soon, anyway. I'm looking for a job. Maybe I'll be a nanny or something like that."

Nanny?

"You have any more food?"

I'm not sure why I tolerate the girl. I could squish her like a bug. Instead I dig into my purse and hand her a bag of tortilla chips.

"Thanks." Tearing open the bag, she inhales a fistful of chips. She chews with her mouth wide open, making me feel a little sick.

"Can't you eat somewhere else?"

"Sure. Have a dollar so I can buy a Coke?"

I pull my last dollar from my wallet and dangle it before her eyes. "If I give you this, will you promise to leave me alone for the rest of the day?"

Her eyes sparkle. "I promise. I'll do anything you want."

I wave the bill in front of her eyes. "What I want is for you to get lost. Understand?"

"Of course." She snatches the bill from my hand. "Thank you!" With that she skitters down the street, her duffel bag thumping behind her feet.

Setting down my book, I take a quick bite of my sandwich and feel a poke to my upper back. I look over my shoulder into the drug-slit eyes of a twentysomething homeless man. His dirty-blond dreadlocks nearly reach his knees.

"Give me a dollar, and I'll leave you alone." He laughs. He's missing his two front teeth.

"Get lost," I say, hunkering down.

"Come on. Please? Help a veteran out?"

"I'm out of money. Go away."

"Fat bitch," he mutters, staggering off.

My anger flares, and I play a round of my favorite game. What's the worst? The very worst? It doesn't take long to imagine. How about an office job—something horribly dull. Add to that a nagging wife, snotty children, and a degenerative disease. The perfect recipe for a miserable life.

I polish off my sandwich and a can of warm soda. Right before the courthouse clock strikes two, I head back inside to finish my research.

I start with human bones. I figure it must be close to impossible to get ahold of those, but I'm surprised to find I'm wrong. Within minutes I come across a website that markets itself as a natural history retail store specializing in all types of human remains. Are you kidding me? You can buy human bones off the internet? According to the site, the answer is yes, unless you live in Georgia, Tennessee, or New York. How sick is that?

I scroll through their offerings until I come across the page with partial skeletons; I scroll down some more and find what I'm looking for: fragments of a skeleton from the 1800s. I doubt it's Indian, but it's old enough to stop construction in its tracks. And it's relatively cheap at two thousand bucks.

Next I head to eBay searching for trinkets. I come across twenty Chumash shell beads and an "authentic" arrowhead. Twenty dollars for the lot. I want to purchase right there and then, but I can't leave any kind of trail. I'll have to buy a cash-loaded credit card that can't be traced back to my name. Then I'll open a PO box with my fake ID at the nearby Mail Box Express.

I leave the library so excited I can't think straight. I take the long way home, trying to clear my brain. Money won't be a problem. I've been stashing my savings under my bed in case I need to leave town in a hurry. The cash card I can purchase on Sunday. The PO box during lunch break on Monday. If I pay for overnight shipping, I could have everything I need by the end of the week.

I try to think through the weaknesses in my plan, the various ways I could get caught. But like filing the anonymous complaints, I'm betting I'll come out clean. No one will ever guess what the boring fat girl was up to. Still, I have to be careful. Plot out my many moves, especially on the night I stash the bones. That's where the most danger lies. I'll have to do some site surveillance. Tonight.

"Hi there."

I spin around. Mimi again. "What are you doing here?" I hiss.

Swaying her shoulders back and forth, she giggles like a little girl. "I don't know."

"Well, scat. Get away. Go back to wherever you're from." Hell if I need some grimy panhandler knowing where I live.

"I'm not from anywhere. I don't have a home."

I lift my cell phone. "Either you leave, or I call the police."

"No," she says backing away. "Please don't do that. I just thought you were my friend."

"Either you get out of here, or I call 911. And if I do, I'll make up a story to land your ass in jail."

"I'm going." She sags like a broken rag doll, turns, and plods back down the street.

For the briefest of moments, I don't like myself. And then I shake off the feeling and keep walking.

Kathi

"Arthur?" I haven't seen him since the day at the salon. I don't want to see him right now.

"We meet again," he says with a smile.

"Well, yes." I edge away from the pawnshop door.

"What are you doing downtown?"

"Shopping."

"Way up here?"

"There's a boutique I like."

"Which one? Maybe Eileen shops there."

"I'm sorry. I can never remember its name." Tucking my purse tight under my arm, I look into Arthur's handsome face. His eyes have a way of crinkling at the edges like they're always on the verge of a smile.

"I bet you gals don't like to share your secret shopping spots. Am I right?"

"You're right." I try to relax and smile.

"I'm a smart guy . . . have you had lunch?"

"Why, no."

"Great. Then you'll lunch with me."

I glance around. "I can't . . . I shouldn't . . ."

"Why not?"

"Well . . . is lunch appropriate? I mean, where is Eileen?"

He loops his arm through mine. "Of course it's appropriate. We'll call it a business lunch. Have you been to SIMPLE yet?"

"No . . ."

"Then you're in for a treat. It's country vegan food. A nice young couple owns the place. I referred them to Rich last year, and he was able to help them with an SBA loan. I attended their open house but haven't had a chance to sample their lunch menu."

I glance over my shoulder, thinking this isn't the best of ideas. But Arthur pulls me along, his step so jaunty I soon match mine to his. SIMPLE's interior is constructed from repurposed barn wood, which gives the restaurant a rustic, country feel. Rows of green vines trail from the ceiling; bales of hay are piled against one wall. Stained glass windows reflect a rainbow of colors across the polished concrete floor. The tables are made from rusted sheets of metal set atop old plumbing pipes. The air is fresh, the wait staff charming, the customers young and hip. I'm feeling overdressed until Arthur introduces me to the pretty hostess, who fawns over my designer pantsuit. After a smattering of small talk and a glass of vegan wine, I'm beginning to feel at ease.

I've never tried vegan food before, so I have no idea what to order. Arthur suggests an arugula beet salad with a crushed-cashew dressing.

"So how are you, Kathi?" he asks over his glass of wine. The light shines on him in such a way that his sea-green eyes spark gold.

"I'm fine," I reply, thinking of the $3,000 hidden in my purse.

"You look quite stunning today."

"Me? Stunning?"

"Yes." He laughs. "You. You're doing something different. Maybe with your hair? I can't quite put my finger on it."

I smile. No need to share my secret. He might think me a little weird. When the salad is served, I take a bite and nod in approval.

We chat through lunch, sharing stories of mutual friends. I tell him about the trip we took to Hawaii last summer. He brags about his teenagers, Seth and Sadie. They attend year-round boarding school at nearby Cate.

"Doesn't that bother you," I ask, "not having them at home? I mean, it just seems like time passes so quickly with children, and one day—poof—they're gone."

He nods. "It *does* bother me. I can't tell you how much I miss them, especially in the evenings. Unfortunately, to keep peace in our house, I had to agree."

"You mean it was Eileen's idea?"

Arthur sighs, and his shoulders slump. "Yes. Eileen likes the house to be kept a certain way. And you know how kids are. They just can't help leaving their things everywhere. And she's so busy with her fund-raisers—she doesn't have time to shuttle them around. I offered to bring in extra help to keep them at home, but she refused. She even gave away our family dog. Said he shed too much, and with the kids gone, what's the use?" Arthur pauses, and his sadness washes over me. He shakes his head. "I honestly don't know how you handle life without Rich. Eileen is rarely home, so it's almost like I'm a widower. It's hard. Really hard. Especially at night. How do you do it?"

I shrug. "I don't know. I guess I try to stay busy. Think about the upside as much as I can."

"Don't you ever get lonely?"

I drop my voice. "All the time."

He nods. "Me too. In fact, there are times I feel a little dark. Depressed, I'd guess you'd call it. I've even considered seeing a counselor, but what will therapy change? The truth is I don't like coming home to an empty house. I miss having someone to confide in. To share meals with. To go over the events of the day. You understand what I'm talking about, don't you?"

"I do." I can't believe Arthur is opening up to me. No man has done that in years. Decades, in fact. Not since Rich and I were first dating. "I'm so sorry. I know it's hard."

"I can't believe I'm telling you this. I'm not one to share my feelings, but you're such a kind and lovely person. And I know you understand what I'm going through. It's not like I can talk about it with Eileen. Or with any of my guy friends."

"It's a difficult subject. That's true."

He hesitates. "This may be none of my business, and it's probably too soon to think of such a thing, but have you considered dating again?"

"Oh no." I shake my head. "I don't think I'm ready. And I wouldn't even know where to begin."

"There are those dating sites. Tinder? Bumble? Or eHarmony for older people like us."

"I would never want to meet someone through the internet."

"Agreed. If I suddenly became single, I would want to get to know a woman the old-fashioned way. Invite her to lunch or dinner, just like we're doing here."

I drop my gaze. Is he suggesting . . . ? Just the thought makes my insides flutter, which is wrong since he's a married man.

The waiter arrives and clears our lunch, and Arthur orders us vegan cappuccinos. Once they're served, we settle back. I didn't taste a thing, but it doesn't matter. It's so nice to have lunch with a friend, one who doesn't judge me for Rich's purported sins.

"I don't mean to pry," Arthur says after a while. "But I saw you exit the pawnshop. Are you sure everything's all right?"

I struggle to come up with a good story. "A friend left a ring there. She was too embarrassed to retrieve it, so she asked for my help."

"Good. I feel better knowing it's not you who needs the money." His eyes search mine. "Or is it?"

"Of course not." I look away.

He reaches out and pats my hand. "You can tell me the truth," he says softly. "I'm good with secrets. No one will ever know."

There's a part of me that doesn't want to tell him. Another part that totally does. I've been so sad, so alone these past few months. And he's one of the very few to have reached out his hand. I take a deep breath. "Well . . . it's embarrassing to admit, but yes, I *do* need money. You saw my stack of bills. I'm completely, totally broke."

"So you sold something?"

"Rich's Rolex."

He nods. "Not a bad choice unless it was a family heirloom. I assume your money problems are only temporary?"

"Absolutely."

"Can your son help you in the interim?"

"Jack?" His name bursts from me with a squawk. "He has no money. He's a starving actor."

Arthur cocks his head with interest. "Really? Rich mentioned he'd been promoted to coproducer of his series."

"I guess I don't know about that." I flutter my hands and then dig for my cell. "Oh, goodness. It's late. I should get going."

"Of course. Are you late for an appointment?"

"Well, no . . ."

"Then can you spare a few more minutes of your time? I'd like to talk to you about the file you gave me, the one labeled Casa Bella."

"Is there a problem?"

"Yes. I'm afraid there is."

January 7, 1989

It's Jack's first birthday, and I'm praying that Rich arrives home in a good mood. I know he works long hours, but does that mean he should be grumpy all the time? I've bought a bottle of wine, and I'm making beef stroganoff—his favorite. Tonight's the night I plan on bringing up THE subject. I know he SAYS he doesn't want another child, but I think deep down he does. I just need to convince him that my bout of postpartum depression won't ever return.

Crystal

"You look tired this morning," Dipak says. He's perched on the edge of his chair wiping a spill from his beloved Topman ultraskinny suit.

"Thanks," I reply, keeping my eyes fixed on my computer screen.

"I'm not being mean."

"I didn't say you were."

"Oh, leave her alone," Eric chimes in. "She's in one of her moods. Let's get some coffee."

"All right. Want anything?" Dipak asks me.

"No."

I *am* in one of my moods—that's true. It's Monday, and I'm not interested in chatting with my ex–best friend Dipak, who spends his every waking moment drowning in wedding plans. He and Shelby got engaged over the holidays. Only five months of dating and wham, bam, they're a permanent team. They're planning a small reception in Santa Barbara followed by a huge ceremony in Shelby's hometown of Pacific Palisades—I never would've guessed she was rich. After that comes the three-week honeymoon in India, where Dipak can show off his American bride to his extended family. Most of the planning goes on right here in the office. I'm disappointed in Dipak. He's traded in his former hardworking self to become a member of team Frick and Frack.

Feeling sullen and depressed, I open up the Casa Bella file. One foggy night over a month ago, I placed the bones and shells on the project site and followed that up with an anonymous tip. As far as I can tell, nothing's happened. Nada. Zip. Another good scheme swallowed into the abyss like the complaint letters sent to the feds over three months ago. Seems like Rich walks on water, and I can't bring him down.

I'm filing away Casa Bella's latest construction drawings when Kevin hurries through the door. His pasty face glows apple red, and his comb-over stands on end.

"Where are the Casa Bella files?" he barks.

"The construction file's right here."

"Hand it over, and get me the others. I need to review them right now." He drops into my seat and pages through the file as I rummage through the cabinet for the rest. "Hurry," he says. "We don't have much time."

"What's up?" I set a stack of files in front of him, trying not to breathe in his sickly sweet scent.

"I need to make sure everything's in order."

"My files are always in order."

His hands fly through the paperwork, and then they slow down. "What's this?" he asks. He points to a statement of information on the primary investing entity, VSA LLC. He flicks through a few pages and then stops. "Damn," he mutters. "What's this doing in the file?"

"What do you mean?" I ask as innocently as I can.

"We don't usually gather information on the syndication investors."

"Sorry. I thought we did."

"We need to get rid of this."

"We do?"

"Kevin? Crystal?" Vanessa bobs into the office followed by two stern-looking men carrying empty storage boxes in their arms.

"Surprise audit," she says in her high-pitched voice, a strained smile pasted across her orange-tinted face.

Kevin's shoulders slump. He slaps the file closed and stands. "What files do you need?" He sounds defeated.

One of the two men reads from his phone. "We'd like all of the files associated with the following entities: Ten Corners LLC, SIMPLE, Arthur Van Meter, Casa Bella LLC, Richard Wright. There will be more, but that's enough for now."

I can't believe my luck. I have to swallow my grin. That's no regular list. This is no normal audit. The FBI has arrived. My work is about to pay off.

"We'll need a conference room, of course."

"Of course." Vanessa teeters and totters and grabs hold of the wall. "Please follow me." The men stack the files in the boxes and hurry out the door. Kevin follows close behind.

I can barely contain myself when Dipak and Eric return from their jaunt. I try to pull Dipak out of the room to tell him what's up, but he stops me before I can.

"Check this out." He drops the *Santa Barbara Times* on my desk. And there it is, the double whammy. The lead article details the discovery of a Chumash grave at the Casa Bella construction site. It goes on to say that the project will be delayed indefinitely until an archeological review is completed.

"How long could that take?" I ask.

"The article says months, if not years."

"Van Meter's in a shitload of trouble," Eric says. "The general contractor accused him of ordering a cover-up of the find."

"What does Van Meter say?" I ask, quickly scanning the article.

"He denies any knowledge of the grave and blames the contractor. Says the guy did the hiding because he couldn't afford to stall the project."

"I wonder who's telling the truth."

Dipak jumps in. "Doesn't really matter because the project is screwed. Someone at the bank will take the fall for this."

"I'm guessing Kevin," Eric says with a smile. "Just you wait. I bet I'll be promoted to senior VP by the end of the first quarter."

I would take that bet and double down. But no need. It's time for me to take a seat, sit back, and enjoy.

Kathi

"Casa Bella?" My words echo loudly in the near-empty restaurant.

Arthur lowers his voice. "Yes. The file you gave me from Rich's office. I should've returned it sooner, but I thought it better to have this discussion in person in case your phones are being tapped."

"Tapped?" My heart begins to thrum. "Is that a possibility?"

"With everything going on, I'm afraid it is."

I think back on my conversations. Could I have said something incriminating? Or embarrassing?

"I don't understand," I say. "Just what is going on?" I can't control my fluttering hands, so I grab on to my napkin and hold tight.

Arthur leans back and folds his arms. "I think it's time for me to be completely honest with you."

"You haven't been?" My stomach drops to my feet.

"In certain ways, no. The truth is Casa Bella is my project."

"Yours?" I twist my napkin into knots. "What do you mean?"

"I mean I was the developer on the project. I owned it. I managed it."

"But . . ." I try to focus my swirling thoughts. "Why didn't you tell me when I showed you the file?"

He takes a deep breath. "I guess I was a little taken aback. You see, your husband was a longtime referral source. We've worked together on a number of projects. I've paid him quite handsomely over the years. He helped sell out the Casa Bella syndication, so in truth, I thought you knew."

I stare at Arthur, trying to understand. Paid? Paid my husband? What is he talking about? For god's sake, Rich was a bank president. Why would he have been involved in Arthur's projects? And if he had, why wasn't I ever told? "So you lied to me?"

"I didn't lie . . ." He rubs his forehead. "I figured you knew about Rich's side business, that the two of you were a team. When you showed me that file, I thought you might have an angle."

"Of course I didn't."

"I know that now."

My thoughts swirl faster than a whirligig. I snatch at them. I need them to slow down. "The work you did with Rich . . . was it legal?"

"Sourcing investors? For a regular person, yes. I have a number of legitimate sources, from accountants to lawyers. But for a bank president to be involved with a client's project? I always wondered about that. I mentioned my concerns to Rich, but he wasn't interested in my opinion. He said it would be a problem only if the regulators found out, and they wouldn't. Even if they did, he believed they were too busy and too dumb to investigate minor schemes."

"Rich made good money at the bank. Why do something illegal and risk everything we own?"

"He made good money, but not enough to live the Montecito lifestyle. So he supplemented his income in other ways. You have to understand he thought the Casa Bella project was a sure thing. He'd make some fast cash for sending over a few investors. Then we ran across those Chumash bones, and the project imploded."

"Chumash bones?" I search Arthur's face. "That was *your* project I read about in the *Times*? *You* dug up the burial site?"

Arthur nods.

"My god." Is it possible Arthur isn't the man I think he is?

"You have to understand," he says in a mournful tone. "My general contractor dug them up and tried to hide the discovery from me. I was shocked. Completely sideswiped. Couldn't believe I had hired such an unethical man." His shoulders sag. "You don't know how difficult this has been. I'm not just talking about the money—and, believe me, I lost my shirt. But I've never seen myself as just a developer. I'm much too altruistic for that. I've thought of myself first as a housing advocate expanding homeownership for the working class. And then there's Arthur the patriarch, taking care of his flock. No one had ever lost a penny on my watch. And then my project blows up." His voice begins to tremble. "I've hurt so many people. And now, well, it seems I've hurt you too."

I believe him. And I can't help but feel sorry for him. He looks like a lost child. "Please don't worry about me. I'll be fine."

He hesitates, and his eyes fix on mine. "There's something more."

My stomach begins to churn. "What?"

"The problem I mentioned with the file?"

"Yes?"

"I found a receipt made out to an investor, Mabel McCarthy. It's for a million dollars, and it's signed by Rich. Problem is he only invested half of that in my project."

I think back on the file and the $500,000 scrawled across the top. "So where's the rest?"

"I was hoping you might know."

"Me? Of course I don't."

Arthur stares at me sadly. "Then it's possible the money was stolen."

"Stolen?" I drop my napkin on the ground. "By whom?"

"By Rich."

He's talking about Rich. My Rich. My husband for close to thirty years. It's one thing if he cut a few corners at the bank. But if he were the type of man to do something so disgusting, wouldn't I have known? I shake my head. "Impossible."

"Unfortunately, all of the evidence points to him. The thing is last week Mabel's attorneys contacted my lawyers. They've asked that we provide the paperwork for the million-dollar investment, but of course our papers reflect half of that. They're going to want to know what happened to the rest of the money. I'm afraid their questioning will lead them to you."

"Me?" Beads of sweat form on my brow. "But I don't know anything about that money."

Arthur sighs. "I want to help you, Kathi. I really do. I think the answer is to find that missing half million and give it back."

"How would I do that?"

"Did Rich ever mention anything about the investment? Indirectly, I mean. Maybe you overheard something he said on a phone call or at a party with friends."

I rack my brain. "I don't think so . . . except . . ."

"Except what?"

"The FBI found two hundred thousand dollars in our safe deposit box. I have no idea how it got there. They thought it came from our home equity loan."

"Really?" Arthur slowly nods. "All right, then. That's a starting point. If it's Mabel's money, we need to find the remaining three hundred thousand. Any ideas?"

"No. None at all."

"I suggest you think hard on the subject. Let me know if you come up with any clues."

I feel like I've been punched. Kicked while I'm down. My voice fades to nothing in my ears. "Maybe we should tell the police," I try. "Maybe they could help."

He leans back, arms folded. "Tell them what? That you lied about the Casa Bella file? That you forgot to tell them you gave it to me?" He shakes his head. "I'm afraid if you do that, they'll arrest you, Kathi. And then they'll arrest me as your accomplice. No. It's best to wait until we find the missing money."

"At least I should tell Leo about this."

"Leo Silverstein?" He makes a face. "That's your lawyer?"

I nod, thinking I really need another drink.

"You know he's not a criminal attorney, right? He handles simple business transactions. I highly doubt he understands the complexities of Rich's crimes." He lowers his voice. "I'm not one to spread rumors, but I've heard he's suffering from early-onset dementia. He totally screwed up a simple transaction for a friend of mine."

I think back on our meetings. Leo never seemed distracted or confused, just irritable every now and then.

Arthur continues. "The best thing we can do is keep our search secret. In the meantime, I promise I'll do everything in my power to help you."

"Thank you." Tears spill from my eyes. "I just don't understand how Rich could've done such a thing. *My god!* How could he betray that poor woman? How could he betray me?"

Arthur shakes his head. "I'm sorry. I really am. I know what it's like to be betrayed."

"You do?" I scour his face. So handsome. So honest. So kind. Who would ever betray such a man?

"Unfortunately, yes. I wasn't going to tell you, but since we're sharing secrets . . . Eileen and I have separated."

"Separated?" I glance at his ring finger. It seems shameful to feel elated, but I do.

"Yes."

"I'm so sorry."

"Don't be. It's been a long time coming."

"But you seemed like the perfect couple."

"*Seemed* is the operative word. We've been fighting nonstop about everything. Money. The children. And then I found out she's been having an affair with the club tennis pro. It's been going on for some time."

"That's terrible."

"Honestly, it's not her first. Over the years I've done everything to keep us together, but this latest indiscretion has forced my hand." He leans forward, dropping his voice. "Promise me you won't tell anyone. It's not yet public knowledge, and for my children's sake, this secret has to stay between us."

"I promise."

Arthur gazes at me with the saddest of eyes. "I knew I could trust you. I could tell the first time I met you. We're the same, you and me. We're two of a kind. Maybe we can help each other through these difficult times." He reaches across the table and takes my hand. His fingers are dry and rough to the touch. Manly hands. Worker hands. Rich's were always soft and moist. "What do you think?" he asks. "Can we be there for one another?"

What do I think? After all of the awful things that have happened to me, I think there's finally a break in the clouds.

June 26, 1989

So I got the silent treatment all weekend. As Rich puts it, he's "pissed." He says it was a waste of time and money to get a babysitter and take me to dinner. A waste? It was our second anniversary, for goodness' sake. He was the one who got grumpy when I couldn't fit into his favorite black dress. Is it my fault that Jack cried the entire first year of his life? I could barely get dressed, let alone cook healthy meals or work out. And so what if I sneak a Twinkie every now and then? My treats are often the only sliver of happiness I can find in my dull and dreary life.

Of course I added fuel to the fire by having a little too much to drink. Then I brought up the baby subject again. That's when Rich went ballistic. He was so mean I walked out of the restaurant and continued walking down the dark street. And the saddest thing? Rich just let me go! What kind of man does that? I could have walked all the way to Iowa, and he wouldn't have lifted a finger. When I finally got scared and turned around, I found him sitting motionless in the car. He didn't even look at me. Just started up the motor and drove us home without uttering a single word.

Crystal

A hush has fallen over the bank; a web of fear has spread wide. The FBI entourage that showed up last month doubled in size and then doubled again. They've taken over the executive conference room, where they keep the door shut day and night. They open it every now and then to bark out requests for files or food or for an employee to hustle to their quarters. They've grilled Kevin four times, Eric twice. Even Dipak spent an hour with them last week, although he refused to tell me anything about the meeting. Said he didn't plan to spend the next ten years in jail, which is what they are threatening if anyone spews. I expect to be called, but it hasn't happened yet. I'm carefully grooming my words to get ready for when it does.

This must be what it feels like when there's a murder in a family and fingers are pointed all around. No one knows for sure what's going on, but from the files being pulled and the questions asked, Rich and Vanessa must be wetting their pants. Rich looks pale and thin these days. He hurries through the bank with his shoulders slumped, less man than cowering dog. Vanessa has the same look, only worse, and spends most of her time with the investigators. I'm guessing she's ready to crack.

I followed Rich after work one day and saw him duck into the Huntsman Pub. It's one of those forever-twilight taverns where alcoholics occupy entire days. Vanessa followed not ten minutes later, teetering like a drunken sailor down the street. They must have been too scared or too smart to communicate by email, text, or phone. I wondered how much they would drink. Getting Rich arrested with a 911 call would tie a ribbon around my plans.

The phone rings and wakes me from my daydream. "I'm transferring a phone call to you," a distant voice says.

"Who is it?" But the phone goes silent, and I wait the requisite ten seconds for the two beeps and a click. "Welcome to Pacific Ocean Bank," I say, our required greeting. "This is Crystal Love. How may I help you?"

"You may help me by having a drink with me."

"I can't," I choke. "I'm busy."

"How about I stop by the bank?"

"*No!*"

Dipak lifts his head and glances at me with a questioning look. "It's nothing," I mouth.

"It's one or the other," Marco says in my ear.

I hesitate, but there's no choice. "I'll meet you at Oyster."

"Perfect. I'll see you at five thirty."

"Today?"

The phone line goes dead.

"You got a date?" Dipak asks, smiling.

"None of your business," I reply.

Marco sits at a corner table of the Oyster's glassed-in courtyard studying the local paper. He's dressed in casual clothes: jeans and a form-fitting T-shirt that exaggerates his broad chest. He jumps up when he sees me and even pulls out my chair. Several people glance our way, and their eyes linger. I know what they're thinking: *What's the Italian stud doing with the Bakersfield blimp?* I drop into the tiny metal chair, and it squeals. Marco acts like he doesn't notice. He holds up the paper and chuckles.

"Guess we're not in Kansas anymore."

"Guess not."

The feature story in the *Times* is on the Prince of Wales, with an oversized photo of the prince dressed in riding gear. He's in town for the weekend to compete in an international polo tournament. "Never thought I'd live in a place like this. You?"

"Nope."

"Is outside okay? Not too cold?"

"It's fine. I can't stay for long."

"Busy?"

"Yes." I don't like Marco's eyes searching my face, so I focus on the view.

Oyster sits at the foot of the Santa Barbara Harbor. Its courtyard looks out over a sea of blue and white yachts. The ease of parking and extended happy hour make it a draw to tourists and locals alike. The crisp winter day has warmed into a near-balmy evening. A few pinkish clouds hover in the darkening sky; a flock of pelicans soars through the air. There's an amateur cluster of ukulele players huddled in a circle, strumming songs from the sixties. Their voices are terrible, but the music isn't bad. They look like they're having fun.

The waitress shimmies up and takes our order: two beers and a platter of fried calamari. Marco ordered the food, not me. "So how are you?" he asks once the drinks arrive.

I pick up my beer, my hand trembling. "Fine, I guess."

"You guess?" He takes a long pull from his beer and continues to study me.

I won't look at him. He knows too much about my past. I nibble on a chunk of deep-fried calamari and watch a mother stroll by with two kids. She's pushing the little one in a stroller while the older one prances by her side. They're laughing like the world is a blessing. Laughing and singing songs.

I take a second calamari. And then a third and a fourth. Marco frowns, so I keep it up.

"You ever hear from your grandma?" he asks.

"Never."

"She pass on?"

"I don't know." My thoughts drift back through the years.

I didn't mean to hurt Granny. I really didn't. I came home from school that day more upset than ever before. A poem I'd written for my birth mom had slipped out of my folder during English—the only class I liked in eighth grade because Mrs. Montrose treated me nice. Then I came across rich-bitch Glenda in the cafeteria sharing my private words with her friends.

"I look for you in every face I see," she shouted in a singong voice across the room.

"I look for your eyes, the way they shine;
Your smile so warm it melts my sorrows;
Your step so light and firm;
Your voice so sweet and . . ."

That's when I hit her. Hit her hard on the mouth. I'm pretty sure I broke her tooth, because I cut my finger to the bone. Then I dropped my books, wrapped my hand, and lumbered the long and lonely mile home. I kept my eyes downcast when some high school boys yelled something nasty at me from their speeding car.

Granny wasn't home when I got there. She worked as a bookkeeper and never made it back before five. So I circled the living room, the telephone ringing over and over until I finally took it off the hook. Then I inhaled a quart of ice cream and a pack of Oreo cookies while watching an episode of *Lizzie McGuire*. I usually liked Lizzie, but not on that day. She only pretended to be awkward, but it wasn't the least bit true.

She wasn't fat. She wasn't ugly. She had parents. She had friends. What is the worst? The very worst? Those words kept buzzing in my head.

I turned off the TV and started pacing again. Granny was going to kill me, for sure. Somewhere along the line I grabbed her secret stash of cigarettes and lit one up. I didn't like cigarettes—not the taste or the smell—but they gave me a sense of power. At some point I snatched a stack of Granny's favorite gossip magazines and got a small fire going in the sink. Once that was done, I began circling again, stopping at the flowery kitchen curtains Granny had hung a few days before.

I pressed the cigarette against the silky fabric, thinking I'd make one tiny little hole. But the flames blew up in front of me, and I fell back, not knowing what to do. I heard Granny's screams before I saw her. She pushed me away and started whapping at the curtains. First the sleeve of her jacket caught fire, and then the flames ran up her arm and exploded in her hair.

"I didn't mean it," I cried to the men who loaded her into the ambulance and whisked her away. Granny survived the fire but was permanently disabled. She moved into a convalescent home. I never saw her again.

"What about your parents?" Marco asks. "You guys in touch?"

"No."

Both Alan and Anna showed up at juvie that night. I saw them in the outer hallway. Anna glanced my way once, but Alan never looked back. And that was the last I ever heard from those losers. They pitched me from their lives just like my birth parents had.

"I lost track of you after you left Bakersfield," Marco says.

"Lost track?" I focus on his face, on the arch of his brows, the wide brown eyes, the steel jaw. He was the probation officer assigned to me the first day following the fire, and he stayed by my side through the years of detention hell. "You've been checking up on me?"

"Not exactly." He hasn't touched a calamari—must've bought them just for me. "But you were one of my first cases. I've stayed interested.

Was happy to hear you finished Bakersfield College and worked your way into a decent career."

"There wasn't much choice in the matter," I say, using a napkin to wipe the grease from my fingers. "It's not like I had family to support me."

"You did get the short end of the stick with that adoptive family. I don't think the judge would've put you in juvie for so long if you had somewhere else to go."

"Yeah, well, life sucks sometimes." I take another bite.

"Not always." He tilts his head in such a way that I'm swept up in a memory of a long-ago crush. I slug down some beer to clear my throat.

"So if your life was working out, why change it?" Marco asks. "Why move to Santa Barbara?"

I tuck the memory away. "I could ask you the same thing." I reach for the last calamari, but Marco snatches it away. He tosses it into his mouth and chews it up.

"So your new job's a good one?" he asks.

"As good as it can be." I finish off my beer.

"How about your last job?"

"In Bakersfield?"

"Yeah."

"It was okay."

"So why'd you leave?"

"Why do you care?"

"Just interested."

Out on the boardwalk a bunch of kids toss bread to the seagulls, and hundreds of squabbling birds have appeared. They dip and dive, wings flapping, beaks flashing. Soon the kids run off screaming, their parents following behind.

"I guess I wanted to start over," I say. "You of all people should know that my life in Bakersfield wasn't exactly peaches and cream."

"I know that." He leans back and folds his thick arms against his chest. "I thought you might've been upset by the death of Mike Simms. He was your boss, wasn't he?"

"Yeah. So?"

"Let's just say I've taken an interest in the case."

My body goes hard, and my breathing slows. I need to be careful. Very careful. "I *was* upset. Mike was a mentor to me."

"He was?"

"Yep."

"That's a surprise."

"Is it?" I push my beer away.

"I've done some checking around. Some of your former coworkers say that Mike wasn't the nicest of guys. He could be mean. Liked to tell the kind of jokes that put people down."

"I don't remember that."

"Racist jokes. Jokes about the elderly and the disabled. He could be especially harsh about a woman's looks. Any of this ring a bell?"

"I don't know. I just worked for him. We didn't socialize after hours."

"They mentioned he seemed to enjoy harassing you."

"I never noticed."

"They say he was relentless. You became the center of his daily comedy routine."

"I wouldn't know."

"Once he left a scale on your chair along with a box of day-old doughnuts."

"It was a joke."

"So it didn't hurt your feelings?"

"No."

"I find that hard to believe."

"You can believe whatever you want. I just went to work every day and did my job. I didn't get involved in the office gossip."

"But Mike was your mentor?"

"He was."

"Were you shocked when kiddie porn was discovered on his work computer?"

"Of course."

"And disappointed?"

"Yeah . . ."

"Well, you weren't the only one. It shocked everyone who knew him. They seem to agree that he was a jerk but not a perv."

"So?"

"So this is one of those cases that I can't get out of my head. Guy downloads kiddie porn at work. Guy gets caught. Guy kills himself."

"I thought he died in a car accident."

"That's what the investigators thought at first, but things just didn't add up. So here you have a college-educated banker with a squeaky-clean background. Granted, he could be mean, but he was clean. Not even a single speeding ticket to his name. And he's a senior vice president at a bank. He would've known that his work computer, like all bank computers, was under constant scrutiny. So why download porn? Why not view it at home or on his cell, where there's less chance of getting caught?"

"Maybe he did."

"The police searched his phone. And his home computer. They searched his entire house. All they found was a box of old *Playboy* magazines. Don't you find that odd?"

"I suppose . . ."

"I just wish *I* could've interviewed Mike before he drove into that wall."

"So you're saying it wasn't an accident?"

"There was no sign he tried to step on the brake. In fact, witnesses say he sped up."

"Why would he do that?"

Marco shrugs. "He'd lost his job. His friends. He must've known any court case would drain his savings. Guilty or innocent, it didn't matter. Life was over as he knew it. And desperate men are known to take desperate measures. It appears he staged his death as an accident hoping his family would collect on his life insurance. Unfortunately, it didn't work. Kelly lost her home and had to take the kids and move in with her parents."

"Kelly?"

"Mike's wife."

"You know her?"

"We dated a little in high school." Marco finishes off his beer, his eyes leveled on mine. "We went our separate ways after graduation, but since the tragedy we've reconnected. Not in a romantic way. I don't have the temperament to take on Mike's kids. But Kelly's a nice woman in a very tough situation. I admire her. She's handled these terrible events with grace. But she's like a bulldog. Unrelenting. She just won't let this thing go. She calls me at least once a month asking for help to solve Mike's murder."

"Murder?"

"It's a stretch, but in a roundabout way you could call it murder. If someone planted the porn on Mike's computer with the intent to destroy him, at the very least that person would be charged with manslaughter."

I swallow. I'd been careful. So very careful. "So what do you want from me?"

"Funny you should ask." He leans forward. "I was having drinks with a group of friends the other night. I suppose they're more like acquaintances than friends. Anyway, I met up with a bunch of guys from my evening workout class, and one of them tells this story about how a young guy got fired at your bank. Seems he sent a porn photo to everyone at work. You hear about that?"

"Of course. I worked with him."

"His name was Tyler, right?"

"Yes, Tyler."

"What department was he in?"

"Mine."

"Wow. Well, it seems this Tyler swears he never sent the photo, and he can't figure out how it happened."

"He probably drunk dialed."

Marco nods. "See. I knew you could help me."

"What do you mean?"

"It's the second time you've been involved in something like this. You're something of an expert."

"I wasn't *involved*."

"Sorry. Poor choice of words. What I mean is it's the second time a coworker of yours has been fired for questionable online activity. And both of them claim they didn't do it. So I'm just trying to understand how something like this could happen. Assuming they weren't lying—and I'll admit that's a stretch of an assumption—how easy is it to get ahold of a coworker's password?"

"Very."

"How's that?"

"Almost everyone writes them down."

"But wouldn't that be against bank policy?"

"Yeah. But we have so many passwords they're hard to remember."

"I'll bet you don't write yours down."

"I don't."

"I knew it. You're far too bright for that." His eyes narrow the tiniest bit. "How about you and Tyler? You two get along?"

"We got along fine."

"Was he a mentor?"

"I wouldn't call him that."

"He ever tease you?"

I rustle in my purse and pull out my cell. "Sorry. I have to get going. I'm meeting up with a friend."

Marco stands, like the gentleman he pretends to be. "That's too bad. I'd hoped we could spend more time together. I thought you might have some additional insight into Mike's case."

"I don't know what more I could tell you." I drop a twenty on the table.

"Next time it's on me," he calls out as I rumble away.

I hurry to my car and fumble for my keys. I'm about to drive off when a knock on the window startles me.

"You left these." Marco holds up my sunglasses. I roll down the window and reach for them, but he doesn't let go at first.

"I would like to talk to you a little more. I'm sure you'd be happy to help the wife of your former mentor."

"Sure. Anytime. Just call me."

"How about we set a time next week?"

"I'm busy next week."

"How about the week after that?"

"I'll have to check my schedule."

"You do that." He smiles. "And by the way, do you still play that game of yours? The one you played with your grandma?"

"Of course not." I grab my glasses, roll up the window, and floor the accelerator, almost colliding with a waiting car. I zoom out of the parking lot, my heart banging in my chest, sweat dripping down my back.

What is the worst? The very worst that can happen to Marco? I know the answer. He'd better stay away.

Kathi

I'm scared! I'm excited! Arthur is coming to dinner tonight. At my house. *My* house. He called yesterday to say he just *had* to see me but couldn't afford to trigger the local gossip machine. So I invited him over for a home-cooked meal. Well, almost home-cooked. I've never been a good cook. Expensive takeout is as close as I get.

Was I too forward? I don't think so. I'm a widow, and he's separated. It makes perfect sense. Not that I think it's a date. We're just friends, of course. At least for now. But who knows where the night might lead?

I've almost used up my $3,000, but I've used the money very well. Eight hours of housecleaning including windows, inside and out; two days of gardening; a mani-pedi; a cut and color; a stunning tropical bouquet; a fully stocked refrigerator and cupboard; and a mini Saks shopping spree. Of course, I can't be expected to slave over a meal, so my favorite caterer has supplied our dinner: a portabella and Gruyère quiche paired with pistachio-endive salad. Add a couple of bottles of fine wine into the mix, and I'm nearly broke again.

And then there was the full Brazilian wax—painful and embarrassing, but I've heard it's all the rage. It seems crazy and gross, but who am I to say? Not that I plan to take off my clothes. No plans for that at all.

But what if something should happen? What if we get carried away? It doesn't hurt to be prepared, does it?

Arthur had to spend the day in LA, so he suggested we dine at nine. I was disappointed at first, as I'd imagined us lounging on the terrace watching the sun melt into the sea. The sunset is so beautiful this time of year, a mix of rosy orange and gold. But now I realize the timing couldn't be better. A near-full moon brightens the sky. A warm breeze ruffles the leaves. Crickets chirp, frogs croak, and the distant lights of Santa Barbara twinkle in lovely shades of pink and blue.

It takes everything in me to delay my first glass of wine. I don't want to look flushed or sound slurred, so I force myself to wait until eight before I pour a half glass of Pinot. I sip it slowly and don't allow myself to gulp. I put on some nice classical music and spin around a few times. Coming to a stop in front of the living room mirror, I take a good look at myself. I spent half the day choosing the perfect outfit and settled on a sleeveless pink top with white jeans and gold sandals. My look says casual yet chic. Artless yet sophisticated. Self-confident yet innocent. It's perfect in every way.

I may not be stunning like Eileen or even beautiful. I'm short and a little stubby. No one would ever suggest I modeled in my youth. But I'm still pretty, in that fresh-faced farm-girl sort of way. I can understand why Arthur might like me. I really can. I finish off my wine and pour another half glass. Less than eight ounces total. I can handle that.

Shortly after nine, Arthur roars into the garage. I left a space for him like he asked. The doorbell rings, and I rush to greet him.

"Sorry I'm late," he says, stepping inside. "Do you mind if I shut the garage door?"

"Not at all." It seems impossible, but he's even more handsome than I remember. His smile is brighter. His eyes kinder. His lavender polo shirt is fitted tight enough that a surprising six-pack shows through. He laughs when he notices my glance.

"Believe me: they don't come naturally. That's a lot of years spent in the gym."

I swallow and nod like a fool, searching for a witty response.

He sets down a slim bottle of port. "I've brought you a hostess gift."

"Thank you," I say, pinching my wrist.

"You're welcome. Do you mind if I have a glass of whatever you're drinking?"

"Of course. I'm sorry. I should've offered."

"No worries. I'll get it." He pours himself a glass, and we settle on the couch.

"So how was your day?" I ask. "Did the producer like your script?" Arthur has just completed his first screenplay and made a pitch today to some Hollywood insiders. We have so much in common it's breathtaking. He's a writer, just like me.

"I think so," he says with a modest grin. "They're supposed to get back to me next week." He looks around the room with interest. "I like your sleek, contemporary look."

"Thank you."

"Do you always leave your pocket doors open?"

"On nice evenings like this."

"They must be a bear to clean."

"They are."

"I've always liked the look, but Eileen wouldn't allow them. She worries about intruders and bugs." He chuckles. "She also thinks a mountain lion might wander in, even though we live at the beach. I suppose you have a security service to keep tabs?"

"We do—or at least, we did." I picture the unopened bills. "I haven't seen them around lately. It could be I'm not a client anymore."

"Then you should be careful. I worry about a single woman living alone."

"It's very safe here. I have lots of neighbors."

"Good to hear. Now, tell me about that painting above the fireplace. Is that an original?"

I focus on the oversized square canvas splattered with purple-and-orange splotches. "I believe it is. Rich had an interest in midcentury modern art."

"And you don't?"

"Not really. Do you?"

"I prefer the French impressionists. Renoir, for example."

"Exactly." I almost clap my hands. "The impressionists are my favorite. So soft and soothing. I would've loved to have lived in one of those old Victorian homes near the mission. You know the ones, with gabled roofs and wide lawns? I adore the old wood floors and high ceilings with those beautifully intricate moldings. I would've filled my home with all kinds of French art."

"You would have missed out on the Montecito address."

"I don't care about that."

"But Rich did?"

"Very much so."

"We have a lot in common, don't we?" Arthur leans back and sips his wine. "This Pinot is quite good. Just the right hint of pepper and spice. Perfect for a summer evening." He crosses his legs. He's wearing black designer jeans and Teva sandals. His toenails are nicely manicured; his fingernails perfectly buffed. I've never spent time with a man who looked and acted so hip.

Arthur sets down his glass. "Our Montecito home is also contemporary, but the design was never my choice. Eileen decided where we lived and how we decorated. It was important to her that we follow the trends. I just went along for the ride."

I nod until my neck hurts.

His gaze washes over my face. "Please tell me if I'm getting too personal, but did you ever feel boxed in by your marriage? Like you'd been handed a set of plans that never belonged to you? Like you wanted to escape to a life filled with art and beauty, but you were imprisoned by your past choices?"

"Yes," I say breathlessly.

"Me too." He looks despondent. "In many ways I've been living someone else's dream. I've been living the life of a coward."

"But that's not true! You're not a coward. You're a wonderful and sensitive man."

"How can you know that, Kathi? We've only just met."

"I can tell the kind of person you are. You're, like, well, this may seem silly, but you remind me of the hero of my novel. You're a good man caught in circumstances beyond your control."

"You're a writer?"

"I started writing again after Rich passed away."

Arthur nods. "It wasn't until my marriage fell apart that I began to work on my screenplay. I've been wanting to write for years." He sets his hand on my knee, and it lingers there for a moment. "I can't tell you how nice it is to be with a woman who has interests outside of shopping and parties."

A shiver runs up my spine. I picture Arthur pushing me back onto the couch. Unbuttoning my shirt. Covering my body with kisses. I want him so much it's an ache, a yearning. I look deep in his eyes and see passion there, but he doesn't make a move. I'm guessing he's too much of a gentleman. Should I help guide the way? I purse my lips and slouch forward, but Arthur picks up his wine glass and returns his attention to the artwork.

"I think I recognize the artist. It's possible your painting could be worth upward of fifty thousand."

"Really?" I ask, my face steaming with shame.

"I believe so." He gazes at the random splotches with ongoing interest. "A friend of mine deals in these sorts of things. He could appraise the work, if you'd like."

"That might be helpful."

"So how about that dinner?" he asks with a smile. "I'm starved. It's been a long day."

"Well, yes, of course." I'm relieved to be moving on. "I thought we'd eat out on the terrace, if that's okay with you."

"Perfect. Now, if you'll direct me to the bathroom, I'll wash up."

I head out onto the terrace, beating myself up. I'm an idiot. Why would a man like Arthur Van Meter ever be interested in me?

June 30, 1990

The doctor confirmed what the box tests said. I'm pregnant and healthy as a horse. Healthy as a horse? Does he say that to the thin women or just to the chubby ones? The point is there's little chance I'll lose the pregnancy, and I'm not sure if that makes me happy or sad. Now that I've gone and done it, I'm actually scared to death. I don't think Rich will change his mind, but I won't have an abortion. I WON'T! He can't make ...... can he? Just in case, I'm going to keep my pregnancy a secret for as long as I possibly can. I won't even tell Aunt Genny. If I wait long enough, Rich will just have to accept it. There will be nothing he can do.

Crystal

March 11, 2016

It's been two months since the FBI arrived, and I'm one frustrated snitch. A few people have gotten burned, but not as much or as fast as I'd like. Two board members have resigned. The controller's been fired. Kevin's been reassigned to postfile review. Yet Rich struts about like some cocksure rooster. I don't get the attitude. Who's he paying off?

There's an information gap, one I can't breach. Lots of gossip flowing—mostly fake news. George has ordered us to keep our heads down and go about our business, but with corruption rumors dogging the bank, customers have scattered like rabbits from a fire.

With Eric out sick and Dipak on vacation, the Stable is extra quiet today. I won three of my ten solitaire games. So when I happen to see Rich slipping out the door, I decide to be a Friday-night snoop. He doesn't notice the invisible girl, of course. Plus he has his cell phone glued to his ear. When he skirts the bank parking lot, I start to get excited. Maybe there'll be a Vanessa hookup, and I can document their sins for the feds.

But Rich has his own master plan. He saunters past the downtown bars and winds up at the scene of my crime. My heart begins to thrum. Casa Bella. This could be even better. I follow him through the project shadows, where mounds of dirt and rocks loom overhead. He climbs the steps to the shed and bangs on its metal door. After a moment, he slips inside, and I stealthily close in. Crouching beneath the open window, I catch some undecipherable mumbling followed by Rich's angry voice.

"You swore you wouldn't contact me."

There's a muffled response, and then Van Meter must move near the window because his words abruptly ring clear. "Should I have stopped at the bank instead?"

"Of course not. You know the feds are crawling up my ass."

"I do. They paid me a visit last week. They were asking a lot of questions about the investors. They found it strange that so many were your neighbors and friends. Even stranger that a handful were bank customers."

"You didn't say anything, did you?"

"Not yet. But I might."

"What does that mean?"

Van Meter chuckles. "You're a bright boy. Guess."

"Stop playing games and tell me."

"All right. I want money."

"Don't we all?"

"Of course. But your situation is better than mine. You're still being paid a salary, while I've lost my shirt and more."

"It's not my fault you dug in the wrong place. I lost a million on your mess."

"Mere pennies to me. I've lost more than that."

"Not my problem." Rich's voice is getting screechy.

"You can make it your problem, or I'll talk. I'm sure the feds would love to hear about the commissions. I doubt you reported them as taxable income."

"You willingly paid me under the table. If you spew, you'll incriminate yourself. *You'll* be the one to go to jail."

"Not if I turn state's evidence. They've offered me immunity."

"You wouldn't dare."

"Wouldn't I?"

I can't help but swallow a chuckle. Rich must be wetting his pants.

"You're a motherfucker," Rich says.

"That's a poor choice of words."

There's a long pause. "So how much do you want?"

"You stole half a mil from that old lady. How about you give me half of that?"

"Fuck you."

"You're free to leave."

"Maybe I will."

"And maybe I'll spill."

Rich stays silent for a few beats of my heart. "All right," he says. "I might be able to get you something."

"That's fine, assuming 'something' means half by Monday."

"That's impossible. I can't get to that money right now."

"Then our discussion is over."

Rich doesn't say anything for so long I wonder if he's left by a back door. When he finally does speak, he sounds like a pouting child. "Okay. I'll get you your money, but I'll need at least a week. It's been stashed away, and it'll take me some time to get it back."

"You have until Monday."

"You're crazy."

"It's Monday, or my lawyer arranges a meeting with the feds."

"You're an asshole, you know that?"

"So we have a deal?"

Rich hesitates. "I suppose."

"Good. I'll meet you at the bird refuge parking lot at nine p.m. sharp. Bring the money."

"You want to meet near that homeless camp? Are you crazy? I'm not going there at night."

"You have a better idea?"

"Not at the moment."

"Then we'll do this my way. The camp's been cleared out, so it's dark and quiet. No one will see or hear us."

"Hell . . ."

"Agreed?"

"I guess."

My back is aching, so I straighten up, thinking I've gotten enough scoop for one night. The rest can wait for Monday. There's a tap on my shoulder, and I jump.

"Hi there. Remember me?"

Holy shit. It's the homeless girl. I put my finger to my lips.

"I'm Mimi."

"Shush."

"Why? What's wrong?"

I wave her off and race away as fast as I can. There's a shout, and I hear the men tumbling from the shed.

"Have a dollar for dinner?" Mimi calls in her squeaky voice. She follows me, taking two steps for my every one. "Or maybe two? I can get a Big Mac combo with that."

I hurry around the corner. "I've seen you here before," Mimi says breathlessly. "There's a nice little cubby under the shed. It's a great place to sleep. No one bothers me there. It's small, but I fit in just fine."

"Go away."

"Just a dollar? Or fifty cents?"

"Get lost."

"I saw you that night," she calls out. "I saw what you did."

I stop and spin around, my heart hammering. "What?"

She jogs up to me, her hair frizzing around her face. "It was late," she says. "I was sleeping. You woke me up."

"You're wrong," I insist. "I've never been here before." I want to break her into little pieces. Squash her like some bothersome bug.

"I saw you put those bones in the pit. And the shells too."

Is it possible this homeless twit could mean death to my well-laid plans? I want to grab her. Shake her. Toss her into the street. But instead I just grind my teeth and flex my sweaty hands. "What is it you want?"

"Have dinner with me."

"That's all?"

"That's all."

"All right. But only this once."

"Great. But not McDonald's. I want a real dinner with a yummy drink."

I stare at her hard. "Okay."

"*Fun.*" She twirls in a circle and tosses her duffel bag high into the air. It lands with a thump. "Where to?"

A car cruises in our direction, its headlights blindingly bright. I raise my arm to block the glare. It's Van Meter's car. A Land Rover. I feel his wicked eyes fixed on mine.

There can't be many places I can take a homeless girl to dinner, so I rack my brain until I remember Gino's. I went there once with Dipak to take advantage of a two-for-one dinner coupon. It's mostly a dive bar, but there's a back room where they serve decent Italian food.

We set up shop at a tippy plastic table in a near-empty room and order drinks at the bar. The bartender doesn't look at me twice, but he cards Mimi. The girl's clothes are dirty, and her hair's a ratty mess. Sweat and urine scent the air. He stares at her license long enough to write a short story. Then he hands it back and takes our order.

"What can I get you?"

"A Dirty Shirley," Mimi says.

The bartender makes a face. "Dirty Shirley?" he repeats.

"Yep."

"What's that?" I ask once we take our seats.

"A Shirley Temple with vodka." Mimi claps her hands together. "I hope it comes with real cherries. That's my favorite part."

"Just how old are you?"

"Sixteen." She giggles.

"No, really. How old are you?"

"How old do you think I am?"

"I don't know. Thirty?"

"Not even close."

When the drinks arrive, Mimi takes a sip from her tumbler, and her face lights up like it's Christmas in March. "It's been so long," she murmurs, taking another careful sip. "I just want to savor every moment. This is a magical night." She picks up the menu and reads.

Maybe for you. Not for me, I think. It's at least ten minutes before the waitress returns to take our order.

"You ready?" the waitress asks. She's pale and stiff and obviously not happy to have a homeless girl in the room.

Mimi licks her lips and continues to scour the menu.

The waitress rolls her eyes and taps her foot. "I don't have all night," she says.

"Beef lasagna," I say.

"And you?" She points her pen at Mimi.

"I guess I'll have the spaghetti alla puttanesca, if you please."

"Aren't you the elegant one?"

"Why be mean?" I ask.

"Why bring her to Gino's?" she replies.

"She has as much a right to be here as anyone else."

"Actually not." The woman points to a sign on the wall. WE HAVE THE RIGHT TO REFUSE SERVICE TO ANYONE.

"I'm guessing that's not legal," I say. "I'd be more than happy to check with the city."

The woman's nostrils flare, but she steps away without another word.

Mimi giggles. "Thank you for that."

"She's a bitch."

"I'm used to people being bitchy. Not so used to people being nice."

We don't speak much until dinner arrives. Then I watch Mimi inhale her food. Well, *inhale* is not quite the right word. She eats fast but has near-decent manners. Twirls her spaghetti between spoon and fork.

"Where'd you learn that?" I ask.

"Cotillion."

"What's that?"

"It's where my mom took me to learn good manners. Like how to properly eat and dance. Your mom never took you to cotillion?"

"I didn't have a mom."

"That's sad."

"I suppose."

"Well, my mom made me go there for six weeks every summer for three whole years."

It's like Mimi has shape-shifted. Morphed from a homeless girl into someone else. "You from around here?" I ask.

"Montecito."

"Really?" I'm betting she's lying like she lied about her age.

"Yep. I grew up in a mansion on Pepper Hill. Right off of East Valley Road. I went to Mount Carmel Elementary and then Bishop High for a year until . . ."

"Until?"

She takes another bite and smiles sweetly. "Until my stepfather raped me one too many times, and I stabbed him through the heart with a knife. Everything went downhill from there."

"You killed your stepfather?"

She nods. "My mom wasn't happy about that. I kinda screwed up her life. After the trial she remarried and moved to Taos. She said her new husband wanted nothing to do with me, so when I got released, it

was into a group home. I didn't like the other girls, so once my probation was up, I started living on the streets. I've been there ever since."

The story sounds an awful lot like the plotline of one of my true
crime books. "You ever see your mom?" I ask.

"No," she says cheerfully. "But she sends a card to me through my
ex–probation officer each and every Christmas. Sometimes there's a
hundred dollars inside. Sometimes not a single cent. I think she's still
angry with me for messing with her life. I'm clearly not the daughter
she'd hoped for."

Clearly.

Mimi licks her lips. "Are you going to finish your lasagna?"

"No, you can have it." I push my plate her way. "So what happened
to your finger?"

She gobbles a forkful of lasagna and shrugs. "I got attacked by this
homeless guy's dog. At least that's what the police told me."

"You don't remember?"

"No."

"You think you would."

Her face grows sad. "It happens to me sometimes. My mind just
wanders away. Sometimes for days. Sometimes for weeks. When I wake
up, people tell me about the things I did, but I never know for sure. For
instance, I have no memory of killing my stepfather. I'm sure I did it,
but there's no picture in my head."

"Probably a good thing."

"Yeah, probably."

"Are you on meds?"

"No. I don't like how they make me feel." She finishes up my meal
with an extra lick of her fork. "How about dessert?"

"You're still hungry?"

"Aren't you?"

"Not really. But you can order dessert. I'll wait."

Mimi mows through a chocolate pudding. Then an apple pie with vanilla ice cream piled high. By the time she's done stuffing her face, it's nearing ten, and the dining room is empty. Drunken laughter billows from the bar. I ask for our check and pay the bill. I'm hoping the food has been enough to shut the girl up.

"I want to play the game," she says, her voice lowering. She's morphed again. Her eyes have narrowed; her air of silliness is gone. There's a look about her, as if she's part fox.

I'll have to be as careful as I can. "Game? What game?"

"The one you play at the construction site."

My heart skips a beat. "I don't play any games."

Her head falls back, and she laughs. "Don't be a liar pants. Of course you do. And now I'm your friend, so I want to play too."

There's a dribble of ice cream coating her chin. Bits of dried food stick in her hair. Her foul scent seems to grow stronger, and suddenly I want to retch.

"I'm tired," I say. "It's been a long day. I'm still in my work clothes. I want to go home and get some sleep."

"I have something to show you." She digs in her duffel bag and slaps her four-fingered hand on the table, leaving a small shell behind. "You know the game I'm talking about. It's the one where you wear funny glasses at the library and tuck your hair into a hat. And then you dress in black and visit the construction site in the middle of the night. You look both ways. You climb into the pit. You dig a hole with a shovel. Then you drop in a bunch of bones and shells and cover them up. You climb back out."

I swallow, my throat gone dry. If it's been this easy for her to figure me out, then what will stop someone with a brain? I've been sloppy. I've been stupid. Mimi jabbers on.

"So the next day the tractor man starts up his motor, and it's just about the first place he digs. He tells the pretty man about his find, and they argue for a long time before they put the bones in a bag. But you're smarter than they are, so when the city people come, they find the spot in the corner where you hid some more."

My mind whips up and down and around dark corners, searching for a way out of this mess. Maybe it's the beer. Maybe it's the hour. Nothing comes to me. "Let's say there's a game. Why would I want to include you?"

She suddenly looks older. Harder. Her voice deepens. Her pale eyes glitter like diamonds. "Because we're friends, of course."

"I have enough friends."

"Not that I've seen."

"You've been following me?"

"When I'm bored."

"Get a life."

She leans forward and rests her chin in her hands. "If you don't let me play the game, I'll tell a policeman what you did. A couple of them hang with us a lot."

I think about Marco's job. Doesn't he work with the homeless? "Are you threatening me?"

"I don't mean to. I just want to play."

It dawns on me that there's more than one Mimi sitting across the table. There are two or even three living inside that shrunken head. She's a schizo or psycho or maybe something worse. But I can't just flick her away. "What do you want from me?" I ask. "Money?"

She leans back and shakes her head. "I want a friend to play with. I want to play *your* game."

"What if I tell you the game is over?"

"I heard the men tonight. I know what they said."

I stare into Mimi's eyes. What is the worst? The very worst? But the worst has already happened to Mimi. There's nothing more I can do.

"All right," I say, crossing my arms and dropping my voice. "I'll admit it. I have been playing a sort of game. It's a game of good people versus bad."

"And you're a good person?" she asks eagerly, speaking like a child again.

"Of course. But it's way too dangerous to talk about here. The bad people could be listening."

"They could?"

"Yes." I flick my gaze toward the grumpy-looking waitress. She's slumped against the far wall, pecking at her phone. "Check out the waitress."

Mimi looks around. "Yeah?"

"She's a bad guy."

"Really?"

"She's probably relaying information right now."

Mimi's eyes grow wide, and her voice drops to a whisper. "Are you telling me we're surrounded by spies?"

"They're everywhere. They've even infiltrated the police."

"They have?"

"Yes. To be honest, it wasn't that I didn't want you to play the game. But it's not just any game. It's something so dangerous that if you mention a word about it to anyone, we'll both end up dead in a ditch."

"I won't tell. I promise. I just want to help you out."

"Okay, then. We're a team."

"A team of good guys?"

"Yes. We're the good guys. Now let's get out of here."

"Okay. But first can you tell me one itsy-bitsy thing?"

"What's that?"

"Tell me your name."

I work my brain around a few lies, but I finally give up. If she's seen me around the library and followed me to the construction site, I'm guessing she knows where I live and work. "My name's Crystal Love."

"That's pretty," she says. "Pretty like your face."

"And what's your name?"

"Mimi McCoy."

"That your real name?"

"Yeah."

We get up and push our way through the bar and out onto the quiet street. The night has turned leaden, the air scented with seaweed. The foghorn bellows like a cow. A drizzle dampens my face. I survey the top of Mimi's frazzled hair, where beads of moisture have formed. An old adage comes to me. *Keep your friends close and your enemies closer.*

"Are you cold?" I ask.

"I'm always cold," she replies, her duffel bag thumping from behind. "You get used to that when you live on the street."

"So why don't you come to my house? You can take a shower and sleep on my couch."

She pauses midstep. "I don't want you to get the wrong idea. I'm not a lesbo. I just want a friend."

I force a laugh. "It's nothing like that—I promise. I just thought that now that you're in on the game, it's safer if we sleep in the same place. And I'm sure you could use a little break from the streets. We're friends, remember? You told me that."

Mimi glances over her shoulder. "You think we're being followed?"

"I know we are. You need to stay close to me. I'm worried for your safety."

I start walking away, and she skitters up from behind. "How far?" she asks.

"Just a few blocks. Why? You tired?"

"Are you kidding me? I can walk ten miles in my sleep."

"There's just one thing. We need to be extra quiet. My landlord doesn't allow overnight visitors."

"I'll be as quiet as a snowflake."

"And you'll need to shower. That way if she sees you, she won't guess you're from the streets."

"A real shower? I haven't had one of those for so very long." She takes a few quick steps. "But what about my clothes? They stink. They're awful. I can't pretend to be anyone else if I'm wearing these."

She's right, of course. I'll have to do some shopping. "You can sleep in one of my T-shirts, and then tomorrow I'll get you some clothes."

"Really? You'd do that for me?"

"Yeah. Now that they've seen you with me, there's no telling what they'll do. So you'll have to dress like a normal person and do everything I say. Think you can do that?"

"I can!" she exclaims.

"Not so loud."

"Sorry. I promise to be quiet from now on."

Kathi

I serve dinner on the terrace. The moon glows high overhead. Far out on the darkened ocean, the lights from a half dozen oil derricks shimmer and shine. I'm a little bleary from the wine, but there's no need to chatter right away. Arthur is telling me about his screenplay, one of those Bruce Willis–type things where buildings burn and people die and a rogue policeman saves the day. It's not the kind of movie I like, but I get caught up in the story anyway.

"That's a lot of death and destruction," I say when he finishes up.

Arthur laughs. "That's true. But there's also a love story. The guy saves the girl."

"And they live happily ever after?"

"Of course."

"Perfect. Who do you see in the lead roles?"

"I think we're getting ahead of ourselves, but maybe Brad Pitt and Jennifer Lawrence?"

"So older man and younger woman?" I try not to show my disappointment.

"I'm told that's what sells these days. Now, enough about me. Tell me about your novel."

I take a bite of quiche and almost choke. Am I crazy, or do I taste the Gruyère? "It's just a little story," I say. "Nothing grand like yours."

"I'd like to hear about it."

"Well, to start with, it's a romance novel."

"Romance?" His eyes light up. "Are you kidding me? That's where the money is. I would write one if I could."

"Really?"

"Really. Give me your pitch."

I've studied writing magazines long enough to know what a pitch is, but I can't help fumbling for my words. What should take only three or four sentences drags on. "And they live happily ever after," I finish up, my face all sweaty and warm.

"That's great," Arthur says. "I have a producer friend who might be interested in purchasing the film rights to your novel."

"You do?"

"I do. And those rights can go for hundreds of thousands of dollars. Even millions."

Millions? I flash on how lovely my life would be if that happened. I could pay off all my debt and sell this house and buy a home I truly love. Travel the world with a man like Arthur. I picture us sharing a meal at a Paris café and feel a little faint.

"Do you have an agent?"

I come back to earth. "No, but I've contacted Harlequin."

"So your plan is to cut out the middleman?"

"I suppose it is."

"Brilliant. More money direct to you. Well, when you're ready to share some pages, I'd be happy to give you my input."

"You have time for that?"

"For you? Yes. I do."

"That's so kind."

"Actually, it's selfish." He reaches out to brush my cheek. My heart skips a full beat. He smiles and drops his hand. "Now . . . about our conversation the other day . . ."

"Yes?" I linger on a bite of salad. Is that garlic in the dressing?

"Have you had any luck locating Mabel McCarthy's money?"

"No. None." Even the pistachios taste salty. What in god's name is happening here?

"No revelatory thoughts on where it might've gone?"

I shake my head.

"Don't you care to learn the truth?" He sounds a little frustrated.

"Of course . . . it's just . . . does the endive taste bitter to you?"

"Endive always tastes bitter."

I take another bite. "It does, doesn't it? I don't like it."

"Then why did you serve it?"

"Because . . . well . . . I guess I don't know." I giggle.

"You don't know a lot of things."

I set down my fork. Is he being mean?

Arthur tenses and peers into the darkness. "Did you hear that?"

"What?"

"Footsteps?"

"No . . ." Mr. Calico darts into view. "Oh, look. It's just my neighbor's cat." The little guy heads inside.

Arthur frowns. "You allow him in your house?"

"Why, yes. Don't you like cats?"

"I'm allergic."

"Oh. He doesn't come around very often."

"Let's hope not." We finish our meal in an uncomfortable silence, and then Arthur seems to perk up. "Let me grab that hostess gift. It's a very rare port."

"Oh, but I really shouldn't—"

"But I insist. I was lucky to find it for a great price at Montecito Liquor. It's the perfect way to celebrate our special night."

Our special night. "Well, then, yes, I'll have a glass." It's not like I have to drive anywhere. But Arthur does. Unless he doesn't. My pulse begins to race. "Let me clear the table first."

"Absolutely not. It's my chance to serve *you*. Please just sit and relax. Did you have a dessert planned?"

"Just plum sorbet."

"Perfect. I'll be right back."

I think to argue, and then I don't. How nice to have a man take care of me. Rich never cleared a plate in his life. My favorite Albinoni adagio drifts from the outdoor speakers. I relax into the haunting melody and smile upon Arthur's return. He sets down two heaping bowls of sorbet followed by my mother's holiday wine glasses filled to the very brim.

"I found this beautiful crystal in the cupboard," he says. "I hope you don't mind if we use it."

"Not at all. I inherited the set from my mother. It was one of the few fine things she owned. I like to bring them out on special occasions."

"Of which this is one."

"Yes, it is."

"Now, let's toast."

"To what?"

"To us."

I raise my glass and take a sip of the port. I try not to grimace. It's horribly bitter. Maybe the bottle has gone bad?

"Your turn to toast," he says.

"Oh no . . ."

"I insist."

"Well then . . . a toast to your screenplay. I bet it will make a wonderful movie." There's a tingling on my tongue. Is that how it starts? How I relearn my sense of taste?

"And to your romance novel. I know it'll be a resounding success."

I take another sip of wine and then another. Now my tongue feels numb. From far off the train horn sounds. Within seconds the metal beast charges through the flats of Montecito, its wheels screeching around a curve.

"That must be hard for you to hear," Arthur says.

"I used to like it. Not anymore."

"How could you?"

Bats dart across the moonlit sky. A barn owl screams from above. A breeze bathes me in warmth, and I want nothing more than to sleep.

"I wonder what it takes to step in front of a train," Arthur says.

"What?"

"I don't think I'd be brave enough to do it. Would you?"

"Of course not."

"Did they find drugs in Rich's system?"

"No." I don't like the turn in the conversation. "Are you suggesting . . . ?"

"Suicide? I guess I am."

"He didn't do that." I set down my glass. "He wouldn't."

"No? Then what? Murder?"

"Of course not. It was an accident." My voice is fading.

"You believe that?"

"I do."

"Was he drinking?"

"They found a little alcohol in his system. Not much." The lights of Montecito begin to move beneath my feet. The stars overhead join them, whirling past me like some crazy carousel. The moon spins like a top.

"It's getting chilly," Arthur says. "Let's head inside."

I wobble to my feet. How embarrassing. I've had far too much to drink. I tip to one side and then tip to the other. Then I stumble and hit the ground.

"Here, let me help you." Arthur gathers me in his arms and lifts me up. "Well, there's a surprise. You're heavier than you look." He staggers into the living room and drops me on the couch. His lips grow close enough to kiss as his warm breath mingles with mine. I should feel excited, but I only feel dizzy, my limbs as heavy as lead. Something bad is happening. Could it be a stroke? I open my mouth to beg for help, but not a single word comes out. The air squeezes from my lungs, and my heart lunges in my chest. *For god's sake, help me. Help me, please.*

"Kathi? Kathi? Kathi?" Arthur's head floats above me like a balloon, expanding and contracting with each breath. This must be the end. I'm about to die. *Don't just stand there. Do something. Call 911!*

"Kathi?" Arthur snaps his fingers in front of my eyes. I try to answer, but the lights go out.

September 30, 1990

I fainted at the grocery store and ended up in the emergency room. I begged the doctor not to tell Rich I was pregnant, but he only frowned and shook his head. Afterward, Rich dropped me off at home and didn't return for two whole days. I cried until I made myself sick. Could there be anything worse?

When Rich finally showed up this morning, he refused to listen to me. Wouldn't let me kiss him or touch him. Just gave me his ultimatum. Either I give up the baby, or he'll divorce me and file for sole custody of Jack. He says he can do that because of the depression. Hiding a pregnancy for six months is proof I'm sick in the head. He's contacted a local adoption agency and says if I want to stay married, I have to keep my pregnancy a secret and give our baby away at birth. How can he ask such a thing? How can I make such a choice? I tried to call Aunt Genny, but he ripped the phone cord out of the wall. He says if I ever tell her about the baby, our marriage will be over. I'm so scared. So lonely. If only I had a friend. But all I have is Rich.

Crystal

I park my car beneath the sagging branches of an ancient acacia tree. The only light comes from slivers of moonlight sifting through the fog. A shallow pond stretches before us—dark, smelly, and fermenting. The dark waters are home to seasonal flocks of ducks and geese kept fat by a handful of zealous locals. I can't see the birds, but I hear them warming their bodies inside the clusters of lakeside willows.

"I don't like it here," Mimi says.

"Then get out of the car and walk home."

"I won't leave you alone. It's not safe."

"I can take care of myself."

Mimi twists in her seat. "You don't understand. See over there? Between the railroad tracks and the freeway? It's where mostly bad people live."

"I thought it got cleared out weeks ago after that drunk stepped in front of the train."

"It did. It gets cleared out at least once a year, usually after a fight or when someone's found dead. But eventually the ruckus dies down, and the homeless find their way back."

"You ever live there?"

"No way." She sounds offended. "I may be homeless, but I have my standards. That place is dirty and violent. It's filled with addicts, mentals, and predators who have nowhere else to go."

"Well, hopefully we don't come across any of them tonight."

"I have my switchblade if we do." Mimi lifts her good hand, and a knife snaps from a simple black handle cradled in her palm. Its slender blade glitters, silver like the underbelly of a snake.

"Isn't that illegal?"

"Being homeless is illegal."

"You know how to use it?"

"I do."

"Good." I peer into the darkness and shiver. I'm not sure if it's Mimi's words of warning or the deadly blade or the incoming fog, but the place gives me the creeps.

An ambulance blasts past us on the nearby freeway, its deathly wail a slap in the face reminding me to check the time on my cell. Eight thirty. We'd better get ourselves into position. I want to be close enough to overhear the men. I can't wait to see how this goes down.

"Come on," I say, throwing open the car door.

"Where to?" Mimi asks, sinking low in her seat.

"Closer to the railroad tracks, near the entrance."

"But won't they see us? Hear us?"

"Not if we hide really well."

"Maybe we should stay in the car."

"We have a game to play. Remember?"

"But I'm hungry."

"We'll get something later at Taco Bell."

"Yippee!" She slips out of the car.

"Keep quiet, and follow me."

I creep over to the clump of trees and bushes that line the entrance to the lot. Tendrils of fog slip around me, bringing a chilling cold. Drips of moisture have pooled on the leaves, slapping the ground with every breeze. After making our way through a patch of bamboo, we settle onto a graffiti-covered rock.

"What part of the game is this?" Mimi asks, wiggling back and forth.

"The part where we wait to find out the truth."

"Fun." She's quiet for a moment but then starts squirming again. "After the truth, can I have two burritos and two tacos? I'm really, really hungry."

"You can if you shut up."

"All right."

The ocean sits on the far side of the pond. The waves crash in the distance.

"I'm cold," Mimi whispers, reaching for my hand.

"Don't touch me," I say, shaking her off.

"Why not?"

"I don't like to be touched."

"Never?"

"Never."

"That's kind of weird."

"Whatever."

A car drives by, its headlights blurred by curling mists of fog. I hold my breath, but it's just a police car on the prowl.

"I think my ducks live here," Mimi says in a wistful tone.

"What?"

"My pet ducks, Yin and Yang. Before my real dad went away, he bought them for me. I was probably eight or nine."

"Oh." Enough with the sharing.

"My mom didn't like them. Said my dad had only done it so she'd be forced to think of him every time she cleaned up their crap." Mimi leans forward, flicking her blade in and out. "Maybe that was true. When I got them, they were so tiny I could fit them in the palm of my hand. I loved them so much I would cover them with kisses. I remember my mom saying if I didn't stop all the kissing, I'd kill them with my love. But I didn't stop, and they got bigger and bigger, and pretty soon they wouldn't fit in the cage anymore. So we put them out in the garden, where they ate my mom's favorite flowers and pooped all over the place."

"So how'd they end up here?"

Mimi sighs deep and sad. "One day my nanny took me to the movies, and when I got home, they were gone. My mom said they'd make friends at the bird refuge and have a much better life. That was a lie, of course." Her voice breaks, and she wipes her eyes with the back of her hand. "I wanted to see them, but my mom said I'd gotten too attached. Sometimes I come here and look for them. They're all white, except Yin has a black spot under her eye and Yang a red mark on his face." Mimi starts to whimper, and I stiffen. I don't want to feel anyone's pain. I have more than enough of my own.

"Do you think they're still alive?" she asks hopefully. "Do you think I'll find them one day?"

My heart softens. Just the tiniest bit. "Yeah, I think you'll find them."

"Will you come look with me?"

"Someday, sure. Now, let's concentrate. Remember—we're on a secret mission."

Mimi sighs and snuggles a little too close. But I don't push her off. Instead, I shut myself down and suck it up and get more and more nervous inside. Where the hell are they? Have they changed the time? Traded texts without my knowing? Water drips in the misty darkness. Ducks rustle and quack. A lone owl screeches and dives, crashing into the bushes and swooping back up holding something wriggling in its talons.

"I hope that's only a mouse," Mimi says. "Not some poor baby duck."

"Hope so."

"I bet it's a mouse. Yes, it has to be. Momma ducks would protect their babies at night, don't you think?"

"Yep." My teeth chatter. The dampness chills me to the bone. I'm getting ready to call off our vigil when a shadow flits across the road.

"Look there," I whisper, pointing at the street. "See it?"

"No."

"Over there."

"Maybe."

"It's Van Meter."

"Who?"

"The pretty man."

"He's walking?"

"Must be. His beach house isn't far from here."

"How do you know?"

"I just do. Now, no more talking. The game has begun."

"All right," she drops her voice. "I'm just so glad to be playing. And I'm glad you're my friend."

"*Shush.*"

Van Meter stands in the shadows, arms folded, foot tapping. His head tilts up and to the side in his cocky-cool way. Another five minutes pass before Rich pulls up in his convertible. It's a red Corvette Stingray, the kind that proves a man is a man. He climbs out of his car, and the two men circle like dogs preparing to fight. There's a pulsing rhythm of an argument, but their words dissolve in the wind.

I tap Mimi's arm. "We need to move closer." We creep through the bushes, Mimi's switchblade clicking, until we're less than a stone's throw from the men.

"I'm asking you nicely," Van Meter says. "Remove your shirt, or I leave."

"My shirt? Are you crazy?" Rich asks, slurring. He's been drinking. Not the smartest move on this night. "Why would I need to do that?"

"Heard a rumor your lawyers tried to contact the feds. It's possible you're wearing a wire."

"That's fucking bullshit. Who told you that?"

"It doesn't matter. I'm asking you to remove your shirt. You can either do so or suffer the consequences. It's your choice."

"Maybe the feds have *you* wired. I should ask you to do the same."

Van Meter turns and begins to walk away.

"Wait." Rich tugs at his tie and then rips at the buttons of his dress shirt. He flings his shirt over his shoulder and spins around. "You happy?"

Van Meter nods. "Now bend over. I need to pat down your pants."

"Hell if I'll let you touch me."

"As I said before, it's your choice."

Rich hesitates. "Okay, damn it. Just make it quick."

Van Meter moves his hands up and around Rich's butt and crotch and smoothly down each leg. "You pass," he says with a laugh. "It's no wonder you need the Corvette. Damn, your package is small."

"Fuck you." Rich pulls on his shirt.

"You've already fucked me."

"It's not my fault those bones showed up."

"Maybe not. But it *is* your fault that the feds have come sniffing at my door."

"How's that?"

"You left a trail of stinking bread crumbs that led them right to me."

"They would've found you anyway. You and your Ponzi schemes."

"You're the one who steals from old ladies."

"I didn't steal a fucking thing. I borrowed her money for a short-term investment. I had every intention to give it back. Everything would've been fine if your project hadn't gone belly-up. Now, well, it's different. I *need* that money. I *can't* give it back."

"Do you ever take responsibility for your mistakes?"

"Do you?"

Van Meter stiffens. "I've had enough of your stupidity. Get me my money, and I'll move on."

Rich sways back and forth. "First . . . I have a proposition."

"I'm not in the mood for bargaining."

"You need to hear me out."

Van Meter folds his arms. "I'll give you one minute. Go ahead."

Rich lowers his voice. "I need you to alter the syndication documents. Show that Mabel McCarthy invested a million with you, not half."

"You want me to forge a set of documents?"

"No. Just alter the ones you have."

"I can't do that."

"You have to. She's been calling me. Leaving messages. She wants her money back. She'll contact the police before long, and when she does, they'll pay you a visit. If we can show them the money was legitimately lost in your sunken project, then it's a sad story, but no one can deny that a ten percent return comes with a sizeable risk. But if they think we made off with the money and used it to pad our nests, well, that's a different story. One that could land us in jail."

"*Us?* Why would they think *I* was involved in *your* theft?"

Rich chuckles. "Let's just say I'm not the idiot you think I am. I've left a few clues to tie you in. Figured it couldn't hurt."

"But I haven't touched a cent of it yet."

"*Yet* being the operative word."

"And if I walk away tonight without the money?"

"My lawyers will know how to spin this, whether or not you take the cash. I can see the headlines now. *Gullible bank president conned by local developer into swindling widow's inheritance.* If you're lucky, you'll get probation, but I doubt it. I'm thinking five to ten."

Van Meter makes fists like a boxer raring to fight. Then he drops them. "All right," he snaps. "I'll make the changes to the documents. Now, enough with your blabbering. Go get my cash."

"We have a deal?"

"Do I have a choice?"

"Honestly? No. You don't." Rich staggers to his car, returning with a canvas bag. "Here you go."

"Not here, you idiot. Follow me." Van Meter heads for the clutch of shadowy trees that lines the railroad tracks. Rich hesitates and then follows. We creep along behind the men, nerves gnawing at my throat. In the distance a train rumbles along, sounding its warning horn. When Van Meter reaches the tracks, he turns to face Rich.

"All right," he says. "Let's see it."

Rich holds out the bag. Van Meter takes it and peers inside. "What the hell?"

"Consider this a down payment. I'll give you the rest when you follow through on your promise."

"How much is in here?"

"Fifty thousand."

"That wasn't our agreement."

"I repeat. You'll get the rest when I see the documents."

"Fuck that. Our deal is off."

"Then return my money."

"Are you kidding me?" Van Meter begins to walk away. Rich grabs him by the arm, and Van Meter shakes him off. "Let go of me, loser."

"*No!*" Rich lunges for the bag. "I want my money."

Van Meter rears back and punches Rich hard in the face. Rich stumbles and falls across the tracks. His head hits the rail with a crack. "No one makes a fool of me, you double-crossing asshole." He lifts his foot high and smashes it down on Rich's face. The train light is flashing, the ground vibrating. Van Meter stands for a moment, considering. Then he tucks the bag under his arm. "Die, creep," he mutters under his breath. He looks over both shoulders and then hurries away, his back straight and stiff.

"*Holy Christ*," Mimi hisses. "We've gotta help him. He's gonna die."

"*Wait!*" My heart thrums. My gorge rises. I watch Van Meter get swallowed by the shadows and then count to twenty. "All right," I say. "Let's go."

We scuttle from the bushes and onto the tracks. Rich looks like a bloodied corpse. The tracks ping, and the train's horn blows. This wasn't part of my master plan. I grab Rich's arms and pull. He's heavier than I ever would've guessed.

"I can't budge him!"

Mimi tugs him by a leg. "I think he's stuck on something."

One of Rich's bloodied eyes flutters open. The other one doesn't seem to work. "Help me," he whispers.

I try yanking him in the other direction. "His foot is caught between the ties," Mimi says. "Or maybe it's his belt."

"Cut it off."

Mimi's knife flashes. She slices through his belt. The train's horn blasts through the night, its light whipping like a strobe. Rich grabs hold of my arm.

"Don't leave me," he gasps.

I tug with all the strength left in my body, but still, the man won't budge. "Get up," I yell. "Save yourself."

"It's too late," Mimi cries, pummeling my back. "Let's go."

"*No!*" Rich howls.

"*Move!*" Mimi screams.

"Wait!" I put my face in Rich's as Mimi grapples with my arms. "I'm your daughter. The one you gave away in Reno."

Rich's good eye widens and then closes. "Just save me," he begs.

"Why'd you do it? *Why'd you throw me away?*"

"*Please!*"

"Move!" Mimi lunges, knocking me over. We tumble off the tracks and roll away in the dirt, coming to a stop in a tangled bundle. The train bursts by us, screeching like a flock of Satan's demons.

There's a humming in my ears. A thrumming in my bones. A slick of wetness dampening my face. A howl bubbles up in my throat and bursts like a missile from my lips.

"It's okay," Mimi says, hugging me tight. "But we can't stay here. They'll be coming soon. We don't have much time." Taking hold of my hands, she helps me up, and we stumble our way back to my car.

Kathi

I awaken to a blurry brightness and a gnawing, grinding pain. An axe has split my head. Lightning sparks my eyes. The room is dim with shadows. Could it be afternoon? I roll over and try to sleep, but a rustling brings me back. Crumpled papers rest near my head. They look like pages torn from my journal. But why would I do that? I start to crush them in my fist but reach for the light instead. December 25, 1989. After several moments, bile rises in my throat.

They're garbage. I don't need this. I throw the bedcovers aside and force myself to stand.

After staggering into the bathroom, I shred the pages into tiny pieces and flush the evidence away. Then my gaze shifts to the mirror, and my knees almost buckle. *I'm naked.* That's impossible. I always sleep fully clothed. Running my hands along my stomach, I finger a raised, crusty patch. I scratch and sniff. I smell sex. Sex? *Sweet Jesus!* What's happened? I honestly don't understand.

I force myself to think. *Think!* Where was I last night? Oh yes, I was here. Arthur came over. We had dinner. I served quiche and an endive salad. He brought wine. And . . . and . . . and . . .

I drop to my knees, grab on to the toilet, and retch until my ribs rebel. Then I fall backward onto the cold tile floor and stare at the spinning light. I have a vague recollection of being carried and falling across the couch. Of lips coming close. Of Arthur's caring eyes. There's darkness after that.

Oh my god, this is it. No more wine. *I swear!* Or maybe just a little. One full glass. That's it. Not a goblet. Just a regular-sized glass. I'll fill it to the brim. I promise no more than that.

I heave myself up and peer into the mirror. My eyes are sunken in shadows, my pasty face framed by my bushy brown hair. My breasts look shrunken, my privates pink. I run my finger across the scar that stretches like a smile from hip to hip. I hate it. I bet Arthur did too. I'll bet that's why he didn't stay. A shadow of a memory pokes through the fog, but it just as quickly fades. I run my tongue across my lips. They feel horribly cracked and dry, and there's a fetid taste of vomit rummaging around my mouth.

Taste?

Fumbling for my perfume, I spray it on my wrist and breathe in the orange-blossom scent.

No! It can't be.

I coat my toothbrush in toothpaste. I begin to brush. An explosion of mint fills my mouth, and my knees almost give out. That's it. It's over. I've lost my secret to success. No more designer dresses. No more hollowed-out cheeks. It won't be long before I return to my former pudgy self.

I cry until my tears run dry and then force myself to shower. The scents swirl around and sicken me like the fumes of rotting fruit. Coconut shampoo. Mango conditioner. Peach shaving cream. It's all too much. Too much! I towel off, pull on a robe, and drag a comb through my knotted hair. Then I head downstairs in the hope I'll be able to sort everything out.

It's five o'clock. That's impossible. But the kitchen clock doesn't lie. The sun hides behind the fog. It's gray and dreary outside. Mr. Calico has made himself at home on a corner of the living room couch. *The couch?* Another sliver of a memory drifts through my mind. I picture Arthur's handsome face. He told me about his screenplay and asked about my book. He said something about cats. He doesn't like them. He's allergic or something like that.

Did I do something embarrassing? Did I say something wrong? Did I get so drunk I asked for sex? No. That's not me. I'm sure of it. But why is my mind so dim? In a frenzy I search for my cell phone and find it under a pile of rumpled clothes. My beautiful designer blouse and jeans, wrinkled and stinking of wine.

I stare at my cell phone for the longest time. I almost don't want to know. I get up my nerve and scroll though the handful of texts. When I reach the final entry, my heart breaks out in song.

Last night was wonderful. Call me. Love you.

Last night was wonderful? How great is that? I spin in circles like a little girl. He likes me! He wants me to call him. He even used the word *love*. Is that possible? Do I deserve him? Could he be with a simple girl like me?

I brew a cup of tea, and for the first time in months I can taste the mint. I add lots of honey and bask in the sweetness that awakens my long-lost tongue. I search the refrigerator for the remains of the quiche, but we must have finished it off. So I rummage in the freezer and spy an ancient piece of coffee cake tucked in an ice-crusted plastic bag. Oh. *Just this once.* It's a celebration.

I head upstairs to get dressed while my perfect pastry bakes. A sugary scent wafts to the upper floor, causing my stomach to growl. I pull on a pair of jeans and a pink T-shirt and apply a layer of shimmery makeup. I have to look good. What if Arthur stops by? He's almost my boyfriend now.

Skipping downstairs, I slather butter on the coffee cake and try my best not to drool. When I take a bite, the sugary dough rolls up and around my tongue. It's like spring has come to winter. Summer has been cooled by fall. The upside to getting my taste buds back? Food is a delightful treat. But I must be careful. Watch my calories. It's important I maintain my weight.

Licking the last of the crumbs from my fork, I head out onto the terrace, relax in my favorite chair, and fondle my cell phone. Finger the buttons. I return to the text and read it out loud. Last night was wonderful. Call me. Love you.

Does that really mean what it says? Could it possibly be true? I shiver, take a deep breath, and tap out Arthur's number. My call goes directly to voice mail. And so does the next. And the next and the next. And the next one after that.

Crystal

July 16, 2016

It was on a Tuesday four months ago that management announced Rich's untimely demise. The news hit the bank like a gunshot. Wednesday brought a bank-wide audit. Thursday followed with a series of layoffs. By Friday, a new president was installed: Matt Brown. Big and bald with shifty eyes, he constantly straightens his tie. All of these moves must've been in process—Rich's death just sped them up.

Within days of Brown's arrival, he called an all-hands meeting and announced a series of changes. Said the employees could either get with the program or leave with a two-week severance. I was tempted to take the money and run, but I'm tethered to my job by unease. I have to be careful. Very careful.

There's Van Meter to worry about. And the press has the train's grainy video. The footage caught two homeless women leaning over Rich right before the accident occurred, one as big as a lineman, the second as small as a child. Were they urging him off the tracks or forcing him to stay down? Opinions have been flowing on both sides, but it's no wonder the police are on the hunt.

Van Meter saw us on the street that night. Could *he* put two and two together? Would he hurt us if he did? I've convinced Mimi to stay away from me during this dangerous stage of the game, so she's back on the streets and keeps her distance. But there's the problem of her chattering mouth. What if she spews our story, and it makes its way to Van Meter's ears? Or to Marco and his uniformed minions? Now there's a frightening thought.

Now, here I am, four months later, still waffling. One day I'll feel guilty about Rich, and the next I want to take out the wife. The part of me that wants to let go says I've done enough to ruin her life. Led a crazed man to kill her husband. Sank his reputation in the mud. Sent a letter to the son outing his dad. Blew their financial security to bits. But then there's this nagging voice that says my work here isn't finished. That the wife deserves her own brand of punishment. That the worst has yet to be done.

Not long after the funeral, I visited the wife's home in the hope I would see things more clearly. I crouched outside her window and watched her guzzle a box of cheap wine. After she passed out on a pile of trash, I considered snapping a few choice photos. Then a train sounded in the distance, and I saw Rich on the tracks again. I stumbled away from the house that night barely able to breathe.

Now I've reached midsummer, and I've decided on one last try. See if a visit helps me to make my decision. If not, I'll move away.

So on a warm evening in mid-July, I slip on dark sweats and take a spin to the promised land. After parking my car in the Upper Village, I make the two-mile trek up the road and arrive at the wife's house, sweaty and winded. The side gate clicks behind me as I sneak into the backyard. The flash of a critter dashing past me jump-starts my heart until I see it's just a calico cat. But it's the buzz of startled voices that nails my feet to the ground. Visitors? That's strange. The wife's usually all alone. I count to twenty before I move again and peek around the side of the house.

What the fuck?

I've been sideswiped. Sucker punched. Quite possibly I've been duped. How else to explain Van Meter breaking bread with his victim's wife?

A hundred scenarios flash through my mind. Is she prey or partner? Colleague or pawn? Is he setting a trap, or are they celebrating success? Whatever's going on, this is dangerous. What if Van Meter catches me? I should leave. No, I can't. I won't. I want to know the truth.

I creep my way through the shadows until I have the couple in my sights. They seem to be having a nice enough chat until the wife wobbles to her feet. She takes a few steps and topples, hitting the ground with an ugly thud.

Van Meter acts like he doesn't give a damn. He finishes his dessert and sips his wine, folding his napkin before he stands. Then he scoops the wife in his muscular arms and nuzzles her drooping neck. Something's wrong. Not natural. The wife's as limp as a corpse. I slink to the far side of the pocket doors to watch the action unfold.

The wife lies splayed across the couch as Van Meter yanks off her clothes. There's pretty music playing in the background, which gives the scene the feel of a nightmare. He's not fondling her in some sexy way. He's handling her like she's meat. He snaps off her bra and panties and drops them to the ground.

"You're old," he says. "And not my type. Know that? Of course not. You're too dumb." He snaps his fingers. "You in there? Oops. You might've had too much."

Too much what?

He runs his hand across her breasts and squeezes. I can't help but wince. "Do you feel this?" he asks. "No? Hmmm. Definitely too much. Don't die on me, okay? Let me know if you can't breathe."

Backing away from the door, I tiptoe to their dinner spread and take a nip of Van Meter's wine. It's heavy and sweet but not poisonous. Then I dip my tongue into the wife's glass, and bitterness floods my mouth. Scumbag. He's drugged her. What the hell could he possibly want? Money? Sex? Revenge?

Whatever. Truth is I should leave.

A series of nagging thoughts stops me in my tracks. He killed Rich. Will he kill the wife? Will he then move on to the son? The smartest move may be to leave this place, but for whatever reason, I don't.

I sneak back to the open doors. Van Meter is ranting, but I can barely catch his words. Something about Rich. And money. Money? *Of course.* He's after the old lady's missing money. I doubt the wife has a clue. And why get her naked? What's the deal with that?

Van Meter gets up and heads in my direction. I edge behind the bushes, praying he doesn't look my way. He picks up the wine glasses and returns inside, where he rinses and slowly dries them. Then he pours a tall glass of red.

"My, this is good," he says. "Much better than your boxed crap, don't you think?" He drains his glass and, without warning, hurls it against the wall. It shatters into a million pieces, leaving a bloody stain behind. "Now where's my money? Huh? That's all I want. If I find it, I'll let you live. Just kidding." He chuckles and slaps her face. Then he slaps it harder. "Oh dear, has it come to this?" He picks up her panties and presses them against her face. "Oh, Kathi, you're such a moron. Don't make me repeat my past."

My heart beats loud in my ears. *No way. Not again.* I won't let him steal another game and send it spinning out of control. But what can I use for a weapon? A tree branch? A chair? A rock? What about the tool set next to the fireplace? I might get to that in time. But then Van Meter stands and drops the panties and begins to rub his crotch. Can I stop him from rape? How? Should I call the police or play the part of the coward and slink off into the night?

I'm relieved when he moves away from the wife to search the house. He looks behind the artwork, rummages through the bookshelf, and eventually heads upstairs. I've almost gotten up the nerve to check on the wife when he jogs back down. He pauses to peer in the mirror and carefully arranges his hair. Then he turns to the wife.

"Found these," he says gleefully, holding something sparkly in his hand. "Three carats, at least. Better than nothing. Now, I'm going to take you upstairs and snap a few photos—a memory of our wonderful night. They might be useful one day. After that, it'll be time to wrap things up. I promised Eileen I'd be home by midnight, and I never go back on my word."

Lifting the wife in his arms, he carries her upstairs and, after what seems like hours, jogs back down. He does another quick search of the house before heading out a side door. Moments later, the garage door rumbles, and a car speeds into the night.

I hurry up the stairs to find Kathi posed like a porno mannequin on the unmade master bed. Her eyes are closed, her hair mussed, and her limbs spread extra wide. I push her legs together, gagging at the crud pooled on her stomach. *Ugh!* He did that? Really? What a twisted mess of a man.

I think to clean her up, but I don't have it in me, so I pull back the sheets and turn her on her side instead. She's so small, so helpless. Less adult than an abandoned child. A pool of conflicting feelings swirls like dirty dishwater in my gut. I order myself to leave, but some part of me refuses to go. I finally settle on waiting until dawn and disappearing before she wakes.

I missed dinner, so I head downstairs and finish off the quiche. It's the best I've ever had. Then I pour myself a warm glass of chardonnay and can't help but neaten up. I clear the table and wash the dishes and pick up the pieces of shattered glass. I rub at the wine stain, straighten the paintings, and return a few books to the shelves. Turning out the lights, I carry my wine upstairs and settle in the chair by the wife's bedside. That's when I notice the pile of leather-bound books stacked on the nightstand. I open the first to discover a child's handwriting scrawled across the face.

Kathi's SECRET Journal—1979.

Wow. That's a find. A key to the wife's heart.

I skim through the sadness of the first few journals and slow when she hooks up with Rich. Moving on to her life as a mother, I almost take pity on the abused wife. The words make me strangely happy. They confirm what I've come to believe, that the wife was controlled by a monster. She was both kindly and sweet.

But then I reach the near-final entry, and my heart all but stops. *December 25, 1989.* I think I know what's coming. But I'm wrong. I never expected this. Anger wells inside me, making monsters of my hands. I want to break her into pieces. Mush her into sauce.

"No!" I howl. "How dare you? How could you? *How could anyone be so cruel?"*

Tremors rake my body. My insides split in two. Saliva fills my mouth. I spit it on her sham of an innocent face.

Ripping the final entries from the journal, I stuff them in her hand. Then I thunder down the stairs and into the night without pausing to shut the doors. Stumbling out the gate, I sob my way back to my car. *What is the worst? The very worst?* But there's no need to craft an answer. Van Meter will take care of that.

Kathi

"I'm disappointed in you, Kathi."

The hospital room is dim. I can barely see Rich, only the outline of his body perched on the edge of a metal chair. His legs are crossed, so too his arms; his jaw is set tight as stone.

"We had an agreement, remember?"

I'm exhausted from the labor and fuzzy from the drugs, and I'm hooked up to all sorts of bells and whistles that won't give me a minute of peace. There's a whirring behind my head, a throbbing near my ear, a whooshing where the pump drains gunk from my stitched-up wound. I didn't want a cesarean. I begged them to stop, but after twenty hours of hard labor, they'd given me no choice.

"The baby's too big," the doctor insisted. I continued to struggle until a nurse gave me a shot while saying a few kind words in my ear. "If it's the scar that worries you, it'll be worth it. That fading line will become a sweet memory you'll carry with you forever."

"Kathi?" Rich says. "Are you listening to me? Good. Now, please do what you promised, and hand the baby over. The adoption rep has been waiting for hours. Give her a break. It's Christmas Day."

I tighten my grip on my bundle of joy. "I don't care. Tell her to go home."

"All right, then." The tension builds beneath his words even though he's trying hard to sound nice. "But you really should sleep," he continues. "You must be exhausted. The doctor offered to increase your Demerol dosage. You know you like that drug."

"If I sleep, you'll take my Rose away."

"Stop calling her that. You shouldn't name her."

"I'll name my daughter if I want."

Rich makes a frustrated sound and jumps to his feet. "I've had enough. I'm going to grab something to eat. Hopefully you'll have come to your senses by the time I return."

He leaves the room, and I snuggle Rose close. She smells of sugar, of mown grass, of fresh ocean air. Her eyes are shut, her lips pursed, her dark hair thick and wavy.

"You're mine," I whisper, my heart blooming with joy. "I'll never give you away."

I must have slept, because I awaken to a brightly lit room with baby Rose tucked in a bassinet by my side. Rich stands just outside my hospital room conferring with the adoption rep. I don't like her. She's pushy, and her hair is dyed a shade of orange that looks hideous against her pale skin. The two of them glance my way and stop their whispering. Then the woman nods at Rich and slinks off.

Rich approaches my bedside. "Sweetheart . . ."

I throw my arm across the bassinet. "Stay away, or I'll scream."

"Don't worry," he says nicely. "No one will take the baby away, including me. You have to give her up willingly. We both have to sign the adoption papers."

"That's never going to happen."

Rich pulls up a chair and sits beside me. He tries to take hold of my hand. "Kathi," he says in a loving voice. "I know the past few months have been difficult. And I haven't been very supportive. I'm terribly sorry about that."

"Then let me keep my Rose."

"But all the arrangements have been made. Her new parents are waiting."

"I don't care. They're your arrangements. Not mine."

His eyes narrow, but his tone stays nice. "I'd like to show you something that might help with your decision."

"There is no decision." I can't believe I'm defying Rich. I feel a sense of power.

"Maybe not, but will you do something for me? Please? Just a little thing? I think I deserve that much."

I don't trust him. He's brighter than me. And I know I'm not thinking clearly.

"Please," he repeats, giving my shoulder a rub.

I bite my lower lip. "All right."

"Good. The nurse's aide will help you into a wheelchair, and then she's going to take you for a ride."

"With Rose?"

"Of course. I have an appointment to speak with the pediatrician. I'll meet up with you in a few minutes."

"You'll meet me where?"

"At the viewing window."

It takes some time to disconnect me from the tubes and equipment. Then the nurse's aide lays Rose in my arms, swaddled in a pink blanket.

"Shouldn't she wear a cap?" I ask, eyeing her bush of dark hair.

"I'm sorry," the woman says. "We don't have one large enough to fit her head."

"It's not that big, is it?"

"Not for a baby her size."

"She's large?"

"At eleven pounds? God, yes. She's the biggest one I've ever seen."

I take in Rose's features as I'm wheeled down the hall. I don't remember Jack looking so odd. She's puffy and swollen, almost purple. There are rolls of fat ringing her neck. She kind of looks like a monkey.

Not perfect and sweet like Jack. For a second I wonder if they made a mistake. Put the wrong child in my arms. But no. This is my baby, and I love her. I'm holding my big baby Rose.

We reach the viewing window, and the aide tells me she'll be right back. I look at the rows of babies, all snugly wrapped in pinks and blues. A gray-haired woman steps next to me. She taps at the window and smiles. "There's my granddaughter, Ella," she says, pointing to a tiny baby resting in the far corner of the room. "Which one is yours?"

"This is my baby," I say, holding up Rose with a smile.

The woman frowns. "She looks so much older. When was she born?"

"Last night."

"Last night? Really? How much does she weigh?"

"Eleven pounds."

"Eleven pounds? My god. That's twice Ella's weight. *Ralph!*" She signals at a balding man slouched against the far wall. "Get over here and check out this baby. You've never seen anything so big in your life."

"Isn't it time for lunch?" he whines.

"You've got to see this first."

The man slogs over and leans close, his breath stinking of cigarettes and onions. "Damn," he says. "That's one hell of a baby. Is he healthy?"

"*She's* healthy, yes."

"She? Wow. Maybe she'll be the first gal to play for the Steelers." He laughs so hard he nearly falls over.

"Mind if we take a picture?" the woman asks, holding up her Kodak. "I'd love to show this to my friends."

"No." I cover Rose's face with my hands. "You can't take a picture."

"Well, *excuse me* for asking." She grabs her husband's arm. "People are so rude these days. Come on, Ralph. Let's go eat."

I stare at the couple until they disappear down the hallway and then take a good look at Rose. She does look older than the babies in the window. That shouldn't bother me, but it does.

"I'm back," Rich says, giving my shoulders a quick rub. "How are you feeling?"

"Tired."

"That's understandable." He moves to the window, and for several moments he stares at the neat rows of babies. "Cute kids," he says, turning to me. He crouches down and places his hands on my knees. "Kathi?"

"Yes?"

"You need to prepare yourself." His handsome face grows sad.

"For what?" My breathing begins to come hard and fast.

"The doctor is concerned about the baby's size."

I tighten my grip on Rose. "She's just big. What's wrong with that?"

"It's not just her weight. It's something worse."

My lips move, but I can't make a sound.

"She may have a condition called macrosomia."

"Macrosomia?" I say the word slowly, panic rising like water in my chest.

"Yes. It's a rare condition that results in a large birth. It's highly likely this baby has a genetic disorder. It could take months to know for sure."

"My god . . ."

"Even if she doesn't, there could be long-term complications with her health."

"But—"

"You have to admit she doesn't look right."

I scour Rose's face. Her eyes are open, her lips moving. I can't deny she's verging on obese. "So . . ."

"So the adoptive family is still willing to take her."

I turn my head away. "I don't want to talk about that."

Rich wraps his arms around my shoulders. "I'm sorry, sweetheart. I truly am. Sorry for everything I've put you through these past few months. I didn't realize how important a second child was to you. I was horribly selfish. I won't ask you to forgive me. I don't think I can ever forgive myself." He takes a quivering breath.

I've rarely seen Rich cry. My heart reaches out for him. "It was my fault too," I say. "I shouldn't have stopped taking the pill without telling you."

Rich straightens, his blue eyes searching mine. "I was so scared of the financial implications. But I'm not anymore. I've received a job offer in Santa Barbara. My new salary will be more than enough to cover the cost of raising a second child."

"That's wonderful news."

"It is." His eyes shimmer with tears. "But you have to understand: we can only afford one more child."

"I'm fine with that."

He wipes his eyes with the back of his hand. "So tell me. Is this the child you want?"

"Of course."

"It doesn't bother you that she's not normal?"

"She *is* normal."

"No, she's not."

I shake my head, confused. "So what're you saying?"

"I'm saying that I *do* want a second child with you. I want a daughter, a beautiful daughter that I can proudly walk down the aisle one day. But is this the right child? I mean, look at her."

"Oh, Rich . . . don't make me . . ."

"Everything is already in place. We can follow through with the adoption and have a healthy child next year."

"But I couldn't—"

"Think about it, Kathi. How will we handle a child with a genetic disorder? What will that do to us? To Jack? All of our time and money will be spent on this child, and for what? No college. No marriage. No grandchildren. Or . . . we can give her up and try again. We can have the daughter of our dreams."

I stare at the pretty babies in the bassinets and then return my gaze to Rose. She yawns, and her face scrunches up in an unattractive way.

"You promise?" I ask in a whisper, looking deep into Rich's eyes. "You promise I can have another?"

"I'll swear on a Bible if it helps."

"All right, then." I close my eyes and hold out my arms, and Rose disappears from my life.

PART THREE

Kathi

"It's called ghosting," Jane tells me, sipping her nonfat latte.

"Ghosting?"

"When a man you're dating suddenly disappears. Not that I've dated in ages, but I've read about it online. I try to keep up with the cultural trends. One day Franklin won't be here, and I can't wait forever to get back on that horse. I'm no spring chicken myself." She leans forward with anticipation like she's about to inhale a piece of cake. "Now, who is it? Who's the lucky guy? I promise I won't tell."

We've met for coffee at the gluten-free deli that fronts the trendy Busy Bee gym. There's a steady stream of beautiful people coming in and out of its copper-colored doors, mostly young and white and wealthy. They all look confident and self-assured. I pull my stomach tight, but it does no good. The growing bulge won't disappear.

Jane is dressed in a pair of gold leggings and a tiny, form-fitting top. Her tan arms are carved with muscle, her stomach flat as a board. Pink cheeks glow from the hour-long workout; the sheen of sweat wipes years from her skin. It was take-a-friend-to-workout day, so she invited me along. I thought maybe the exercise might cheer me up, but I've never felt so out of place. Couldn't hide my age in the many mirrors. Couldn't keep pace on the stationary bike. Couldn't do ten girl pushups, let alone a single man's. Couldn't curl ten pounds more than twice.

I take a sip of my latte and then another. The bitter sweetness coats my tongue. Every day more flavors return. Every day another pound piles on.

"It wasn't a date, really," I say.

"Not a date?" She looks confused for a second and then claps her hands like a child. "Are you telling me that prim and proper Kathi Wright had a night of gratuitous sex?"

My cheeks grow warm, and I look away as she claps her hands again.

"I'm so proud of you, Kathi. I really am. Was it your first time after Rich?"

"It wasn't like that."

"No?"

"I actually like the man. I thought he liked me."

Her eyes grow sad, and she reaches out and gives my hand a quick pat. "Oh my dear, I'm so sorry. You mean you fell for this mystery man?"

My eyes water, and I wipe away a tear. "I think I did."

"How long has it been since you've heard from him?"

I shrug. "I don't know. Three weeks. Maybe four."

Actually, it's been twenty-eight days since the night Arthur slept in my bed. At least that's what I think happened. I can't see through the haze of the evening, so I've built a story line in my head. It follows the general path of my novel, which I've set aside for now. When the door shuts to the bedroom, I don't see what happens next. I only feel a shiver of excitement, the pang of anticipation, and another feeling I try to dismiss. Something dark and dirty.

"Have you called him?"

"A few times."

"And texting?"

I nod, ashamed.

"Oh dear. There's your mistake. Never show a man you're interested. Let him think he has to hunt you down."

"Too late now, I guess."

"There are plenty of men out there who'd be interested in a woman like you." Jane squints, and her voice drops. "There she is. *No!* Don't look." She stirs a packet of sweetener into the dregs of her latte. "It's that backstabbing bitch Eileen. Let's pretend we're talking about something funny. I don't want her to think I give a damn."

Jane launches into a silly story while the gorge rises in my throat.

"There," Jane says, her smile fading. "She's gone. I can't believe Eileen's working out here. I'm going to have to find a new gym."

"You two never made up?"

"We didn't, and we won't. But I can tell you it's because of her I've started reading the local paper again. It makes me happy to see how much trouble Arthur has gotten into. I hope they both end up in jail."

I shift uncomfortably in my seat. "You can't always believe what you read in the *Times*."

"Of course. That was dense of me." She eyes me closely. "You probably know more than I do. Wasn't Rich involved somehow?"

I shake my head. "I'm sorry. I'm not supposed to speak to anyone about Rich's case."

"Oh, of course. I don't mean to pry. I just can't believe a man as smart as Rich got taken in by a con man like Arthur Van Meter. And to involve you . . . oh my god, Kathi. I know we haven't spoken about it, but how terrible to have the police raid your house."

I should keep my mouth shut, but I can't help myself. "I'm not sure Arthur is a con man. There's no proof he did anything wrong."

"No proof? Are you kidding me? Concealing Indian artifacts? Losing his investors' money? Franklin knows an awful lot of people who've been sucked into Arthur's investment schemes. Luckily, my husband's way too smart for that."

"Yes, I suppose. I just don't wish the worst for anyone."

Jane eyes me sadly. "That's what I like about you, Kathi. You have such a kind heart."

I'm careful with my next words. I don't need her sniffing out the truth. "So how long have they been separated?"

"Who?"

"Arthur and Eileen."

Jane shakes her head. "You'd think that would've happened by now, wouldn't you? I've heard the opposite is true. Suddenly they're doing better than ever. In fact, last week they chartered a jet and invited half of Montecito to Kauai to watch them renew their wedding vows. Apparently, it was a huge spectacle that included fireworks, a roasted pig, and hula dancers. How tacky is that? For a time I thought Eileen and I might make up. But when she didn't invite us to the ceremony, it was the last straw. The very last. To not be invited. To be dissed like that. Well, I wish the two of them hell on earth."

I struggle to my feet.

"What's wrong?" Jane says. "You look pale as a ghost."

"It's the heat. I'm feeling a little faint. I need to go home . . ."

June 30, 1991

This is my last entry. I'm giving up journaling. I no longer want to record the history of my life. Rich and I have come to an agreement, and he's been a changed man ever since. We will keep this past year a secret from everyone, including ourselves. It helps that I never made friends in Reno. That I never told Aunt Genny. No one will ever know about the baby. It's like she never happened.

I lie in bed at night and picture building a wall, brick by brick. It will divide the before from the after, housing nine months in between.

It's sad to think I can never have any more children. The infection took care of that. But Rich is right. There is no need to adopt and bring an outsider into our family. We must focus our attention on our beautiful boy.

The good news is that Rich has taken an important position at a prominent Santa Barbara bank. He's getting a pay raise and a promotion. We've saved enough to buy a starter home with a sneak peek of the ocean. Rich says one day we'll exchange it for a bigger place with an even better view.

I'm so excited to get started with my new life. Rich said I can decorate Jack's room however I want. I'm thinking blues, of course. Or maybe I'll play with a few shades of green. I'm so busy. So VERY busy. There's no time to think of anything else. The moving van comes tomorrow. When we drive off, I plan to never look back. So it's good-bye, dear journal. I'm going to miss you. But it's time to get on with my life.

Crystal

It's nine in the morning, and my day is already a disaster. There's a note sitting on my desk.

We have to meet. Call me as soon as you can.

I've been avoiding Marco's calls and emails for months. He seems to think he has power over me, and it's just possible he does. Mimi and I have met a few times in secret, late at night. She's told me the police have been questioning the local homeless, trying to drum up information on the witnesses to Rich's death. From her description, I'm sure one of them is Marco. I've begged her to keep her distance, but she says that's difficult to do. She's also not convinced the good-looking cop who gives out extra change is one of the bad guys. I'm not sure how long her promise to keep her mouth shut will last.

I pick up the note again. Call you? Are you kidding me? If you had half a brain, you'd stay away. I slump in my chair and sort through the mail, depressed by the empty hours ahead. Then Dipak walks in with a file box, his face all sad and glum.

"What's up?" I ask, knowing full well what an empty box means but not wanting to let myself go there.

"They're letting me go," Dipak says.

The breakfast burrito I downed that morning does a double flip in my stomach. "What're you talking about? Who's letting you go?"

"King Matthew Brown, of course. Well, he didn't tell me himself. He's too much of a chickenshit for that. HR called me in this morning. They've given me an hour to pack up my things. I should've taken the severance pay when they offered it. They aren't paying out a dime anymore." He drops into his chair. "I'd like to tell my clients, but I'm not allowed to touch the computers. Maybe you can send a few emails for me."

This can't be happening. Not to Dipak. He was only an innocent bystander. Now he's become a sacrificial pawn in my retribution game. "Have they already yanked your access?"

"Hell yeah."

"Jerks."

"Assholes."

"Did HR say why you're being fired?"

"Laid off, thank you."

"Sorry."

"That's all right. Seems I'm part of a new round of cost-cutting measures. There are at least a dozen getting the boot today. My guess is Brown is whittling expenses to the bone so he can sell the bank and collect his megabonus."

"Do you think they know we sent the letters?" My mind whirs back and forth.

He lifts his finger to his lips and shakes his head. "I need another job, okay? So just be quiet and let me pack my box. I'll meet you for lunch if you want. We can talk about it then."

I get up and stand with my arms crossed, watching Dipak clean out his desk. In the time it takes him to empty his first drawer, I begin to second-guess myself. What if Van Meter knows that I saw him on the tracks that night? What if Marco is hot on my trail? I mumble some sort of apology to Dipak and stumble out of the office. Then I hurry down the hallway and into the bathroom, where I puke my guts away.

I bring turkey sandwiches to Alice Keck Park, but Dipak refuses to eat. Instead, he's brought a quart of malt liquor wrapped in a crinkled brown bag. He says it's the strongest thing he could get, short of a bottle of hundred-proof vodka.

"How can I tell my parents?" he says, dropping his head in his hands. "They'll be so embarrassed. So ashamed."

"I'm sorry," I say, unwrapping my sandwich and taking a big bite. I'm the opposite of Dipak. When I'm upset, I can't help but eat. "How do they expect to run the bank without any employees?"

"They don't seem to know or care. With all the bad press the bank's gotten, the loans and deposits keep running off. I can't argue they need to do something, but shouldn't they whittle down senior management?"

"That'll never happen."

"I know. So the sick thing is Shelby got her notice too. It's a bloodbath over there. I bet they've laid off half the staff since March." He looks at me with his sad brown eyes. "It's just such a bummer. We had everything planned. We were saving up to buy a starter home. And now this."

"I wonder why they kept me."

"Come on. We both know you're George's pet." He takes a slug of his beer and wipes his mouth with the back of his hand. "Sorry. That was mean. The truth is you're smarter than me. And more efficient. Hell, you're smarter and more efficient than just about anyone I've ever met. And you were right about all the crap that was going on. Jesus. What a mess."

"So there's no severance pay?"

"Hell no. George pulled me aside before I left. Said he tried to do something for me. He knows it's not fair, but Brown shut him down.

Said the employees were the ones who got the bank into trouble, and they don't deserve to be rewarded."

"That's ridiculous," I say. "You know as well as I do that it was Rich who tanked the bank."

"With Shipwreck Barbie's help."

"He couldn't have done it without her. And the board members, of course."

"And don't forget the CFO. He had to know what was going on. I heard he's leaving with a severance package worth well over a million."

I shake my head. "Isn't that how these things work?"

"Yeah, management screws everything up, but it's the workers that take the blame."

"I'm sorry," I say. "Maybe we shouldn't have sent those letters." Or maybe I shouldn't have pressed Dipak to send a letter. For all I know he's been outed, and that's why he lost his job.

"Don't blame yourself," he says. "With all the corruption going down at the bank, the shit would've hit the fan at some point."

"I know. But . . ."

Dipak drains his beer and lobs it into a nearby trash can. "You think we killed him?" he asks, wiping his mouth with his sleeve.

My heart speeds up. "Who?"

"Rich."

"Of course not. Why would you say that?"

"If he committed suicide because of the filings, isn't that partly our fault?"

"I don't think he committed suicide."

"Really? Then what? He was murdered?"

I shrug. "He had lots of enemies."

"Like?"

I consider what to say next. I've been wanting to place a rumor to get the evidence pointed in the right direction. "Like . . . well . . . like Van Meter."

"Arthur Van Meter?"

"Yeah."

"No way."

"Why not?"

"He's too nice a guy."

"Because he's white, rich, and good-looking?"

"Exactly. Why risk that?"

"Maybe he's crazy. Insane."

"I don't see it."

"The thing is . . ." I choose my next words carefully. "Rich had invested money in Van Meter's Casa Bella project."

Dipak looks up. "No way."

"Yep. It's true. He did it through an LLC."

"You think the feds know?"

"I know they do."

"So even without finding the Chumash bones, the project might've been stopped?"

"Bank president forms secret corporations to funnel funds into a client's multimillion-dollar project? That has money laundering written all over it. As well as bribery, extortion, and fraud."

Dipak doesn't look convinced. "So you're saying Van Meter killed Rich because . . . ?"

"Because of money. When his project got stalled, Van Meter was in a shitload of trouble. What if he decided on blackmail as the answer?"

"Blackmail is one thing—"

"And then for some reason Rich didn't pay him."

"You're writing that novel again."

"Am I?"

Dipak thinks on this for a while. "No. It makes no sense. Van Meter has everything going for him. Looks. Money. The trust fund wife."

"I suppose." I tossed the rumor out there. There's not much more I can do. "So you're not mad at me?"

Dipak shakes his head. "I'll be fine. George says he'll give me a good reference. I know he feels bad about how things turned out. He's the only good guy left standing except for you."

I peer at Dipak, wondering what he'd think of me if he ever learned the truth. That I'd been playing him like I played the others. That he was a pawn in my master game. I feel a sudden surge of remorse. Am I really such a monster? A lowlife snake in the grass? "What if you stay, and I move on?"

"You serious?"

I gnaw at my lower lip. "I am. I've been thinking of leaving town anyway."

"Back to Bakersfield?"

"No. I want to try someplace new."

Dipak seems to consider my offer but then shakes his head. "Thanks, but no. What's done is done. I'm not going to beg for my job back. Anyway, I might find something closer to home. There's a small bank in Mojave that's been looking for a branch manager. A headhunter's been calling me for months."

"Mojave? You hate it there. You said you'd never go back."

"I know, but with everything going on in the world, it might be a good time to stay close to home."

"Because . . . ?"

Dipak's face grows haggard. Like he hasn't slept in weeks. "I take it you don't follow the news."

"Not really."

"Well, my parents are a little spooked. Last week someone spray-painted *Go home, Muslim* on the motel's front wall."

"You're not even Muslim, are you?"

"We're Hindu. But try telling that to some nutcase with an AR15 in his hand."

"You're exaggerating, Dipak. It's not that bad."

"You think? You're not on Facebook, right?"

"Nope."

"Or any other kind of social media?"

I shake my head.

"Then you have no idea how bad it's gotten out there."

"Maybe I don't want to know."

"I suppose that's a choice. Anyway, I don't blame my parents for being scared. And what do I have to lose? Shelby's moving home too, just until we can make enough money for a down payment on a house. Then we'll find a place of our own. It'll be a hell of a lot cheaper in the desert compared to here."

"There's a reason for that."

Dipak grimaces and picks up his cell. "I gotta go. Shelby's parents are coming tonight. I promised I'd help her pack."

I stand and face him, feeling lost and alone. If only there was something I could do to get his job back. Give him a second chance. I consider speaking to George, but what exactly would I say?

"I'll miss you." I order my eyes to stay dry.

"I'll miss you too." Dipak reaches over and hugs me, and I don't even flinch. He's so little that it feels awkward. But then again, it feels nice. "I'll be sending you an invite to the wedding." His eyes search mine. "You'll come, right?"

"Sure," I lie.

"Promise?"

"I promise."

"Good. Until then."

He walks off, and I settle on the bench and stuff the rest of my sandwich in my mouth. Everyone always leaves me. I'll never be anything but alone.

A spider crawls across my neck. I jump and spin around and almost slap Mimi's face. "What're you doing here? We're not supposed to be seen together, remember?"

"I saw him." Her eyes glow.

"Saw who?"

"The bad guy. You know. The one from the train."

"Van Meter?"

"Yeah. I like to spy on him when he comes downtown. He does all sorts of weird things. Today he followed you from the bank."

"Shit." My mouth goes dry. "You sure it was him?"

"Yep." She points at a tall man hurrying down the street. It doesn't take a genius to recognize Van Meter's stride.

"Double shit."

"He was hiding in the bushes behind you. I hope you didn't tell any secrets. He probably heard everything you said."

I think back on my words. If he did overhear us, he'll know that I know.

Mimi crouches and eyes Dipak's untouched sandwich. "Can I have that?"

"Sure."

"Yay."

I picture Van Meter smashing his foot into Rich's face. Fear creeps up my spine. "We have to be careful," I say. "The bad guy might try to hurt us."

Mimi mumbles through a mouthful of bread. "Of course," she says. "Or maybe I'll hurt him first." She pulls out her knife and flicks it open. The blade glitters in the dappled sunlight.

I wonder again at the many faces of Mimi. Is she an innocent? Or a killer? Or some weird combination of both? I get an eerie feeling that I'll know the answer very soon.

Kathi

September 2, 2016

Leo's office smells like old leather. I never noticed that before.

"I'm glad you could finally make it in to see me," Leo says, a frown pinching his haggard face.

"Sorry it's taken so long to get back to you." I've been avoiding Leo's calls ever since Arthur told me about the dementia. Of course, now I have no idea who or what to believe.

"I left quite a few messages."

"I know. I've been busy." Tick. Tick. Tick. I frown at the ugly clock.

"With what?"

"With . . ." What have I been doing? Oh yes. "I've been working on my novel."

"Are you getting close?"

"To finishing?" I shake my head. "Not quite."

"Well, it's nice you've found a hobby."

"It's not a hobby. I'm hoping it becomes my life's work."

"Of course." Leo pages through my file. "Are you getting out and doing things?"

"Yes. Quite a bit." I try to sound perky, but I hear the failure in my tone. Oh, why won't Arthur reach out? I'd forgive him for lying about the state of his marriage. My heart aches with a schoolgirl crush.

"Well, I must say you're looking healthier. Not as . . ."

"Thin?"

"Pale."

"Thank you." *Healthy* is a code word for *fat*, but it's not like it matters anymore.

Leo lowers his brow and leans forward. "Well, I have news—some of it good and some of it . . . well, some of it might be rather difficult to hear. Where shall I begin?"

"I guess you should begin with the good news. Maybe it'll cheer me up."

"All right. The good news is that the feds have determined you didn't access the safe deposit box on the morning of Rich's death."

"Finally. Why'd they change their minds?"

He retrieves a grainy photo from my file and hands it to me. "This was taken of a woman entering the vault on the morning of Rich's death. She forged your signature on the entry log. The forgery was quite good."

I peer at the photo and recognize my wide-brimmed hat and Gucci sunglasses. And even the cut of my dress. But the way the woman stands with her hips thrust forward? That's clearly not me.

"Who is this?" I ask.

"Look closely." He points to the woman's heels.

"Why, they're barely shoes . . . more like spikes."

"Exactly. Know anyone at the bank who dresses that way?"

I shake my head. "I don't think so."

Leo takes a deep breath. "The woman in the photo is Vanessa Allen."

"Vanessa? From the compliance department? I don't understand."

"The FBI was able to identify her through a fingerprint they found inside your safe deposit box. They now believe that Rich gave her the key."

"Why would he do that?"

"We'll get to that in a moment. First, I want to ask you a few questions. I'm trying to make a case for the feds dropping the charges altogether."

"Go ahead." The ormolu clock chimes four, only an hour away from a glass of wine.

"Tell me about the day you signed the home equity documents."

"But that was over a year ago."

"It may be important to your case."

"All right." I lean back in my chair and close my eyes and try to picture that long-ago day. "I remember I was upset because Rich told me about the signing at the very last second. I had to cancel my appointment at Claudio's, and they charged me two hundred dollars to *not* cut my hair."

"So he was rushed? Irritable?"

I blink a few times. "He was always rushed and irritable at work. But as usual, I did what he said. When I arrived at his office, I found him in a terrible state because the bank notary was out sick. He ordered George to fire the poor girl."

"But eventually they found someone . . ."

"Yes. Vanessa notarized the documents."

Leo writes something in my file and looks up. "Did it seem strange that the head of compliance would do that type of work?"

"Not really. Vanessa was a founding employee of the bank. She'd do anything for Rich. He called her his work wife."

"And that didn't bother you?"

"Are you asking me if I was jealous?"

"Or worried?"

"Well, I wasn't. I trusted Rich. And anyway, she wasn't his type."

Leo leans back in his chair. He can't hide the pity in his eyes. "I hate to be the one to tell you this, but Vanessa was deeply involved in Rich's scams. She has confirmed that the money found in the safe deposit box belonged to Mabel McCarthy."

The old fuzzy feeling starts up again. "How would she know that?"

"The morning of Rich's death, he asked her to retrieve fifty thousand dollars from the box."

"But why?" Nothing makes sense.

"She doesn't know, or at least she won't say. She swore she gave it to him. That money has not been found."

"But why would Rich use Vanessa? Couldn't he have gotten the money on his own?"

"He knew he was under investigation, that his time as a CEO was coming to an end. He'd grown extremely paranoid—and rightfully so. His every move was being monitored. For whatever reason, he needed money that morning, so he took some clothes from your closet and had Vanessa disguise herself as you."

"It still doesn't explain—"

"I think it does, Kathi. I think that the truth is right before your eyes, but you don't want to see."

"See what?"

Leo clears his throat. "Rich and Vanessa were having an affair."

An explosion rips through my heart. "I should go."

"Take a seat, Kathi."

"But—"

"I want you to sit."

I ease back down on the chair.

"And please stop humming."

"Am I humming?"

"I know you don't want to hear this, but it's important you do."

My hands are gripped so tight my nails cut through my skin.

"Rich and Vanessa were having an affair. It had been going on for quite some time."

I sink low in my chair, my mind awhirl. Flashes of scenes come before me. Late nights at the office. Extended conferences. Perfume on shirts. Discreet phone calls. No interest in sex. My thoughts tumble this way and that until I'm sickened by anger and grief.

"Are you sure?" I ask in a trembling voice.

"Unfortunately, yes."

An image of Vanessa floats before me, all smiling, thin, and blonde. She was so very nice, always complimenting me on my outfits.

"And it wasn't just a casual thing," Leo continues. "They were planning to get married, but Rich was worried about the impact a divorce would have on his wealth."

"Divorce?" I struggle to get out the word.

"Yes. His plan was to divorce you and leave you with next to nothing."

"I don't believe you."

"Unfortunately, it's true."

My thoughts whirl until they blur.

"As you know, California is a community property state. That means fifty percent of the family assets belong to you."

"So how could he steal them?"

"He was devious about that. Over the past few years he's taken out loans against the vacation home, cars, and boat and funneled the money into an account he maintains in the Cook Islands. It's why you are so far in debt."

"So he was planning to leave me with nothing?"

"Next to nothing, to be exact."

My anger hisses like a steam engine. My heart beats through my chest. "I hate him."

"Unfortunately, there's more. The missing million dollars from your home equity loan? We discovered where that went too. It was funneled through shell companies into an LLC, where it was invested into a local construction project. Casa Bella."

The pounding in my ears grows louder with every breath. "Are you sure?"

He nods. "I hired a forensic accountant who was able to follow the trail. The bad news is that the million dollars is lost. The good news is that he's located the Cook Island accounts. It'll take some time, but eventually that money will be returned to you. Once you sell your assets and retire the debt, you'll be financially sound."

"I don't believe this . . ."

"You don't believe what?"

I grab a wad of tissues from my purse and begin to shred them into bits. "Arthur would've told me about the investment."

"Arthur?"

"Arthur Van Meter."

A harsh look crosses Leo's face. "Don't tell me you've had contact with that man."

I lift my chin. "Is that a problem?"

"Yes. He has a terrible reputation. He's been sued for fraud."

"He's not like that."

"He's not?"

"No. And I don't believe he knew that Rich invested our money in his project."

Leo picks up a stack of papers and slaps them on the desk. "Don't be stupid, Kathi. I have the evidence right here. You're welcome to review it."

"I don't want to."

"You can't avoid the truth."

"Can't I?"

A frown overtakes Leo's face. "What's wrong with you, Kathi?"

I stare at him, thinking I've never really liked him. "I just can't believe what you're saying about Arthur. I won't believe it. He's been there for me. He offered me help and friendship when no one else would." I nearly choke on my words.

"If he offered you help, it's because he wanted something from you. That's it. At the very least he's a crook. He may be something worse. I'm concerned he made contact with you."

I think back to the morning at the market. "I believe I made contact with him."

"I'm guessing he manipulated the situation. That's what men like him do."

I want to cover my ears. "He was kind and gentle. He was helping me."

Leo clears his throat. "He's a narcissist, Kathi. And a sociopath. That's how he gets away with so much. No one can believe the handsome guy with a movie star smile can do anything wrong. But whether or not you want to believe it, Rich created a number of shell corporations and invested a million dollars of *your* money without *your* knowledge in the Casa Bella project. The ultimate intent was to hide the funds from you, which is basically a form of theft. And my guess is Van Meter was in on the plan. Rich probably paid him handsomely to keep his mouth shut. We'll take legal action against him. So I suggest you stay away from that man. Can you do that for me? Please?"

"Is there a chance you're wrong about any of this?" I ask, feeling defeated.

"I'm afraid not. Along with the forensic accounting, I have Vanessa's deposition right here. She wired the home equity money to Van Meter and then attempted to cover her tracks."

"Oh." I'm trembling so hard I feel sick. "So you're telling me I've been scammed by both of them . . . both Rich *and* Arthur?"

Leo gets up, comes to my side of the desk, and sits in the adjacent chair. He reaches out and takes my hand. "I'm sorry about all of this, Kathi. I know it's hard to believe, but things are looking up. The charges against you are due to be dropped, and we'll retrieve your money soon. Before you know it, you'll get your old life back."

My shoulders slump. "I have no life."

"That's not true, Kathi. Things look dark at the moment, but they'll get better over time."

I tug my hand from Leo's and swipe at my tears. "I find that hard to believe." I sink deeper in my chair. There is no upside to any of this. My path forward is bathed in shadows. I fumble for my purse.

"Just a moment, Kathi. There's one more issue we need to discuss."

"I can't take any more."

"It's about Jack."

"What about him?"

"Let me get you some water."

"I don't want any."

"Well, I need some. I'll be right back."

Crystal

August 14, 2016

At the end of my work day, I step out of the bank to find Marco lurking at the front door. I'm tired. I'm hungry. I have a headache. Marco is the last person I want to see.

"You haven't returned my calls," he says.

"I've been busy." I push past him.

"Wait up." Marco matches his step to mine. "You've become quite the walker."

"Good for me."

"Have time for a drink?"

"No."

"Where are you headed?"

"Home."

"Mind if I tag along?"

I stop in my tracks and fold my arms. I've always pictured Marco as a giant of a man, but in truth he's shorter than me. "What do you want?"

"To talk."

"I have things to do."

"I think you should hear me out."

I can't avoid him forever. It's not like I'm unprepared. "All right," I say. "But just one beer. Where to?"

"How about Playa Verde?"

"Works for me."

We take seats at an outdoor booth on the restaurant's shaded terrace. It would typically be crowded at this time of day, but a clammy fog has rolled in.

"This all right with you?" he asks.

"Fine."

He babbles on about some Bakersfield gossip that is of no interest to me. When our beers arrive, he stops with the chitchat and goes in for a premeditated kill. "So I hear things have been rough at the bank."

I bite into a stale tortilla chip and almost spit it out. "In what way?" I try dipping a chip in the ruby-red salsa. It's too bland to help.

He folds his arms and leans back. "You're short on time. Right?"

"Right."

"So let's be honest, you and me. Not only do I read the papers; I have access to information at work."

"Then I'm sure you know more than I do."

"I know that Richard Wright was up to no good. He forged financials, committed bank fraud, and possibly stole the savings of an elderly neighbor."

"As I said, you know more than I do."

"Maybe. Maybe not."

"I'm just a low-level worker."

"Well, low-level or not, it seems strange that wherever you go, a questionable death turns up."

"Wherever I go? Are you kidding me? I've only had two jobs in my life. I can't help it if a couple of bad things happened. Bad things happen every day."

"So it's all a coincidence?"

"All what?"

"Where were you the night of March 14?"

"Are you interrogating me?"

"Just interested."

"I was at home."

"Can anyone verify that?"

I shrug. "My landlord's a snoop. She might've noticed. But she's old, and it's been so long I doubt she would remember."

"So you weren't anywhere near the train tracks? You weren't there that night?"

"You're suggesting *I* was one of the homeless women?"

"Because if you were trying to help, that's one thing."

"Do I look homeless?"

"The video footage of the accident is crappy, but one of the two women was, well, rather large."

"So?"

"So I've spoken to everyone in the local homeless community. Not one of them will admit to being involved or point a finger at anyone else."

"Why would they?"

"There's a ten-thousand-dollar reward."

"Well, if you're suggesting I was involved, you're wrong."

"You sure?"

"I'm sure." I set down my mug with a thump. "So we've had our chat. Are you good? Can I leave?"

"I have something I want to show you." He takes a paper from his pocket, unfolds it, and pushes it my way. "I assume you know about this."

I stare at the birth certificate long enough to work out my next move. "How'd you find it?"

"It wasn't hard."

"Have you told anyone?"

"Not yet. I wanted to speak to you first."

I sigh and bat my eyelashes like I'm a sexy actress. "Yes, I suppose there is something I'd like to tell you."

He leans forward. "Go ahead."

I dig into my purse and extract a copy of a photo. I hold it up, and Marco's eyes grow wide. "Welcome to your past," I say.

"What the hell?"

I'm dangling a copy of a photo of a slutty-looking girl standing next to a twentysomething Marco. He grabs the paper from my hands and rips it into pieces. I almost want to laugh at the emotions scurrying across his face. "Of course, I have plenty of those," I say.

"What's this about?"

"The mistake men like you make is that you don't understand how teenagers work. They can't keep a secret, even a special one. That's especially true in juvie, where the girls are bored and have a limited supply of friends."

"I don't understand."

"No? Well, let me help you remember. You see, I had a crush on you back then. You were so sweet. So handsome. You acted like you cared. Not that I was surprised when you chose Mindy over me. I wasn't an idiot. She had that killer body. Fourteen going on twenty-one. She was a total flirt, and you took the bait. It didn't take long before she began bragging about how you'd chosen her as your gal. She had quite the mouth. Got into the dirty, grimy details. For instance, I happen to know you preferred her from behind. I remember that clearly because I so wanted to be Mindy. Every night I'd pray you'd take me in that way."

"You're disgusting." Marco shoves his chair back and stands. "This is total bullshit."

"Sit down," I order. "You're the one who wanted this chat, and we're going to finish it or else."

Marco hesitates and then drops in his chair. I know he wants to kill me. There's that look in his eyes. Plus, his hands are bunched into fists.

"Mindy didn't just spew to me," I continue. "There were a half dozen girls who knew what was up."

"It's all lies."

"You keep telling yourself that. Anyway, you'll be interested to know I found Mindy. Are you surprised? I was. What with the wild life she led as a teen, I was sure she'd be dead by now. Unfortunately, things haven't gone well for her. She's not so pretty anymore. She lives in a run-down mobile home in Palmdale with three mousy kids and a meth-head boyfriend."

I take a moment to enjoy the look on Marco's face. "I drove all the way out to see Mindy," I continue. "I wanted to chat with her about old times. You'll be glad to know she doesn't hold a grudge. She has fond memories of that year. Doesn't view what you did as rape, although others might have a different opinion. A man in your position of power? A policeman, for god's sake. I'd say that's the worst. Anyway, she's not seeking revenge. But the meth has taken a toll on her finances. She'll do anything for a few extra bucks, so I took her on a shopping spree at Kmart. She was so appreciative she wrote out a statement, and I had her signature witnessed by a notary. Has an official stamp on it and everything. I made a copy for you."

I slide over the grimy envelope I've been carrying in my purse for weeks. "Of course, the original is hidden someplace special, someplace you'll never find. I've also left a couple of copies with a good friend. She's instructed to give one to your supervisor and one to the local paper should anything happen to me."

Marco pulls the statement from the envelope, scans the page, and sets it down. "So what do you want?"

"Your silence in exchange for mine."

"That's all?"

"And you'll stop with your snooping. You'll leave well enough alone."

"How do I know you'll stick to your end of the bargain?"

"As far as I can tell, this is even stephen. You keep your mouth shut, and I'll do the same."

Marco stares at me with so much hate my heart speeds up. I finish off my beer and set it down. "Well?"

"I don't think I have much choice in the matter."

"You're right. You don't."

"I'll agree to keep quiet, but first I'd like to ask a few questions."

"Fire away."

"Did you download porn on Mike Simms's computer?"

I shrug. "Next question."

"And spam your coworker's email?"

I shrug again. "Anything else?"

"How about your father's death? You have a hand in that?"

"The sperm donor? Not his death, no."

"But other things."

"I may have pushed things along, but he deserved it."

"You filed the complaints that led to the SAR?"

"Would it be wrong if I did?"

"But why?"

"Why not?"

"I'm not following."

"What does it matter? But I *can* tell you this. That was no suicide. Richard Wright was murdered."

Marco's eyes open wide. "Who did it?"

"I can't say. But the murderer *is* out there. You just have to look. Now, I've got to get going. Do we have a deal?"

"Do I have a choice?"

"No." I shove my chair back and stand. "You'll be happy to know I'll be going away soon. I don't like it here anymore."

"Back to Bakersfield?"

"Somewhere new. I'm going to start over. Find a new life. I don't want to be me anymore." I start to walk away.

"You can't do that, you know," he calls out, his voice sounding mournful and sad.

I pause and look back. "I can't do what?"

"You can't leave your past behind. It'll turn up one day."

I stare at him, a defeated man. What's the worst? The very worst? Was it digging up Mindy? Or forcing him to face his true self?

Kathi

The clock strikes five. I've been in Leo's office for over an hour. I want to get out of here and go home. Curl up in a ball and drink myself into a coma and never wake up again.

The clock ticks away as I stare at Leo's empty leather chair. I don't want to think about Rich or Arthur. How many ways can I be betrayed? And Jack? I've tried calling. I've tried texting. I've "liked" his Instagram feed. Reached out to him on Facebook again and again until he blocked me. I wish I could see him and hear his voice, touch his hair. I wish he would listen to what I have to say. I'm ready to admit I made a mistake, the biggest mistake of my life.

Why didn't I ever think about you, Jack? Why didn't I worry about how you'd feel? Why didn't I tell you about the family secret? I've done so much wrong I can't make it right. I'm paying for my sins right now.

I pull my wallet from my purse and retrieve a fading photo of Aunt Genny and me taken at the Iowa State Fair. We're dressed in old-fashioned costumes. I'm wearing a frilly farm dress with an oversized bonnet that swallows my thirteen-year-old face. Aunt Genny stands beside me dressed in a Civil War uniform, a fake shotgun resting in her arms. I remember attempting to smile until the photographer told me not to grin. He said in the old days people didn't smile in their photos. I remember thinking that was fine because my smile was fake anyway. My parents were gone. I might never smile again. I feel the same way now.

I wipe away the tears with the back of my hand and return the photo to my wallet. Does my baby Rose ever feel this way? Has she ever felt lost and alone?

"Here you go," Leo says, returning with two glasses of water.

"I don't want any."

"Well, take it anyway. It'll do you good."

I take a few sips, my hands trembling. Water splashes across my dress. "Thank you," I say, tears blurring my eyes.

"You okay?" he asks.

"I'll be fine." I set down my glass.

Leo hands me a box of tissues and settles back into his chair. "About Jack," he says.

"What about him?" I can't help but expect the worst.

"He's asked me to pass on his plans to you."

"Plans?"

"Yes. It's been a tough year for him too. Not only did he lose his father, but his TV series just got canceled. He's decided to make some major changes in his life."

I swallow. "Major?"

"He and his girlfriend have sold their belongings. They leave for India tonight. They plan to spend a year living in an ashram. They'll be out of contact during that time."

"He's giving up his career?"

"For the time being, yes."

"And he has a girlfriend?"

"Alisa. He met her at yoga class."

"He does yoga?"

"Apparently. He said he needs time to find himself. His father's death has been a huge blow. And the accusations have only made things worse."

"But India? An ashram?" I start breathing hard. I can barely catch my breath. "Why would he do that? Why would he give up his life in Hollywood and move so far away?"

"I think you know." Leo pulls off his glasses and gives his eyes a good rub. "Jack told me about the family secret, about his father's long-ago affair. The secret of his half sister. He's terribly upset—and rightly so."

There's a whooshing in my ears. I want to run and hide. But if there ever was a time to tell the truth, that time would be now. "There is no half sister," I say.

"Now, Kathi—"

I take a deep breath and clear my throat. "There's no half sister because . . . because the child we gave away . . . well . . . she was my child too."

Silence washes over the room. Tick. Tick. Tick. Leo's mouth opens and closes like the jaws of a beached fish. "So she was born before Jack? Before you two were married?"

"No," I say in a tiny voice. "She's two years younger than Jack."

"I don't understand."

I clench my hands together. "You see, I made a mistake. A terrible mistake. I was young. Stupid. Rich wanted to lead a certain kind of life, and I just nodded and followed along."

Leo shakes his head. "You gave up your daughter because . . . ? Why don't you help me here?"

I open my mouth to blame Rich, but the truth clogs my throat. I have to stop living in denial. It's led me down a terrible path. "We moved to Reno right after college when Rich took his first banking job.

Jack was born shortly after." I'm trembling to my toes. "He was a dif-ficult baby, and Rich was rarely home. I was lonely and depressed and thought another baby might be the answer. Rich absolutely refused. I stopped taking the pill anyway and got pregnant. By the time he found out, it was too late for an abortion. He gave me an ultimatum, and I caved."

"So it was Rich's fault." Disgust consumes Leo's face. "You think you know someone, and then you don't."

I straighten my shoulders and look Leo directly in the eye. "No. In the end it was *my* choice. I agreed to let her go."

"*Your* choice?"

I work my hands together until they feel ripped and raw. "The adoption couldn't have happened if I hadn't signed the papers."

"So Rich forced you?"

"Manipulated? Yes. Forced? No." Tears stream down my face, and I don't try to stop them. "In the end . . . well . . . in the end I didn't want her. I didn't want my baby Rose."

"You can't mean that."

"It's true. She was big, and, well . . . she was different. She didn't look like the other baby girls. Rich told me the doctors were worried that there might be health problems, possibly a genetic issue. Looking back, I think he lied. He also told me he'd changed his mind and we could have a second child. He gave me the choice of settling for Rose or choosing a future baby. I rolled the dice and chose the future. I chose wrong."

"Meaning?"

"Two weeks later I came down with a horrible infection—no chance for babies after that. And you know what? I didn't once complain because I knew I deserved it. I had no right to a second child."

Leo refuses to look at me. Tick. Tick. Tick.

"So you see"—I rush on—"it wasn't just Rich. I did something terrible. And now I want to right that wrong. But I need your help."

He shakes his head. "So you gave your child away because she looked . . . different? Tell me you were deathly ill or that your marriage was broken. That's something I can comprehend."

I drop my head in my hands. "I know it sounds horrible—"

"It doesn't just sound horrible. It *is* horrible. Honestly, Kathi. How do you live with yourself?"

I fix my gaze on my lap. "I'll tell you how you live with yourself. You pretend that it never happened. You lock the entire incident away. And that's what we did. That's what *I* did. For close to three decades we never spoke of our child. And then Rich died, and somehow Jack got wind of our secret, and I've been forced to face my past."

"To clarify, Jack learned of only one part of your secret."

"Yes. He thinks he has a half sister. He doesn't know the full truth."

"I find this hard to believe." Leo's voice has grown stone cold.

"I understand if you hate me. I hate myself. But now I want to fix my mistake. Start over. I want my daughter back in my life."

"I would say the odds of that are next to impossible."

"But why? I've heard stories about adopted families finding each other. They seem to live happily ever after."

"Those searches were different than yours. They didn't end with the discovery of an intact family that willingly gave up a child."

I focus on the gilded angels perched on the edge of the clock. "You're judging me."

"What did you expect?"

"I don't know. Your understanding. Or at the very least, your help. I just want to find my baby girl. Make up for the lost years. Maybe she'll find it in her heart to forgive me. But I need your help. Please? I want to find my baby Rose."

"I don't know . . ."

"I'm begging you."

"I'll have to think it over."

I stare at Leo, comprehension dawning. I think I made a mistake. There will be no forgiveness coming. No assistance. There's no upside to confessing my sins. "All right." I stand and stumble out of the room and down the hallway, a knife stuck in my heart.

Crystal

"Can I come over?" Mimi begs. "Please. I haven't seen you in so long."

"It's only been a week, Mimi."

I've just spent an hour after work at the library with Mimi nipping at my heels. I haven't told her, but I gave my two weeks' notice today. I'm done with Santa Barbara. Done with Bakersfield. I'm going to move to a place where I can reinvent myself. Somewhere cheap and warm with a large population so I can hide the old Crystal away. The new Crystal will be different. Thinner. Smarter. Nicer. There'll be no more playing the game. I've narrowed my search to El Paso and Tucson. Either should give me what I need.

George was not happy with my resignation, but of course he understood. Told me that if he was young enough to start over, he would do the very same thing. I accepted the reference letter he wrote for me, but I'll never use it. I intend to change my name and cut all ties with my past.

I'm going to road trip my way to my new life, so this morning I had my Civic's threadbare tires replaced. I picked up the car from the mechanic at noon and left it at a nearby parking garage. It'll be a luxury not to have to walk home on a sweltering evening when the Santa Anas blow through.

"Please," Mimi begs, tugging at my sleeve. "We could watch TV and eat popcorn. Wouldn't that be fun?"

I feel bad about leaving Mimi behind, but there's no room for her in my new life. I have to take care of myself. I don't plan to tell her today. Maybe next week or the week after that. Or maybe I'll just disappear. Here today, gone tomorrow.

"Okay," I say. "We'll watch a movie at my house, but you have to shower first. You know I hate that homeless smell."

"Yay." Mimi spins like a top with her hands in the air. "But I smell better today, don't I? The shelter has really nice showers."

It's true. Mimi *has* been cleaner since she scored a bed at a transitional women's shelter. Still, I'm tired and was looking forward to a quiet night, but it seems mean hearted to send her away.

"I love you this much," Mimi says with a giggle, spreading her thin arms wide.

"I like you too."

"Really?"

"Really."

"That makes me so happy."

"Good. Now, let's go." We head into the shadows of the multistory parking garage, and Mimi taps me on the back. "Look over there," she whispers. She points at the woman who stands wailing at the far entrance to the garage. Rich's red Corvette is hitched to a black tow truck. The driver ignores her cries.

"Why would they take her car?" Mimi asks.

"I don't know, and I don't care."

That's not quite true. I pulled the wife's credit report last month, and it confirmed what I had guessed—the woman's a walking financial disaster. No surprise the Corvette's getting repossessed. She'll lose all her cars soon enough.

"Let's go," I say, climbing into my Civic.

"You're being kinda mean," Mimi says, sliding onto the passenger seat. "She was your dad's wife, after all."

"I told you not to talk about her, didn't I?"

"You did."

"So don't ever mention her again." I made the mistake of pointing out the wife a couple of weeks ago when we saw her slip into a restaurant near the park. I don't know why I opened my mouth, but I've been paying for it ever since. Literally paying. Whenever Mimi brings up the subject, I hand her a dollar to make the subject go away. I hand her one now, but she won't stop jabbering.

"Look, she's crying. We have to help her."

She *is* crying. But what do I care?

"Come on. Her husband got killed by that bad man. I'll bet she's terribly, horribly sad. We should help her. Please?"

I pause and consider. Maybe I should make one last pass at the wife. I might get a kick out of telling her. Watch her squirm like a worm on the hook. "Okay. But she can't see us together. I don't need her figuring us out."

"You think she'll know we were the ones on the tracks?"

"Maybe."

That's not really true. I doubt the wife's bright enough to put two and two together. But it might spark a rare thought in her head to see a bank employee hanging with a homeless gal. "There's also the problem of your big mouth," I say. "I'm not sure I can trust you to keep it shut."

"My lips are sealed." She makes a motion like she's locked them with a key.

"Why don't you just spend the night at the shelter? We can do something tomorrow."

"But you promised we'd do something today. Don't make me go away. Please. Please. *Please.*"

I think for a moment. "Okay, then. You can come with me, but you have to climb into the trunk."

"The car trunk? Won't I die in the heat?"

"It's cooling off," I lie. On a Santa Ana night, it only grows warmer. "Anyway, if she needs a ride, it won't take long. Her house is only twenty minutes away."

"You'll let me out after that?"

"Of course."

"Promise?"

"Promise." I pop the trunk, and Mimi climbs in and snuggles like a child. I hand her a half-empty water bottle and a bag of stale chips. "You have to be quiet," I say. "This shouldn't take long."

She smiles up at me. "I kinda like it in here."

"Good." I shut the trunk and lumber down the ramp. The wailing's stopped, and the wife now sags against a cement pillar.

"You okay, Mrs. Wright?"

She straightens, wiping her eyes before pasting on a crooked grin. "Yes, I'm fine. I'm sorry. Do I know you?" Her eyes are red, her makeup smeared. Stains spot her dress.

"I'm Crystal Love. I work at the bank. We've met before."

She taps her forehead. "Well, of course we have. Stupid me." Grabbing a wadded tissue from her purse, she wipes her runny nose. "You're the loan analyst with the delightful name. But you look different. You've lost some weight, haven't you?"

"A little . . ."

"Well, it's very becoming."

"Thank you, Mrs. Wright."

"Please call me Kathi. Mrs. Wright makes me feel old."

"Sure. Can I help you with something, Kathi?" I try not to choke on her name. "Do you need a ride?"

"That's sweet, but no. I'm fine. Now, if you'll excuse me, I must find a restroom somewhere. It's so hot I'm melting. My makeup has got to be a mess. Maybe the museum will let me step inside. My husband used to be on their board of directors, and I'm sure they'll . . ." Her voice drifts off as she shuffles away.

"Wait a minute," I call out. "Wasn't that Mr. Wright's car getting towed?"

Kathi turns to face me, a look of horror in her eyes.

"What happened?" I ask.

"I . . ."

"Did the battery go dead?"

"Yes. Yes. That's it. The battery."

I can't help rubbing salt in the wound. "You must've left something inside the car. I heard you shouting at the man."

She works her hands together. "Why, yes, I left my . . . my notebook. That's right. I probably overreacted, but I'm a writer, you know. Romance novels. I keep my notebook near me at all times in case an idea pops into my head. Anyway, I guess the driver couldn't hear me. He had his windows rolled up and was playing that awful rap music. I find it so very offensive and . . ." She pauses with a look of confusion, like her brain's not connected to her tongue.

"Let me give you a ride home. It's hot out."

"I can't ask you to do that. I live in Montecito, you know. I can take a taxi. Or one of those Uber things."

"You have an Uber account?"

"Do I need one?"

"Or cash for a taxi?"

She peers into her purse. "Stupid me. I spent all my money on lunch and left my credit cards at home."

"Then follow me." I don't wait for her answer and head for my car, smiling when her heels clickety-clack behind me. I climb into my seat. "Sorry about the trash," I say as she settles into hers.

"No problem." She shoves aside the fast-food wrappers with her designer heels and giggles. "You should see the inside of my car. I haven't had it washed in months. The car wash is so expensive, don't you think?"

"I wouldn't know." Kathi's perfume is chokingly sweet, like she bathed in a vat of moldering orange juice.

She gives me her address and tries to buckle herself in.

"Sorry," I say. "That seatbelt's broken."

"Isn't that dangerous?"

"Not if I don't crash."

"Oh, you're joking."

"Of course."

She giggles again like some crazy woman, but when I pull onto the freeway, she grows quiet.

"Don't be nervous," I say as I speed around slower cars. "I'm a good driver."

"Of course you are." Her jaw is clenched, her body stiff, her arms folded tight.

"You all right?" I ask.

"I'm fine." Her breathing speeds up and doesn't slow down until I pull off the exit to Montecito. She gives me directions, followed by a tidal wave of chatter. "I know I sounded crazy in the parking garage," she says. "I was really nervous about Rich's car getting towed. Of all the things to happen. I never drove it before today."

"Why's that?"

"Rich didn't want me to. He was afraid I'd scratch it."

"So he was the boss of the family."

"Oh yes, I suppose he was." She lets out another giggle. "It's true I'm not the best driver. I only took his car today because I needed to get to a meeting with my lawyer. I would've driven the Volvo, but it's . . . it's in the shop."

"That's too bad. What's wrong with it?"

"Oh, you know. Car problems. Engine kind of things. And it's European, so it's hard to find parts. I have no idea when I'll get it back."

"So what will you do?"

"Well, I have an Audi, but it doesn't seem to work."

"Maybe it needs gas."

She's quiet for a moment. "Are you making fun of me?"

"Of course not."

"It's okay," she says sadly. "I would make fun of me too."

I consider giving Kathi another smart-ass reply, but I glance at her and don't. A single tear travels the length of her broken face. Now it's my turn for breathing funny. I grip the wheel and stare straight ahead. We don't say another word until I pull into her driveway.

"Can you come in?" she asks.

"It's been a long day."

"Just for a moment? Please? I could use some company."

Her sadness washes over me. I think I might puke. "Okay," I say. "But I can't stay for long."

Kathi

September 2, 2016

"I forgot to lock my car," Crystal says when I open my front door.

"No need for that around here."

"You can never be too careful. I'll be right back."

"Fine. I'll leave the door unlocked. Just come on in."

I wait until she moves off and then rush through the living room to the kitchen and pour what's left of a boxed chardonnay into an empty bottle of expensive wine. I'm not sure why I feel the need to impress this girl, but I do. Recorking the bottle, I hide the box in the oven and stick the bottle in the fridge. Then I push open the glass pocket doors and step outside. The Santa Ana blows so hard the trees are nearly bent. The scent of dried manzanita hangs thick in the air. The blazing sun dips behind a wind-whipped purplish sea.

"It's pretty out here," Crystal says, stepping up from behind.

"Thank you. I've always loved this view." Crystal towers above me like a house. If she were thinner, she'd be beautiful in that supermodel kind of way. Her skin is flawless, her cheekbones striking. She has the very brightest of blue eyes. They remind me of Rich and Jack. I'm suddenly sad again.

"Are there fish in that pond?" she asks.

"There used to be a few koi before the cats and raccoons cleared them out."

"That's too bad."

"Yes, it is."

"Do you ever worry about wildfires?" Crystal gestures toward the rugged ravine that skirts the south side of the house.

"Of course, especially on a night like this. We've had two close calls in fifteen years, but we've been lucky and escaped the infernos."

We, I think. There is no *we.* There never really was. The sadness creeps across my soul, and the view morphs to waste and ruin. Rotting leaves coat the pond. Scorched weeds edge the bricks. Cat poop fills the fire pit. I'm overwhelmed by a longing for escape. "Can I get you an appetizer?" I ask, almost choking on my grief. "Crackers and a little cheese?"

"No, thank you."

The train horn sounds in the distance. The sun inches into the sea.

"I didn't realize you could hear the train from here," Crystal says. "That must be hard to take."

"Yes, well. It is what it is." I glance at her from the corner of my eye. Who is she to hint at Rich's death? I think I'll ask her to leave. But that means I'll be alone with my thoughts. "I'm sorry," I say. "I'm not being a very good hostess. Would you like a glass of wine?"

"Why not."

We head inside, and I apologize for the heat, telling a little white lie. "The air conditioner's broken again. It just never seems to work." Of course it hasn't worked since before Rich passed, but I would never admit to that.

"You're lucky to even have one," she replies. "Tonight my apartment will feel like an oven."

"Where do you live?"

"In a converted garage downtown."

"Is it nice?"

"It's cozy."

Cozy. That sounds perfect. Something small with lots of books. Maybe one day I can live somewhere like that. I pour two glasses of wine and take a seat on the living room couch. I expect Crystal to follow my example, but instead she wanders the room.

"When was this taken?" she asks, pausing before a framed Christmas photo.

"A couple of years ago."

"You do these every year?"

"We do. I mean we did. My son refused this past Christmas. Said he was too old to be a part of the annual card."

"He's handsome. What's his name?"

"Jack. He's an actor. You might've seen him on TV. He has a recurring role on *Revenge*."

"I don't watch TV."

"I guess young people have other things to do these days."

"I guess we do."

She says something else, but I'm no longer listening. Leo's words swim through my head. Jack's show had been canceled. He's on a plane heading to India with the girlfriend I've never met. He won't be back for at least a year. He left without saying goodbye.

"Another glass?" I ask, holding up my empty one.

"Not yet." Crystal's glass is close to full.

"Well, I'm going to have a tiny bit more. Friday night is my time to splurge. Not that I work, but I think I deserve a preweekend treat. I'll be right back." I cross to the kitchen and refill my glass to the very tippy-top. I gulp the golden liquid and quietly refill it. Then I wobble back to Crystal, who's staring at the photo with a frown.

"He looks a lot like Rich," she says.

"Yes, he has Rich's beautiful blue eyes."

"Are they anything like mine?" She turns and faces me.

"They are," I say, peering close. "You're very pretty, you know. You're lucky to have such wonderfully thick hair. If only . . ." I have to be careful here. My thoughts are parting ways with my tongue.

"Only what?"

"Oh, nothing."

"I bet you were thinking I need to lose a few pounds."

"Of course not. You're beautiful the way you are."

"You believe that?"

"I do."

She nods, looking pensive. "I thought Montecito women only worshipped size two and below."

"Some people are like that, but not me."

"That's good to hear."

There's something I don't like about her attitude. I really should ask her to leave. Feign a headache or some such thing. I shift uncomfortably in my seat.

Crystal sets the frame on the coffee table and picks up her wine glass with a smile. "Did you ever wish you had more children?" she asks.

"What?"

"More children. Did you want them?"

She's being awfully nosy. "Doesn't everyone?"

"Not really. I mean, lots of people have problems. Like they're poor or crazy or impotent or barren. But you and Mr. Wright were healthy and wealthy and educated. You seem like the kind of couple that would've had at least two children, if not three or even four."

"We had our reasons."

"Like?"

I want this woman out of my house. She's weird, if nothing else. "We would've had more children, but unfortunately we couldn't."

"Couldn't?"

"Couldn't."

"Medical?"

"Yes."

"That's sad."

"It is. Or it was. I guess I've gotten over it by now."

"But let's say you had a daughter. Would you have loved her no matter what?"

"Of course."

"Even if she were fat or ugly?"

"What a strange question."

"I'm sorry if I'm being intrusive. I'm just interested in the whole parenting thing. Maybe I'll have a child one day. Not now, of course. First I have to get thin and snag a husband. But when I do, I want to get things right. And it seems that a lot of moms want their daughters to be pretty and slim. Smart, too, but I'm guessing pretty is more important. Am I right?"

"No . . ."

"Really? So if you had a daughter and there were issues with her looks, what would you do?"

I speak slowly, trying to keep the slur from my words. "I would help her to be the best she could be."

"That's sweet. Do you consider weight an issue?"

"Only if it gets out of hand."

"What if she was fat? Would you send her to weight camp?"

"Only if she wanted to go." I set down my glass with a clink. If she won't leave, maybe I will.

"What if she didn't want to go?"

I roll my tongue around my words. "I suppose I would eliminate any junk food in the house. I would only serve nutritious meals."

"But if that didn't work. Would you take her to a specialist?"

"If I thought that might help." I pick up my cell phone. "Oops. I forgot I'm meeting a friend for dinner. I have to get ready." I stand, but Crystal continues like I hadn't spoken.

"So if she didn't go to a fat camp and she didn't lose weight, would you be embarrassed to show her off to your Montecito friends? How about cotillion classes? I'll bet the heavy girls get fat shamed there. Would you feel bad watching that happen to your daughter? Would you cringe when she didn't get asked to dance?"

"I would find a way to help her," I say primly. "There are secrets to getting thin."

"Are there?"

"Yes. I have personal experience with that."

"So you were a fat kid?"

"I gained a few pounds later in life, but they're mostly gone now."

"Yes, you're quite trim."

"Trim or thin?"

"Thin."

"Oh good. Anyway. You've been so very gracious, and I so appreciate the ride . . ."

Crystal doesn't take my hint. Instead she plops on the couch with a sigh. "I always wished I had a brother."

"You don't have any siblings?" I ask, not caring if she does.

"Not really."

"What does 'not really' mean?"

"I was adopted, and my *faux* parents didn't have any more children together."

"You call them 'faux' parents?"

"They weren't very nice."

"Oh."

"In fact, they were quite mean. Ended up they didn't want me. After they got divorced and remarried, they started all-new families, and each had a new set of kids."

"So technically you *do* have siblings."

"No. Technically, I don't."

"I'm so sorry." The heat and the wine are making me woozy. "Have you tried to search for your biological parents?"

"I have."

"And?" I perch on the edge of the couch.

"I found them."

"Was it wonderful?" I ask breathlessly.

"No. I didn't like what I found." She drains her glass. "I'll have that second glass of wine now."

"Oh. Are you sure? It is getting late, and I have to get ready—"

"I'm sure."

"Then wait right here." I stagger to the kitchen and refill the wine glasses and return. There's a look on Crystal's face that says she's judging me. I can't understand why. I've been the perfect hostess.

"Where are you from?" I ask, not that I really care.

"I grew up in Bakersfield, but I was born in Reno, Nevada."

"Reno?" I slump forward.

"Something wrong?" she asks.

"No. Nothing."

"Maybe the heat's getting to you."

"Yes, that's it." I wipe my brow with the back of my hand.

"Anyway," Crystal continues. "You asked me about my family. I typically don't like to share."

"Then maybe you shouldn't."

"But I'm ready to tell my secret. I've never done that before."

"You don't even know me."

"That's okay." Her blue eyes sparkle. "I feel like I've known you for years. And I'll bet you'll understand. You see, I went looking for my birth mother expecting the typical story. I found something else."

I don't want to hear any more. "You should go," I say, standing up.

She lowers her voice to a whisper. "You see, my mother wasn't single or poor or crazy. She just didn't want me. That's it. She gave me away because I looked different. Isn't that the saddest thing you ever heard?"

My heart begins to race. I think I might faint. Then a voice calls out, and I jump. I blink twice, thinking I must be seeing things. Arthur stands at the pocket doors holding what looks like an unconscious child in his arms.

"Look what I found in the trash," he says. The child lifts her bloodied face.

Crystal

"Arthur!" Kathi sways from side to side. "Is it really you?"

"Of course it is, my love." Van Meter is dressed in black and wears a blazer despite the summer heat. There's a sharpness to his tone. A tightness to his features. A glitter in his eyes. I glance from him to Kathi. She must be shit-faced. Can't she see what he holds in his hands? He smiles big and wide. "I've missed you, Kathi. I so enjoyed our romantic dinner. And the lovemaking, wow—that was out of this world."

"Arthur." Kathi lowers her gaze.

"Forgive me. That was in poor taste. No man should kiss and tell." Mimi moans and lifts her head again. Her mouth is bloodied, her right eye swollen, her left arm strangely bent.

"Let her go," I say softly.

Van Meter's eyes narrow. "Why, hello there. It's Crystal, isn't it? From the bank? Fancy meeting you here."

"You're hurting her."

"Who? This?" He jiggles Mimi, and she moans.

"What's going on here, Arthur?" Kathi asks, finally gaining a clue. "Who is this girl? What's wrong with her?"

"This homeless maggot? Why don't you tell us, Crystal? Feel free to fill us in."

"Crystal?" Kathi's bleary eyes meet mine. She looks scared and confused. "Do you know this girl?"

My heart pounds through my chest as my mind works the odds. What does Van Meter know? What did he see?

"I found this maggot lurking by the terrace," Van Meter says. "When I tried to grab her, she tripped and hit a rock. I believe she hurt her arm." He wipes his forehead with his sleeve. "It's sure hot out tonight. And these winds? We better hope the arsonists stay home. It would be a terrible night for a fire."

"But I don't understand," Kathi says. "Who is she? How did she get here? And what were *you* doing out there?"

"We'll get to that." He gives Mimi a shake. "First, I must ask for your forgiveness, Kathi. I should've called you weeks ago. I hope that night was as good for you as it was for me, but I've been in a terrible place of late. Kind of depressed. Yes, depressed. Depressed about so many things. First and foremost would be the death of my good friend Rich. That, of course, goes without saying. But then there's the implosion of my lovely Casa Bella. That one is almost harder to take."

He drops Mimi to the ground and hauls her into the house by one arm. "Can you believe my bad luck? Of all the ways my project could have gone sideways, I never would've guessed Native American bones. Chumash bones, for god's sake. Give me an earthquake, fire, or flood. I can understand those, and so can my insurance agent. But human remains? Hell. You got me there." He laughs, but his eyes stay dark and flat. "But you want to know something? It's the craziest thing. I just found out the joke's on me. Can you guess why? Huh? Can you? Kathi? Crystal? How about you, little maggot? No? No one wants to guess? Okay, then. I'll tell you. The lab just confirmed the bones are pure Caucasian. Caucasian. Damn. Can you believe that? Not a single Native American gene anywhere to be found."

"Well, that's a good thing, right?" Kathi says. "You can start building again."

"Oh, Kathi." Van Meter drags Mimi to the fireplace and releases her with a shake. She squeals like an injured mouse. I want to punch him in the nose. "I know you're naive, but please don't act stupid. You must know that the investor money is gone and the loan has been called. And you know what? I can't help but be pissed as hell." He drops to his knees and pulls plastic handcuffs from his pocket and slips them over Mimi's wrists. She moans when he yanks them tight. He does the same thing to her feet and then stands and glares at me. "How tall is your little maggot?" he asks.

"Her name's Mimi."

"Mimi? Mimi the maggot? How very sweet. I'm guessing she's five feet max. And you? Well, you're a behemoth. That jogs my memory about something I saw in the news. Hmmm. What could it be?"

I glare at him like I don't give a damn, but I'm shivering inside.

He turns his attention back to Kathi. "Anyway, we're both in a jam, aren't we, sweetheart? We're both totally fucking broke."

Kathi looks at him, confused. "Aren't you and Eileen doing fine?"

"Why? Because my bitch wife has a trust?"

"Isn't it partly yours?"

"Unfortunately, it's family money." He laughs a little too long and loud. "And we split, remember?"

"I heard you renewed your vows."

He shrugs. "I made a futile attempt to secure my financial future, but Eileen's no dummy. She left me when I couldn't pay the hotel bill. What an embarrassing moment. Even my kids think I'm a schmuck." He places his hands on his hips and stares me down. "So now. Let me finish the rest of my story because I'm hoping someone here can fill me in."

"I don't know anything about anything," I say. "I just gave Kathi a ride home."

"Whatever. Let me finish. And please don't move while I do." He pushes his blazer to one side and traces his fingers across a handgun. "You must know by now I'll use this. It won't take much, you understand?"

I swallow, my throat stone dry. "Yes."

"Louder."

"Yes." Fear smothers my hatred. I can't let myself fall apart.

"Good. Anyway, I received some additional information from the lab." He reaches out and gives Kathi's shoulder a rub. "Focus here, Kathi. You're a writer. If this were a novel, it would be a key plot point."

"I don't understand what's going on," she says, plucking at her wrist. "Why have you tied up that girl?"

"You don't need to understand. Just sit back and pay attention." He gives her a push, and she falls back on the couch. "Now listen carefully. The real surprise is that the bones didn't come from just one person. Apparently, they're a mix from a dozen poor souls. So concentrate a moment. What does that tell you, Kathi?"

She bunches up her forehead like she's actually trying to guess. "That a lot of people died in that spot?"

"Strike one. Try again."

"It used to be a cemetery?"

"Strike two."

"I don't know . . ."

"Strike three. No surprise there. You're not the brightest crayon in the box. So I'll just have to tell you. It means some schmuck of a human being bought the bones off the internet and buried them at the construction site."

"Why would anyone do that?"

"That's what I'd like to know. But the schmuck wasn't as smart as she thought she was. She didn't know there was a tiny identifying symbol stamped into each and every bone. I traced the purchase back to a recent shipment to a private mailbox in Santa Barbara. The person that ordered the bones used a cash-loaded credit card to disguise their identity."

Kathi's mouth hangs open. "But who would do such a thing?"

"I've been trying to sort that out. At first I thought it might be the crazy neighbor. Then I spoke to a very nice gentleman at the local Mail Box Express. For a hundred bucks he gave me a description of his customer. Apparently, she looks a lot like your friend Crystal."

I can't stop the flush that spreads across my face.

"Thought so. Now, Crystal, would you be so kind as to take a seat next to your friend?"

I consider running for the open doors. Van Meter laughs and nods. "Go ahead and try it," he says, drawing his gun and aiming it my way. "Let's see how fast a fat girl can run. But I'm warning you: I'm a regular at the shooting range. You'll be dead before you step outside."

"Arthur?" Kathi wobbles to her feet.

"Sit," he orders, swinging the gun her way. He waits for her to collapse on the couch before turning back to me. "I'm serious," he says. "You know what I'm capable of."

I grit my teeth and ease down next to Mimi. She smiles with her pale-blue eyes. "It'll be okay," she whispers. "He doesn't scare me."

"How sweet is that?" Van Meter laughs. "The gimp consoling the giant. Now, Crystal, please heave that body of yours onto your knees, and hold out your wrists."

I do what he says, gazing out to the garden, where darkness has settled in. Scattered lights flicker from far off. Would anyone hear me if I screamed?

"Good girl." He yanks my wrists together and snaps on the plastic ties.

"That's too tight," I say, my fingers tingling.

"Sorry about that."

"I don't understand." Kathi rubs her hands across her face as if she's sweeping cobwebs away. "Can you please explain what's going on?"

"Oh, Kathi," Van Meter says. "You might consider slowing down on the drink."

"But I've only had one glass this evening."

"Really?" Van Meter strides to the kitchen and throws wide the oven door. "So what do we have here? Hmm?" He pulls out a box of chardonnay. "Someone must have confused the oven for the refrigerator. I wonder who that could be." He grabs a wine glass from the cabinet and fills it to the top. Then he walks over to Kathi and refills her glass from the box. "Damn it, Kathi, don't hoard the good stuff. You should share it with your friends. Otherwise people will start calling you a drunk. You don't want nasty rumors to spread."

Kathi plucks at her wrist. "I can't understand how that happened. Maybe the housekeeper put it there?"

"Housekeeper? Ha. When's the last time this dump got cleaned?" Van Meter sighs deeply as if his feelings are hurt. "I'm disappointed in you, Kathi. We're supposed to be lovers. You should be truthful with me."

"I *am* truthful."

"Sometimes." His face hardens. "You should know I've been worried about you, living on your own in the secluded foothills. No husband. No son. No gardeners. Letting your security service go. I've been worried enough to stop by every now and then to watch you from the terrace."

A look of horror crosses Kathi's face. Her hand creeps up her neck.

"I know. You must be thinking about the nights you passed out drunk on your kitchen floor. But honestly those nights aren't as bad as the ones where you collapse in your garden. You do realize coyotes and raccoons are out and about. And don't get me started on what could happen if you were visited by a wolf of the human kind."

"But . . ."

Van Meter waves her off. "No need to deflect. I'm not judging you. You know what they say. People living in glass houses shouldn't throw stones. And I'd be remiss if I didn't acknowledge that I'm crawling with human flaws. Speaking of flawed humans, have you figured out where Rich's money is hidden?"

Kathi nods like a puppy dog. "Leo said it's in a bank on some island."

"Leo?"

"My lawyer."

"Didn't I tell you not to speak to him?"

"Yes, but . . ."

"But what?" He shakes his head and then eyes her slyly. "Did Leo say you would get your money back?"

"In a few weeks."

"Good to hear."

My hands throb, and Mimi's close to passing out. We can't take much more of this. "Can we finish this up?" I ask. "Please? Mimi needs help. Her arm's broken."

Van Meter makes a sad face. "Poor little thing. But I don't think that's such a good idea. You just be patient and take care of your friend."

"There's nothing you need from us," I say. "Please just let us go."

"And let you hurt Kathi? Are you crazy?"

"She wouldn't do that, would she?" Kathi asks, her eyes growing large.

"Yes, my love. She had plans to hurt you. Thank god I intervened. But it's not up to me to convince you. Let's give Crystal her turn." Van Meter regards me with a wry smile. "Feel free to get in a more comfortable position. I want you to tell Kathi the story about your chance meeting this afternoon."

"It *was* a chance meeting," I say. A rush of warm wind blows through the open doors, scattering dried leaves across the rug.

"Then maybe you can explain who was hiding in your car trunk."

I shake my head. "No one," I insist.

"Is every woman I know a compulsive liar?" He walks over and taps my head with his gun. "I'd hate to do anything to your pretty face. It's the one part of you I like. Now, let's tell Kathi the truth about today."

The words slip out before I can stop myself. "How about I tell her the truth about Rich?"

Van Meter slaps my face. My ears ring like a tuning fork. A metallic taste coats my tongue.

Mimi pushes herself up on her elbow. "I'll kill you if you do that again."

"Shut up, maggot. You too, Kathi. Stop your crying." He grabs his wine glass and drains it and then downs Kathi's. "I'm sick of women. All of them. Scheming, nattering, useless women. They're taking over my life."

"We're sick of you too," Mimi says.

Van Meter gives her a swift kick in the side. She moans once and grows silent. He turns to me and lifts the butt of his gun above my head. "Another word on the Rich subject, and I'll hurt you bad, understand? And then I'll hurt your friend. Got it?"

"Got it." I wish him dead.

"Good, because I can't take much more of this. My patience is wearing thin. For reasons unknown you've fucked with me and destroyed my project, so it's my turn to destroy you. To start with, tell Kathi the truth about your visit." He strokes the side of my face with his gun.

"Mimi was in the trunk of my car," I say flatly, not looking Kathi's way.

"And she was there because . . . ?"

"Because I could see Kathi was in trouble. Her car had been towed."

He knocks my head with the gun. "I said the truth."

"That is the truth."

"Why didn't you want her to meet Mimi the maggot?"

"Because . . . I don't know."

"Let's be honest. You thought she might recognize the two of you from the video footage."

"No."

"Well, I sure did. Are you listening, Kathi?"

"Yes . . ."

"Then stop your blubbering. Sit up and pay attention. Good. Now, go on, Crystal. What happened next?"

"I drove Kathi home."

"And?"

My voice sounds strangled. I can't help it. I think I might throw up. "She invited me inside."

"Did you happen to mention the maggot hiding in the trunk?"

"No."

"And you let her out without Kathi knowing."

"It's not like it sounds. It was too hot to leave her in there."

"Right. Did you hear that, Kathi? Because the next thing they planned to do was kill you."

"That's not true."

"Just like they killed Rich."

"We didn't kill him. You did."

"Shut up." He presses the gun to my forehead. "Tell Kathi that you and the maggot are the women the police are looking for. You were there the night of Rich's death. You held him on the tracks."

"Crystal?" Kathi asks, her red-rimmed eyes growing wide.

My gaze moves from Kathi to Van Meter and back again. "It's not true," I say, thinking my truth is stranger than his fiction.

"You killed Rich?" Kathi asks. "You lied and told me Rich was your mentor, when you actually hurt him instead?"

"No, Kathi. You have to believe me. I didn't . . . I wouldn't . . ." But I did lie. I did hurt him. And I made every effort to hurt her too. My game used to be so clean. So pure. How had it come to this?

"She was blackmailing Rich," Van Meter says. "She found out about Mabel's stolen money and knew he was hiding it in the safe deposit box. She demanded a payoff, or she'd rat him out to the feds. That's why they were at the train tracks that night. She killed him. And tonight they came looking for the rest of the money. They planned to kill you too."

"That's not true," I cry. "*You* killed Rich. Mimi and I saw you. You took his money and threw him on the train tracks and ran away. We tried to save him."

Van Meter knocks my head again. There's a hush in the air. A buzz in my ears. I may have peed in my pants.

"Now, Kathi," Van Meter says. "Think hard. If it didn't happen like I said, what exactly were Crystal and Mimi doing there that night?"

Kathi stares at me, waiting. I open and shut my mouth. And then I open my mouth again. But no words come out.

Kathi

What *were* they doing on the train tracks? I try to catch Crystal's eye, but she's staring off into the night. A purple lump swells on her forehead, and blood flows freely from her lip. Could she? Would she? I try to focus my thoughts, but they're swirling around like bits of fruit in a blender. "Why were you there?" I whisper.

Crystal licks her bloodied lip and glances at Mimi. "It's kind of hard to explain."

"Try," Arthur snaps.

"I . . . we . . ."

"Case closed." Arthur folds his arms.

"So it's true?" I ask, my ears ringing. "You hurt Rich?"

Arthur makes a face. "Let's dispense with the euphemisms, shall we? Crystal killed Rich. And you are next on her list."

My stomach churns. My throat closes. There's a sour taste in my mouth.

"You're a liar," Crystal says, her face reddening. "We did everything to get Rich off the tracks. But he was stuck and barely conscious, and we didn't have enough time. *You* were the one who put him there. *You* were the one who could've saved him."

She sounds so earnest I almost believe her. But it's Arthur's word against hers. "Then why were you there?" I repeat.

Crystal looks down. "It's . . . well, it's complicated."

"Not that complicated," Arthur says. "You had dug up dirt on Rich. He gave you fifty thousand to keep your mouth shut, and you killed him to cover your tracks."

"That's not true," Crystal says, almost spitting. "And I can prove what a monster you are. The night of your dinner with Kathi, I was here. I watched you from the garden. You drugged and stripped her, and you took photos. I bet they're still on your phone."

Photos? I think I might throw up. I stumble to my feet. "I need to use the bathroom."

"Not now." Arthur gives me a push, and I fall back on the couch. "It's amazing what lengths this woman will go to."

"He searched your house," Crystal continues. "He stole your earrings. Big ones. Three carats, he said. And then he jerked off and left you for dead."

Arthur whaps his gun against Crystal's head. She doesn't cry. Doesn't moan. Her blue eyes just narrow to slits.

"Once again you're fabricating a story," he says. "But you also admit to trespassing on Kathi's property the night of our special dinner. Why? For what purpose? Were you planning to kill her? Was the maggot by your side?"

"*No!*" Crystal's tone begs for understanding. "Kathi, you have to believe me."

Arthur traces his gun across her forehead. "So then tell us. If it wasn't to rob and kill Kathi, why were you here that night?"

"I wanted to warn her about you."

Arthur chuckles. "How very admirable of you. But if you were so worried, why didn't you call the police?"

Crystal hesitates. "I—"

"Or warn Kathi in the morning?"

"Because—"

"Or warn her the next day or the next or the day after that?"

"I can explain."

"Then go ahead. We're waiting. We don't have all night."

Crystal looks at me, her voice pleading. "You just have to believe me."

Arthur's lips twist into a smile. "Let's move on to another interesting subject. Why don't you tell Kathi about the letters you sent to the feds? The ones that ruined Rich's life?"

I search Crystal's face for the evil. "You did that? You sent the letters?"

"Yes, but—"

"But why? Rich didn't even know you. Why would you want to ruin him?"

Crystal opens her mouth to answer, but Arthur jumps in first. "It's nothing complicated," he says. "These two are grifters. They travel from town to town and target some wealthy family and proceed to take them down."

"Is that true?" I ask, searching Crystal's face.

"Darling," Arthur says. "This woman is a compulsive liar. We can't believe a word she says." Arthur takes a seat next to me and pulls me close. He kisses me softly on the cheek. It feels odd. Awkward. My nose burns with his sweaty scent. I try to pull away, but he wraps his arm tight around me, the butt of his gun resting on my shoulder. "I know it's been a difficult night," he says. "And I know I've said some harsh words. But I needed to wake you up. You had to see the truth. I'm just glad to have been here to save you."

I take a big, snuffling breath. "So now what?" I ask. "Should we call the police?"

Arthur shakes his head. "Tell me. What would they do?"

"They'd arrest these women. Send them to jail."

He taps my shoulder with his gun. "I don't recommend it. Not at all. I'm thinking that Crystal could ruin us with her outrageous accusations. If she's willing to blame me for Rich's murder, she'll be willing to blame you too."

"But no one would believe her. I've never hurt anyone in my life."

"We know that, but you're already under investigation. What if the police think you're involved? Not only would you be forced to drain your assets to cover the legal fees; you would probably end up in jail. No. I think we need a more permanent solution." Arthur gets up off the couch and begins to pace. "A solution that doesn't involve our financial ruin, one that may actually give us a future. And that's what I want, Kathi. I want a future with you."

"You do?" That surprises me. I'm so confused.

"Yes. I care about you, Kathi. I'm attracted to you. I want you in my life."

"Liar," Crystal mutters.

Arthur fills up my wine glass and hands it to me. "Drink this down, sweetheart. It will calm your nerves."

I take the glass, my hand shaking so hard wine spills across my lap. I know I shouldn't have more to drink, but I swear I can't stop myself. I take one gulp. And then another and another until I finish it off.

"Good girl," Arthur says when I set down the glass. "Now, I have an idea that might work. It's a little extreme, but honestly, Kathi, when I think through the options, losing your home is what will get us to our dreams."

"My home?"

"This property is insured for what? Five or six million?"

"I wouldn't know. Rich took care of that."

"Of course he did. I'm guessing if the house burns, the insurance will pay off your loans, and you'll net at least a million or two. You could live downtown in a pretty Victorian and have the life of your dreams. And I'd be there with you every step of the way."

Reality seeps through the fog. "But how would that happen? There isn't a fire."

"There could be."

"I don't understand."

"You don't need to. Just get up and take my gun."

"But—"

"*Get up!*" His caring tone is gone.

I wobble to my feet, and Arthur pushes the gun into my hands. The metal feels cool against my skin. "But I don't know anything about guns. I've never held one before."

"It's easy. Hold your arms out straight. See this trigger? Put your finger on that. Pull it if either of them makes a move."

"I don't think I can do that."

"If you don't, Crystal will kill you. I promise you that. Now, give me just a moment. I have to step outside and get things started. If one of these butchers makes a move, you must shoot. It would be self-defense, you understand."

"I couldn't. I wouldn't."

"Don't forget they killed your husband and nearly destroyed your life. They've taken everything from you. They're evil. They're vicious animals. Don't believe a single word they say."

I take aim at Crystal and think of all that I've lost. Maybe Arthur is right. Maybe I could shoot.

Crystal

Kathi stands a few feet away, head bobbing, makeup smeared beneath her eyes. She's holding Van Meter's gun and shuddering like an off-kilter washing machine. My hands have swollen into balloons. It's possible they could explode. But there's no time to wallow in the pain. "He's going to kill us," I say to Kathi. "You have to let us go."

The gun barrel wobbles in my direction, but she doesn't say a thing.

Mimi pushes herself up with a groan. One arm is purplish yellow. Blood oozes from a cut on her cheek. "He's a liar," she says. "He's a bad man through and through."

"Don't talk to me," Kathi replies, her eyes fixed above our heads. "I don't want to hear anything you have to say." A cat wanders in from outside and winds around Kathi's legs. "Why, Mr. Calico," she says, nearly tipping over. "What are you doing here?" She rights herself and gives the cat a quick pat. "I think you'd better leave."

"We saw him," Mimi continues. "We saw that Arthur guy punch your husband and leave him for dead. Me and Crystal only tried to help, but we couldn't pull him off the tracks."

Kathi wobbles a bit, and the cat heads to the kitchen. Kathi's gun is now backlit by a hellish orange glow. Panic grips my stomach. Smoke eats my nose.

"You have to believe us, Kathi. Mimi is right. Van Meter was the one blackmailing Rich. It wasn't an accident. He wanted him dead."

"You're a liar," Kathi says in a trembling voice. "Why would he do that? It makes no sense."

I try a different tack. "Okay, then. What if Van Meter is right? What if we *are* Rich's murderers? Does that mean you're above the law? Would you really let him kill us? Would you let us burn to death?"

"He won't do that."

"Look behind you. He's building a fire. He plans to burn this place down." I'm trying not to panic, but the smoke is getting thick.

Kathi glances over her shoulder. "It's just the house he's after."

"You've had too much wine. You're not thinking clearly. On a night like this any fire will burn from the mountains to the sea. Hundreds of people will die. Van Meter will say it was your fault. You'll spend the rest of your life in jail."

"You're trying to scare me. I know it."

"It's the truth. Please listen."

"Stop talking."

"If we die, you'll be a murderer too."

"You won't die. Arthur will take you with us."

"He won't. We're the witnesses to his crime."

"*I said no talking.*" She lifts the gun and aims, but I don't believe she'll shoot. I have no choice but to continue pushing on.

"At least call the police and turn us in."

"Arthur said not to."

"Because he's guilty."

"*Stop talking,*" she cries. "I don't want to hear any more."

"He doesn't love you. He never has. He's just wants your money. Once he gets it, he'll get rid of you just like he's getting rid of us."

Kathi weaves from side to side. "It's a trick. You're trying to confuse me."

"Crystal is telling the truth," Mimi says. "You have to believe her."

Flames burst from the fire pit. A shadow heads our way. I have only seconds to save our lives. It's time to tell the truth.

"I'm your daughter!" I yell. *"I'm the one you gave away."*

Kathi's jaw sets tight. "What a terrible thing to say."

"It's true! I came to town seeking revenge, not murder. I wanted justice for my rotten childhood. I wanted you to hurt like I did. To know what it's like to have no one. To have nothing. To be out in the world alone. It's a game I play. A terrible game. This time it went too far. *I'm sorry.* I truly am. I may be a bad person, but I'm not a murderer. Arthur Van Meter is."

Van Meter steps through the door, a flaming branch in his hands. "Come on, Kathi. Time to go. We have to leave fast." He tosses the branch on a pile of magazines. They quickly burst into flames.

I raise my voice again. "Don't let him hurt me, Mom. *I'm your baby girl.*"

Kathi

September 2, 2016

"*Let's go*," Arthur yells.

"We can't leave them," I say, swinging the gun his way. The flames have burned through the magazines and now shoot up the wall. Mr. Calico bursts from the kitchen and shimmies up Arthur's leg.

"*Get the fuck off me!*" He grabs my foster kitty and slams him against the wall.

"*No!*" Mr. Calico lands on his feet and limps out the open doors. "How could you hurt him?"

"Cut the bullshit," Arthur says. "It's just a goddamn cat." His handsome face has dissolved into meanness. I haven't seen this side of him before.

The heat in the room rises, and smoke chokes the air. I keep the gun fixed on Arthur's chest. "Tell me something," I order Crystal. "Something that proves you're my daughter."

Arthur takes a step toward me. "Give me the gun, you dumb old bitch."

"Stop or I'll shoot!" My insides go hard. The trembling recedes. "*Tell me something*," I yell. "*Anything.*" I can't look at Crystal, but her voice crackles above the flames.

"I'm Rose, and you're my mother. I was born twenty-six years ago on Christmas Day."

"That's not enough."

"My eyes are blue just like Jack's."

"Lots of people have blue eyes."

"This is your last chance," Arthur shouts, his face an angry red. "Hand over the gun, or you die."

"*I'm Rose*," Crystal repeats. "I'm your daughter. I look just like Rich's sister. *Think!* Can't you see Ann in me?"

I glance at her from the corner of my eye, and the resemblance is suddenly clear. How had I never noticed? How could I have been so blind?

Arthur lunges, and I pull the trigger. The recoil sends me falling to the floor. Arthur drops to one knee and groans. Blood runs from his shirt. I jump back up and aim again, the gunshot echoing in my ears.

Crystal lurches to her feet. "*Hurry!* We don't have much time."

I should help her, but I can't. My feet are frozen to the floor. And what if Arthur moves? I'll have to shoot again.

"Get the switchblade," Mimi orders, rocking onto her stomach. "Cut the ties."

Crystal grabs a knife from Mimi's back pocket, and the blade flashes open. Gripping her hands tight around the handle, she saws at Mimi's ties until they snap. Then she drops the blade, and Mimi grabs it with her good hand and with one slice frees Crystal's hands.

"Let's get out of here," Crystal says.

The flames are warm against my face. They crackle in my ears. Smoke blurs my vision. But I don't feel the least bit scared. "You go," I say. "I'll make sure he doesn't move." I keep the gun aimed at Arthur. Blood pools on the floor. "Why," I ask him. "Why'd you do it?" His eyes go dim. He tips to one side.

"*You're coming with us*," Crystal yells.

"I can't take a chance he'll hurt you," I reply, feeling utterly calm inside.

"And I won't leave you behind." She wraps her arms around my waist and lifts me high in the air. "Drop the gun," she orders. "Let it burn with the rest."

The gun slips from my fingers, and Crystal carries me out the front door. By the time we reach the road, the flames are roaring down the hill. A firetruck races up, and a dozen firemen leap out.

"Is anyone left inside?" one yells.

"The arsonist," Crystal says, setting me down.

"Is he armed?"

"No. He's injured. He can't walk."

An EMT rushes over. "Are any of you hurt?"

Crystal points at Mimi. "Her arm's broken, I think."

"What about you, ma'am?" he asks me.

"I'm fine."

My eyes stay dry as the sizzling flames engulf my entire house.

Crystal

September 3, 2016

We're waiting in a hospital emergency room for Mimi to get her arm set. After that the police intend to whisk us away to their headquarters, where they'll force us into a chat. But I've been thinking through the angles. What exactly can they do? We're the obvious victims here: Van Meter's helpless prey, three defenseless women attacked by a psychopath who's killed at least once before. At least that's the story we all agreed on before the ambulance carried us away. Stick with the present. Avoid the past. No talk of lurkers near the train. Kathi's called some guy named Leo. She says he'll straighten things out.

After I got my head stitched up, there was no mingling with the masses. Instead they led me to a plastic chair in a small office. There are no windows here, just bright fluorescent lights illuminating the starkest of white walls. The air reeks of antiseptic. The lights buzz like mosquitos on crack. The only reading material is a dog-eared *People* from last year.

A few minutes after I arrived, the nurses led in Kathi, her eyes looking a little glassy. She says they ran a bunch of tests and gave her a shot to help her manage the shock. It's not like we're normal patients. The police stand guard nearby. When I tried to step out to buy some snacks, a uniformed officer offered to help. He had a smile stuck on his pretty-boy face, but his hand rested on his gun. He walked me down a crowded hallway where a group of nurses chattered about the fire. At least a dozen people had been brought to the hospital with mild to severe burns. One broke her leg escaping from a window before her beach house went up in flames. Seems I was right that the fire could burn from the mountains to the sea.

I take a sip of a Coke, gnaw on a chocolate bar, and tap my feet. I've always liked the feel of sugar water bubbling around my mouth.

The room is so small that my knees nearly touch Kathi's. She was calm when we arrived, but now she shakes like a leaf. Her dress is torn and dirty, and her hair sticks out like straw. She's been plucking at her wrist nonstop, as if satisfying some fearsome, nagging itch. She looks like some crazed homeless woman who's run out of her mental meds.

Above Kathi's head rests a sign listing the top five indicators of child abuse. I focus on number one.

1. Frequent, unexplained visits to the emergency room.

Anna and Alan never took me to the emergency room, but I was most certainly abused. What some parents do to a kid's psyche can be worse than any broken bone. Kathi sets down her uneaten candy bar and pipes up in a scratchy voice.

"Crystal?"

"Yeah?" Should I mention the streaks of mascara darkening the shadows beneath her eyes?

"Can we talk?"

"Be my guest." I fold my arms tight and work to zipper the fraying seams of my heart.

"You won't leave me, will you?"

"Leave you?" It must be the drugs talking. Has she forgotten I brought the wrath of god upon her family? Blew up her perfect life?

"I mean, after it's over. When we're done with all of this. Will you stay in Santa Barbara?"

I shrug. "I don't think so. There's nothing for me here."

She takes a quivering breath. "But where would you go?"

"Maybe Arizona or Texas. Somewhere big and warm."

"Can't you stay here?" She drops her gaze and scours the floor. "Can't you stay with me?"

I hesitate before I speak. "I told you I'm the one who screwed you, right? Van Meter might've been the murderer, but I lit the fuse."

Kathi's voice shrinks so small it could fit inside of a thimble. "I think . . . well . . . I think you did what you had to. And I think we deserved it. What Rich did . . . what *I* did to you . . . it was totally selfish. It was wrong." She reaches out and takes my hand, and I quickly pull mine away. I don't like that she's getting mushy. It doesn't fit with the story in my head.

"It's better if I leave."

"But we just found each other."

I slowly shake my head. "No. You just found me. I've known about you for years."

She looks at me in confusion. Maybe the shock drug hasn't worn off. "Please stay," she says. "I need you. I need my family. So does Jack. He wants you in his life."

"You think?" Wait till he hears what I've done.

"Yes. He's horribly angry at me for keeping you a secret." She looks up at me, tears blurring her eyes. "He won't speak to me. He's left the country. I may never see him again."

So there it is. "You want to use me to get your son back."

"No. That's not true. No matter what happens with Jack, *I want you*. I want my daughter, Rose."

Her words cut through the seams of my heart. Blood rushes to my face. I think I want to slap her, but Kathi's contrition fumbles on.

"We did something terrible years ago, and now I'd like to make it right. Please give us a chance to start over."

I stare at the list above her head. There's no saving that little girl. Her hurt is way too deep. "It's not as simple as pressing reset. In real life, there are no do-overs."

"There could be. I mean . . . we could start over from here. From today forward. I want to make up for my mistakes. I want to be the mother I should've been. I want you back in my life."

"Back? I never *was* in your life."

Kathi shudders like I punched her. I feel kind of bad about that. But I'm going to tell her what I know, and we'll see what happens after that. I search her tortured face. "I read your journal entries," I say. "I know why you gave me away."

"*No*," she says, raising her hand to her mouth. "You read my journals?"

"All of them. Including the last one. I know why you didn't want me."

She grapples at her hair. "But that hospital entry is just a couple of lines. It doesn't tell the whole truth."

"It told me enough."

"But when I wrote those words, I thought Rich was being honest. That there was something wrong with you."

"You were too lazy to out his lie?"

"Too tired. Too depressed. Too confused. Too ignorant. I was all of those combined."

"But even so, you were willing to give me up because . . . why? I was big? I was swollen? I was *different?*"

She drops her head in her hands and sways back and forth. "I know it sounds terrible. I admit I was weak and naive. And I was depressed. Horribly so. My mind wasn't working right. Somehow I lost myself in Rich. I'm just finding my way out now." Kathi looks up, her eyes pleading. "I hope you can see there's an upside to all we've been through. I lost my husband. I lost my home. But those things don't matter. Because I found you."

I gulp down my Coke and finish off my chocolate, my mind working overtime. I can picture the words from her journal entry. *Big. Swollen. Different.* But I've had my revenge on this woman, and in the end, she saved my life.

"I can only promise to stay a few weeks. We'll see how it goes after that."

"Thank you," she says, a smile lighting her face. "Thank you so very much." She begins to pluck at her wrist again. "There's one more thing I have to tell you."

"What's that?"

"I love you."

I open my mouth to answer. Then I shut it just as quick. "Do me a favor. Don't say those words again. I'm not ready for them yet."

Kathi nods. "I understand. I won't push you. We'll take this one day at a time."

Epilogue

KATHI

August 1, 2020

"It's here—it's here!"

"What's here, Mimi?"

"Your new novel. We just got the box. Can I open it? Please? Please? Please?"

"Of course."

I stand over Mimi, smiling at her excitement. She's such a sweet girl. So kindhearted. It's like having a child at home. She rips open the package, and a dozen candy-colored copies of my latest novel fall out: *Honest Love at Play*. It's the second in my *Honest Love* series. Last year I self-published *Honest Love at Work* to fantastic online reviews. Its Amazon sales ranking topped twenty-five thousand, which is amazing for a first try. I'm certain this one will do even better and that Harlequin will beg to take me on.

"Can I have a few to sell at the piazza?" Mimi asks.

"Of course."

She brushes her hand across the glossy cover, her fingers lingering on my pen name. "It's funny how you use Crystal's old name."

Crystal goes by Rose these days. Rose Taylor Wright. She changed it on the day of the double adoption. Mimi opens my book to the dedication page.

To Jack, Rose, and Mimi. The three loves of my life.

"That's sweet," she says.

"It's true."

She returns to her easel, and I sort through the rest of the mail. Picking up a legal-sized envelope from Leo, I pour a glass of ice tea, head for the terrace, and settle into my favorite lounge chair. Mr. Calico lifts his head and stretches. Then he yawns and falls back to sleep. He spends most of the time curled in his basket. He's old, and his bad leg bothers him. He doesn't move around much anymore.

I take a sip of tea and stretch out my legs, all toned and tan. I've gained a few pounds since we moved to Sicily, but I'll work them off in no time. Our rock-walled rental is set hundreds of steps up from the harbor cove. It's at least another three hundred steps into town. Our villa is cozy—three tiny bedrooms and one bath—but we enjoy some of Taormina's most breathtaking views. White clouds race across an indigo sky. Tiny boats bob in the turquoise sea. Happy chatter floats up from the throngs of tourists who swarm the white pebble beach below.

I open Leo's envelope and sift through the documents. A copy of the sales contract for the Aspen property. A summary of my various investment accounts. A handful of business and personal letters. He's included an article clipped from the *Santa Barbara Times* about the sale of Pacific Ocean Bank to a Chinese conglomerate. It went for pennies on the dollar. The article goes on to weave a lurid tale that reads like the front page of a tabloid. It tells of Rich's greed and fall from grace, along with his gruesome murder on the train tracks. The piece finishes with Arthur's attempt to silence the witnesses in a devastating fire that killed an elderly neighbor and consumed hundreds of homes. Poor old Mabel McCarthy. No one deserves to die that way.

Inside the package there's a handwritten note covered in Leo's messy scrawl.

Sheila and I are engaged. We plan to be married next summer. Honeymoon in Taormina? Sheila wants to meet you. She says she's your biggest fan.

My biggest fan? Wow. So exciting. Who knew I'd ever have fans? I think on this until the doorbell rings, and I head inside.

Rose stumbles in carrying a backpack and two bulging bags of groceries in her strong arms. She's dressed in khaki shorts, a sleeveless T-shirt, and hiking boots. A red baseball cap is pushed low on her head. Her blue eyes sparkle beneath the rim.

"I think I got everything you asked for," she says. "You sure Jack will eat mussels?"

"He's says he's given up on the vegan thing." I'd love to reach out and give Rose a hug, but she still prefers not to be touched. I grab a bag brimming with fresh vegetables and blow her a kiss instead. "How was work?" I ask.

"Nice. I took some Americans up the trail to Castelmola. They bought me lunch and gave me a good tip." She whips a hundred-dollar bill from her pocket and waves it at Mimi. "Want this?"

"Yay." Mimi jumps up, clapping her hands in the air. "I can buy lots of pretty pastels with that." Mimi paints miniature landscapes and sells them cheap to the tourists in the nearby town square.

"That's a hard climb," I say to Rose. "Could your tourists handle the heat?"

She nods. "They're part of a running group touring the south of Europe. They were actually in very good shape." Rose works for an adventure tour business that specializes in hikes in and around Taormina. Not the career I pictured for my daughter, but I've learned to keep that thought to myself. "Tomorrow I'm leading a hike up Mount Etna," she says.

"Tomorrow?" I turn to her. "But won't that take all day?"

"Most likely."

I slowly unpack the groceries and drop a bag of fresh mussels into the sink. "But Jack will only be here for a short time. I was hoping we could spend the day together."

"I wish I could, but I can't."

I give my wrist a pluck. "But Rose. He's your brother. He's flying halfway across the world to see us."

She folds her arms and makes a face. "I thought he was flying halfway across the world to attend a friend's wedding. We're just a stop along the way."

"Now, Rose—"

"And he didn't give us much notice, did he? I can't just bail on work."

"How could he? He's so very busy with his career."

"And I'm not?" Her cheeks redden. "I'm going for a swim."

"Now? But Jack will be here soon."

"Don't worry. I'll be home in time for dinner." She hurries into her bedroom and returns with her workout bag. "Back in a couple of hours."

"Go ahead," I say, as if I mean it. "We can prepare dinner all on our own."

"You mean Mimi can," she replies with a not-so-nice laugh. The front door closes with a thump.

Mimi looks up from her easel. "I don't like it when you fight."

"We're not fighting."

"But you're not happy."

"I'm always happy."

"Hope so." She sets down her paintbrush and hurries across the room to give me a hug. "You can help me with the *zuppa di cozze*," she says. "There's lots of scrubbing and chopping to do."

"Thanks, Mimi. I'd love to."

After I've cleaned the mussels and chopped the tomatoes, I retreat to my bedroom for a short rest. I'm a little irritated by Rose's attitude, but I quickly shake it off. Tonight! *Jack arrives tonight!* I'm so excited I could sing. My mind flips this way and that, thinking about the chores I haven't finished. Set out clean towels. Sweep the floor. Brush away a cobweb or two. I finally give up on the idea of rest and get up and search through my drawers. There I retrieve my very first journal, one of my few possessions to survive the fire. I open the smoke-infused pages and retrieve my favorite Polaroid. I like to look at it every now and then. It reminds me of how far I've come.

The photo is of Aunt Genny hugging me tight at the entrance to her farm. Snow coats the ground, poinsettias line the porch, and hundreds of lights twinkle overhead. Our first Christmas together. It was a sad one. You can see it in my downcast eyes. "It's going to be okay," I whisper. "You're going to be happy one day."

"Kathi?" Mimi calls. "Can you come out here? I want to set the table extra pretty."

"Be right there." I replace the Polaroid between the pages, a smile lifting my heart. The upside of dark? I got my children back. And what could be better than that?

CRYSTAL, A.K.A. ROSE

August 1, 2020

The workout kicked my ass. It's the last one before my first-ever triathlon—a short course—to be held at the end of the week. I'm a slow but steady runner and fairly strong on the bike. But swimming? That's my weak link. You'd think I was bulky enough to float like a log, but I have to work double time, or I sink to the bottom like a stone.

Swimming has become my favorite challenge. It channels my energy and keeps me focused. Holds my inner demons at bay. My team holds their daily practices on the open water, swimming from cove to cove. The first time I joined in, I nearly drowned. Since then I've gradually improved.

"Join us for a beer," Salvatore calls out from a crowd of near-naked studs. Salvatore is our unofficial coach—he bartends at my favorite café. Tall and wiry, he's a terror on the bike, runs a 5:30 mile, and glides through the water like a seal. He always seems to be smiling, which makes him the polar opposite of me.

"Sorry," I reply, wrapping up in a towel. "My brother's arriving from the States tonight."

"Next week, then?" he asks, his face full of hope.

"Sure. Maybe next week." I jog up the narrow steps, wondering if that's his way of asking me out. He's been hinting around the past few weeks. Not sure how I feel about that. The thought makes my stomach churn.

When I arrive home, Jack's already there. Dressed in all black, he looks like a model—no one would guess we're family. We share blue eyes but little else. He's long and lean, with an easy laugh, and wears his dark hair up in a bun. His chin is hidden beneath a trim goatee that Kathi clearly doesn't like.

"Did you grow that thing for a movie?" she asks Jack shortly after I arrive.

"No. I grew it for me."

She tilts her head, eyes narrowing, as if examining a piece of art. "I think it makes you look older," she says.

"I think it makes me look good." Irritation scurries across Jack's face and settles into his thin shoulders. *Been there, bro*, I almost say. He winks at me like he knows.

This is the fourth time I've met up with Jack, and I'm beginning to feel at ease. Like he's almost become my real brother. Like I'm not scared of him judging me.

We dine on the terrace beneath a star-studded sky, party voices wafting from the bars below. The table is set with a dozen candles that flicker softly in the evening breeze. The soup is beyond good—the mussels steeped in garlic, the tomato broth fresh and salty. It goes well with Mimi's homemade bread and a jug of our neighbor's white wine.

Jack entertains us with stories about his upcoming movie, the gnat-like paparazzi, and his most recent crush. Mimi describes an elderly patron who buys a painting from her every week. Kathi tells a funny story about two romance novelists locked in a power struggle over a blog. Her face is flushed but her smile serene, as if she has everything she could ever want. She slowly sips on her single glass of wine—that's her absolute limit these days. When there's a lull in the conversation, she turns to me with a sudden look of concern.

"You're awfully quiet tonight, sweetheart."

Warning bells go off in my head. "I'm not quiet," I say. "Just listening. That's what some people like to do."

"Was Salvatore at practice tonight?"

My shoulders stiffen. "Yeah."

"Salvatore?" Jack smiles and arches an eyebrow. "Does Rose have a Sicilian lover?"

I draw into myself like a snail that's been poked. "No. He's just a friend."

Kathi giggles. "That's not true. He has a crush on her. I can see it in his dreamy brown eyes."

I snatch a piece of bread from the basket and slather it with a wad of butter. Then I take a huge bite and stare at Kathi, daring her to say another word.

"Are you still hungry, sweetheart?" she asks, her smile all but sucked away. "If so, mussels are better for you than bread."

"I'll eat what I want," I mumble, stuffing the rest of the bread in my mouth.

Jack glances from Kathi to me, a worried look settling on his face. "Sorry, Rose," he says. "I shouldn't have teased you. Obviously it's not a joke."

"Whatever. It doesn't matter. If you'll excuse me, I'm tired. I'm going to bed." I stand, clear my plate, and head directly for my room. After shutting the door, I plop on the bed and ball my hands into fists.

What is the worst? The very worst?

Those words can still engulf me in anger. I let them sizzle and burn until humiliation quenches the flame.

It's nearly midnight when I creep from my bedroom and cross through the darkened house. I quietly step onto the terrace and settle into a lounge chair. The ocean oozes its spicy evening scent; the parties have all quieted down. A full moon hangs high in the sky, painting silver across the sea.

"Can I speak to you, sweetheart?" Kathi whispers, poking her head around the open door.

"Why not," I say, feeling foolish. Jack must think I'm a jerk.

Kathi takes the seat next to me and immediately starts in. "I'm sorry," she says in a shaky voice. "I shouldn't have mentioned Salvatore. Or anything about the bread." Her head droops to her chest. "I really don't know what comes over me. Why I say such stupid things."

"And I'm sorry I got upset. You didn't say anything wrong."

"Yes, I did. I embarrassed you in front of Jack." She sniffs and wipes her eyes with the back of her hand. "Can you forgive me?"

"Of course." I take a deep breath, wondering why this family stuff has to be so horribly hard. "It would help if you didn't ask me about my private life. Or tell me what to eat."

"You're absolutely right," Kathi says, her head bobbing. "I'll try to never do that again. It's just that sometimes I can't help but worry."

"Well, you don't need to worry about me."

"I know that," she says in a soft voice. "But worrying is something that all good mothers do. It gets mixed up with love somehow. I can't always control it." She reaches out and takes my hand, and I surprise myself by not pulling away. Instead, I curl my fingers inside of hers and let their warmth slip into mine.

ACKNOWLEDGMENTS

Thank you to Robert Dugoni for paying it forward;
Steven James for sharing technique.

Phil Morreale, my patient first reader;
Cynthia Wessendorf, who smoothed later drafts.

Jessica Tribble for "getting" the voices;
Leslie Lutz for making words sing.

Monte Fligsten for insights on counsel;
Daniel Calderon for parsing police raids.

Jessica Therkelsen for sage advice;
Ali Morreale for drumbeats of support.

The women in my life who made the difference;
the friends and family who rooted me on.

And above all, thank you to Rebecca Scherer:
friend, cheerleader, agent extraordinaire.

ABOUT THE AUTHOR

Photo © 2017 Linda Blue

Catharine Riggs lives and writes on California's central coast. A graduate of UCLA with an MBA from Drake University, Riggs is a former business banker, adjunct college instructor, and nonprofit executive who spends her free time traveling and exploring the outdoors. *What She Gave Away* is her debut novel. She is currently at work on the second novel in her Santa Barbara suspense series.